SEEN IT ALL
and
DONE THE REST

Pearl Cleage

A NOVEL

SEEN IT ALL
and
DONE THE REST

ONE WORLD · BALLANTINE BOOKS · NEW YORK.

Seen it All and Done the Rest is a work of fiction.
Names, characters, places, and incidents are the products of the author's
imagination or are used fictitiously. Any resemblance to actual events,
locales, or persons, living or dead, is entirely coincidental.

2009 One World Books Trade Paperback Edition

Copyright © 2008 by Pearl Cleage
Interview copyright © 2008 by Carleen Brice
Discussion questions copyright © 2009 by Random House, Inc.

Published in the United States by One World Books,
an imprint of The Random House Publishing Group,
a division of Random House, Inc., New York.

ONE WORLD is a registered trademark and the One World colophon is a
trademark of Random House, Inc.

RANDOM HOUSE READER'S CIRCLE and colophon are
trademarks of Random House, Inc.

Originally published in hardcover in the United States by One World Books,
an imprint of The Random House Publishing Group,
a division of Random House, Inc., in 2008.

LIBRARY OF CONGRESS CATALOGING-IN-PUBLICATION DATA
Cleage, Pearl.
Seen it all and done the rest : a novel / Pearl Cleage.
     p.   cm.
ISBN 978-0-345-48113-9
1. African American actresses—Fiction.
2. Female friendship—Fiction.
3. Atlanta (Ga.)—Fiction.   I. Title.
PS3553.L389S44 2008
813'.54—dc22   2007040822

Printed in the United States of America

www.randomhousereaderscircle.com

2 4 6 8 9 7 5 3 1

Book design by Mary A. Wirth

TO DEIGNAN,
WHO NEVER CEASES TO AMAZE ME.

This one's for you.

You were wild once. Don't let them tame you.
—Isadora Duncan

Remember that you, yourself, are America.
—Alice Walker

SEEN IT ALL
and
DONE THE REST

ONE

We were already on our second round of drinks, and Howard had shown no sign of calming down. In fact, I think his indignation was rising along with his voice. At least we were sitting outside. That way the noise floated up and away rather than bouncing off the walls and driving the other patrons crazy. The International Sky Café has a nice little patio where you can drink and smoke unmolested and that's where we had been encamped for the last hour and a half, almost two. The outdoor seating promised that the pungent smell of world-class ganja would gently surround anyone passing by, and practically guaranteed a contact high if you lingered. Marijuana and hashish are legal in Amsterdam, and it is not uncommon to see people sitting in outdoor cafés, reading newspapers and having a little smoke with their morning coffee, but Howard and I weren't smoking today. We were ordering champagne by the glass and trying to make sense of what had just happened.

"I've been thrown out of places for being too black, too queer, too loud, too drunk, too hip, and too *too,* but I have never, *ever* been tossed out on my ass for being *too American!*"

Howard was working himself up into a pretty good rant, but we were entitled. We had been asked to leave the funeral of an Iraqi director who had been a close friend and collaborator of ours for years. The problem was that Halima's relatives were there from Baghdad and the war wasn't just a blurb on the six o'clock news to them. It was real. Even though she died in a boating accident, nowhere near a war zone, her family was still outraged at the presence of Americans, *any* Americans, soldiers or not.

"It wasn't a question of degrees, Howard," I said. "It was a question of citizenship. They were pretty clear about that. *No Americans.* Period."

Thirty years ago, our pain at the loss of our friend and our general sorrow about the fucked-up state of the world around us might have spun us into a long afternoon of passionate, awkward, *just need to feel alive* sex, ending in a good long cuddle, maybe a nap, and an evening out laughing too loud, drinking too much, and not giving a damn. The fact of Howard being unapologetically gay would not have been part of the equation. At those times, it wasn't about gender. It wasn't really about sex. It was about comfort, connection, and an unequivocal affirmation of life. This happened frequently when too many of my friends were dying of AIDS in the early days of the epidemic. Being a practical sort, even in the midst of panic and confusion, I learned to put my diaphragm in and pack condoms before funerals, just in case.

Howard was still fussing. "I'll tell you one thing, missy, this is my first and last time being tossed out of somewhere for being an American. An *American*! Can you believe that?"

His voice rang with equal parts incredulity and indignation. The very idea that he, Howard William Denmond, Jr., born and raised on the south side of Chicago, Illinois, could be mistaken for a first-class American citizen was beyond the scope of Howard's experience or comprehension. We were *black* Americans, after all, not the other kind, and we were not used to being held accountable for their sins.

"So I look like John Wayne to you?" Howard was on a roll. "Can't they see that we're *niggas*?"

We spend so much time defining ourselves as outsiders when we do get invited to the party, sometimes we can't remember why we even wanted to go. I raised my eyebrows at him.

"Oh, excuse me, missy. We're *Negroes*, okay? African Americans! *Jigaboos!* Take your pick! All I'm saying is, we're not *real* Americans!"

It suddenly occurred to me that in all the confusion, I hadn't had a chance to share my other bad news. It never rains but it pours.

"Try telling that to François," I said.

"What are you talking about? François knows it. He's been around black folks so long he's practically an honorary spook himself. If it wasn't for that damn accent, we could pass him off as a Louisiana Creole and nobody would be the wiser."

"He fired me."

Howard was waggling his long, slender fingers at the waiter to indicate we were ready for another round. My words didn't register at first.

"He what?"

The waiter, gliding between the tables like a dreadlocked Fred Astaire, nodded to acknowledge Howard's gesture and disappeared.

"Fired me," I said, draining the last of my champagne in preparation for another. When I turned fifty, I decided that the only alcoholic beverage I would consume would be champagne. Now I can spend all that time I used to waste looking at the wine list looking for a new job.

Howard frowned at me across the tiny table. "He can't fire you!"

"Well, he took me into his office, closed the door, took my hand, and told me the board didn't want me to open the season. What would you call it?"

"The board?" Howard snorted derisively. "That's absurd! Beyond absurd! Since when does the board make artistic decisions? They wouldn't even have a theater if it wasn't for you! And François would still be directing those wretched little pieces he used to do in that awful space by the train station."

It was an awful space, and most of the work that was presented there was distinguished by its passionate intensity, not its artistic excellence.

"I did some good work there."

"*Exactly! You* did! Not François and the rest of that crowd. *You!*"

Howard snapped his fingers for emphasis as the waiter appeared with our drinks, scooped up our empties, and then stopped to peer at me quizzically. I knew that look. He just realized that he'd seen me in a movie, or at a film festival, or on a stage somewhere. The idea that I could have stopped in to have a few too many glasses of champagne in the café where he happened to be working was not something he had ever considered. In New York or L.A., I could walk down the street stark naked and not get the time of day, but here in Amsterdam, or London, or Paris, even Rome on a good day, I'm a recognizable face if not a household name.

"You are a bona fide star, missy. What possible reason could he give for firing you?" Howard said, not even noticing the waiter.

"Would you believe for being an American?"

Howard choked on his drink and started coughing like a maniac.

"Excuse me," the waiter said, seeing his break and jumping in before Howard could catch his breath.

"Yes?"

"I'm sorry, but . . ." The waiter was ignoring the presence of other thirsty customers as if we were alone in the room. "But are you . . . are you Josephine Evans? The *actress*?"

As opposed to Josephine Evans the pig farmer. I nodded, smiled, reached out to shake his free hand. "Yes, I am."

"Thank you," he said, his eyes filling up with tears. "Thank you, thank you, thank you!"

"Well, you're very welcome," I said, wondering what I had done to deserve such unabashed adoration.

Howard, fully recovered, was grinning at me like the Cheshire cat. "So you know Ms. Evans's work?"

The waiter nodded. "Oh, yes! I've seen every play you've done since 1992. You're the reason I became an actor."

An actor-slash-waiter, I thought. "How old were you in 1992?" He looked like he was barely old enough now to be legally serving us drinks.

"I was *ten*," he said, sounding breathless and amazed. "We were in a play together."

That could mean only one thing. The only play I've ever done with children was *Medea* and I got to kill them at the end. A lot of actors will tell you never to work with kids or animals because they're too cute or too fidgety, and in either case, you can't compete. I thought that was good advice the first time I heard it and I still do, but the kids are on stage for only a minute or two in *Medea,* and she's so wonderfully crazed by then, there is no way any kid, even a seriously cute or terminally twitchy one, can compete with that.

"*Medea,* right?"

He nodded.

"Were you my son?"

"Yes!" He almost gasped in his delight. "I was the older one. The one she stabs first. I can't believe you remember me after all these years."

"She never forgets a line or a face," Howard said, reaching in his pocket for a pen and a piece of paper which he slid across the table to me. He knew the drill. *Smile, acknowledge, autograph, say goodbye.*

"Well, my son, you grew up nice," I said, teasing him gently, pen poised above the scrap Howard had provided. "Would you like an autograph?"

"Oh, would you mind?" he said, still ignoring the increasingly impatient people nearby, hoping to catch his eye for a refill.

"What's your name?" I said, unprepared for the crestfallen look my question elicited. *Oh, my God,* I thought. *This sweet baby actually thinks I remember his name after fifteen years!*

I twinkled at him in a way that once would have been flirtatious but, since I'm old enough to be his mother, was only sweetly conspiratorial. "You know how we theater people are," I said apologetically. "I only remember your character's name. Do you want me to sign it that way?"

His smile returned. "Yes, of course, that would be fine. Oh, no, that's not good. Then no one will know it's for me. You better go on and make it to Julian."

"To Julian," I wrote, "a great actor and a wonderful son, your loving mother, Medea-slash-Josephine."

He read it, smiled as if we now had an official private joke, bowed slightly, and backed away as if he were leaving the presence of royalty.

"See? That's just what I mean," Howard said, taking a sip of his champagne.

"About what?" The exchange had been pleasant, even routine, but suddenly I felt exhausted. The events of the last two days had finally caught up with me. I considered going back on my resolution and ordering up a vodka on the rocks with a splash of lime, but I don't want to be unemployed *and* drunk on the same day.

"About the idea of them firing you being beyond absurd."

"They fired you."

He snorted dismissively. "They fired me for destroying those hideous costumes, not for being an American."

He was right about that. Six months ago, a guest director with more ego than experience had clashed mightily with Howard about his designs from the first day of rehearsal. Nothing pleased the guy, and although he had no talent or experience as a costumer, he demanded changes up until the day before the official opening. After a while, Howard gave up trying to reason with the man and just did whatever was requested. If the director said he wanted a bustle on a miniskirt, Howard whipped it up and handed it over. The actors were mortified.

"What are you going to do?" I said the night before the opening after I'd watched a dress rehearsal and realized the costumes were even worse than anyone could have imagined. "Your name is still listed on the credits."

"Don't I know it," Howard said calmly, hand-stitching a piece of pink silk with great concentration. "Pick me up at seven thirty tomorrow, okay?"

The next night, Howard dawdled around so long getting ready that by the time we got there, they were halfway through act one. I figured he was just putting off looking at those terrible costumes as long as he could, but when we crept up to the balcony to sneak a peek at the show, I was amazed to see the actors going through their paces, beautifully dressed in Howard's original designs. Seeing my surprise, he put his fingers to his lips and led me outside around to the back of the theater. There in a pile of ugly orange, yucky yellow, and inappropriate purple were the hideous costumes the director had requested, neatly cut to ribbons.

Of course, François had to fire him for unprofessional conduct, but his costumes were so fabulous, and the story was so good, he'd been working nonstop ever since.

"Tell me François's exact words."

"Your firing makes a much better story than mine," I said, trying to move on.

Howard raised one eyebrow in a way that people who didn't know him found intimidating. "His *exact* words, missy."

I couldn't resist trying to lighten the moment by doing the accent. François was a Frenchman, raised in Spain, who had been living in Greece for a decade before we arrived in Amsterdam on the same rainy afternoon almost thirty years ago. He walked up to me at the airport, looking very hip and European, told me he was a director, and asked if

I was an actress. Of course I was. I fell in love with him immediately. We lived together off and on for five or six years. At that point, we decided to stop driving each other crazy and just be friends.

In an attempt to be all things to all people, not one of his finer qualities, François deliberately rolled all his accents into one so that nobody could quite figure out where he was from. "I'm a citizen of the world" was his habitual response to direct questions, and most people let it go at that. That's one of the best things about theater people. It's our job to make stuff up. Characters, accents, costumes. The specifics of real time, real place are less important to us than the integrity of heart and sweetness of soul. Nobody held François's accent against him. We had all come from somewhere else. Many of us had come from someone else. But once we found each other, we became members of the same tribe.

The most passionate relationships we ever had occurred in the context of rehearsal and performance. Our lives outside the theater often seemed flamboyant and extravagant, but that was only because when you spend three hours a night doing Shakespeare, Ibsen, Sophocles, Wilson, Hansberry, you have to live your real life at that emotional level, too, or risk boring yourself to death until showtime. If anyone appreciated the necessity of reinvention, Howard and I did. Plus, we both loved François, even after he had sent us packing. You can't forget all those years of friendship, love, struggle, collaboration, and sex just because the world was going stone crazy and there wasn't a damn thing you or your friends could do about it.

" 'Josephine,' " I said, exaggerating the famous accent until I sounded like a combination of Pepé Le Pew, the cartoon skunk who thinks he's Charles Boyer, and Arnold Schwarzenegger, the actor who thinks he's the governor of California. " 'You know I love you . . .' "

Howard groaned. "He didn't go there, did he?"

I plowed ahead. " 'But we've gotten some calls at the theater. Some letters. The board just thinks this isn't a good time to have an American actress open the season this year. They're afraid it sends the wrong message.' "

"The wrong message to whom? Do they think you set American foreign policy in between performances?"

I was still doing François, but it wasn't as funny as I had hoped it would be. " 'You know, Josephine, I would not be where I am today if it hadn't been for you.' "

"At least he had the guts to say it."

"But he didn't have the guts not to do it," I said in my own voice, amazed to feel my eyes filling up.

"Fuck 'em," Howard said, pretending he didn't see me blinking back the tears.

"Be sure you tell François that the next time you see him, will you?"

"This is all the work of that little Cuban floozie if you ask me."

François's new girlfriend was a Cuban actress who had joined the company two years ago and was both talented and beautiful.

"She's not a floozie and she hasn't got that kind of influence over the board anyway."

"They don't deserve you."

I took another swallow of champagne to soothe my frazzled nerves. "He took great pains to tell me that they were prepared to let me keep the apartment and pay me half salary even though I wouldn't be playing such a visible role."

When I said that about the apartment, Howard looked as shocked as I had felt. I'd been living there so long, I had almost forgotten it technically belonged to the theater. Apparently, François's memory was a lot better than mine.

"What did you tell him?"

"I told him I wanted all of it in writing so I could show it to my lawyer."

"Good for you! I didn't even know you had a lawyer."

"I don't. No job. No lawyer. I'm batting a thousand." I could never remember whether a big number or a small number was better in baseball. "Is that the bad one?"

Howard smiled and patted my hand. "I'm not a big sports fan, sweetie. I couldn't tell you."

"Well, whatever is the worst, that's what I'm batting."

We just looked at each other. This was bad and we both knew it.

"Should I act like a real American and go over there and kick his ass for him?" Howard said.

"Would you?"

"With pleasure. All you have to do is say the word."

"I'm not there yet," I said, "but hold yourself in readiness."

"Can't you teach classes or something?"

I looked at him.

"What? You'd be a fabulous teacher."

"I'm a fabulous actress, remember? I don't have the patience to teach."

"Maria Callas gave private lessons."

Callas was Howard's favorite opera singer of all time, but the legendary diva's voice classes were famous for making mincemeat of those who came to worship her.

"She made people cry and slash their wrists," I reminded him.

"Nobody slashed their wrists."

"That's because they had to leave all sharp objects at the door."

"Okay, okay," he said. "I get it. Teaching is out. So what are you going to do?"

The truth was, the funeral had come up so quickly on the heels of my demotion that I hadn't had time to really consider the question. It would take me a minute to process the possibilities and come up with a plan that would feed me creatively and put champagne on the table.

"I have no idea."

"You still going to do your trip?"

I was leaving for Atlanta in two days. My granddaughter had been on the periphery of a high-profile murder case that consumed Atlanta gossips for months and exposed her to a level of scrutiny and speculation for which she was unprepared. Shell-shocked, she had withdrawn from college in the middle of her senior year. Her mother was worried and so was I. Howard loved Zora almost as much as I did. *Almost.* He's the one who taught her to speak French and took her to her first Paris fashion show. She'd been flying to Europe to spend part of the summer with me for almost ten years, but this year she told me she just wasn't up for the trip.

"Of course."

"Good for you," Howard said. "Strategically, it's absolutely the right move. Leave your outrage hanging in the air and haul ass back to Atlanta until I can sort things out here."

Is that what I was doing? *Hauling ass?* "I've never run from a fight in my life."

"This isn't running, sweetie. This is a strategic withdrawal."

"What is there to sort out?"

"Everything," he said. "Did you not participate actively in the conceptualization and actualization of the Human Theatre Company?"

"François had the theater when I met him. You know that. Technically, it's his. He can do anything he wants to with it."

"Fuck technically. I'm talking about truth. Did you or did you not?"

"Yes, I did."

"Were you planning to stop performing before François's surprising announcement?"

"Of course not. Not yet anyway."

"Not yet? Not *ever*. Great actors are ageless, sweetie. You're just hitting your stride."

"I can't see myself doing *Medea* when I'm sixty."

"Then do Clytemnestra. Do Rose Maxson. Do Lena Younger or that three-hundred-fifty-year-old voodoo girl in August Wilson's last opus."

"Second to last. There's one more after that."

"You're missing my point, sweetie. Our board used to be like us. Artists and a few rich eccentrics and, if we were lucky, somebody who owned a café close by. Now they're a bunch of stone-faced bean counters who wouldn't know a piece of art if it hit 'em in the face." Howard's voice was rising again.

"Calm down," I said. "We don't need to be thrown out of anyplace else today."

Howard ignored my suggestion. "Just because it's no longer me and you and François and Halima sitting up in my funky little apartment, dreaming and drinking and smoking bad dope, doesn't mean this thing we created now belongs to them. Fuck that! Let's fight for it!"

"How are we supposed to do that?"

"Who knows? For now, you go to Atlanta. Spend time with Miss Zora and help her get that lovely little head screwed on right again. Rest and play and have fun while I figure out our next move. How are your finances?"

"I'm okay," I said, but the question set off alarm bells in my head. I'm okay only in the sense that as long as I had my regular stipend coming in from the theater and my beautiful little rent-free apartment, I could live at the level to which I'd become accustomed and continue to follow what Jack Nicholson called the universal rule of show business: *the one who's working pays.* Since I'd been working regularly for the last thirty years, I'd paid for hundreds of meals, rivers of wine, oceans of beer. I'd loaned money for rent knowing I'd never get it back, paid for round-trip tickets home on the only working credit card in the group, and been glad to do it. That was the beauty of the rule. It gave those of us in a notoriously fickle profession a way to handle emergencies without having to humble ourselves to outsiders with straight jobs who always feel obligated to lecture you on the precariousness of your financial situation, like you don't already know it.

The fact of the matter is, my finances are nothing to write home about. I haven't got any savings to speak of. I own a duplex in Atlanta that my mother left me, but I have no idea what it's worth, and I've got a couple of thousand bucks stashed here and there as a hedge against being a broke old lady, depending on the kindness of strangers. I always kind of figured that I'd add more to it later so I'd wind up with a bigger nest egg, but I just never got around to it. It occurred to me in a sickening flash that if I couldn't work this out with François, I might have to start auditioning for parts again, which would be a nightmare. An audition at twenty-five is one thing. An audition at fifty-eight is something else altogether. That's why those Hollywood girls cut their faces up and shoot them full of Botox like that. Trying to turn back time.

"Come to Atlanta with me," I said, feeling suddenly more vulnerable than I wanted to. "We'll only stay a couple of months, I promise. François will come to his senses and we'll be back by spring."

Howard shook his head. "I refuse to visit any country where you can't smoke a joint with your morning cappuccino without getting hauled off to jail. It's not civilized. Besides, I promised the ghost of Langston Hughes that if I ever got my black ass out of Chicago, they wouldn't have to worry about Howard Denmond setting foot on American soil ever again. As long as I stay here, I'm living the life I dreamed about. Back there, I'm just one more black faggot with a little style."

"You could never be just one more anything."

"Could you?"

"I don't know," I said. "How about one more glass of champagne."

"Your wish is my command." He waved at Julian, our waiter-slash-actor, who was already hovering with a bottle of something French, which he said was on the house.

"Why are you so good to me?" I said when Julian had poured us two glasses, made another small bow, and disappeared.

It was a rhetorical question, but Howard answered it anyway. "Because you're my best friend and I can't bear to see them treat you this way. Plus, you're a star, sweetie. You've opened and closed the season every year for the last decade. George Bush doesn't cancel all that out by being the biggest fool on God's green earth."

"All right. I will leave myself in your capable hands."

"Good! This shouldn't take long, I promise."

"Do you already have a battle plan?"

"Of course. First, I'm going to remind them of who you are. I may also let slip that you've had a very attractive offer from The Red Bird Workshop."

The Red Bird was the new kid on the block, and François was already worried about them stealing his audience. "I have?"

Howard smiled. "Leave everything to me, sweetie."

"I guess at this point, I don't have much choice."

He leaned over and patted my hand. "Have I ever let you down?"

"Never."

"Well, I'm not about to start now."

"Good."

"I know one thing."

"What's that?"

"I'm going to miss you like crazy," he said, his voice cracking just a little. "Jesus! I didn't even cry at the damn funeral!"

"You didn't have time," I said. "We got tossed out too fast."

Howard grimaced. "What a day! That already seems like a hundred years ago!"

"A hundred years and counting."

Over the next two hours, what had started off as an angry drowning of our sorrows evolved into a wonderfully teary bon voyage party and a picture-perfect ending to an absolutely terrible day. All I needed to do now was call Zora and tell her I was on my way.

"Well, let's have one last toast before we drag our drunk asses home," Howard said, dividing the last corner of the dark green bottle between us.

"Good idea," I said. "What are we toasting?"

"Here's to being real Americans." He raised his glass and grinned across the table at me. *"Who knew?"*

TWO

⋅

*T*he test of a decision you make when you've been drinking champagne is whether or not it holds up in the morning when you're drinking coffee. To my great relief, I woke up at dawn and felt exactly as I had the night before. It was time to head for Atlanta. Zora needed some life lessons her sweet mother couldn't teach her, and I needed distance and time to clear my head. It was a fluke that I came to Amsterdam at all. One of the women in the touring cast of Ntozake Shange's play *For Colored Girls Who Have Considered Suicide When the Rainbow Is Enuf* got pregnant and couldn't travel. I auditioned, got the part, got my passport, said goodbye to my son and his father, and hopped on a plane, heading for a twelve-city tour, all within ten frantic days.

I was in heaven. It was a great company of actresses who all had more experience than I did. Their work was so good it made mine get better just to keep up. All the characters in the play are identified in the script only by the colors they wore: the lady in yellow, the lady in blue, the lady in green, the lady in purple. I was the lady in red. My big climactic scene at the end of the play required me to describe watching my former husband, Beau Willie, drop our two screaming children out of a tenement window while the whole neighborhood watches. I did this six times a week, including a matinee on Saturday. It was a hell of a way to spend an evening, but the truth of those black girls' lives that we were putting on the stage rang so true every time we spoke it out loud that audiences gave us standing ovations every night. The reviews were rapturous, and everywhere we went, the ladies who made up the cast, including me, were treated like the reincarnation of Josephine Baker—times five. Berlin, even with all of its ghosts, loved us. Lisbon couldn't get enough. Rome begged us to stay longer. London couldn't resist us, although they tried, and Paris was a dream come true. Then we went to Amsterdam.

The minute I stepped off the plane, I knew I was going to stay longer than the ten days we were scheduled to be here. A lot longer. I had no idea how I'd work it out with my son's father, who was no longer my lover but continued to be a wonderful and loving presence in his son's life, but I knew I'd have to find a way. There was just something about the place that felt like home in a way that Atlanta never had. The only time it came really close was the night Maynard Jackson got elected the city's first black mayor, but that was one day, one spectacular event. This was something else. This was a feeling of personal freedom that I had never known before, even in New York. I felt like I had permission to follow my imagination wherever it might lead me. For the first time, there were no forces, seen or unseen, attempting to put me in one box or another because I was a woman or because I was black. Nobody in Amsterdam gave a damn.

Howard said it was because after you come face-to-face with Hitler, you don't sweat the small stuff. We had just been on a tour of the Anne Frank house, so Nazis were very much on his mind, but I knew what he meant. My more cynical friends said there simply weren't enough black folks around for us to be a problem. *Yet.*

"Right now, we're still exotic to them," Denise said one night after the show when we were having drinks and I said I could see myself living there. "You wait until we aren't all superstars or jazz musicians and see how much they love us."

Denise had no patience with white folks, especially white men. Playing the lady in yellow who has the great monologue about losing her virginity in the backseat of a great big Buick, she was a vibrant, cocoa-brown butterfly with great big eyes and a manner so effortlessly flirtatious that there were always several enraptured men waiting at the stage door after every show, convinced she had been speaking only to them. She laughed at their adoration, signed their programs "all my love," and never let them buy her so much as a glass of champagne, explaining to anyone who asked, "They bought a ticket, not a date."

She was convinced that white male interest in black women was always based on a racist idea of our supposed sexual promiscuity rather than on our own undeniable fabulousness. I tried to suggest that maybe we ought to give ourselves more credit than that, but she just snorted and waved her hand at the waiter for another Pernod.

"You wait until we start taking their jobs," she said. "That's when they'll show their true colors."

At the time, I thought she was merely a victim of outmoded American attitudes about race, but that was a long time ago. These days, race riots in Paris and terrorist plots in London make race as complicated an issue here as it is in the States. Not to mention religion. When you add the current wave of antiwar, anti-American sentiment to the mix, it becomes not only complex but exhausting. Even in the light of day, my decision to spend some time in Atlanta seemed like the best move I could make, and in life, just like in theater, timing is everything. Right now, it was time to call Zora.

The phone rang four times before she cleared me with the caller ID and answered.

"Mafeenie?"

When Zora was a toddler, *Mafeenie* was as close as she could get to Grandma Josephine, and it had stuck. Her voice sounded sleepy, although it was early afternoon, Atlanta time.

"Hey, darlin'! Did I wake you?"

"No, I'm just . . . watching a movie."

I heard the tinkling of ice and, in the background, the sound of the Mayor of Munchkin City reading a proclamation to the bedazzled Dorothy.

"Don't you ever watch anything but *The Wizard of Oz*?" I teased her, hoping she wasn't sipping anything stronger than a Coke. Cocktails alone in the middle of the day made me nervous, especially since her mother had called a week ago to tell me she thought Zora was drinking. I could hear the terror in Jasmine's voice. She had suffered so much with my son, Zora's father, before he drank himself to death. I think the idea of battling the same devils in his daughter was more than Jasmine's gentle spirit could comprehend.

"It's a classic," Zora said, sounding defensive.

"I'm just teasing," I said gently. "How've you been?"

"Okay. Where are you?"

"I'm still in Amsterdam."

"Is everything okay?"

"Everything's fine. I just wanted to let you know I'm headed your way."

"To Atlanta?"

"Don't sound so surprised," I said. I hadn't been home since her father's funeral six years ago. Since then, she had always come to see me, until last year when all that mess happened. Now I could hear the faint sound of the Munchkins singing one of their many welcome songs. Zora had slurred the T's in Atlanta ever so slightly. If she was drinking Coke, it had rum in it.

"You hate Atlanta."

"But I adore *you*," I said, "so that puts me about even."

"What's going on?"

I gave her the no-worries version of my current condition. "François and I are not seeing eye to eye on some things at the theater, and until we get them straightened out, I'm on leave."

"*From acting?*"

"Don't sound so shocked," I said, soothing myself as much as I was soothing her. "It's just temporary. I'm trying to give François and the new board enough time to come to their senses and let me open the season."

"You always open the season."

"They're mad at Americans, so they've decided not to let me."

"American *actresses*?"

"Americans, period. Because of the war."

"They blame you?"

"They blame us."

"François, too?"

"François's in love so he can't be counted on to do the right thing. His new girlfriend thinks I'm too old to do *Medea*."

"How old is she?"

"Medea or the girlfriend?"

"The girlfriend, Mafeenie!"

"Thirty-six." Although I hated to admit it, she did have a point. Medea's violent madness is completely explainable during the passionately messy childbearing years, but postmenopause, the killing of the children is just bad mothering. "She wants to play the role herself."

"Is she any good?"

"Not that good," I said, hoping it was true. "Howard suggested this might be the ideal time to let them miss me for a while, so I've got a month or so off, and I thought since you couldn't come here last summer, the mountain would come to Muhammad."

"For a month?"

She sounded less than enthusiastic about the prospect, but I chose to interpret her tone as simple surprise. "Too much time or not enough?"

"No, no," she said quickly. "It's fine. It's just that I'm working these crazy hours at the vet center and I gave up my apartment, so you know . . ."

She let that "you know" dangle in the air between us, and I realized that she didn't want me to stay with her. Too bad. There was no way I was going to go to Atlanta specifically to see my granddaughter and check into one of those elaborate Atlanta tourist hotels or camp out at a sad little motel near the airport, full of the ghosts of disappointed business travelers and the women who love them.

"Your mother told me you were house-sitting a mansion," I said. "Can you put me up?"

"It's not exactly a mansion. It's one of those West End gingerbreads."

West End was a southwest Atlanta community primarily known for three things: first, several blocks of perfectly restored Victorian homes, complete with the latticework around the front and back porches which had earned them the name *gingerbreads*; second, the five schools of the Atlanta University Center, including Spelman College, from which Zora should have graduated last May; and, third, Blue Hamilton, their homegrown godfather who had abandoned a promising career as an R&B crooner to oversee the neighborhood's twenty-odd blocks and guarantee the peace and security of all the people who settled there. The violent scandal that had splashed on Zora's feet last spring was an aberration in a neighborhood that was usually so peaceful it boasted a twenty-four-hour beauty shop where clients came and went at all hours with never a thought that they might not be safe. I had a whole scrapbook full of pictures of an apartment Zora had there for the last two years, including some of her working in the big garden out back. She loved that place, but she said it had too many memories so she was looking for a new one.

"Do they really have a pool?" I said. Jasmine had described it in great detail. Something about a mermaid mosaic on the bottom that had to be seen to be believed.

"Yeah." Zora sounded a lot less enthusiastic than her mother had.

"Has it been warm enough there for you to get in it?" It was the middle of February, but Atlanta is known for its mild winters, especially these days when winter was becoming an increasingly distant memory.

"It's heated."

"You're kidding."

"Nope."

"Well, you lucked out, then. I remember how much you loved the pool at that villa Howard had in Nice. The house was an absolute wreck, as I recall, but we couldn't hardly get you out of that pool long enough to eat and sleep. I thought your fingers were going to be permanently pruned."

In the silence that greeted this grandmotherly attempt at sharing a treasured memory of one of our best summers, I heard the tinkling ice in Zora's glass again and the faint twittering of the ever-excited little people as Glinda the Good Witch made it abundantly clear that Dorothy was right: They weren't in Kansas anymore.

"Are you still swimming every day?"

"Not really," she said. "I don't have time, you know . . ."

That *you know* hung there just like the other one. "Well, I'll swim in it. How's that?"

"Fine, I guess," she said with an audible sigh. "When are you coming?"

Her lack of enthusiasm was starting to really bother me. I decided to cut through the bullshit before I got mad, never a good option, especially when dealing with ex-lovers, bad directors, and fragile grandbabies. I took a deep breath.

"Listen, sweetie," I said, "I know you've had a lot going on in your life and—"

"That's a nice way to put it," she said, and laughed a little, but it wasn't a good laugh. "You sound like Mom."

She meant "well meaning, but clueless."

"Well, we're both a little worried about you if that's what you mean."

"I don't mean anything," she said, sounding exhausted and annoyed. "I'm just saying . . ."

Her voice trailed off and whatever she started saying remained unsaid.

"I'm going to ask you a question and I want you to give me an honest answer."

"Okay."

"Is this a bad time for a visit?"

She exhaled again, loud enough for me to hear it. I waited, hoping she wouldn't ask me not to come. I know I'd told her I wanted an honest answer, but only if it was in the affirmative.

"There's no bad time for you to visit, Mafeenie. You know that."

"Thank you, darlin'," I said, relieved.

"So when are you coming?"

"Next week, if that's okay."

"Still traveling incognito?"

I laughed. "Old habits are hard to break."

It's not really that I travel incognito. It's just that I've been moving around the world on my own for so long, I've got it down to a science. One of the things I eliminated early on was the airport greeting. As environments go, airports are among the worst when it comes to saying hello or goodbye to someone you love. Everybody's rushing around, security is directing you one way or another, and the lighting is awful. Under those conditions, I don't want to meet anybody and I don't want to be met. My preference is to give people a rough idea of when I'm coming and then call them when I light somewhere. That way, I can move on my own rhythms, changing and adjusting as the mood strikes me without feeling any pressure to arrive before the flowers wilt or in time for the midnight show.

Whenever Zora came to see me, we always traveled this way. We'd show up in Paris or Madrid or Havana and call my friends from our hotel. They invariably chided me for not letting them meet us at the airport. I would apologize and tell them to join us for dinner, where all would be forgiven before we had opened the second bottle of champagne. Zora would have a Shirley Temple.

"I'll call you when I get in."

"My schedule is crazy at the center," she said, "and sometimes I have to turn off my cellphone, so if you don't reach me, just catch a cab to the new Paschal's and I'll meet you there."

The old Paschal's restaurant had been a popular Hunter Street watering hole for forty years before they moved to a new location a few blocks from the concrete and glass monstrosity that is the Georgia Dome. Legend has it that the late Mr. Paschal single-handedly kept the Atlanta office of the Student Nonviolent Coordinating Committee from starving to death by keeping them supplied with his famous chicken sandwiches whenever the staff was broke and hungry, which was often.

"No problem," I said. "That way I can get a glass of champagne and something to eat until I lay eyes on you."

I could hear the faint cackling of the Wicked Witch of the West, who had just landed in Munchkin Land in a puff of green smoke, highly pissed, and looking for her sister.

"Get back to your movie," I said.

"Travel safe," Zora said.

"Don't worry. I'll just click my heels together three times like I always do. Love you!"

"I love you. Mafeenie?"

"Yes, darlin'?"

"I really am glad you're coming."

"Me, too," I said. There was nothing on Zora so broke we couldn't fix it. *Together*. That's what grandmothers do.

THREE

•

*A*rriving at the airport early to comply with all the new regulations and security measures, I breezed through all checkpoints, flashing my passport like the good American citizen that I am. When I presented myself at the gate for my flight to Atlanta, the agent shyly requested an autograph and told me the flight was almost empty so she could upgrade me to first class. I signed: *To Chloe, with great appreciation for your kind assistance. Peace & Love, Josephine Evans.*

"My granddad used to sign his letters like that back in the sixties," she said, smiling as she tucked the paper safely away in her uniform pocket.

"We all did," I said. "Some of us just never stopped."

She walked me all the way onto the plane and handed me over to the smiling young women who were greeting the first-class passengers and offering them pillows and a beverage before the back cabin had even begun to board. I settled into an aisle seat with no one scheduled to claim the window beside me and accepted a glass of champagne and a pillow. There were only three other people in first class and a dozen in coach. There was a man one row up and across the aisle from me who ordered a double scotch on the rocks, drank it, and fell asleep almost before the captain turned off the FASTEN SEAT BELT sign. The bright-eyed flight attendant tucked a blanket around him like he was a toddler known for kicking off his covers and asked me if I'd like a magazine. Of the ones she offered, *Vogue* and *Vanity Fair* were the ones I chose, but I wasn't really interested. I flipped through a preview of spring fashions that was heavy on baby doll dresses and ballet flats, scanned an article on "the new Hollywood," which looked a lot more diverse than the old Hollywood but had the same penchant for big-breasted blondes with bee-stung lips and heart-shaped behinds.

I closed the magazines and snuggled a little deeper into my soft leather seat. I wasn't really sleepy, but it was late, and the hum of the jet engines and the soft snoring of the man-baby across the aisle were hypnotic. I turned off my reading light, leaned back, and let my mind mull over the events of the last few days. The truth is, this wasn't the first time I had felt that anti-American thing nipping at my heels. It's been building ever since the invasion of Iraq when the president started trying to bend the rest of the world to his will the way Rudolph Valentino's tyrannical father does in that silent movie *The Sheik*. It's one of my favorite oldies. Zora loves it, too.

It takes place in some unnamed desert somewhere. At the beginning, the dad is really pissed off about something, so he takes a length of pipe that just happens to be lying around his tent and folds it over like a pipe cleaner. This gesture is intended to demonstrate to his son, played to smoldering perfection by Rudy himself, who is in charge. Valentino, of course, takes the pipe, dark-rimmed eyes blazing in defiance, and straightens it right out again to show his father that times have changed around the oasis.

I think that's what happened to our president, too. After 9/11, he started bending every pipe in sight, while people whose blazing eyes have nothing to do with the skill of makeup artists and creative lighting, bent them right back. I was in Paris doing one more *Medea* just before the invasion, and there were massive antiwar demonstrations every day. Early in my career, I played the idealistic Princess Antigone, up against the amazingly stubborn King Creon, more times than I can remember, so I had a clear understanding of the implacability of power. Watching the news conferences and angry speeches, I knew there was a strong chance that we were already beyond the possibility of diplomacy and persuasion.

At first, Howard and I just watched from the balcony of the hotel, but after a couple of days, I decided I had to be a part of it. Howard, who had only come in for a long weekend to see the show and do some shopping, thought I was crazy for getting involved. When I reminded him that it was, after all, our country against whom they were protesting, he just snorted.

"Speak for yourself, Miss Betsy Ross," he said. "If I wanted to march up and down the street, hollering at white folks, I would have kept my black ass at home in the first place. No thank you!"

So we arranged to meet for dinner after the show, and Howard went back to catching up on his beauty sleep. I joined the throngs of men, women, and children who were carrying signs that said, "Stay out of Iraq!" and "U.S. Out of the Middle East!" and some fairly angry things about George Bush, his father, and one about his mother that I won't repeat since she never ran for office and so is of no concern to me. They were also carrying posters with various photographs of the president, sometimes altered so that he had little devil horns like goat bumps on his forehead or blood dripping off his little pointed teeth. There were some classic peace signs, white on black background, and one saying "war" in a red circle with a line through it.

I fell in with a group of young women who had skipped the day's classes at their university to join the marchers. We all got along great. Everybody spoke English and French so we could really talk in both languages, which we did. When people recognized me, they would smile and applaud, or come over to shake my hand, or take a picture and compliment the artist while striding along beside the activist. That was back when the demonstrators were really mad at our government, but they still had faith in us to change it, which we did. But people around the world still don't see enough evidence of that change, which is why they're losing patience with us.

So I wasn't really surprised by what happened at the funeral, or by the board's decision to replace me. It hurt my feelings more than anything else. But now all that is in the capable hands of Howard Denmond, whom I trust to make it right before I run through my savings and have to figure out how to make an honest living doing something other than acting. Howard was right. We had been through all manner of dramas over the past twenty-plus years, and he has never let me down.

Comforted by that thought, I must have dozed off because when I woke up, they had lowered the lights and the only activity in the cabin was taking place a few rows ahead of me, where a young couple with identical shiny blond heads was giggling together between kisses. From where I was sitting in the dark across the aisle behind them, I could see the boy whispering in her ear and hear the girl laughing softly as she shushed him. He took her hand and pressed it to his lips in an urgent, sensual way that made me know exactly what was coming next. And why not? Making love on airplanes is practically a sexual rite of passage in the modern world, and this flight was so empty, they didn't even have to crowd into the tiny bathroom to escape their fellow passengers' prying eyes. The snorer had not moved a muscle and I'm sure they had no idea I was even awake. The girl's head dropped out of sight and the boy groaned softly and leaned his blond head back against the seat.

I was never a big sex-on-the-plane kind of girl, although I had my moments. It's much easier for women to give pleasure in such close quarters than to receive it. Upright airplane seats seem tailor-made for fellatio, while trying to find a way to reciprocate would challenge even the most determined and flexible suitor. I knew I was invading their privacy by not turning away, but somehow I felt like they didn't really care. Half the thrill of this kind of thing is the idea that somebody might be watching.

After a few minutes, the boy let out a little gurgling half groan and pressed his head against the seat. For a moment, neither one moved; then the girl sat up, pushed her hair behind her ears, and looked around. When she saw that I was awake, she grinned conspiratorially. I grinned back just as her beau pulled her back down into his arms for a long grateful kiss.

I was grateful, too. Not for a chance to play the voyeur at thirty thousand feet, but because that's one of the things I really like about people. We don't care how many rules you make, we're going to find a way to fall in love and have sex on airplanes and make babies and laugh and cry and live free. That's just something we do, and all the wars and all the governments and all the armies you can put together to stop us won't make one bit of difference. Especially when you're moving along effortlessly at five hundred miles an hour and the flight attendants are half dozing and the cool-looking older lady that's watching has probably seen it all and done the rest. That's how she got to be so cool.

FOUR

•

*P*aschal's had changed its location, but the food was exactly the same: high in calories, high in cholesterol, and absolutely irresistible. My flight arrived on time and I caught a cab into the city, arriving at just before nine. I left a message on Zora's cellphone, as instructed, and took a small corner table in the bar area where they had the television turned to CNN. I ordered a glass of champagne, but when I hadn't heard from Zora by the time I finished it, the smiling waiter who said his name was MacArthur, "like the general," had no problem serving me the same great meal I would have gotten in the dining room.

A half hour later, while I waited for my peach cobbler and a cup of coffee, I thumbed through a copy of *Dig It!*, the homegrown gossip sheet that had been Zora's nemesis since her name surfaced in the scandal. Jasmine had told me how furious Zora had been to find herself in its pages, but I had never seen a copy before. It was free from the box right outside the front door, sandwiched between *The New York Times* and *The Atlanta Sentinel*, both of which were sold out. *Dig It!* was free. The paper made its money in ads. *Looking Good While Being Bad!* the headline screamed across the front in big red letters. As I flipped through it, there were many people I didn't recognize. I wondered if that was because I'd been away so long or just that so many of these "celebrities" looked barely old enough to vote, much less to be called stars. Most of them seemed to come from the world of very recent pop culture with an emphasis on reality television and rap music.

I was beginning to wonder if Zora had gotten my message, when I turned the page, and there she was, splashed across the cover feature on "Looking Good While Being Bad." They got that right. In every photograph of her, Zora looked absolutely beautiful. There she was, dancing with an attractive young man in a crowded nightclub. There she was, having drinks with him the same night, smiling seductively. She obviously had no idea she was being photographed. There were also several of her entering or leaving the campus at Spelman, wearing huge sunglasses and shielding her face with her hands. One photographer even secretly snapped her leaving the West End News. In that shot, she looked drawn and tense.

MacArthur brought over my pie and coffee and I smiled my thanks, but I couldn't stop staring at Zora. She hadn't even looked that unhappy at her father's funeral, but I guess that was a moment for which she had time to prepare. This was a violent disruption of her life that she didn't see coming until she crashed into the middle of it and found herself surrounded by enough paparazzi to be a Hollywood starlet out with Paris Hilton for a night on the town. Poor baby. She didn't even know that the worst thing you can do is try to hide your face. It just makes them more determined to get the shot of you hiding.

The copy read: "Even in the middle of one of the most scandalous moments in Atlanta's recent history, Zora Evans, the mystery coed of last year's biggest, sexiest murder mystery, managed to look good enough to eat!"

"Mafeenie, I can't believe you're reading that trash!"

Zora's voice sounded indignant and embarrassed just above my head. I looked up to find her standing behind me, frowning like she had caught me performing a very unnatural act in a very public place. She was alarmingly thin and her hair was pulled back tightly from her face.

"My darling girl," I said, tossing the offending tabloid aside and rising to embrace her. "You're here at last!"

She felt like skin and bones. *How much weight had she lost?*

"And not a minute too soon," she said, hugging me tightly in spite of my choice of reading material.

I leaned back and looked at her without breaking the circle of my embrace. "How are you, darlin'?"

"I'm fine," she said, squirming a little under my unrelenting scrutiny.

She had lost fifteen or twenty pounds easily and her usually creamy smooth complexion looked sallow and muddy. With no hair to soften her newly narrow face, her cheekbones jutted out, sharp and heartless.

"How much weight have you lost?"

"Can I order a drink before you begin your interrogation?" she said, wriggling free and flopping into the seat across from mine.

"Of course you can," I said. "Jet lag has ruined my manners! Are you starving? Order something to eat!"

"I'm not hungry," she said as MacArthur hurried over with a menu. She barely glanced at him. "Stoli on the rocks."

"Coming right up," he said.

Zora ordering vodka was even more of a surprise than her weight. I had never seen her drink anything stronger than a glass of opening-night champagne. The copy of *Dig It!* I'd tossed on the table had fallen open to the editor's column, which ran beside a photograph of a handsome young man with big brown eyes and very white teeth. Zora tapped the picture with her fingertip.

"I threw a drink in that guy's face once."

"You did?" I was impressed. Drink throwing is a dying art in the modern world.

She nodded. "I walked in here one day and there he was sitting at the bar watching the Braves game and drinking a beer. Next thing I knew . . ."

She shrugged her shoulders as if what happened next had been beyond her control.

"That's a difficult gesture to pull off," I said. "How'd it go?"

She shook her head and grimaced slightly. "Not so well, actually. I felt a little silly afterward."

"That's why it's a hard one," I said, understanding completely. "It always feels good while you're doing it, but once it's done, there's that whole moment after to deal with when you're standing there, still trembling with righteous indignation, and the other person is sitting there with stuff dripping off their face, looking at you like you have just lost your entire mind."

"Exactly!"

I nodded sympathetically and took one more bite of my peach

cobbler. It was harder to lose an extra pound or two these days so moderation was key, but this pie was too good to resist.

"That's why you can't just stand there after you've done the deed," I said. "Toss the drink, put down the glass, and go. One smooth motion."

"How many times did it take you to figure that out?" she said, closing the magazine and tossing it down on the chair beside her. It fell open again to the page that was crowded with her picture, but she ignored it, so I did, too.

"Oh, two or three, I guess."

She was looking at me like she used to when she was a kid and everything that came out of my mouth surprised her.

"What?"

"Most grandmothers can't critique your drink-in-the-face moves like that."

"I'm not most grandmothers," I said. "And thank God!"

She almost smiled at that, but she seemed to have forgotten how.

"I'm sorry I didn't get your message earlier," she said. "My supervisor makes us turn off our cell phones if we're talking to a vet."

"Good for her," I said. "Cell phones are the work of the devil. I was doing *Fences* last year and right in the middle of Rose's big scene where she finally gets to tell Troy all about his sorry self, a cell phone went off right in the front row."

"You make it sound like a bomb or something."

I resisted the impulse to tell her that in my world, it was close enough. Her tone surprised me. I had thought she would find it funny, but her response sounded more like a reprimand.

MacArthur reappeared with a little white cocktail napkin and set her drink down in front of her. As thin and bedraggled as she looked, he couldn't help stealing a little glance. Even on her worst days, Zora's beauty shines through.

"What did you do?" she said, taking a big gulp of her drink.

"I stopped the show."

"Oh, God! You didn't." She still sounded more annoyed than amused.

"I waited. I tried to talk over it, but it just kept ringing. Finally, I turned around and just stood there until this fool finished fumbling through her coat pockets and found the damn thing."

Zora took another swallow of her drink. She grimaced a little, as if she didn't really like the taste of it, but whatever it was she did like was worth the sacrifice.

"The worst thing about it," I said, "other than completely wrecking my big scene, was that her ring tone was playing 'Little Red Corvette.'"

"I love that song," Zora said, like I had just slammed Prince's artistic genius.

"I love it, too, but not in the middle of my big scene!"

Zora drained her glass. "Did she turn it off or answer it?" She was shaking the glass gently back and forth in a gesture that reminded me of her father more than the dimple in her chin or her hazel eyes.

"I wouldn't be sitting here today if she had answered it," I said. "I'd be in jail for assault and battery, and you'd be marching around with a sign saying 'Free Josephine Evans.'"

At least she smiled at that, but she was busy looking around for MacArthur. She wanted a refill.

"How long have you been drinking straight vodka?" I said, knowing she was a grown woman and could drink whatever she liked, but unable to hold on to the question any longer.

"Not long," she said.

"You like it?"

"Not much, but Dad said with vodka, it's better to take it neat so you can keep track of how much you've had."

Now I truly loved my son, but taking advice about alcohol from a man who drank himself to death seems unwise. For most of his twenties, my son thought staying drunk was the way to address the emptiness. When he married Jasmine and they had Zora, I think he hoped family would be the cure. He even joined AA and went to meetings before rehearsals, but he always went back to drinking. After a particularly horrendous weekend, Jasmine went to the bank, withdrew her half of their savings, packed up her daughter, and left. She drove to Florida and invested her money in a tiny beachfront motel, where they rang a bell every night at sunset to honor the end of another day and tended to attract a laid-back clientele of regulars who didn't require pampering. Zora grew up there, raised by a mother who adored her and a father who visited occasionally.

When he got so sick he couldn't work, he came to the front door of the motel one evening, like he was just another traveler looking for a few nights' rest, and never left. When he died, Jasmine and Zora invited me to come for the service and I did. We rang the bell at sunset and scattered his ashes in the ocean behind the motel. I wept a little for the distance I had allowed my work to create between my son and me. I couldn't deny that I had chosen to live my life without making any real space for him in it. There were reasons then, and there are reasons now, but the end result was he left his daughter behind with Jasmine, the same way I had left him in his father's care, without a backward glance.

She deserved better, I thought that day, watching Zora standing beside her mother in a long white dress, eulogizing her father as if he couldn't have been more perfect if he tried. The next morning, I invited Zora and Jasmine to come to Amsterdam for the New Year's Eve celebration that would usher in the new millennium. That way, I explained, if the doomsayers were right, at least we'd be together at the end. Jasmine said that was a pretty depressing reason to fly thousands of miles across the ocean, and how about if they came because there was no place else they'd rather be? They stayed a month and the three of us got closer than we'd ever been.

Maybe that was why the way Zora was looking so hard for MacArthur to refill her drink order made me feel so sad and so scared that I opened my mouth to tell her that whatever she was looking for probably wasn't hanging around in the bottom of a cocktail glass, but I hadn't seen her in so long. It would probably be better to head home and get settled in before I started dispensing unsolicited advice.

"Well," I said, "you're grown. You can drink whatever you want, but can we do it at your place? I've had all the pie I can afford to eat, but if we sit here much longer, I'll have to polish off the rest."

I spoke quickly because MacArthur was headed toward us and Zora was already wiggling her glass in his direction. My request took her by surprise.

"What?" She looked at my half-eaten pie and back to me.

"You ready to show me your house?" I said, reaching for my credit card as MacArthur waited patiently for instructions.

"Oh, yes! I'm sorry. Of course we can go. Sure, sure . . ."

MacArthur left us to run the card; Zora tipped her glass back one more time to sip the watery remains of her drink and stood up.

"Is this all you brought?" she said, glancing at my small pile of luggage.

"Travelin' light," I said. "Just like always." She slung my carry-on over her shoulder and tucked the garment bag over the pulling suitcase's extended handle like a pro. I taught her well.

I signed the check and included a generous tip. MacArthur repaid my largesse by holding my coat in a courtly gesture I'm sure he learned from a gentlemanly grandfather or an old copy of *Playboy*.

"Thank you," I said, slipping my arms into the silk-lined sleeves quickly. Zora was standing beside the table and I couldn't help noticing that even her hands were too thin. She looked tired and tense and irritable.

"Excuse me, miss?" MacArthur's voice floated tentatively in Zora's direction. I imagined him peeking around from behind me like a kid on the first day at a new school. Zora ignored him.

"Miss?"

I stepped away from him and waited for her to answer.

"Are you talking to me?" she finally said, real nasty, like even the idea of such an exchange was insulting to her.

MacArthur was not dissuaded by her tone. He picked up the copy of *Dig It!* lying open in the chair beside where Zora had been sitting and pointed to the picture of her dancing ecstatically with her doomed companion.

"Is this you?"

Zora didn't blink. "No."

FIVE

•

$\mathcal{Z}$ ora was house-sitting in the heart of West End, just a few blocks away, and she drove home down Ralph David Abernathy Boulevard, the neighborhood's main commercial strip. It had been almost ten years since I'd been in Atlanta to handle the family business when my mom died, and I was happy to see that things still looked good around here. This community is unique. No trash in the streets, good lighting everywhere, and an absence of predators. We stopped at a red light near the neighborhood mall and there were still people shopping even though it was almost midnight. There was a line at the sub shop on the corner and at the twenty-four-hour hair salon; business was booming. Every chair was occupied as patient women flipped through old magazines and waited for their stylist to beckon.

I always love the ebb and flow of sisterhood that forms in salons between those being served, those waiting to be served, and the anointed ones we have trusted with our crowning glory. I wear my hair short because it's easy and I like the way it looks. Puts the focus on my face. I used to shave my head and that was always fun, although if everybody adopted such a look, stylists would have to close up shop and then where would we gather?

The woman at the all-night florist next door to the salon was constructing an elaborate window display featuring an amazing bunch of tropical blossoms that looked like they would have been at home in a window box in Martinique. I made a mental note to visit the shop as soon as I got my bearings. I had no idea what to expect at the house Zora was watching, but there's always room for fresh flowers. There were people visible through the windows of the West End News, browsing through the magazines or drinking coffee at the tables near the big front window. It reminded me of the International Sky Café, except I didn't see anybody smoking. A young woman with a backpack came out the front door, looked up at the big full moon, and headed off with a private smile of appreciation.

Zora took a left and eased the car carefully through the quiet tree-lined streets. It wasn't the season for the famous gardens to be in bloom, but I could see them everywhere, already turned over, mulched, and fertilized in readiness for spring. A few brave souls had put in winter collards, but most of these gardeners didn't plant until Good Friday, traditionally the day to put your plants in the ground. The woman who started the West End Growers Association used to live across the hall from Zora in her old apartment building and had a huge garden there that started on one side, wrapped around the back, and was legendary, according to Zora, for the size and sweetness of its tomatoes. Zora had sent me some great pictures of her and some other women working in that garden, and they looked like they were having a ball.

"Is Blue Hamilton still the man to know around here?" I said.

"He's the one," Zora said. "That's his house right there."

She was pointing at one of the larger Victorians. It was beautifully restored and even had a little gaslight burning out front. An impressive magnolia rose up from the middle of the carefully manicured front lawn. I met Blue Hamilton in Paris once, years ago when he was married to a friend of mine. We all went to dinner and I couldn't stop staring at his eyes. I apologized to my friend when we were alone later and she just laughed. That was before he became West End's godfather.

"Didn't he get married again?"

Zora nodded and turned onto Oglethorpe Street. A woman walking a big dog waved, and Zora waved back but didn't slow down.

"A couple of years ago," she said. "He and his wife just had a baby. They're in Trinidad for a while so Blue can help his friend write a song for Carnival."

That surprised me. Was the godfather finally tired of his task?

"So who's watching the store?" I said.

Zora pulled over in front of another big gingerbread, turned off the motor, and popped the trunk. She considered the question and then shrugged her narrow shoulders.

"I guess we are."

SIX

•

W hen you said you were house-sitting, I pictured you in a cozy little bungalow with a manageable yard and a front porch swing," I said as Zora gave me a tour of the place where we were staying.

"I told you it had a heated pool, remember?"

"But you didn't tell me it was so . . ."

"Fabulous?" she said, borrowing my favorite word, but the fact of its fabulousness didn't seem to give her any pleasure.

The place was beautifully and expensively decorated in soothing earth tones with enough colorful accents and eclectic pieces of art to keep it from being boring. There were lots of windows and high ceilings, and the uniform color scheme created the feeling that one room flowed into the other with no visible effort at all. The art was mainly oversize abstracts except for the kitchen, which had one whole wall covered in photographs of smiling, healthy-looking people.

"Which one is your landlord?" I said, stopping to look at the pictures but not recognizing anybody.

Zora pointed to a couple standing in front of a plateglass window that said *The Atlanta Sentinel* in big white letters and underneath, "Tell the truth to the people."

"Louis and Amelia," she said. "She's a lawyer and he publishes *The Sentinel.*"

"Is that Louis Adams?" The man's face looked vaguely familiar.

"Louis Adams, Jr.," Zora said. "Do you know him?"

"He was a couple of years behind me in high school. I remember the paper. His father was a force to be reckoned with. A real race man."

"Louis is like that, too, but Amelia's teaching at a university in Beirut for two years, so Louis went with her."

The woman standing next to him in the picture was tall and slim with a very close-cropped haircut and a great big smile. Nobody with any sense would let that smile go off into the world alone for two whole years. Louis, Jr., sounded like the perfect combination of race man and romantic.

"So they left you holding down the fort?"

"Well, they had another woman staying here, but her reserve unit got called up for Iraq," Zora said, as we walked from the kitchen back to where my bags were still standing by the front door. "Want to see your room?"

"Absolutely," I said, "And then I want to see that pool you promised me."

She bumped my big pulling suitcase up the stairs behind her while I brought up the rear with my carry-on and the garment bag. I followed her into the third door on the left near the end of a long hallway. It was a lovely, peaceful room. All blond wood and beige comforters. Over the head of the bed was another one of the abstracts that I had noticed downstairs. This one had lots of turquoise and other shades of blue. It was like having a little unexpected piece of sky in the room.

There was a rocking chair by the window and a small table and chair in the corner. The curtains were closed, but Zora put my bag beside the bed and went over to pull them back.

"Come look," she said.

I tossed my things on the bed and went over to stand beside her. Below me, I could see the meticulously landscaped backyard, which boasted not only some of Georgia's famous pines but a few hardwoods and a magnificent magnolia every bit as impressive as the one we had seen in Blue Hamilton's front yard around the corner. A stone walkway lit by small lanterns wound its way from the back porch steps to the pool, twinkling mysteriously in the darkness. I'd have to get closer to see the mermaid, but it was beautiful, even from a distance.

"It's almost too beautiful to swim in," I said, already looking forward to dipping my toes in the warm water. "Almost!"

Zora seemed pleased that I liked the room, and she smiled at me for the first time that night.

"Thank you, darlin'," I said. "It's perfect."

She let me hug her, but I could still feel the tension in her body and she didn't hug me back with much enthusiasm. I gave her a quick peck on the cheek and then released her.

"Do you want me to help you unpack?" Zora said, opening the closet to reveal a row of padded hangers and one of those canvas shoe organizers swinging on the back of the door.

"I'll do it later," I said. "Where's your room?"

Zora hesitated for just long enough to make me wonder why. "Down at the other end of the hall," she said, but she didn't offer to show it to me.

"Long hall," I said.

"My room's a mess."

"This is Mafeenie, darlin'. I don't give points for neatness."

"That's not how I remember it," she said. "The same summer we had that pool, you used to check under my bed every single day to be sure I'd swept."

That must have been one of my best acting jobs ever. She still didn't suspect anything!

"I wasn't looking for dust, darlin'. I was checking for snakes."

"Snakes?"

"Howard found a good-size green garden snake curled up under his bed the first week we got there. The caretaker said they were just looking for a cool spot and that they weren't poisonous, but the only way I could get Howard to stay was to promise to check under every bed every day to make sure there weren't any more snakes."

"And you never told me?"

I grinned at her indignation so many years after the deception. "I just did."

Zora looked at me without blinking for a minute and then she started laughing. It was so good to hear the sound of it that I started laughing too and once we got started, we couldn't stop. I laughed so hard my sides ached. Zora had tears running down her cheeks, and we still couldn't stop laughing. I sat down on the edge of the bed and tried to get myself together. Zora's laughter had segued into a slightly hysterical chuckle.

Now this was more like it! We always had fun together. Whatever funk she was in would just have to find another place to spread its gloom.

"If I had known that was such a funny story, I would have told it an hour ago," I said.

Zora was still grinning. "You should be ashamed, Mafeenie. You deceived an innocent child."

"I apologize," I said. "But if I had told you what I was really doing, you would have packed your little suitcase as fast as Howard did!"

"You're right," she said. "I just can't believe the two of you kept that secret for this long."

"My ability to keep a secret is legendary."

"What about Howard? He tells me everything!"

"I threatened his life."

"Why? We could have found another place for the summer."

"Not one with a pool, speaking of which . . ." I stood up and reached for her hand. "If you're not going to show me your room, then how about introducing me to that mermaid?"

"You got a deal," she said, not letting go of my hand when she stood up. "Mafeenie?"

"Yes, darlin'?"

"I'm sorry for being such a bitch at Paschal's. I'm really glad you're here."

"Me, too, darlin'." And this time when I hugged her, she hugged me back tight.

SEVEN

Zora made me a cup of mint tea, poured herself another vodka, and took the bottle with us when we headed outside. Of course, I clocked it, but I didn't say anything. She led the way down the small path from the house to the pool. It was past midnight and the air was cool enough to justify the two Mexican blankets Zora had instructed me to scoop up from a big basket near the back door.

The area around the pool was tiled in the same shades of deep blue as the painting over my bed, and at the bottom there was indeed a beautiful, life-size, brown mermaid whose long black hair curled around her face and spread over the floor of the pool in tendrils that seemed to ripple gently in the soft light. In one hand, she held a large conch shell and with the other, she covered her pubes delicately, demure for all her nakedness.

"It's beautiful," I said, walking over to stare into the mermaid's black eyes and admire her mysterious smile. I wondered if she ever disengaged herself from the bottom of that pool when nobody was looking and did a few languid laps in the moonlight. "Is there a story?"

Zora shrugged. "Some rich white guy built it to impress the neighbors."

I didn't belabor the point, but I knew there was more to it than that. Why a swimming pool rather than a Cadillac? Why that particular blue for the tiles? Why a mermaid and why was she brown? The old Zora would have enjoyed speculating on the options with me, but this bony stranger seemed almost bored with the beauty in her own, albeit temporary, backyard.

We pulled a couple of the striped canvas pool loungers as close as we could to the edge of the mermaid's domain, each holding our drink of choice as we gazed into the water. Zora had placed the vodka bottle carefully out of sight, but we both knew it was there. We just sat there for a few minutes, looking at the mermaid. The ice in her glass tinkled softly, but I tried not to focus on it.

"I've really missed you, Mafeenie," Zora finally said into the stillness.

"Me, too, darlin'," I said. "I can't believe it's been so long. How are we ever going to catch up?"

"I don't know."

There was a slight tremor in her voice and I wished suddenly that I had called her more often in the months we'd been apart. I'm old-fashioned when it comes to personal communications. I know e-mail is faster and cell phones are omnipresent, but I don't like either one. The intrusion of electronic devices always annoys me so Zora and I tend to write long letters in between visits, but not lately.

"Maybe we should just go for it," I said.

She looked at me with some apprehension. "How do you mean?"

"Just start talking. Don't try to organize it or anything. Just tell me what your life has been like since the last time I saw you."

She laughed a little, but it wasn't a good laugh. "Well, my life has been pretty shitty since the last time I saw you."

"All of it?"

"Not all of it, I guess."

"Okay, good. Go on."

She hesitated. "Should I talk about the shitty part first or the other part?"

"Start with the other part. It gives the shitty part too much power if you put it right out front. Tell me the good stuff first."

"Okay."

Then there was a very long pause. I pulled my blanket a little closer around my shoulders and waited. There was no hurry, but the longer the pause went on, the more concerned I got. I took a deep breath, savoring the smell of the mint tea, enjoying the warmth of the cup in my hands, admiring the mermaid, trying not to rush the moment.

"I think I should start with the shitty part," Zora said finally.

"Why is that?"

"It's easier to remember since there's a lot more of it."

Poor baby, I thought. *You've had a rough time.* "Good enough. So tell me everything."

She hesitated again. "All of it?"

"I can stand it if you can."

"I've never really talked about *all* of it."

"Well, here's your chance," I said.

Another pause, not quite as long as the other one, but long enough.

"I don't know where to start."

Zora never had any problem talking to me. We had covered every imaginable topic during our summer road trips from her mother's spirituality, to her father's demons, to her first period. Nothing was off-limits and she knew whatever she shared with me, stayed with me. I was the Las Vegas of grandmothers.

"Start with the trip to D.C.," I said, "where you first met the guy."

Zora's antiwar activities had taken her to Washington for a conference, where she met a young army deserter who was fine enough to attract her attention at the train station, which set the whole thing in motion. They talked over coffee and she gave him a number in Atlanta to call if he ever needed some help dealing with the army, although by the time they parted company Zora was already smitten with his con-man's charm and hoped he'd call for more personal reasons.

When he showed up in Atlanta, broke and jobless, he started cruising the gay clubs as a hustler for hire. One of his customers turned out to be the son of a popular politician, who had an oblivious wife and an adorable two-year-old child at home already. After only one disastrous date, where he ended the evening so drunk he could hardly make it home, Zora realized the guy was not the conscience-driven antiwar hero she'd convinced herself he was, and cut him loose.

His reaction was to seek sex and solace in the arms of a young prostitute who counted among her regular customers a gangster who was more possessive than made any sense, under the circumstances, and who shot the poor boy dead in a loft belonging to Mr. Married-for-show-only. When the cops arrested the young husband and father, all hell broke loose, and Zora blamed herself.

Zora looked stricken. "You know about that?"

"Your mother told me that's where you met him, and I know you were trying to do something good and that it ended badly."

I also knew it had been a rumormonger's mother lode. Atlanta hadn't seen anything as juicy since a popular race leader's coke-dealing girlfriend was arrested after assaulting his wife on his mother's front lawn. That one had included love letters signed in blood and mountains of drugs, but this one involved the suicide of Blue Hamilton's right-hand man, the secret life of a mayoral front-runner's bisexual son, the confessions of a stripper named Brandi, and a cold-blooded murder masquerading as a crime of passion. Jasmine told me Zora was cast as the hazel-eyed beauty whose antiwar activism was, as one *Dig It!* headline screamed, "more deadly to a young soldier than the bombs of Iraq."

"That's pretty much everything," Zora said in a small, tight voice.

"That can't be everything," I said, "because there's nothing in there to make a woman lose thirty pounds, ruin her complexion, and start drinking vodka at all hours."

She drained her glass defiantly in one big gulp and looked away. "Would it be better if I was only drinking at lunchtime?"

It was time for some tough love. "It would be better if you would let that young hustler who got shot rest in peace and let the old fool who killed himself find his reward in paradise."

Zora sat up then and turned toward me, her lovely face a thundercloud. She took a deep breath and I realized I had gone too far. Tough love is one thing but I was definitely dippin'.

"Mafeenie," she said, her voice like ice, "you know I love you and I'm glad you're here, I truly am, but I'm going through some things right now that you can't be part of. You can't figure it out for me and you can't fix it. It's *my* stuff and I'll deal with it, but you have to respect my boundaries, which I know is not your favorite thing, but I really need my space right now. *Okay?*"

I wondered if she'd given this same speech to Jasmine, who, being the progressive mother that she is, probably felt bound to respect it. I, on the other hand, had no intention of staying out of Zora's business. I claim grandmother immunity anytime it comes to Zora's mental health or physical safety. This was obviously one of those times. Of course, I didn't have to tell her that.

"Okay," I said. "I promise not to meddle."

"I'll hold you to it," she said, still sounding firm.

"How about this," I said, hoping to lighten up the moment. "If I don't keep up my end of the bargain, you have my permission to throw me into that beautiful pool."

"With all your clothes on?" I could almost hear a small smile.

"Every stitch."

"It's a deal." She held out her glass and I clinked it with my cup to seal the deal.

She leaned over to refresh her drink with another splash of vodka and settled back in her chair. "Your turn."

"Well, like I told you on the phone, I'm lying low for a while so Howard can mount a big campaign and bring me back in triumph," I said.

"Absence makes the heart grow fonder?"

"Exactly, plus I need to check on the duplex. The new people who are supposed to be handling it keep giving me the runaround."

"Mom said they stopped sending checks."

This was the first I'd heard about any break in payments to Jasmine. From the beginning, I'd directed the company to send any money they collected in rent straight to her for Zora's education. I'd never needed it to live on, and since my son didn't have any life insurance, I was glad I could pick up the slack.

"Since when?"

"Right before I withdrew from Spelman. I guess that's why she didn't tell you."

"Well, she should have."

"She said they sent a letter that said nobody was living there, but as soon as they got some new tenants, they'd be in touch."

"That's almost a year ago."

At six hundred dollars a month for each apartment, that was almost fifteen thousand dollars that they were explaining away so casually. What were they trying to pull?

"Don't tell her I told you, okay?" Zora said. "I didn't mean to start anything."

"You didn't start anything," I said. "But it's time to get this stuff straightened out. They're fooling around with your inheritance."

Zora laughed a little hard laugh when I said that and sat up. "Well, tomorrow's my long day, so I've got to get some sleep. . . ."

"I thought today was your long day."

"We're really shorthanded at the center," she said. "More and more of these guys are coming back every day, women, too, and they need somebody to talk to."

Zora had been working for a veteran support group at the Morehouse School of Medicine, but her boss fired her after her name popped up in the paper one time too many, so she had found another, smaller group to work with. They seemed to specialize in long hours.

"What do they talk about?"

"They used to talk about benefits, housing, taxes," she said, letting go of my hand and standing up. "Now they want to talk about their bad dreams. About what they saw over there. What they did."

No wonder Zora was depressed. Listening to war stories all day and drinking all night. This was no way for her to live.

"I'm working on a project that's really going to help a lot."

"What's your project?"

"I'm putting together a website where the soldiers can be in touch with counselors at our place twenty-four hours a day by using an interactive feature on the site," she said. "Late at night is the worst time for most of these guys. That's when their dreams wake them up and they need somebody to talk to right then, but we're closed, so most of them find a porn site, which, trust me, is not the best antidote to war dreams. If I can get it all worked out, they'll be able to talk to us live 24/7."

I admired Zora's dedication to her work and her skill with the computer. I don't even own one. The only thing that worried me was the work itself. Zora was channeling other people's nightmares for a living and I could see it was taking a toll on her.

"You have to be careful with a job like that," I said.

"I know. My boss always says when you look long into the abyss, the abyss also looks long into you."

"Your boss quotes Nietzsche?"

"He used to be a philosophy professor over at Morehouse, but he lost the stomach for it."

"For philosophy?"

"For Morehouse."

Many Spelman students, matriculating on an all-girl campus, have ambivalent feelings about their brother institution, an all-male enclave just across the street from their elegant, tree-lined campus.

"Tomorrow's my day to open so I'll be out before seven," Zora said. "And I'm trying to get a presentation together about the new website for a conference here this weekend, so I won't be home until after ten. I'm sorry, but I warned you it was going to be crazy!"

"No problem," I said, admiring her commitment to the difficult job she had chosen. "I'll use the time to explore the neighborhood and get my bearings."

"There's not much to eat in the house, but up on Abernathy there's . . ."

I held up my hand. "Please! I have found a way to feed myself from Trinidad to Transylvania. I'll be fine."

Zora gave me another small smile. "What were you doing in Transylvania?"

"Looking for Dracula, what else?"

She leaned down and picked up her blanket and threw it over her shoulder. "Good night, Mafeenie," she said, leaning down to kiss the top of my head.

"Good night, my darlin'," I said, as she started up the path to the house.

"*Je t'aime*," she called back over her shoulder, addressing me with the perfect French accent Howard taught her when she was fifteen and tired of sounding like an American.

"I love you, too," I said, and heard her close the back door behind her as she went inside. I was alone and the yard was silent and wonderfully peaceful. I wondered how the people who lived here had been able to leave it to head off into a war zone. I hoped they were the kind of folks who carried their peace with them. The trip was catching up to me now and I indulged a giant yawn, but I still didn't feel like going inside, so I curled up under my blanket instead and waited to see if I could catch that mermaid having her midnight swim.

EIGHT

•

ora was as good as her word. In the morning, I heard her moving around quietly and then the sound of her little Civic as she pulled away just before seven. It was still dark outside and I gave myself permission to turn over and go right back to sleep, which I did. The best way to avoid jet lag is to let your body handle the transition on its own terms. Those last few hours were exactly what I needed and I woke up at nine thirty feeling refreshed and ready to explore. I had unpacked last night when I finally gave up on the mermaid and came inside at three thirty and it was nice to be able to open the closet and see my things hanging neatly like they belonged there.

I reached in for black pants and a turtleneck, my current street uniform of choice, slipped on a pair of my favorite walking shoes, and grabbed my coat. I had poked around in Zora's kitchen last night and although it was beautifully appointed with an impressive array of gleaming appliances and a ring of copper-bottom pots hanging over the stove, the only things in the refrigerator were a few bottles of water, a couple of Styrofoam containers that I didn't even bother to open, and a jar of kosher dill pickles. The freezer held a half-empty bottle of vodka. Part of my mission today was to find the nearest grocery store and stock up on everything. But first I needed some caffeine and a paper to be sure I hadn't missed anything really awful while I was sleeping. I tucked the extra key and a couple of dollars into my pocket and headed for the West End News.

The day was chilly, but it felt good. The sky was blue and cloudless. I took a deep breath of the morning air and geared my pace to a stroll not a stride. Left to my own devices, I'm a fast walker, but I wanted to get a feel for the neighborhood, and that calls for a different speed altogether.

The houses on each side of Zora's temporary digs were Victorians, too. One with a big, wraparound porch and the other with the most elaborate curlicues I'd seen so far. The street was empty except for two young men coming toward me about a half a block away. They looked to be in their late teens, with big hooded jackets and blindingly white tennis shoes. I wondered if they were on their way to school or on their way to work. I hoped those were the only two choices, although I wasn't really concerned. I was always pretty good at being able to distinguish between the good guys and the bad guys and these two were laughing and talking like old friends, not coconspirators.

Besides, I knew I was invisible to them. Women my age no longer show up on the scan of men under the age of forty-five. This is, for me, a very recent development and I'm still trying to figure out how I feel about it. Until a couple of years ago, I was used to men not only wanting to talk to me, but wanting to sleep with me, but it's all different after fifty. I tried not to admit it, but reality has a way of making you see the truth. One night at a reception, when I was just shy of fifty-five, a handsome young thing was chatting me up in a corner, and I was chatting right back, when he leaned over, put his lips against my ear, and confided that he had always had a thing for older women. It took me a minute to realize he meant *me*, which pretty much killed the mood I'd been working on. I excused myself, claiming a sudden headache, went back to my room, crawled into bed, and pulled the covers up over my head. *An older woman?* This would take some getting used to.

And it did. It still does. There's really nothing that compares to the realization that men are not looking anymore. Oh, if you're standing on the stage with a light on you, they're looking, but I mean out in the world where you're just a real person, trust me, no men are looking. I'm not complaining. It's just a fact. Even if you are truly stylish, they're only looking at your clothes, which also means they're probably gay. But the look from every straight man you pass that evaluates you as a possible sexual partner? That look is gone and it isn't coming back.

That made me sad at first. Not so sad I considered shooting Botox into my face or sewing bags of saline solution into my body to make my breasts look bigger, but definitely a little nostalgic. At first, it was hard to adjust. I'd see a young man approaching and suck in my stomach out of pure habit even though I knew he would probably not pay me the slight-est attention as we passed like ships in the cross-generational night.

Then I realized that all this new invisibility had an upside. I could stop considering random men's sexual evaluations when I encoun-tered them on the public streets. I no longer had to wear high heels, tight pants, or low-cut dresses unless I wanted to. Not that I've always dressed to please men, but as long as there was the possibility of more intimate contact, I wanted to please the eye, as well as stimulate the sex and boggle the mind. But without that possibility, I could simply dress for comfort, protection from the elements, and my own amusement, which is what I began to do. The more I did it, the more I liked it; now I don't even suck in my stomach anymore. The young men passed me deep in conversation without giving me a second glance and I walked the rest of the quiet block with the double satisfaction of having my theory of invisibility check out one more time and of knowing I truly didn't care.

I walked on, enjoying my solitude and wondering if I should fix Zora something special for dinner to tempt her appetite and how far I'd have to go to find some fresh food. It didn't take long for me to find out. When I turned onto Abernathy, it was already bustling with peo-ple on their way to work, doing some shopping, or catching up with friends at the barbershop. The twenty-four-hour salon was as full as it had been the night before. Across the street, I saw a small market that I hadn't even noticed yesterday that was already welcoming a steady stream of customers. If they had a decent produce section, I was home free. Now all I needed was a cup of espresso and a newspaper. Zora had assured me that the West End News had both.

Stepping inside, I felt like I was suddenly back in Amsterdam, ex-cept the cappuccino didn't come with an invitation to roll your own. There were racks of papers and periodicals from all over the world and students with backpacks ordering the daily special blend to go. There were people sitting at small tables, catching up like Howard and I used to do every day of our lives. At the counter, there were two men who seemed to be regulars arguing about the sorry state of one or another of Atlanta's sports teams while the large, serene-looking man behind the counter refilled their cups without being asked.

Stacked near the front door were *The New York Times*, *The Atlanta Journal-Constitution*, *The Washington Post*, and *The Atlanta Sentinel*. I grabbed one of each. There were also copies of several international papers. I picked up *Le Monde* and the London *Times* and moved over to the counter to place my order.

"Here or to go?" the counterman said with a smile. He reminded me of those fat Buddahs I collected for a while—if Buddah had worn a spotless white apron and a pair of perfectly pressed black pants.

"Here," I said, looking around for a seat near the window. I spotted a tiny table tucked into a little nook out of the path to and from the counter. It had a perfect view of the street.

The man behind the counter nodded. "I'll bring it right over."

"Thank you," I said.

I sat down and scanned the papers to see which one caught my eye. *The New York Times* and *The Washington Post* were both full of the latest war news. *Le Monde* had French election coverage, and the London *Times* was clucking its tongue over the latest escapades of the doomed Diana's grown sons. The headline in the *Constitution* trumpeted the city's declining crime rate and praised the mayor for her innovative approach to community policing. All important stories, but none that seemed particularly suited to accompany my morning caffeine, so I sat back and just gazed out the window. It felt good to be here. I can't say it felt like home, but it was close enough.

My Buddah with the big white apron came out from behind the counter and brought my espresso, complete with the little lemon twist that isn't required but is always missed.

"We've got some lovely croissants this morning," he said, trying to tempt me.

"No, thank you," I said. "This is fine."

"Well, just let me know if you need anything. I'm Henry."

"Josephine," I said.

"Welcome to the neighborhood," he said, heading back to his post where two girls with backpacks and iPod headphones in their ears were waiting to pay for their coffee. I wondered if they were together and, if they were, if they talked around the music, or just walked along together, each one in her own universe of separate sounds.

I took a sip of the strong, hot brew and realized he knew his customers well enough to spot a stranger immediately. That's the thing about West End that I always enjoy. It feels more like a small town than a big-city neighborhood with skyscrapers in its backyard and a rapid-rail system carrying people to the busiest airport in the world fifteen minutes away. I wished for a minute that my mother had bought her duplex over here, before I remembered that when she bought the place, black folks weren't allowed to buy these houses.

As I sat there, sipping my espresso and getting my bearings, the door opened and a woman entered in a long, dark green skirt, a bright orange shawl, and a pair of hot pink Chinese slippers with roses embroidered on each toe. Her short, curly hair was pulled away from her face and behind her, she trailed the faintest scent of patchouli.

"Good morning, Miss A," Henry said as she stepped up to the counter. "The usual?"

"Good morning, Henry. Thank you."

The woman looked to be about my age, give or take a year or two, and something about her looked so familiar I almost smiled and said good morning. Did I know her? I grew up in Atlanta, but I almost never see anybody from those days on my infrequent visits and when I do, I can't hardly ever remember their names. What did the *A* stand for?

"You two settle the season yet?" she said, her voice teasing the two at the counter who had nodded their good mornings when she first came in. Their discussion seemed to have ended in a draw that didn't please either one and they were sulking.

"This Negro doesn't know a good first baseman from a hole in the ground," said the one with the houndstooth jacket.

The one in the stingy-brim hat just snorted and rolled his eyes. "At least I know what a shortstop does."

Henry chuckled as he expertly added a sprinkle of cinnamon to the takeout cup of cappuccino, which must have been "the usual."

"Don't get them all riled up again, Miss A," Henry said. "They're running my customers away with all that mess."

She laughed, a sweetly musical sound, as Henry handed her a cup with a cardboard sleeve so it wouldn't be too hot on her walk to wherever she was going. Was it Anna? Adelaide? Ava? Abbie? *Abbie!* Could this be Abbie from D.C.? How long had it been since I'd seen her? Twenty years? Thirty? Was it Amsterdam? Paris? She looked almost exactly the same as I remembered her and she still smelled like patchouli, which was always her trademark scent.

"Sorry about that," she said, handing over five dollars and declining her change. "I thought you two had called a truce."

"Ain't nobody studying you, Henry," the slightly older man said.

"Besides," said the one with the hat, turning fully toward Abbie with a twinkle. "We only come in here to wish you good day, Miss Abbie, and you know that!"

It was her! Abbie Browning, live and in living color. What the hell was she doing in West End?

"Mr. Charles, does your wife know you're out here flirting so early in the morning?"

"No, and don't you tell her," he said, holding up his hands in mock terror. "That woman ain't got no sense of humor when it comes to me."

"She married you, didn't she?" the other one said. "How much more sense of humor she gotta have?"

Henry laughed at that and so did Abbie.

"What do you hear from Hamilton?" Mr. Charles said.

"The song is done and Gina said it's a shoo-in to win the Carnival competition."

The two men nodded in unison and smiled as if hearing that a favorite nephew had just been accepted to college.

"We ought to go down there for the show and surprise them," Mr. Charles said.

The other one rolled his eyes again. "That would surprise them all right. Two old fools trying to keep up with the young folks."

Abbie shook her head. "It's not like that, Mr. Eddie. Everybody goes to Carnival. Old people, young people. The streets are full of all kinds of people dancing and singing and drinking that Trinidadian beer they buy off the trucks. What's it called?"

She looked at Henry, but he just chuckled and patted his ample belly. "Last time I went to Carnival people were still calling me *Slim*. The only thing I remember is all the beautiful girls."

Mr. Eddie poked his friend. "Then Charlie ain't gotta worry about going. Iona ain't takin' him no place like that."

"Shoot, that woman know she ain't got to worry about me," Charlie said. "I got sense enough to know I'm a lucky man."

"You got that right."

"Peachy's still looking for you all to come down and see the restaurant," Abbie said. "There are two seats at the bar just waiting."

"You tell Nolan we'll be down there as soon as it warms up a little," Mr. Eddie said. "We too old to be messing around at the beach in the middle of the winter."

"It's almost spring!" Abbie laughed and adjusted her shawl around her shoulders. "Have a good one, y'all."

"You, too," they said together as if they had rehearsed it.

Mr. Charles tipped his hat as she headed for the door. I stood up quickly.

"Excuse me," I said. "Are you Abbie Browning?"

Standing that close to her, there was no doubt that she was. Like all of us, she was a little heavier and, of course, a few years older, but she had that same bright, curious, wide-open face and that same beautiful skin.

"Yes," she said, turning in my direction. I wondered suddenly if she'd remember me. Paris was a lifetime ago. "Josephine? Josephine Evans?"

The recognition was immediate and the enthusiasm genuine. "Oh, my God! Is it really you?"

"It's me," I said, laughing. "I thought that was you!"

"Oh, my God!" she said again, reaching out to hug me with her free arm. I hugged her back as the three men at the counter watched us like we were a reality TV show being performed for their amusement.

"You haven't changed a bit," I said. "You look great."

"So do you! How long has it been? Twenty years?"

"Close enough." It was probably more like thirty.

"What are you doing here?"

"I just got in last night. I'm spending some time with my granddaughter."

"Who's your granddaughter?"

The three at the counter leaned forward to hear my answer. "Zora Evans."

"Zora's your granddaughter?"

The counter contingent nodded their approval.

"Do you know her?"

"Everybody around here knows Zora."

More nodding.

"Well, she's house-sitting a beautiful place right around the corner with an amazing pool and I—"

"Amelia and Louis's place?" Abbie interrupted me.

I nodded.

"That's right. They're still in Lebanon."

The town was getting smaller by the minute. "Do you know all your neighbors?"

"All I can stand," she said, turning toward the counter. "Have you met the crew?"

"I met Henry," I said, and he nodded, "but not these other two gentlemen."

"Well, I'd better go on and introduce you since they'll have a fit if I don't."

"We ain't studying you, Miss Abbie," Mr. Eddie said, standing up to be properly presented.

"Mr. Charles and Mr. Eddie, meet my friend Josephine Evans."

"Pleased to meet you," they said in unison, and Mr. Charles took off his hat.

"Where you from?" he said, smiling like a man who enjoys talking to women.

"I was born here, but I've been living in Amsterdam for about thirty years."

"I met her in Paris," Abbie said.

"I like Paris," Henry said, leaning on the counter and folding his surprisingly muscular arms as if settling in for a nice long talk.

"What were you doing way over there?" Mr. Eddie said, wrinkling his brow like there could be no more unlikely place for me to hang my hat.

"Hold on now," Abbie said, laughing and holding up her hand. "Me and Jo have a lot of catching up to do! You'll have to wait your turn."

Their disappointment was almost comical. Maybe I was invisible to the youngsters on the street, but these guys seemed to see me just fine.

"Well, let us know if you need anything," Henry said. "You know where to find us."

Mr. Charles and Mr. Eddie nodded and turned back to the fresh cups of coffee Henry was pouring for them.

Abbie smiled at me and her long silver earrings caught the sunlight pouring in through the window. "Do you have time to talk?"

"Absolutely," I said, pointing to the table where my empty cup and untouched newspapers awaited my return. "Pull up a chair."

"Not here," she said quickly, dropping her voice. "They'll be listening so hard, one of them will have a stroke."

"I heard that," Mr. Charles said over his shoulder.

"Ain't nobody studying you," added Mr. Eddie, who seemed to favor that response over all others. "We got more on our minds than you think we do."

"I stand corrected." Abbie laughed and turned to me. "You ready?"

I had no idea where we were going, but finding a long-lost friend so far from home is the best kind of good omen. I grabbed my coat and tucked the papers under my arm. "Ready."

NINE

•

When we stepped outside, Abbie adjusted her shawl and linked her arm through mine like we were French schoolgirls on our way to an early class.

"I didn't mean to snatch you away like that," she said, "but I'm on my way out of town and I wanted to grab a few minutes so we could at least exchange numbers or schedules or whatever it is you're supposed to exchange after being out of touch for so long."

"We can do all that," I said, sorry she was leaving and hoping she'd be back soon. "Where are you going?"

"I'm driving down to Tybee Island for a couple of days. Do you know it?"

"Off the coast near Savannah?"

"That's the one. I have a friend who just opened a restaurant there and commissioned a photograph from an artist who lives up here. We're driving down together to deliver it. Have you met Aretha?"

I shook my head. "I just got here, remember?"

She laughed and squeezed my arm. "You'll meet her and Peachy, my friend who owns the restaurant and . . . How long are you going to be here?"

"A month or so," I said. "I want to spend some time with Zora, and I own a duplex over on Martin Luther King that I need to check on."

"Wonderful." She beamed at me. "For me and for Zora. I think she needs a little nurturing right now, even though she would never admit it."

"I think so, too," I said, pleased her assessment echoed my own. "Were you here when all that stuff was happening last year?"

"I was, but I had some of my own stuff to deal with right then, so I wasn't much help." A shadow of something flickered across her face, but she banished it with another bright smile. "That's a story for an-other day."

"No problem," I said. "Where are we going now?"

"Well, why don't you tell me about the old crowd? Do you ever see Howard Denmond? Weren't you all good friends?"

"I see him all the time, but I meant where are we actually going?"

"Oh! Good lord! I thought you meant conversationally."

"I figure the conversation will take care of itself. I just wondered where we were headed."

"I'm sort of house-sitting, too," she said as we turned off Aber-nathy down one of the tree-lined residential streets. "My niece, Regina, and her husband are on vacation with their new baby and I'm keeping an eye on things. I thought we could go over to my place and talk until Aretha comes to pick me up."

An interesting piece of Abbie's current life fell into place. "Your niece is married to Blue Hamilton?"

"Yes. Two years last Christmas. Do you know him?"

"I know enough about him to know that he probably doesn't need you to keep an eye on things."

"He's a good man." She smiled.

"Everybody says so," I agreed. "Zora showed me their house on the way home last night."

"You should have stopped," Abbie said, sounding disappointed. "I'm always up late."

"I didn't even know you were here yet."

She laughed and squeezed my arm again. "In that case, I forgive you!"

She stopped in front of what I already knew to be her niece's front gate. The house looked even bigger in daylight and the magnolia was even more magnificent. There is no more beautiful symbol of the South than the magnolia tree, but I knew it would drive Howard crazy. Whenever he even sees a picture of a magnolia, he starts humming Bil-lie Holiday's "Strange Fruit" and muttering about lynching parties.

Abbie opened the front door, tossed her shawl on a narrow table in the hallway, and reached for my coat. She stashed it in a small closet while I took a look around. Inside, the house had high ceilings, an abundance of windows, and from what I could see, an appealing mixture of big leather chairs, soft couches with enough pillows to get lost in, and a traditional rocking chair with a high back and a cane bottom. There was also a huge toy chest tucked next to a tiny replica of the larger leather chairs that I assumed belonged to the baby of the house.

In the hallway, there were photographs of family, friends, and faraway places, much like the arrangement in the kitchen at Zora's place. The study off the living room boasted floor-to-ceiling bookcases and a small chess table with the intricately carved pieces neatly arranged in what looked like a game in progress. I never liked chess. It reminds me of baseball. Long stretches of nothing much going on that anybody else can see, interrupted by bursts of excitement when somebody hits a home run or crows "checkmate!" I like checkers.

"Come on back to the kitchen," Abbie said. "I can make us a pot of coffee or we can just share this cup of Henry's famous cappuccino."

"I think I've had enough caffeine for the time being," I said. "How about a glass of water?"

"No problem," she said, leading the way to a lovely, light-filled kitchen with a long table that could easily seat eight, ten if they squeezed a little, more photographs, and two huge wall maps, one of the world and one of the United States. The world map had colored pushpins stuck in it like they used to do in elementary school to show you where a particular story might be taking place in some part of the world you probably couldn't quite pronounce yet.

As Abbie went to the refrigerator, I leaned over for a closer look, my eye unable not to clock the distance between Atlanta and Amsterdam. There was a whole ocean between me and everything that had defined my life for the last thirty years. I suddenly hoped Howard knew what he was doing. I was a long way from home without even a reliable pair of ruby slippers to get me back. What if the theater didn't come around? What if François didn't have the guts to stick up for me? What if nobody else would cast me? What if I really was too old to play Medea?

Abbie's voice broke through the sudden swirl of my worrying like a sunbeam on a cloudy day. "How about champagne instead?"

I turned around to find her holding up a bottle of Dom Pérignon and two graceful flutes. "That is an inspired idea, but are Americans allowed to drink champagne before noon?"

"It's midnight somewhere." Abbie laughed.

"You got that right!" And I laughed, too.

She set the glasses down and opened the bottle easily. I like women who can open whatever they're drinking without looking around for a man to pop the cork. She poured us each a glass and we raised them for a toast.

"To friendship," I said.

"To friendship."

We each took a sip to seal the deal and settled in at one end of the long table to catch up a little.

"You know I think this champagne was meant for you," Abbie said.

"I'm glad," I said, "but how do you figure that? You didn't know I was here until an hour ago."

"I didn't know all the details," she said, "but I've been feeling an arrival for almost a week."

She sounded like the Jedi Master in *Star Wars* who is so highly evolved he can identify even the smallest changes in the universe as disturbances in the Force.

"So you went out and bought a bottle of Dom Pérignon, just in case?"

She smiled and took another sip. "Something like that. I have great faith in my instincts."

I raised my glass. "Then here's to your instincts."

My instincts would probably have told me to get a bottle of André's in case things didn't work out, but I admired her style.

"Things always work out," she said, as if she could read my mind. "Who would have thought I'd run into you at the West End News after all these years, but I did."

"It's so good to see you," I said.

"Ditto," she said and we just sat for a minute, sipping our champagne and enjoying the lovely coincidence that had brought us together.

Abbie was one of those friends I had made when I was traveling so much I literally lived out of a suitcase. François had gotten a grant to do a series of workshops and performances and we never stayed anywhere longer than three weeks. It was exciting and exhausting and taught me more about doing theater than any class ever could have. The process lent itself to the formation of very intense relationships that developed quickly, flamed or sputtered just as fast, and left you either sorry to say goodbye or relieved to be moving on.

I met Abbie in Paris. She was married to a painter who was a good friend of François's and after she saw our opening performance, she came to the show every night. Afterward, the four of us would meet at their apartment, drink cheap wine, and talk about art until the wee hours, when François and I would walk home, make love, and fall asleep in each other's arms so we could get up the next day and do it all again.

François had lots of interesting male friends who I had met on the tour, but the women who adored them fell into two main categories: rich and long suffering; or young and bedazzled. In both cases, when the men were present, these women spent their time glued to the side of the beloved, hanging on his every word, no matter how banal, and waiting to refresh his drink without being asked. Alone, their conversations consisted mostly of reverential reviews of the great man's talent or brokenhearted revelations of frequent and unrepentant infidelities.

But Abbie wasn't like that. She was in love with her husband and she clearly respected his work, but she never seemed to worship him or think his life more worthy of attention than her own. Recognizing a kindred spirit that first night when we talked until dawn almost as if our significant others weren't even there, I invited her for lunch before the show the next day, in addition to drinks with the guys after. For the next three weeks, that became our very pleasant habit. We'd meet at noon, then talk and eat until three when I had to start getting ready for the show.

She was a few years older—I discovered this was her second marriage—but we were being molded and marked by the same movements for change that were stirring people up all over the world. She wasn't an artist, but her perception of herself as "a free woman in process" mirrored my own. We encouraged each other to savor the adventures, to push the boundaries, and to demand of our lovers not only good sex but absolute truth and absolute tenderness, not necessarily in that order.

When our troupe packed up a few weeks later and headed back to Amsterdam, Abbie promised to write and I promised to visit, but we saw each other only one more time before this morning. She came through with her painter on the way to Madrid and confided that she'd be leaving him in Spain and heading back to D.C. for a while. At first, I didn't realize what she meant until she said she intended to file the papers in the United States since he was an Italian and it was much harder to get a divorce there. I expressed my sympathy at the dissolution of her marriage and she looked sad, but not inconsolable.

"He's a lovely man and a great painter," she said, "but he's just not the one."

I had been surprised at the idea of "the one" coming out of Abbie's mouth. I guess I believe in it, too. At some level, we can't *not* believe in it. Great love stories are always built on the quest for, or loss of, *the one*. But Abbie was realistic, just like I was. Maybe more so. When I met her, she'd already been married twice and I had heard through the grapevine later that she'd tried it twice more, once with a cellist and once with a writer, with an equal lack of success. I wondered if she was married now.

"Last time we saw each other, I was still married to the painter," she said, reading my mind again.

"Antonio," I said.

She laughed. "Isn't it funny how I always identified them by their jobs, not their names? The painter, the writer, the guitar player . . ."

"The cellist."

"Same guy," she said.

"Wasn't there one more?"

"Nope. Three's the charm," she said. "I think I'm done. Did you and François ever get married?"

I shook my head. "No. We still work together, though."

"I know. I've seen the reviews."

"Really? Where?"

"Online, of course. All I have to do is type in The Human Theatre and it gives me everything. Schedules, stars, ticket prices. I've kept up with you. What are you opening with next season?"

The question was still too new for me to answer without a little twinge of anxiety. "I'm not sure yet. Part of the reason I'm here is to try and figure that out."

She looked surprised. "Really?"

I nodded. "It's a pretty weird time to be an American. People are mad at us all around the world. I got thrown out of an Iraqi friend's funeral just for being an American citizen."

"You're kidding!"

"I wish I was. That's why the board at the theater hasn't confirmed a schedule yet. I always open the season, but they're afraid to cast me because I'm an American."

She shook her head sympathetically. "Be careful what you ask for."

"I never asked for this!"

"Yes, you did," she said calmly. "We all did. We demanded it. We wanted to be first-class American citizens. And we won! That's exactly what we are, with all the rights and responsibilities thereto, 'til death do us part."

She was sort of starting to piss me off, although I couldn't argue with what she was saying.

"So does that mean I now have to answer for every arrogant white boy these fools send to the White House?"

"These fools," she said gently, "are your fellow citizens and yes, you have to answer for each and every choice they make because there is no *they*. That's the whole point. It's us. All of us Americans together."

I looked at her, sitting there in the little Chinese shoes, and the hippie skirt, looking as bohemian as she ever had, but sounding like Pete Seeger's ghost. "When did you get to be so patriotic?"

"Last summer." She grinned at my surprise. "Me and Peachy drove across the country. I wasn't sure I wanted to do it, but I needed a new perspective and I really wanted to see the redwoods. All my life, I had wanted to see those trees, but I had never gotten around to it, so last summer, we took off down historic Route 66, with Nat King Cole on the CD player, and it absolutely changed my life."

My only driving trip across the country had been with my parents many years ago when there were no hotels or motels for black folks between Gadsden's in Birmingham and the Dunbar in Los Angeles, with nothing but Texas in between. It was memorable in my mind, primarily for the excruciating embarrassment of having to pee by the side of the road while my mother held up a tablecloth to shield me from the curiosity of passersby.

"Driving across the country made you feel like a citizen?" I could hear the skepticism in my voice.

"I know it sounds corny," she said, "but the farther away we got from the cities and the more I saw of all those amber waves of grain and purple mountains majesty, and met all those people who talked about the weather by going outside to actually see it, the more I felt like it was my country, too, in all its messy, multiracial, multicultural madness and I had a right to claim it as my own. You can, too."

She was getting a little worked up, but I couldn't see it. "Go on."

"I felt something shift in how I look at things. How I see myself in relation to those things and to the world. I don't even really understand it myself yet, but I'm planning to go again as soon as I can. You know how much I love to chase a new idea."

Curiosity was one of Abbie's two defining characteristics. Optimism was the other one. In her latest quest to fully embrace our motherland, she had a perfect place to express both. We had fallen back into conversation as easily as we had the summer we met and I realized how much I'd missed her.

"I wish you'd gotten in touch," I said.

"I thought about it," she said, "but I guess I figured we were both probably too busy having our adventures to keep up much of a correspondence and I've always hated telephones."

"Me, too," I said.

"Besides, look at us," she refilled our lovely glasses, "together again, drinking champagne in the morning just like in the old days."

"Tell me you're not the designated driver," I said, remembering she was leaving for her friend's restaurant in a little while.

"Don't worry. Aretha's driving. It's her pickup. I'm just a passenger."

"How big is this photograph anyway?" I said, surprised that they needed a truck to transport it.

"Well, now that she's got it all framed, it's pretty big. Peachy wanted one of those big ornate gold frames they always have in the movie saloons, so Aretha found one. It's huge!"

In those movies, that frame Abbie's friend remembered was usually holding a painting of a voluptuous woman, posing comfortably without a stitch. I wondered if she was going all the way with the saloon motif.

"Is it a nude?"

"The photograph?" Abbie said, and started to laugh.

"What's so funny?" I said as the doorbell announced an arrival Abbie may or may not have felt coming.

"Nothing," she said, still laughing, as she headed for the front door. "Except I'm a little too long in the tooth to be hanging over anybody's bar stark naked, even if the frame is a real antique."

TEN

·

I didn't know it was a photograph of you!" I said when the smiling young woman who introduced herself as Aretha Hargrove carefully removed the protective padding to reveal a larger-than-life portrait of Abbie standing with her back to the ocean and her face to the sky. The frame was, as desired, big and bold and very gold.

"Well, who else is he going to put up in a place called Sweet Abbie's?"

My face must have shown my surprise because Abbie laughed and actually blushed, which was truly charming in a woman our age. It takes a certain amount of innocence to respond with an uncontrollable flush when someone ventures too close to whatever you hold secret or sacred or just plain private and therefore not suitable for public consumption.

"The restaurant is named after you?"

Aretha grinned at Abbie. "She's still in denial, although I don't know how long you're going to be able to keep that going once he hangs this bad boy right inside the main entrance."

"I'm not in denial," Abbie chided Aretha gently, who simply rolled her eyes and leaned against the truck nonchalantly.

I judged her to be in her late twenties, tall and strong looking with a head full of tiny twists held back from her face with a big red ribbon. She was wearing overalls and a T-shirt, but her long neck and easy grace made her look elegant in spite of her paint-splattered work boots and well-worn navy pea coat. She and Abbie had an easy give-and-take and their joking was the kind that can never mask real affection.

"He who?" I said.

"Peachy, the owner," Aretha said. "He's been driving me crazy to get this hung."

"Peachy's a man?" I was sure Abbie had said *she*. Or maybe I just assumed the friend she was going to visit, the friend she'd been with when she had her "I'm an American" moment was a woman.

"Of course, he's a man," Aretha said, turning to Abbie. "You're not in denial about that too, are you?"

"I told you. I'm not in denial about anything. Peachy is a friend," she said to me. "A good friend."

"The best," Aretha said to me sotto voce.

Abbie ignored her. "We've been through a lot together, and when he decided to open this restaurant, he asked me if he could call it Sweet Abbie's."

She shrugged her shoulders and I swear she blushed again. "I told him he could."

Aretha shook her head and her twists jiggled on her head like the ringlets that used to come standard on the better baby dolls. Cheap baby dolls had molded plastic heads with painted-on curls, but as you moved up in price, the hair got better, too, until you reached the most expensive dolls which had rooted plastic hair, usually blond, that could be washed and set on tiny pink plastic rollers. I wondered if Aretha set hers or just tied it back with a bow and let it go its own buoyant way.

"He should have called it Please, Baby, Please," she said. "Since he's only doing it as a love offering."

This was getting more and more interesting. "What kind of love offering?"

"For Miss A," Aretha said. "He's hoping once he proves himself, she'll let him make an honest woman out of her."

I raised my eyebrows at Abbie. Was she really considering taking on a number four?

"I should have told you that Aretha is an incurable romantic. She keeps trying to marry me off."

"I am many things, but an incurable romantic is not one of them. I just know Peachy and I know a little about you." Aretha grinned at me. "We'll talk later."

"I'll look forward to it," I said.

Abbie smiled at us both. "You want to come in, or are we ready to roll?"

Aretha checked her watch. "If we get on the road now, we might be able to get this thing on the wall before he opens for dinner. Should we try for it?"

"Sure. I'll get my things."

Aretha climbed back into the pickup, which was a bright red, perfectly restored sixties-era Chevy, a gift from her uncle Eddie, she told me after I complimented her on it when we first went outside. He had taught her to drive when she was fourteen, and when she left home to come to Spelman, he handed her the keys.

"I was the only girl in my whole freshman class who owned her own pickup," she said, still proud of her uniqueness.

Abbie grabbed a small overnight bag and her shawl.

"Still travelin' light?" I said, echoing Zora.

"High praise from the woman who once hit all the major European cultural capitals in three months with only one suitcase and a duffel bag."

"Those were the days," I said, grabbing my coat, confident that I would spend many more pleasant hours in this house over the next few weeks. I still had a lot of questions about this whole citizenship thing that needed answers, but they could wait until another time.

"No, these are the days," she said, turning to hug me. "I'll be back on Friday. Why don't you come for dinner on Sunday? Bring Zora if she's free."

"I would love to," I said. "Thank you."

Aretha was at the wheel with the motor running as we headed down the front walk. The magnolia was swaying gently in the breeze, the big waxy leaves, dry in winter, clacking softly against each other in the topmost branches. I was loving the feel of this neighborhood. Abbie being just around the corner was icing on the cake.

"By the way," I said, suddenly remembering my day's major mission, "how's that little grocery store across from the newsstand?"

"It's great," she said, opening the passenger door and handing her bag to Aretha, who tucked it behind the seat. "The woman who started all the gardens around here opened it six months ago. The produce is always fresh."

"There's a bakery in there, too," Aretha added as Abbie climbed in and clicked her seat belt into place.

"Sounds perfect," I said.

Abbie reached her arm out the window and I took her hand.

"I'm so happy you're here," she said. "We have so much to talk about."

"I can't wait!" I said. "Have a safe trip."

Aretha tooted the horn as they pulled away and I waved them goodbye as they turned the corner and headed for the interstate. It wasn't even noon and I had already found an old friend, made a new one, shared some champagne, and heard about a man named Peachy who was in hot pursuit of a woman who had just told me that marrying again was the last thing on her mind. Now all I had to do was head over to the grocery store so I could stock Zora's kitchen with something more interesting than a bottle of Stolichnaya. Abbie was right. We have everything to talk about, but in the meantime, a woman's still got to eat.

ELEVEN

·

*T*he grocery store was even better than Abbie had described it. Small and crowded with customers moving carefully between the narrow aisles, it boasted a wide variety of fresh fruits and vegetables, fish and fowl, but no red meat. The bakery offered sliced bread and crusty loaves, along with homemade fruit pies and a beautiful chocolate cake, whimsically decorated with a border of bright pink roses and the word *Yes* right in the middle where *Happy Birthday* usually goes.

I bought as much as I could fit into the reusable canvas bags I bought at checkout to do my part to stop global warming, and headed home a happy woman. I'm not political in the traditional sense, but I think some things are fairly obvious, even to somebody like me. *Peace is better than war. Global warming will kill you.* Once I get it, I do what I can.

The phone was ringing as I closed the front door behind me, and I checked the caller ID, delighted to see Howard's number showing.

"Hey, you!" I said. "Your timing is perfect. I just walked in the door."

"Hey, yourself," he said. "My timing is lousy. I've been calling you for hours."

"I've only been gone two days." I laughed. "Can't live without me, huh?"

"I'm hanging on by a thread already. How was the trip?"

"Uneventful," I said.

"And how's my baby?"

"She's been better, but nothing a little bit of her adoring grand-mother's TLC can't fix."

"Let me speak to her."

"She's still at work. You're stuck with me. Guess who I ran into?"

"Greta Garbo."

"She's dead, remember?"

"So is Elvis, and people run into him all the time."

"Abbie Browning."

"From Paris?"

"Well, she lives here now, but Paris is where we met her," I said, surprised he remembered her. "I'm impressed with your powers of recall."

"Does she still smell like patchouli?"

Now I was really impressed. "Yes, she does! How can you possibly remember that?"

"Please," he said. "She was the only black girl I knew who always, *always* smelled like patchouli."

"How many white ones did you know?"

"Hundreds. Thousands! There was a moment there when after every show, all my costumes would smell like hippie hash bars, but that's not why I called you."

"I thought you called to say you missed me."

"I'm not the only one. I talked to François this morning. He can't believe that you left without giving him a chance to explain."

"Explaining has never been his strong point or mine."

"Well, all that might be about to change. The board is meeting next Wednesday to discuss the season. They wanted you there in case the press shows up."

"Why would the press care about a routine meeting?"

"Because I've alerted them to the strong possibility of unpleasantness."

"You didn't!"

"I most certainly did. How else am I going to get the word out to your many fans that their queen may be in peril?"

I laughed out loud. If I had any doubt that Howard knew what to do to get me back where I wanted to be, his status report obliterated it. "You're my hero."

Howard laughed, too. "Of course I am, but I'm doing this for purely selfish reasons. I'm already dying of loneliness. Without you, everything is a bore."

"You're never bored!"

"I know that, but if I was, now would be the time," he said.

"I miss you, too," I said. "Call me after the board meeting and let me know how it went?"

"I've already got you on speed dial," he said. "Gotta run. Kiss my baby for me! Love you madly!"

"Love you more!"

Which was probably not true. When it comes to unconditional love, me and Howard are tied for first place.

TWELVE

·

When Zora got home at ten thirty, I was in the kitchen putting the finishing touches on what I knew was one of her favorite meals: roast chicken with lemon and tarragon butter, green beans with almonds, and new potatoes. I had also picked up a loaf of crusty French bread, and for dessert, baked apples with whipped cream. The landlord's kitchen was well organized, well equipped, and a pleasure to work in, even for an amateur like me. I've always loved to cook for my friends, and Zora and I had spent a lot of time together in the kitchen. Judging from her dramatic weight loss, she hadn't spent many hours there lately.

I had found a multidisc CD player in the front room and programmed it for random selections, curious about what might come up for my listening pleasure. Exploring somebody's music is as revealing as poking through their closet, and usually a lot more fun. By the time Zora arrived, I had heard everybody from Louis Armstrong to Buckwheat Zydeco and enjoyed them all. I was basting the chicken, singing along loudly to Bob Marley's "Exodus," and wishing I had the patience to grow dreadlocks when she walked in. She gave me a quick peck on the cheek and headed straight for the freezer.

"Hey, darlin'," I said, closing the oven door and figuring another thirty-five minutes should do it. "Welcome home. You hungry?"

"I didn't know you were cooking," she said, pouring herself a drink. "I grabbed a sandwich a couple of hours ago."

"No problem," I said, willing to bet she hadn't eaten anything, although I could smell the vodka already on her breath when she kissed me. "You can sit with me while you have your drink."

"I don't think I'd be very good company," she said, tossing a copy of *Dig It!* on the kitchen counter in front of me. It was today's issue and there she was on the cover, standing in Paschal's draped in my luggage, looking stressed out and skinny, next to a picture of herself looking like she used to, happy, healthy, and effortlessly beautiful.

Scandal takes its toll! The headline blared. *Dig It! exclusive. What a difference a year makes!*

"What is this?" I said, confused.

"There's more," she said. "Page six."

I flipped to it and there we both were, sitting in Paschal's, talking intensely. The pictures weren't great, but they were accurate. Zora looked terrible and I looked concerned. Movie people always say that the camera doesn't lie, and in this case they were right.

At the bottom was a reproduction of the cover photos with comments about the change in her appearance, complete with arrows pointing out the contrast. *Breasts: Last year, full and firm. This year, shrunken and sunken. Booty: Last year, best in show. This year, where'd it go?*

I was outraged at the invasion of her privacy and mystified as to the possible photographer. "Where did they get these?"

"Probably the waiter."

"MacArthur?" I couldn't believe it. "Why would he?"

"Because they pay good money for this crap." She practically spit out the words.

"He didn't seem like that kind of guy," I said.

Hair, said the copy next to an arrow pointing at Zora's severe little ponytail. *Last year, perfect perm. This year, mystery mess.*

"I can't believe they got it out this fast!"

Zora looked at me for a minute and took a swallow of her drink. "You still don't get it, Mafeenie. It's different now. It's fast and it's vicious and it never stops!"

"Welcome to the world," I said, wishing she wasn't already high. Talking to a drunk is counterproductive. Afterward they never remember what you said.

"All right, Mafeenie," she said. "I think now's a good time to show you my room." She nodded at the tabloid on the counter. "Bring that, will you?"

I followed her up the stairs, wondering what I would find behind that closed door. It had taken all my strength not to open it this afternoon, just enough to take a peek inside, but I couldn't have lived with myself after that kind of betrayal of trust. Sure, I was worried about Zora's state of mind, and sure, I was a believer in grandmother privilege, but not enough to risk alienating her forever.

When we got to the door of her room, I thought she might pause for some kind of warning like *don't touch anything,* or *it doesn't bite,* but she walked right in like she had nothing to hide. The room was a little smaller than mine, and it didn't have a view of the pool, but from what I could see, there were no snakes under the neatly made bed at all, just two packing boxes and a pair of fluffy pink slippers. On the night-stand was a photograph of me, one of her and Jasmine on the back deck of the motel, one of her father in costume for his one and only Broadway show, and one of her with Howard in front of the theater in Amsterdam. She set her glass on the dresser and leaned down to pull out the boxes. Curious, I stood there holding the rolled-up copy of today's *Dig It!* and awaiting further instructions.

"Pick one," she said.

"What are they?"

"Just pick one. Any one. Any one at all."

She slurred that just enough to make me cringe so I reached down and pulled out the first thing my fingers touched. It was another copy of *Dig It!* The front cover was split in half, they seemed to like that effect, with a picture of Zora on one side and on the other side, a picture of the murdered vet. He was wearing an army uniform and holding a huge automatic weapon in one hand and what looked like a joint in the other. The headline said: *Doomed vet well known as battlefield doper!* The date at the top was last summer.

Zora was watching me, but she offered no explanation.

"Are they all *Dig It!*'s?"

"It comes out every day," she said. "You'd be surprised how fast they accumulate."

She plucked the back issue and the new one from my hands and knelt to quickly tuck them into place.

"The new one goes in at the back of the section," she said. "The old one resumes its position between *Mystery coed's ties to dead gangster target of police probe* and *Dead vet's shocking secret life lead to coed ultimatum.*"

She was right about one thing. The sheer volume of the coverage was a sickening surprise to me. No wonder she was overwhelmed. She stood up again, reached for her drink, and took a big swallow. When she looked back at me, her lips were set in a tight line. Turns out Zora had snakes under her bed after all.

"Why are you keeping this stuff?" I said. "Aren't you the one who called it a bunch of trash?"

"It's history," she said. "Maybe I'll show them to my kids one day."

"Why would you do that?"

She shrugged her thin shoulders. "Oh, I don't know. Maybe to show them that life is more complicated than they think it is."

I resisted the impulse to tell her life is always more complicated than you think it is. I also resisted a strong impulse to kick the box over. "Why do you care what these idiots say?"

"Because people believe what they read whether it's true or not."

"What difference does it make? People who know you don't think it's true."

"Which would be fine if all I had to do was hang around with people I already know, except that's not the kind of job I have, remember? It's not like I'm a librarian, Mafeenie. I don't just do counseling, I'm starting to represent the organization at conferences and hearings. This kind of crap just makes it hard for anybody to take me seriously."

This wasn't something we had to settle before dinner, but the idea of her pushing those boxes of bullshit back under her bed didn't sit well with me. Sleeping people are so vulnerable because all our defenses are down. Curling up nightly on top of two years' worth of lies and garbage couldn't possibly be good.

Zora sighed deeply. "I practically had to beg my boss for a chance to do the big presentation downtown tomorrow, even though it's my idea, and now this comes out." She shook her head. "I'll be surprised if he still lets me do it."

She looked miserable and resigned, a dangerous, enervating combination.

"It's bad luck to keep that much negative energy around," I said.

Zora looked like she was trying to decide whether or not to remind me that I had agreed to butt out of her business, so I jumped in with a preemptive strike and a smile. "It's my job to spot the snakes, remember?"

She drained her glass and set it down on the nightstand beside the picture of her dad. "I can put them downstairs in Amelia's office with the others if they bother you up here."

The others? "I'll help," I said, picking up the smaller box. It was heavier than I thought it would be as I followed her back downstairs, puffing just a little in spite of myself. "Ever consider burning?"

"Burning?"

"I'm a big fan of burning," I said, remembering how much I always enjoyed doing the climactic scene in *Hedda Gabbler* when the distraught heroine feeds her faithless lover's manuscript into the fireplace, crying out "I am burning our child, I am burning our child," as the only copy goes up in flames.

"Even when I kept a journal, I'd write in it every night when I got home from the theater and burn the pages first thing in the morning."

"What was the point?"

"I didn't want to drop dead and leave that much incriminating evidence behind."

I was only half teasing. Things that start private should stay private.

"Then why bother to write it down at all?"

"The process was what mattered," I said. "It wasn't like I needed to go back and read any of that stuff again."

"What if you forgot something?" she said, flipping on the light in the neat little office we'd only poked our heads into during my initial tour of the premises. She put her box down carefully beside two others next to a beige three-drawer file cabinet. I slid mine in beside it, wishing I had the nerve to feed them all into the jumbo-size shredder I could see near the landlord's desk.

"Then I'd just have to make it up as I went along," I said, stretching my arms above my head to get the crick out of my back. I should have bent my knees before I picked up that much weight.

"That doesn't seem to be working so well for me," Zora said, turning out the light again and heading for the kitchen where dinner was waiting for me and another drink was calling to her.

"Don't worry," I said. "We'll work on it."

THIRTEEN

•

*E*verything turned out great, if I do say so myself, but Zora drank her dinner anyway. Meanwhile, I tried to distract her from *Dig It!* by telling her about my day.

"I ran into an old friend at the West End News this morning," I said. "She knows you."

"Everybody around here knows everybody else. Who's your friend?"

"Abbie Browning."

"Miss Abbie? Where do you know her from?"

"We were friends in Paris a long time ago. I haven't seen her in thirty years and we picked right up like we'd seen each other last week."

"I like her," Zora said. "She's really spiritual. Sort of like a moon worshiper."

"Smile when you say that, or I'll tell your mom," I said.

"Actually, she reminds me a little of Mom," Zora said, tearing off a chunk of bread and nibbling it delicately. "But she's a little more organized. She's got cards and stuff."

"What kind of cards?" I imagined a line of inspirational stationery of the kind Maya Angelou agreed to put her poems on.

"Business cards," Zora said. "They're blue and they say 'visionary advisor.'"

"Is she any good?"

"I don't know, why? Are you looking for some visionary advice?"

"Always," I said. "She invited us for dinner on Sunday. I'd love for you to go."

"I might have to work on Sunday." Zora headed for the freezer and poured another splash of vodka over the ice that hadn't had time to melt. "If I can get off, I'll come."

"You work on Sundays, too?"

She closed the freezer and sat back down. "You used to do two shows on Sunday."

She had me there. "Abbie was driving down to Tybee with another woman who knows you."

"I told you," she said. "Everybody knows everybody."

"Her name is Aretha Hargrove. She's a photographer."

"I know. She took most of the pictures in here."

I had enjoyed spending the afternoon with the smiling faces who had turned toward her camera. The thing that struck me immediately was how happy they all looked. She seemed to have a talent for capturing the moment when joy is visible on the human face. The photograph they were taking down to Peachy was no exception.

"She's good," I said.

"She used to have a studio upstairs from my apartment. We worked in the garden together sometimes. Was Joyce Ann with her?"

"Who's Joyce Ann?"

"Her daughter. She's almost four. I used to babysit for her sometimes, but she gave up her studio and I moved out of that building, so we kind of lost touch."

"Even in this tiny town?"

Zora shrugged. "I've been working such crazy hours."

I started to clear the table, hoping I could tempt Zora wih a rosy baked apple and a big dollop of freshly whipped cream. "She seemed nice. Want some dessert?"

"No, thanks," she said. "I'll stick with what I've got."

"Suit yourself," I said, taking the smallest apple for myself and not going overboard on the cream.

Zora watched me munching and tinkled her ice cubes. "Aretha's probably been in *Dig It!* more than I have."

"What's she doing in that rag?"

Zora looked surprised. "Don't you recognize her name?"

I shook my head. "Why would I?"

"*Married son of mayoral hopeful charged in death of gay deserter.*"

"What does that mean?" I was still confused.

"The married son. That was Kwame. Her husband."

I practically dropped my spoon. If West End was a small town, it seemed to be a lot closer to Peyton Place than it was to Mayberry.

"Are they still married?"

Zora shook her head. "She divorced him, but he still sees Joyce Ann."

Nothing about Aretha said trauma or drama or terminal disappointment the way everything about Zora did. I wondered how she managed to avoid the emotional quicksand that was sucking the life out of my favorite munchkin. Maybe she'd gotten some of Abbie's visionary advice. I hoped I'd have a chance to ask her.

Zora yawned and stretched. "Well, now that I've brought you up-to-date on everything, I've got an early day again tomorrow, so . . ."

"What time will you be home?" I said. "Or will this be a late night, too?"

I didn't mean to sound judgmental, but I probably did because Zora frowned.

"Mafeenie, I told you I'd be working weird hours."

"I know you did, darlin'. I was just hoping you could go by the duplex with me tomorrow. It's just up on Martin Luther King, right near Washington High School."

She looked uncomfortable. "Do you need me to go with you?"

"Well," I said, "I don't have a car and if I can avoid the bus, I'd like to."

"No, no! You know I wouldn't ask you to take the bus, Mafeenie, but I can't get off tomorrow. I was thinking you could drop me off at work and keep the car. I'll get a ride home."

Now it was my turn to hesitate. I hadn't driven a car in Atlanta in years and even though I had a valid license, I wasn't sure I wanted to navigate Atlanta's notoriously fast freeways all alone just yet. On the other hand, I didn't have to use the freeway to get where I was going.

"You sure I can't talk you into coming with me? I promise it won't take long, and who knows? Once we get things organized, you might even want to live there after your landlord gets back."

Zora looked at me strangely, but she didn't say anything.

"What?" I said, not confident of my ability to correctly interpret her expression.

"Nothing, I just . . . I don't want you to hold on to it because you think I'm ever going to live there," she said firmly but gently, like she didn't want to hurt my feelings.

"I was just throwing the idea out," I said. "I can keep renting it like I always have. We'll have some tenants in there by the time you're back at Spelman next year, and after that, you can—"

"I'm not going back to Spelman," she interrupted me.

"What do you mean?"

"I mean," she said, drawing out every word, "that I've decided I don't want to be in school right now. There's too much work to do on the outside. People over there going to class like they don't even know there's a war on!"

She made a sweeping gesture that I assumed was meant to include her former classmates, many of whom were dedicated activists just like she was, tackling issues of war and rap music with equal determination. She was still holding her drink and when she flung out her arm, she splashed some of it on the spotless kitchen floor, where it landed with a liquidy *plop*.

I looked at her. Drinking too much was stupid, but dropping out of college in your senior year was just crazy. "What did your mother say?"

"It's not her decision," Zora said, raising her little chin defiantly. "It's mine."

I took a deep breath. "I know it's your decision, darlin'. I just wondered if you had shared it with Jasmine yet."

"Not yet," Zora said. "I wanted to tell you first."

"Why?"

Suddenly she leaned forward and her eyes filled up with tears. She blinked them back, but she couldn't keep the tremor out of her voice. "Because I want to do what you did, Mafeenie! I want to leave all this bullshit behind and go far enough away to start a life where nobody knows who I am or what I've been."

This was, of course, not an entirely accurate description of what I had done. I found my freedom in a place I stumbled upon by the grace of the goddess, and I had enough sense to stay there and be the woman I was born to be. I wasn't running from anything and I never had the slightest intention of constructing a life where nobody knew who I was or what I'd been up to. But all that was beside the point.

"I want . . ." She stopped and shook her head slowly.

I leaned across the table and touched her hand lightly. "What?"

She looked at me, her face a mask of vodka-fueled misery. "I want my old life back," she whispered. "I just want my old life back."

"Oh, darlin'," I said as the tears splashed over her cheeks. I got up and went around to sit beside her, pulling her close, patting her back gently like she was a baby who needed a burp. "Oh, my poor baby."

When I was a kid, I once saw a TV drama about a mother whose beloved son is killed in a terrible accident. When she has an opportunity to have one wish granted, the heartbroken woman unhesitatingly wishes that her son would come back from the dead, and he does, just as mangled and battered and unrecognizable as he was when he breathed his last breath. The expression on the mother's horrified face when she hears his halting footsteps on the porch and runs to throw open the door stayed with me to this day. The lesson about the impossibility of going back stayed with me, too.

"Listen, darlin'," I said, leaning back but keeping my arm around her shoulders. "Your old life wasn't perfect either. It just looks that way in retrospect."

She brushed the tears from her face and sniffled. "But at least nobody was watching."

"Somebody's always watching," I said. "The trick is to give them something interesting to look at. Put on a strapless dress! Sing something!"

She gave me a crooked little grin. "You know I can't sing, Mafeenie."

"That's the other trick."

"What?"

"If you can't sing, start dancing!"

FOURTEEN

·

*Z*ora's office was part of a dingy little suite of storefronts a few blocks from West End. When we pulled up at the curb, there were already several people inside. One young woman on the phone and two young men waiting patiently in folding chairs that had seen better days. I wondered why so many organizations committed to doing good are equally committed to looking so bad while they do it.

Boasting pricey, renovated lofts on one side of the street, a homeless shelter and a U-Haul on the other, the area reflected an uneasy mixture of earnest gentrification and implacable despair. Looking in the front window past the sign that said: VETSERVE—WHERE YOUR NEEDS ALWAYS COME FIRST, I made her promise to call me if she couldn't get a ride home and assured her that I could find my way without any help from Mapquest.

The new management company had their offices on the third floor in one of those prefab buildings that come complete with a few pitiful little trees and no style whatsoever. Southwest Atlanta was full of them. Even the artwork in the entrance lobby was generic. Bad generic. I got on the elevator with a weary-looking young mother and a small boy whose hand she was holding tightly, as if he might bolt at any second. She pushed the button for two, which seemed to be a floor inhabited strictly by doctors.

The doors closed with a soft hiss and the kid looked at me with large, unblinking eyes. When I smiled, he whispered miserably, "I have to get a shot."

His mother glared down at him, but he didn't look at her.

"It won't be so bad," I lied.

"Yes, it will," he said, still whispering. "I had one before."

"Hush, boy," his mother said as the doors opened for them and she pulled him out to face the terror of the doctor's needle. "She don't care nothin' about all that."

"It's okay," I said, to him as much as to her, wishing I could spare him the routine horrors of childhood, knowing I couldn't. Everybody's got to kill their own snakes.

The management company was the first glass door on the right. Small black letters identified the offices of G. Woodruff and Associates. The smiling receptionist included the name as part of her greeting in case you missed it.

"Welcome to G. Woodruff and Associates," she said. "How can I help you?"

"I'm Josephine Evans," I said. "I'm here to pick up a key."

The young woman had a lovely face, a stylish haircut, and a dark blue dress that was office appropriate but still managed to be sexy. This was a perfect job for her and her twinkle indicated that she enjoyed it, too, but now she just looked confused.

"A key?"

"You manage a property I own at 1839 Martin Luther King. I want to take a look at it."

"Take a look at it?"

Her echo was becoming annoying. She wasn't pretty enough to be this incompetent. Nobody was. Where was the person I spoke to on the telephone yesterday to tell them I was coming? Why hadn't I written down her name?

"I spoke to someone about this yesterday," I said. "She told me I could come in this morning and pick it up."

"Do you remember who it was that told you that?"

I wanted to say, *If I remembered her name, would I have said "some-one"?* but I restrained myself.

"I believe she was Ms. Woodruff's secretary," I said, figuring I'd take a shot. If she wasn't the one, she could find the one. The receptionist's expression conveyed more doubt than relief, but at least she didn't say *Ms. Woodruff's secretary?*

"Have a seat, please," she said, reaching for the phone. "I'll see if I can locate her."

She said it like behind the closed door to the Woodruff and Associate's inner sanctum, there was a labyrinthine maze so intricate that one could get lost for hours, completely unable to contact the front desk. I sat down on the small gray couch and looked at the magazines and newspapers neatly arranged on the glass coffee table: *Fortune, Atlanta* magazine, *U.S. News & World Report, The New York Times, The Wall Street Journal, The Atlanta Journal-Constitution,* and *The Atlanta Business Chronicle.* There were also copies of the company brochure. Ms. Woodruff had sent me a form letter and a copy of that brochure when the former managers closed up shop. There was a picture of the company's owner and her team of what the copy called "real estate professionals." I remember being pleased that I was now in the hands of an experienced black woman who had assembled an impressive-looking multiracial team.

The artwork on the walls featured panoramic views of the Atlanta skyline at various times of the day. Some were the traditional night-time view with red ribbons of light flashing by in a blur on the freeways. Some were the same angle in bright sunshine, downtown now superimposed against a cloudless, impossibly blue sky. But there were several others in black and white that were geared more toward art than advertising. In these, downtown Atlanta achieved a kind of mysterious grandeur almost in spite of itself. They made me think of those magical photographs of New York City that Alfred Stieglitz took before he met Georgia O'Keeffe and started doing those scandalous nudes. The room was pleasant enough, but it struck me as a little cold. Even the bouquet of calla lilies was too perfectly calculated to bring much spontaneous pleasure.

"Ms. Booker will be right out," the receptionist said, relieved to have located the person who could answer the question I had posed. "Can I get you some coffee?"

"No, thanks," I said, nodding at the pictures I'd been admiring. "Who's the photographer?"

She shrugged. "I don't know. I think he's local."

I wondered what it was like to go through life oblivious to your surroundings and devoid of curiosity about them. That ought to be a reality show: *Oblivious and Devoid.*

Ms. Booker was neither. She was totally focused in the way of those people who manage the lives and, more important, the schedules of busy people who sign their checks.

"Ms. Evans," she said, entering the lobby and immediately extending her hand. She was very tall and compensated by wearing flat shoes with her well-cut pantsuit, which was exactly the same color as the couch. I wondered if she would disappear if she sat down on it. "I'm Clarissa Booker, Ms. Woodruff's assistant."

"Josephine Evans," I said.

She sat down beside me, and while she didn't disappear, the effect was still strange, as if at any moment the sofa might swallow her up whole.

"Ms. Woodruff was hoping to be here when you came by," she said, looking concerned. She was holding a small brown envelope with both hands like I might try to snatch it and make a run for the elevator. The address of the duplex was clearly written on the outside.

"No problem," I said. "I just need the key."

"Well, she was hoping that you might talk with her before you go over there."

The way she said "over there" made it sound like I was planning an ill-advised trip to a war zone.

"Is it occupied?"

"No, it's still empty," she said.

"Is there a problem?"

Over Ms. Booker's well-tailored shoulder, the receptionist was watching us without even bothering to pretend she had other tasks to occupy her time. What the hell was going on?

"No problem," Ms. Booker said. "It's just that the place has been unoccupied for a while and there's been some vandalism."

Now she was starting to worry me. "What kind of vandalism?"

She looked pained. "I'm not sure of the specific damage. It's just that when these buildings stand empty, they attract transients."

"How long has it been empty?"

"Seven or eight months. Maybe a year."

That's when they stopped sending checks to Jasmine. This was not looking good, but I was confused. "Why hasn't it been rented?"

"It's hard to keep tenants over there."

Over there. Again with the war zone.

"It was already empty when we agreed to take it on as part of the settlement."

"The settlement?" Maybe this echoing thing was contagious. Now I was doing it. "What settlement?"

"I'm really not comfortable having this conversation with you," Ms. Booker said, clutching the small envelope even tighter. "Why don't we do this? I'll get Ms. Woodruff's book and we'll find a time for the two of us to have lunch and she can—"

"Is that the key?" I said, interrupting her.

She couldn't deny it. "Yes, but—"

"Then why don't we do this," I said, "you give me my key, I'll go take a look at my house, and then I'll be better prepared to talk with Ms. Woodruff."

If she could have figured out a way to swallow that key, envelope and all, I think she would have.

I held out my hand. "Over lunch."

She handed the envelope to me and I stood up. She did too, reluctantly unfolding her long gray self off the couch.

"Thank you," I said. "Shall I call you this afternoon to make the appointment?"

"I'm not sure when she'll be in," Ms. Booker said, wishing, I'm sure, that I'd just go away.

I smiled. "But you'll be here, right?"

She nodded reluctantly. "Right."

"Good."

She waited until I reached for the silver handle on that big glass door. "Ms. Evans?"

"Yes?"

"You should make some noise before you go inside," she said. "If there are transients, it's not a good idea to surprise them."

FIFTEEN

·

*A*s I got closer to my house, nothing looked or felt like it did in West End. From the litter-strewn parking lot outside the grocery store, to the overflowing trash can in front of the gas station, on past the hard-eyed young men in their oversize pants who seemed to be gathered on every corner, this was clearly a neighborhood in distress. A boarded-up house on one corner had been spray painted by desperate neighbors. *Crackhouse,* the big red letters proclaimed. *They sell dope in here!* While I waited at the light, I saw a young man with an unkempt Afro and wearing droopy jeans head around to the back of the place. Obviously, he saw the sign as an advertisement instead of a warning.

I had just passed the Lincoln Cemetery on my left, which meant the house was coming up on my right. The grass and weeds were so high in the front yard that I almost missed the entrance to the long, crooked driveway. One of the unique features of the house had always been the fact that it sat up on the only hill for miles. That's what provided the slope of its expansive green lawn in the front yard and made up for the constant roar of the freeway, whose construction had eaten up most of the back. The house faced Martin Luther King and took up the entire corner lot. A stand of scraggly-looking dogwood trees lined up on one side of the property, separating it from its closest neighbor, an unsavory-looking soul food restaurant at the bottom of the hill, but in no way obstructing the view of the small residential street that ran behind the lot and down toward the freeway.

I pulled up in the yard and looked around. An overgrown lawn was the least of it. There was trash everywhere. All the windows were cracked or broken or covered by plywood and what looked like cardboard. The porch screens were ripped and torn. There was lots of graf-

fiti and what looked to me like it could have been a splatter of dried
blood on one of the outside walls. It didn't even look like the same
place. All the loving care my mother had put into this house all the
years we lived there had been wiped out by the force of sustained neglect, and a despair greater than her optimism could ever have antici-
pated.

I couldn't begin to imagine what I'd find inside, but I had to know.
I clicked the locks and got ready to step out of the car when I remembered Ms. Booker's warning about not surprising uninvited guests.
Sound advice, I was sure, but what were my options? Ring the bell? Call
ahead? Neither one of those made any sense, of course, but what the
hell was I supposed to do now? Sneak up to the window and peek in to
see what I could see? Walk in unannounced and assert my rights as the
landlord to whoever I might find camped out in my mother's living
room? Call the police and ask for an escort? I could only imagine how
that conversation would go: *Excuse me, is this 911? I'm scared to go inside my house because there might be some bad guys in there. Can you
come over and check it out?*

I felt helpless and angry. Angry at Ms. Woodruff for not handling
her business and at myself for not handling mine. The longer I sat, the
madder I got. This place was a problem, not a solution. Down below
on the freeway, or maybe from the traffic speeding by on Martin
Luther King, I heard a horn and then one in response and then another. Now *that* made sense. A loud, indignant noise to announce to
anybody within earshot that you were mad as hell and you weren't
going to take it anymore. I joined the angry chorus, laying on Zora's
horn to protest the mess I saw in front of me. *I don't deserve this and
why did I come here anyway and what kind of grandmother would
promise this as a legacy and who was bleeding on the walls of my house
and where are they now and where am I now, and where is home anyway
and how far is too far and what good is a safe house if it's scarier than
whatever it is you're running from?*

When the back door opened, I jumped about a foot in the air and
jerked my hand off the horn. The man who stepped out didn't look too
scary, but I was shaking anyway. Who was he and what was he doing

there? I popped down the power-door locks with an audible click and watched him through the windshield. He looked to be about forty, but it was hard to tell. He had on a pair of jeans and a brown jacket, both of which had seen better days. His hair was longer than it needed to be and his beard was patchy and turning gray. His ancient high-top tennis shoes looked like he had plucked them from a throwaway pile to get whatever wear he could pretend was left in them. His eyes looked weary but not desperate.

We just looked at each other, neither one of us knowing what to do next.

Finally, I opened the door and stepped out of the car without turning off the ignition. I kept the door between us.

"What are you doing here?" I said.

"Nothing," he said. "Just keeping an eye on the place."

"Keeping an eye on the place for who?"

He looked at me and his eyes narrowed slightly. "Nobody."

"Who else is in there?"

"Nobody."

"Who are you?"

"Who are *you*?"

"I own this place."

He looked surprised. "You do?"

"Yes, I do." My voice sounded a lot more confident than I felt.

"Well, where have you been?"

Now it was my turn to be surprised. Of all the things I had expected, righteous indignation was not one of them. "What?"

"Look at it! How could you just let it go like this?"

This was becoming more surreal by the second. Now the homeless squatter was going to reprimand me for being an absentee landlord? What next? A citizen's arrest?

"I don't see how that's any of your business," I said. "How long have you been here?"

"Couple months," he said. "Give or take."

"Anybody from the management company ever come by to check on the place?"

He frowned again. "What do you think?"

His tone ticked me off a little. "Well, if you were going to camp out here, why didn't you at least clean it up a little?"

"Why didn't *you*?"

It was clear this conversation was over. The person I needed to talk to was sitting behind a big glass door over on Cascade Road. Ms. Greer Woodruff and Associates had some big-time explaining to do.

SIXTEEN

•

I'll wait," I said to the babbling beauty at the front desk who was trying to tell me that Ms. Woodruff and Ms. Booker were both in a meeting and couldn't be disturbed.

"It's going to be a long meeting," she said, clearly not looking forward to the prospect of spending several hours trapped in a room with a madwoman who had blown in like an ill-tempered wind and already raised her voice well above the level of acceptable office decorum.

I didn't give a damn about decorum. I was two minutes away from kicking open that closed door without waiting to be buzzed in and carrying my loud, indignant ass into the inner sanctum to demand some answers to my increasingly indignant set of questions. I took a seat on the gray sofa again and tried to calm down. The receptionist pursed her lips and turned back to her keyboard. She didn't have much choice. She couldn't very well throw me out. I figured I could take her if it came down to it, but she didn't look like a woman to whom public tussling presented itself as an option. She was more likely to figure I'd get tired of waiting and leave on my own.

She could not have been more wrong. I had no place to go and no time to get there. I had trusted Greer Woodruff and Associates to look out for my property in exchange for fees for their services. In return, they had allowed my mother's parting gift to become not only an eyesore, but a haven for neighborhood predators and thieves. They had effectively cut off my only current source of reliable income, not to mention Zora's only real possibility of an inheritance. I wasn't going anywhere until somebody explained to me what was going on.

I picked up *Atlanta* magazine to distract myself and flipped it open right to a big story on Atlanta's growing community of women entrepreneurs. The first profile was of one Greer Woodruff, who the magazine called "a successful Atlanta businesswoman who combines active respect for tradition with a bold vision for the future." You couldn't prove it by me. Her background was impressive. Howard University undergrad, Harvard MBA, public and private sector experience at the highest level, and now president of her own urban redevelopment firm.

In the photograph the magazine ran beside her profile, she was leaning back against her desk with her arms crossed and a pleasant but serious look on her face. She was about my age, broad shouldered, beautifully made up, and dressed for success in a dark blue suit with a skirt, not pants, and a pair of plain black pumps. Her salt-and-pepper gray hair was brushed back from her face in soft waves intended to deflect your attention from the almost masculine cut of her strong jawline.

I tossed down the magazine wondering how long I really was prepared to wait without going off, when the inner sanctum door opened and Greer Woodruff strode into the waiting room, followed by four men and Ms. Booker, who was scribbling busily on a clipboard. Two of the men were wearing very expensive suits that were just a little too flashy for business, as were the too-big-to-be-real, too-big-not-to-be diamond studs the tallest one wore in his ears. Both of them were black and had their hair neatly trimmed and edged up so sharply they must have come here straight from the barbershop. The stark white of their very expensive shirts was even brighter next to their dark skin. One of the other black men was dressed in a BET version of hip-hop chic complete with pants riding so low that the crotch was almost at his knees and a golden dental grille that made his smile a study in conspicuous consumption.

The fourth man was a slender white man wearing a much more conservative and considerably cheaper suit and a grin that can only be described as shit eating. The others were laughing, but the best he could manage was an uncomfortable smile.

"So I told him he should make other arrangements," the hip-hop fashionista was saying. "Or I'd see him on Election Day. Am I lyin'?"

He turned to the white man whose grin didn't waver. "I'm sure the councilman heard you loud and clear," he said. "Loud and clear."

"Damn right."

"I couldn't have said it better myself, Jimmy," Greer Woodruff said, touching the hip-hop guy's elbow lightly as if she was steering him out of her office.

That remark elicited another round of laughter and then her eyes fell on me. There didn't seem to be any flicker of recognition, but her radar picked up the presence of a possible problem and set off a distant warning bell.

"Politics is easy," Jimmy said, trying to extend his moment at the center of attention. "It's the politicians that are a pain in the ass."

Greer Woodruff flickered a look at Ms. Booker, who was surprised and not pleased to see me sitting almost exactly where she had left me a few hours ago. She broke away from the small group and headed for me immediately.

"Gentlemen," Ms. Woodruff said, herding them toward the door and out to the elevator. "Keep me in the loop as you move ahead."

"Ms. Evans," Ms. Booker said, her voice quiet and firm. "I thought I asked you to call for an appointment."

"I'm here to see Ms. Woodruff," I said loudly. "I don't need an appointment."

The group at the door turned as one in the direction of my outraged assertion and Ms. Woodruff frowned and took a step in my direction.

"I'm Greer. . . ."

But before she could finish, the white guy in the group stepped around her, his eyes wide with surprise and delight. "Oh, my God! Are you Josephine Evans?"

Nobody ever recognized me in Atlanta. I was as surprised as he was. "Yes."

"Oh, my God!" he said again while the others looked at him for some explanation of how he happened to know the angry black woman waiting for Greer. "I'm Duncan Matthews. I saw you in *Medea*. Five years ago in Amsterdam. My partner and I were there for two weeks and I saw the show four times. Twice in a seat and twice standing room. Every show was sold out!"

"That was a good production," I said, enjoying his enthusiasm in spite of myself.

"Good? It was amazing! I've never forgotten one second of it. You were magnificent! Absolutely magnificent!"

Greer Woodruff was running through her mental Rolodex and coming up empty. She tapped the man on his back gently. "Duncan? Aren't you going to introduce us to your friend?"

"Friend? Oh, no! I'm not a friend. I'm a fan! A total fan!" He grinned at me and made a small bow. "Greer Woodruff, Jim Nguchi, Matt Lovejoy, Tyrone Parker, I would like to present Ms. Josephine Evans, the most amazing actress in the world."

"Thank you," I said. "You're very kind."

"It's an honor," he said. "That scene at the end where you come out with the blood all over your dress, carrying your dead son? It still gives me chills to think about it. What are you doing here? Are you performing anywhere? Please say somebody is remounting that *Medea*. I'll buy my tickets today!"

The three brothers exchanged looks to see if this was making sense to anybody but the white boy. It wasn't, so they checked their expensive watches as if on cue. Their work here was done. It was time to go.

I smiled at the guy's enthusiasm. "I'm sorry, but there are no immediate plans for that. I'm here on other business."

Greer turned to Ms. Booker, hovering nearby. "Clarissa, will you make sure these gentlemen find their way to the elevator while I take care of our guest?"

"Of course," Clarissa said, guiding them out the door as the elevator bell announced its arrival.

Greer turned to Duncan. "You'd better ride down with them, don't you think? In case there are any loose ends."

His disappointment was all over his face, but she was clearly calling the shots.

He smiled at me once more, reached into his pocket, and handed me a business card. It said, *Duncan Matthews Properties.* "If there's ever anything I can do, please don't hesitate to call on me."

"Thank you," I said, slipping the card in my pocket.

"No," he said, putting his hand over his heart and bowing. "Thank *you.*"

"Mr. Matthews?" Clarissa said, holding the elevator door with one hand.

He grinned apologetically, kissed the hand I offered with a flourish instead of shaking it, and hurried off to regale his friends with tales of my magnificent *Medea*. They would probably think he was talking about the old lady in those Tyler Perry plays, except she would never kill a kid. She might smack one for bad behavior, but nothing terminal. Ms. Woodruff nodded at the receptionist who hit the buzzer so fast she must have already had her finger on it.

"Ms. Evans?" she said with a smile. "Won't you come in? Let's see if we can do some business."

SEVENTEEN

•

*M*s. Woodruff's office wasn't large, but it had enough windows to avoid being claustrophobic. Her antique desk was tiny and tasteful, just like in the photograph. I took one of the chairs provided for visitors and tried to collect my thoughts. She closed the door behind us, sat down, scanned her desk for something she didn't seem to find, picked up the phone, and touched a button.

"Clarissa? Can you bring me that file we talked about this morning? I didn't see it." She moved a few things on the desk around officiously. "Oh! Yes, here it is. Thank you, Clarissa. Tell Marie to hold my calls, would you?"

She hung up the phone and clasped her hands in front of her. "I had no idea you were an actress," she said, smiling with everything but her eyes.

I brushed that off immediately and cut to the chase. "Why didn't you tell me about the house?"

Her smile faded. "I hope we haven't gotten off on the wrong foot."

"I'm afraid we have," I said. "Have you seen it?"

"No, I haven't been—"

"It's a wreck," I interrupted her. "The yard is overgrown and full of trash, the windows are broken, and there are squatters and criminals living there."

"I see."

I waited for her to offer some kind of explanation, perhaps even a plan of repair and recovery, but neither one seemed to be forthcoming.

"Well, what are you going to do about it?"

She raised her eyebrows. "I think, Ms. Evans, that you have the wrong idea about my role in all this."

"I thought your role was to manage the tenants, keep the property in good repair, collect the rent, and deposit it in an account as per my instructions."

She nodded like what I had just said confirmed her belief in the existence of an unfortunate misunderstanding. "That was the job of your old management company," she said. "But they are no longer in business. Responsibility for your property and several others nearby in equally poor condition was acquired by my firm late last year as part of a larger financial settlement, but that is not really what we do."

"What do you mean, not really what you do?"

"We are a real estate development and consulting firm," she said. "We deal primarily with commercial acquisitions and inner-city development. These houses"—she said the word as if the structures to which she was referring were barely worthy of the name—"are in no way related to what we do."

"Then why did you take them on?"

She sat back and looked at me like she was trying to determine how much of the sad story she was prepared to share. "Most of the owners, including yourself, are absentee. We've been trying to reach them, but we haven't always been successful. Your old company's records were often incomplete."

"I've been living at the same place for the past twenty years, and as your friend made quite clear, I am in a highly visible profession. I'm not hard to find."

We looked at each other across her desk for a minute and then she sighed like somebody who's getting ready to give you the bad news.

"Ms. Evans, let me state my position as clearly as I can. We are a three-million-dollar-a-year operation. Managing run-down rentals in bad neighborhoods is of no interest to me whatsoever."

"That's abundantly clear from the look of the place." She wasn't the only one who knew how to adopt a snotty tone of voice and condescending attitude.

"I'm a businesswoman, Ms. Evans, just like you're an artist. I don't have a political agenda. I don't have a social agenda. The only agenda I have is economic."

She opened the folder that I assumed contained the details of the duplex's demise. Her eyes quickly scanned the few papers inside, then she looked back at me. "Unfortunately, your property is in an area that is not slated for any commercial or residential development at this time. The value of the parcel you hold has actually declined in the past few years, and even though your old company sunk quite a bit of money into repairs and renovations—"

"How much money?"

She ran her finger down a line of numbers that I couldn't read upside down. From what I had just seen, they couldn't have spent much.

"According to these figures, close to twenty-five thousand just two years ago."

"Twenty-five thousand? *Dollars?*"

She plucked out the sheet and slid it across the desk in my direction. "See for yourself."

Electrical repairs, $3,500, it said. *New plumbing fixtures, $2,500. Paint, $1,500. Screens and outdoor refurbishing, $2,200. Lawn repair and landscaping, $4,000.* The list went on and on, but I had seen enough.

"This is absurd," I said. "The place is a complete disaster. There is no way they could have done all this."

She nodded sympathetically and replaced the sheet in the folder. "The truth is, they probably didn't do any of it."

"That's what I'm saying."

"Ms. Evans, the reason they are no longer in business is because of this kind of scam. They would spend the funds on hand for maintenance and repairs and leave the properties to fend for themselves."

"That's stealing!" I said, stating the obvious.

She nodded again. "Not to mention stupid, unethical, and easily traced. When they finally declared bankruptcy there was nothing left for creditors or property owners to claim to recoup their losses. We bought the whole thing, lock, stock, and barrel, for some apartments they own over near West End that have some potential, but as far as the individual properties . . ."

Her voice trailed off and she closed the folder firmly. "There's really nothing to be done."

"Nothing to be done?" I was echoing again, but what else was I supposed to do? I had no idea, so I just sat there, hoping something would come to me, but nothing did. This was bad, and the longer I thought about it, the worse it seemed. I had gone from being a well-paid actress with a nest egg to being a slumlord on hiatus in the space of just a few days. My head was spinning.

"I know this is a shock, Ms. Evans," Greer Woodruff said, not unkindly. "And being an artist, business probably isn't your favorite thing, am I right?"

I nodded, hoping she could see a light at the end of the long tunnel suddenly stretching out in front of me.

"I also know that for most of the absentee owners, these properties represented a significant part of their post-retirement planning."

There was no need to tell her that I had done no post-retirement planning since I never figured on retiring. My plan was to keep acting until they carried me off the stage and buried me, preferably in full makeup. I nodded again.

"So, even though all this predates my involvement, I am prepared to do the best I can to set things right."

"What do you have in mind?" I said, hating that I sounded so needy. I cleared my throat.

"I'm prepared to make you an immediate offer for your place. It's not worth much now, but in ten or fifteen years, I might be able to put a package together that—"

"Ten or fifteen years?" *Damn that echo!*

"Even then, there's no guarantee that anyone will be interested," she said. "I just felt that perhaps I'm in a somewhat better position than you are to speculate."

"How much is it worth?" I said. If she made me a decent offer, maybe I could reinvest the money in something more secure and still get my nest egg together. I wasn't retired yet. I still had time to regroup, but I needed some seed money in the worst kind of way.

"As is?" she said.

"As is." No way I was going to throw good money after bad by trying to repair it. My mother had paid forty thousand for it twenty-five years ago. It had to be worth twice that now, if only for the land.

"Fifteen thousand," Greer Woodruff said without blinking.

Before I could stop it, that damn echo leaped out one more time. "Fifteen thousand?"

"I can write you a check today," she said calmly.

"It's got to be worth more than that," I said, shocked.

"Considering location, the condition of the property, and current market values, I think it's more than fair," she said. "It is, of course, your property and you're welcome to do whatever you choose with it. But I would like to be clear about something."

"Yes?"

"My offer is not open-ended."

"What does that mean?"

"It means, Ms. Evans, that when it comes to that particular property, it is a buyer's market."

I could tell she was a great businesswoman because that's what she was giving me: *the business.* I don't know why, but I didn't trust Greer Woodruff as far as I could throw her. There was something else going on and until I knew what it was, I wasn't going to agree to a damn thing. I stood up. "This is a lot to think about. I should go."

She stood up, too, and walked with me as I headed for the door. "I'm sorry we've met under such trying circumstances," she said as we passed through her lobby and out into the hall.

The elevator doors opened as if on cue. I stepped in and punched the DOWN button. "I'll be in touch."

"I'll look forward to it," she said, and gave me that smile again as the doors closed between us.

When I stepped outside, it was still a beautiful day, but I hardly noticed. I knew exactly where I was, but I don't think I ever felt so far from home.

EIGHTEEN

•

W hen I walked into the house, I was surprised to find Zora sitting on the couch cradling a drink in both hands and watching *The Wizard of Oz*.

"Hey, darlin'," I said. "You're home early. I'm so glad!"

That was the truth. I needed somebody to help me sort through the events of a very bad day. I kissed the top of her head since she was slumped down so far I couldn't get to her cheek without major contortions.

"Hey, Mafeenie," she said, without taking her eyes off the screen. "How was the house?"

"It's a mess," I said. "They really just let it fall apart at the . . . you okay?" She didn't look okay.

"Isn't it better to be right?" she said as Dorothy's three newly emboldened friends searched for her frantically in the bowels of the Wicked Witch's castle. "Okay is such a subjective thing. It can change up on you in a heartbeat."

That sounded like vodka insight to me. "What are you talking about?"

She turned her head without lifting it from the sofa and looked at me for the first time since I'd walked into the house.

"My boss told me he doesn't want me to participate in the conference after all."

"What about your presentation?" I knew how hard she'd been working on it and how disappointed she must be.

"Nope. He said it was nothing personal, he just didn't want the kind of publicity I generate to be associated with the program, so maybe it would be better if I stayed away this weekend."

"I'm so sorry," I said, pushing my own troubles out of my mind for a minute.

"You know what else?"

"What?"

"A guy came in today and asked me if I was the chick in the magazine." She turned back to watch the friends first liberate, then embrace Dorothy, then head for the nearest exit as fast as they could run. "When I told him I was, he told me that if I liked vets, he was willing to help me get that booty back in shape with some special push-ups."

Her voice shook a little when she said it and she took another sip of her drink. I wanted to say *I hope your boss threw him out into the middle of Peters Street,* but I didn't.

"What are you going to do?"

She looked at me and raised her eyebrows. "You mean other than lie around the house watching *The Wizard of Oz* and drinking vodka?"

"Well, I was wondering if you were open to other options," I said, refusing to be drawn into an argument about alcohol.

"Like what?"

"Oh, nothing major. A walk around the block. Dinner up at that new Mexican place. We can order shrimp fajitas and I'll tell you about the house."

"Actually," she said, "I can't. I'm going to Birmingham for the weekend. A friend of mine's brother is getting married and since I don't have to work . . ." She glanced down at her watch and frowned. Drunk people are always surprised by the passage of time. "In fact, he should be here in a minute."

"Who?"

"My friend. The one whose brother is getting married. The one who's going to Alabama with me."

She was making no sense and I could hardly hear her. I leaned over to turn down the sound.

"Don't turn it down!" she said. "They're just about to melt the witch. It's my favorite part."

"Mine, too," I said, taking a seat beside her on the couch. "That witch has one of the best exit lines in movie history." And I quoted it, with an appropriately witchy voice. " 'Who would have thought that all my beautiful wickedness could be defeated by one little girl?' "

Zora laughed at that without taking her eyes off the screen. Maybe that's why we both found this scene so satisfying. In spite of the best efforts of the thoroughly intimidating, undeniably powerful, absolutely evil, inexplicably green wicked witch, she was defeated by a girl in a blue gingham dress and a pair of red ruby slippers. Once Dorothy melted the witch and was hailed by the faithless guards and flying monkeys as their new queen, Zora put down her now-empty glass and stood up.

"It's better that I'm going away this weekend, Mafeenie," she said. "I wouldn't be fit company with the conference going on a few blocks away."

"You keep telling me you're not fit company," I said. "Why don't you light somewhere long enough for me to decide for myself?"

"I will," she said, moving toward the stairs. "But I've already promised Jabari, so it's too late to cancel."

"Who's Jabari?"

"He's the one who's coming to pick me up, and he's already late," she said. "But then again, so am I! Just tell him to come in. I won't be a minute."

She took the stairs two at a time and left me to witness the wrap-up of the movie where the Scarecrow, the Tin Man, and the Lion get their rewards from the wizard: brains, a heart, and some courage, respectively. It was funny when you thought about it. All the guys wanted something that would change them, make them better, more able to survive and thrive in Oz, or wherever they decided to settle down. Dorothy didn't want to change anything about herself. She just wanted to get back home. She was already endowed with the qualities that her traveling companions desired. She was smart as well as resourceful. She felt things deeply, loved her friends, family, and adorable dog, and was fearless when it came to defending them from nasty neighbors, green witches, and even the wizard himself. She was complete when we met her, except for one thing: She was mystified by the presence of cruelty and meanness. Her encounter with evil in the form of Elvira Gulch, who was fully prepared to euthanize the adorable Toto for digging in her garden, left Dorothy so confused that she ran away and ended up in Oz, looking for answers all up and down that yellow brick road. Maybe that was what Zora was looking for, too. Some explanation for the bad things that happened to well-meaning women and soldiers who found themselves at war.

Just as Dorothy got ready to click the heels of those famous ruby slippers, somebody out front blew a long blast on a very loud horn. When I went to the front window to see what was going on, I saw a dirty green car with one young man in the front seat and another in the back. They were playing Kanye West loud enough for me to hear it clearly even though all the windows were closed up tight.

> *I ain't sayin' she a gold digga,*
> *But she ain't messin' wit' no broke nigga . . .*

The one in the front laid on the horn again and leaned over to peer at the house. The one in the back peered out, too, bobbing his head in time to the music. Seeing no one coming down the walk, the driver gave the horn another blast, this one even longer and more insistent. *Please tell me she's not riding to Birmingham with these fools,* I thought, as Zora came down the stairs with her backpack and grabbed her coat from the closet.

"He's just trying to be funny," she said, sounding annoyed. "I told him to come up and ring the bell!"

I didn't say anything.

She gave my cheek a quick peck as she headed out the door. "I'll be back Monday. Don't worry. We'll hang out next week, I promise, and you can tell me all about the house."

"Be careful," I said, but I didn't think she heard me.

Zora opened the car door, increasing the volume of the music to a decibel level that made me concerned for her eardrums, tossed in her backpack, and hopped into the front seat without a backward glance. I'm not a religious woman, but I still said a little prayer. Something told me Zora's eardrums weren't the only things I needed to be concerned about this weekend.

NINETEEN

•

here are advantages to living in a house with a heated pool. It's even better if that pool has an amazing brown mermaid on the bottom with flowing curls and a mysterious smile to remind you that there's always more to the story than meets the eye. I had packed a bathing suit as soon as Zora told me about this particular perk of her house-sitting assignment, but this was the first time I'd actually had a chance to use it.

As soon as I shed my robe and slipped into the sparkling water, I wondered what had taken me so long. There are obvious health benefits to doing a series of energetic laps that push your body to its limits and allow your lungs to show you what they've got, but there are equally important psychological benefits to just lying back under the stars and watching the steam come off the warm water and disappear into the cool late February air.

The night was clear, and even in the city, there were an impressive number of stars on display. It only took a couple of hours to drive from Atlanta to Birmingham, so by now Zora would have arrived at her destination. I hoped she was somewhere where she could see these same stars. Somewhere she could take a deep breath and stop running from herself so fast.

But that was unlikely. The mood she was in when she left, and the road-trip energy flowing from the guys who had come to get her, pointed more toward hard drinking, fast driving, and a series of bad decisions. I kicked my feet gently and sent up a little prayer for Zora's well-being. *Next week, we'll hang out,* she kept saying, and I intended to hold her to it. That would be the time to tell her about the duplex after I'd had a chance to think about it. It was, after all, my problem, not hers. What kind of grandmother dumps her troubles on a grandbaby who's having a hard enough time just keeping her own head above water?

That thought made me feel guilty. I was supposed to be here to help her, not join her in some kind of self-destructive pity party. The mermaid's expression suddenly seemed vaguely accusatory. I swam to the edge of the pool, hoisted myself out, grabbed my robe, and headed inside. Only one person could talk me back before I went too far down this road. I went upstairs, rummaged around in my purse until I found my cellphone, and punched in Howard's number on speed dial.

"Your ears must have been burning!" he crowed on the other side of the world. "I just spoke your name this very minute. Where are you?"

"I'm at Zora's place in Atlanta. Where are you?"

"I'm cooking dinner for six at my place. Let me speak to Lil' Bit."

"She's gone to a wedding in Birmingham."

"Alabama?" The idea horrified him.

"No, *England*," I said. "Of course, Alabama. It's just one state over, remember?"

"Alabama isn't just a state, sweetie, it's a state of mind," he said. "Tell me you're not spending Friday night all by your lonesome."

The way he said it made me sound pathetic and not at all like my formerly fabulous self. "Just me and the mermaid," I said.

"What mermaid? Oh, there's the bell. *Somebody get that! I can't leave the pasta!*"

I could hear the sound of one of Howard's famous dinner parties in full swing. Loud music, lots of laughter, and what I knew would be a great big delicious meal.

"I'm making my world-renowned pumpkin ravioli," he said. "Of course, I thought of you!"

"I miss you."

"I miss you, too, sweetie. You okay?"

"I'm fine," I said, realizing this was not a moment when he could indulge me in some good old-fashioned whining about how hard my life was these days, but unable to resist giving him a thumbnail sketch.

"The house is a wreck, Zora's a mess, and I have no idea what I'm supposed to do about either one."

"I thought you said the house was fabulous."

"Not this house. The one I own."

"The duplex?"

"That's the one." A loud burst of laughter made me feel so lonesome I actually teared up. "Listen, this can wait. I was just missing you and wanted to hear your voice."

"I miss you, too, sweetie. These gatherings just aren't the same without you. When are you coming home?"

"You tell me," I said.

"I'm working on it," he said. "Those fools don't stand a chance. Between now and next week, I'm going to have so many folks demanding your triumphant return, Miss Thing won't know what hit her."

I was confused. "Who?"

"Didn't you get my message? That little Cuban chippie who's sleeping with François has floated the idea that she should close the season in a splashy new production of—are you ready for this?—*Medea!*"

I felt like he had kicked me in the stomach. All the air left my body.

"You there?"

"She's not a chippie."

"Stop being so noble. This is Howard, sweetie."

"I'm . . . I just . . . I can't believe it. I've only been gone a few days."

"Time waits for no diva," Howard said. "She saw an opportunity and she's trying to work it."

"What did François say?"

Howard made a rude noise and I could hear the faint ding of his oven timer. "Monsieur LeGutless said he'd let the board decide."

"That's reassuring," I said.

"They'll never agree to it. The American piece is one thing, but your fans would never stand for it. Trust me."

"I do." At this point I didn't have much choice.

"You'd better! Gotta go, sweetie! If this ravioli is not al dente, my rep will be ruined. I love you!"

"I love you more. *Ciao!*"

"*Ciao!*"

So there it was. A perfect storm of bad luck. I was glad that Abbie would only be gone a few days. The way things were going, maybe a visionary advisor was exactly what I needed.

TWENTY

·

$\mathcal{F}$or the next two days, I thought and swam, and swam and
thought, but by Sunday, I was as confused as I had been when I
left Greer Woodruff's office on Friday. Zora hadn't checked in at all. I
didn't want to crowd her by calling, which left me plenty of neutral
space to imagine her floundering around in all manner of unpleasant
circumstances. Dinner at Abbie's was a welcome distraction. She had
offered to come get me, but I told her I'd be fine walking the few blocks
over and she said she'd see me at seven.

I put on a black skirt, a black sweater, and some of my favorite silver
jewelry. When I looked in the mirror before I headed out, I wasn't unhappy with what I saw. It's taken me a few years, but I think I've finally
made peace with what I look like now, at this fifty-eight-year-old moment. A little thicker in the waist, a little broader in the beam, but so what?
Next to the Botox brigade, the thing I find most disturbing is women my
age dieting and exercising away any hint of roundness. Even their necks
get skinny so that their heads are perched up there at the end of the stalk
like perfectly made-up Halloween jack-o'-lanterns. Abbie didn't look like
that. She looked like a real woman with a real life. And so did I.

It was already dark when I stepped outside and stood there for a
minute listening to the wind rustling through that magnificent magnolia. A man and a woman passed the house, her arm looped through
the crook of his with an easy familiarity, and I could hear them talking
and laughing as they walked. François and I used to walk everywhere
we went, but I don't ever remember taking his arm. Or maybe he never
offered it.

Abbie opened the door before I had a chance to ring the bell.

"Come in, come in!" she said, pulling me inside with a quick hug.
"Hang your coat or toss it and come on back to the kitchen. I'm mak-

ing paella and I don't want to miss a step or we'll have to send out for pizza!"

I laughed as she headed down the hallway, her bright red skirt swirling around her ankles. Her tie-dyed shirt was tied at the waist in a style I remembered from the old days. There was a fire crackling in the fireplace, the smell of seafood and saffron in the air, and from the living room speakers, the sound of Ella Fitzgerald singing Cole Porter. I hung up my coat and followed my nose to the kitchen where Abbie was standing at the stove, peeking into her pots with a critical eye.

I was surprised at how much food she was preparing. Why had I thought this was going to be just the two of us? I had a brief pang of disappointment, wanting to ask Abbie's advice about things a little too personal to share with strangers.

"Don't worry," she said. "It looks like I'm cooking for the army, but it's just us, plus Aretha and Peachy."

Her ability to read my mind so specifically was uncanny and a little disconcerting. "Did he like the picture?"

She grinned at me. "He loved it. Hung the thing right inside the front door. Now when you walk in, my smilin' face is the first thing you see."

"I guess that's the end of your anonymity."

"You can't be anonymous on Tybee Island. The whole place isn't ten miles long. Everybody knows everybody."

"Kind of like West End."

"Kind of," she said, adding another bright pinch of saffron to one of the big pots and replacing the lid quickly. "Except West End doesn't have an ocean."

Satisfied that things were under control on the stove, Abbie headed to the refrigerator and took out a bottle of champagne.

"Grab us a couple of glasses, will you?" she said, pointing to the cabinet over the sink. "We'll toast something."

She poured us each a glass and stuck the bottle back in the fridge.

"What shall we toast?" I said.

She grinned and held up her glass. "To the return of the Amazon Queen."

I almost spilled all that perfectly chilled champagne down the front of my favorite sweater. Abbie laughed, clinked her glass against mine, and took a sip. I recovered my equilibrium enough to take a sip, too.

"I can't believe you remember that after all these years!"

"How could I forget it?" she said, putting down her glass and moving toward the cutting board where she had already arranged her salad fixings. I'm a good cook, but a very disorganized one. By the time I get it all on the table, the kitchen is usually an absolute disaster. Abbie cooked like Howard with distinct staging areas for each task. They're the kind of cooks who start the process by running a nice hot pan of soapy dishwater. In Amsterdam, I'm the kind of cook who starts the process by smoking a joint. In Atlanta, a glass of champagne will have to suffice.

"That's the first piece I ever saw you do."

"You're kidding."

"Nope. You were doing that other piece with François at the theater every night, but in the afternoon, you were showing up all over Paris, making these pronouncements from the back of that beautiful black horse."

"Did I have my titties out?"

"Just one, for the herstorical authenticity."

I groaned.

"Don't groan. It was great. You rode up to a café where I was sitting outside having a Pernod, dismounted, and read a communiqué from the Amazon Queen, who, according to what you read that first day, had just returned after a long absence and she was not at all pleased with our progress."

"Can you blame her?"

I really wasn't surprised that Abbie remembered the piece. All false modesty aside, it was a classic. The way it developed was completely spontaneous. One day I was coming back from the theater and I saw a small poster taped to a light pole that said GOD IS COMING BACK AND, BOY, IS SHE PISSED. It made me smile. I figured it was probably true. Gender aside, any god or goddess worth the name would have to be a little bit disappointed in how we turned out. We humans, I mean. The dolphins and the mountain goats seem to be doing just fine.

That's where the piece started, with an image of a big angry female force coming to set things right. It ended with Halima finding somebody who let us use their beautiful horse, and me riding around Paris with a tit or two hanging out and a sword strapped to my back, declaiming my opinions through the persona of a fictional Amazonian warrior woman. She would show up at various points around the city, state the queen's opinions, pass out handbills reiterating the same, and then gallop off into the sunset.

It was an immediate sensation, of course, and probably made my reputation as much as anything.

"Sometimes that seems like another lifetime," I said. "Were we ever really that young?"

"We're still that young," she said, smiling and chopping up some more tomatoes to add to her salad.

She was as optimistic as ever, but I was old enough to know better. I took another sip of my champagne.

"I'm sorry Zora couldn't join us. Is she still working with that veterans' program?"

I nodded. "They're freaking out about the coverage she's still getting in that gossip rag."

"*Dig It!?*"

"That's the one."

"She can't help what they print," Abbie said. "They've got to fill up fifty pages a day. They might say anything."

"Have you ever been in there?"

"No, thank the goddess. I'm not exactly of interest to their prime audience."

"Who is their prime audience?"

Abbie shrugged and leaned back against the corner. Her knife still in her hand, she picked up her champagne and took a swallow. "Young people, bored people, unhappy people with no adventures of their own."

"That's not a very impressive demographic."

"It actually is if you think about it," she said slowly. "Most folks fit into one or more of those groups. Other people's lives, real or imagined, are more exciting to them than their own. So they pick up *Dig It!*

on their way to work, or on their way to the grocery store, and instead of having to figure out what they're going to do to justify their presence on the planet today, all they have to do is see who's hot and who's not. Who's loving who and who's mad about it. It's like a continuing soap opera, except these are real people's lives."

"They're obsessed with Zora. The night I got here, she met me at Paschal's and the next day, there we were having drinks in *Dig It!*"

"The waiter?"

"That's what Zora thinks. Whoever it was, her boss seemed to think the piece compromised her position as a serious activist and gave her assignment to someone else on the staff whose profile presumably isn't so high."

"That poor child has had a year of this," Abbie said, tearing lettuce and tossing it in the big wooden bowl. "I can't believe they're still hounding her. How's she holding up?"

I shook my head. "Not so good." To my great embarrassment, my voice broke a little.

Abbie stopped her salad making and looked at me.

"How are you holding up?"

I tried to laugh, but it came off a little shaky. "I been better."

"Don't worry," she said. "Zora's smart and resourceful. She knows it can't last. Pretty soon, they'll find somebody else to torment. That's not why she didn't come tonight, is it?"

"No," I said. "She's gone to a wedding in Birmingham."

"Well, that's a good thing. She'll be out of town, celebrating with a bunch of people who never heard of *Dig It!*"

"Here's hoping," I said.

Abbie peeked in another pot and looked at her watch. "These Negroes better come on. I am not above starting without them. Are you starving?"

"I'm fine," I said.

"Good, then let's take our champagne in the other room. Otherwise, I'll keep adding stuff until I've ruined a perfectly good meal."

She led the way down the hall to the living room where the fire had burned down to a pleasant glow and Ella Fitzgerald had given way to Nat King Cole. Abbie adjusted the volume for conversation and took one of the rocking chairs. I sank down into the pillows at one end of the cozy couch.

"Did you get a chance to check on your house?"

I rolled my eyes. "Don't remind me!"

"Why? What's wrong?"

I felt like a little background was in order.

"My mother bought the place when we moved here from Montgomery when I was twelve. She left it to me as a hedge against being a broke old woman forced to make a living doing cough medicine commercials."

Abbie laughed softly. "Now that's a good mother. Plan ahead."

"Well, she did, but my management company went out of business and the new one doesn't really have much interest in what they call run-down rentals in undesirable neighborhoods."

"How bad is it?"

"Pretty bad. There are no windows, no tenants, the yard is full of trash. Plus, an indignant squatter read me the riot act for letting the place get so run-down."

"That's awful," she said. "What are you going to do?"

I snuggled a little deeper into the cushions. "I have no idea."

Abbie nodded sympathetically. "What do you *want* to do?"

I loved her for making the distinction. One of the continuing challenges of my life is closing that gap between what I want and what I might actually do.

"Well, I'd like to hold on to it if I can."

"For sentimental reasons?"

"There's that," I said, "but I always liked the idea of owning a piece of property. It seemed like such a grown-up, responsible thing to do, even if I didn't live there. The rent has been paying all of Zora's college expenses, and even though I laughed at my mother talking about that cough medicine commercial, it always felt good to know if worst came to worst, I had a place to call my own."

"You know the funny thing is I remember a cough syrup commercial that they used to show a long time ago and I always loved the woman in it talking about her grandchildren and how this medicine was so good for them."

I laughed and shook my head. "That's because she was probably a great actress trying to get her rent money together!"

Abbie laughed, too, but I could tell she knew I was worried. "Can't you get another management company?"

"Not the way this place looks. I haven't even been inside, but if the outside is any indication, it's a wreck, too. That's probably why what they offered me was so low."

"How much?"

"Fifteen thousand."

"Fifty thousand?"

"*Fifteen*," I corrected her, wishing it had been fifty. I'd be on my way to the bank right now.

Abbie put down her champagne. "Where on M. L. King is it?"

"It's the big white house on the hill a few blocks from the cemetery."

"Near the freeway?"

"Practically runs through the backyard."

She squinted a little, trying to picture it in her mind. M. L. King was still a major thoroughfare through Atlanta's black community, and if she'd spent much time here, chances are she'd driven by Evans Estates. My mother, in a fit of grandiosity, once threatened to have a small sign made that she would post at the foot of the driveway to help people find their way. I managed to talk her out of it, but it became an inside joke between us. *Welcome to Evans Estates.*

"Does it have a great big lawn in the front?"

"It used to. Now it has an overgrown weed field that seems to double as the neighborhood landfill."

"Oh, no!" she said. "I know that place. I've driven by there with my niece. She worked on a project with an older woman who lived around the corner on Wiley. After her house got robbed twice, Regina helped her find a place in West End."

Older meant "older than us." It probably always would.

"The robbers were most likely staying at my place when they did it," I said.

"Oh, Jo, I'm so sorry. And you're right. It is a real mess. Inside, too."

"You've been inside?"

She nodded. "When Regina told Blue what was going on, he thought about buying it, but when he sent a contractor over there with us, to take a look, the guy said thieves had ripped out all the copper wire and dragged away as many of the plumbing fixtures as they could carry. There were big holes in the wall and in the floor, too. Both sides."

"Is that why Blue didn't buy it?"

"Blue doesn't really want to expand out of West End. If he had bought your place, people would have expected him to do more. To do . . . the kinds of things he does over here."

She got up and poked the fire, added another log to it, and sat back down. "He's not really looking to take on any more right now, especially since they had the baby. In Trinidad, Blue can be an artist again instead of . . . you know."

Of course I knew. I had walked over here in the dark without giving it a second thought, hadn't I?

"I'll be surprised if they ever come back here to live," she said.

"So I can't count on Blue Hamilton to reclaim my neighborhood anytime soon?"

"'Fraid not." Abbie smiled. "But even the land is worth more than fifteen thousand."

"That's what I thought, but Ms. Woodruff seemed to think I was being naïve."

"She's being naïve. That whole area is in line for some serious redevelopment," Abbie said. "All that property over there is going to double and triple its value in the next two or three years."

"She said ten."

Abbie shook her head firmly. "Not a chance. Nothing in Atlanta takes ten years. All those folks who left the city to get away from Negroes are tired of fighting the traffic every day to get to work. They want these in-town neighborhoods back. And right now!"

Funny how language sets a tone. *Inner city* sounds dark and dangerous. *In-town* sounds hip and trendy.

"Besides," Abbie said, grinning. "All those neighborhoods are now full of people from all over the world, including black folks. The days of lily-white enclaves protected by privilege from the unwashed masses are gone with the wind. Now all they got is a long commute twice a day and the specter of four-dollar-a-gallon gas."

"How much do you think I might be able to get for it if what you're talking about happens?"

"I don't know," she said. "You should ask Aretha when she gets here. She keeps up with that stuff."

A fabulous photographer with a second career as a real estate mogul? I was liking this Aretha more and more.

"She can also give you an estimate on repairs. She's done a lot of work with contractors."

"How many jobs does she have?" I said, but before Abbie could answer, the doorbell rang.

"That's probably her now," Abbie said, heading for the door. "You can ask her yourself."

TWENTY-ONE

●

I didn't get a chance to ask Aretha anything right then. When Abbie opened the door, she was greeted by both of our dinner partners and another man who looked a little surprised to find himself included.

"I found these guys in front of your house," Aretha said, hugging Abbie hello. "Do they belong to you?"

"Well, this one does," said Abbie laughing and kissing the one who was clearly Peachy on the cheek. "And the other one is welcome. Any friend of Peachy's is a friend of mine."

She extended her hand to the man who was almost a foot taller than she was in her little flat Chinese shoes. "I'm Abbie Browning."

"Louie Baptiste," said the man, bending over to touch his lips lightly to the back of her hand.

"Hey, you heard the lady," Peachy said, grinning. "She's spoken for so don't be kissing on her hands!"

The man looked startled by Peachy's teasing. "I'm sorry," he said. "I didn't mean any disrespect, Miss Browning."

"Don't pay him a bit of mind," Abbie said. "He's just trying to distract me so I won't point out how late he is for dinner."

"It was this Negro's fault in the first place," Peachy said, pointing at Louie. "I've been begging him to come down and help me out at the restaurant, but he's stubborn as a Georgia mule."

Aretha hung their coats and her own in the front closet, clearly a frequent and comfortable visitor.

"So I figured maybe you could talk him into it," Peachy said.

"Not a chance." Abbie laughed and shook her head.

"You don't even know what I want you to talk him into yet, Sweet Thing."

"I don't care," she said. "Talking people into things is not my style. Mr. Baptiste, come in and meet my other guest."

"Call me Louie," he said quickly. I stood up, wondering if he would kiss my hand, too, or if Peachy had scared him out of it for the rest of the evening.

"Louie, meet my friend Josephine Evans. Josephine, meet Louie Baptiste and Peachy Nolan."

"My pleasure," Louie said, but made no move to take my hand.

"Aw, man, it's okay to kiss this one. Go for it!"

I laughed and extended my hand. "How about we just shake instead?"

"So you got a thing about talking somebody into something, too?" Peachy said, grinning, clearly a man who liked to tease. Abbie was standing easily within the circle of his arm.

"I don't have a position against it," I said. "I'm just not very good at it."

"So you say!" He laughed. "I'll bet you could talk the black off a crow."

Aretha came over to give me a hug. "Good to see you again."

"You, too."

Abbie smiled and disengaged herself from Peachy's easy embrace. "Aretha, why don't you come with me and get the glasses? Maybe we can get Peachy to pour some champagne in addition to all that signifyin'."

"I'm your man," Peachy said. "Bring it on!"

He sat down on the other end of the sofa and waved an arm at Louie. "Cop a squat, man. Make yourself at home."

Peachy was a small man with a compact physique and a full head of wavy white hair that he wore just long enough to let you know he considered it one of his best features. He was wearing a rust-colored turtleneck sweater, a pair of softly pleated pants, and a pair of brown and tan two-tone shoes. He looked like a jazz musician. Louie was taller than Peachy, and everything about him was medium: medium brown complexion, medium height, medium weight. His dark hair was cut short and sprinkled with gray and so was the mustache he had let grow in full and bushy. He was wearing a dark suit, white shirt, and sober tie, all of which made him look more like he was going to church than to dinner with friends. His face looked sober, too, like he had more on his mind than Abbie's paella.

"It's good to meet you," Peachy said. "Abbie was real excited that you all just ran into each other at the West End News like that."

"I was, too. We haven't seen each other in a long time."

"Well, now that you're here, don't be a stranger."

"I won't."

Aretha came in with three glasses and the champagne. Peachy quickly took the bottle to do the honors. By the time he refilled my glass, Abbie came in and stood beside him.

"To sweet Abbie," Peachy said, smiling and handing her a glass.

"The place or the person?" Aretha said.

"The person, of course," Peachy said. "No contest."

"I love you, too." Abbie laughed, drank a sip of her champagne, and excused herself, promising dinner would be ready in two minutes.

Peachy's eyes followed her until she disappeared down the hall. "Only reason I even opened the damn restaurant was so she wouldn't think I was spending all my time waiting around for her to agree to marry me."

"How's business?" I said.

"It's great. Too great. We got lines out the door every night. Now when she's got time to see me, I can't see her because I gotta go down to the dock and pick out some shrimp? That ain't right." He turned to Louie, sipping his champagne and gazing into the fire. "That's why I'm trying to get Baptiste to come and help me out in the kitchen, but like I said, he's stubborn."

Louie looked up at the sound of his name and smiled a noncommittal smile. It was clear he had been lost in his own thoughts. "Say what?"

"I said, you're stubborn. Now tell me I'm wrong."

"I came here with you, didn't I?" Louie said quietly.

"I'm just messin' with you, brother. Some of my best friends are stubborn. That woman in there . . ." He jerked his head toward the kitchen. "She is the most stubborn person I've ever met in my life and I couldn't love her more if I tried. So what are you gonna do?"

As if on cue, Abbie appeared in the doorway. "You're going to count your blessings," she said. "Dinner is served."

TWENTY-TWO

•

*A*nother bottle of champagne, Abbie's perfect paella, and lots of laughter made for a wonderful evening. Once we all gathered around the kitchen table, Louie seemed to relax a little, too, grinning and shaking his head whenever Peachy's teasing turned his way. For her part, Aretha treated Peachy like a favorite uncle and he returned the favor by praising the photograph that now hung in Sweet Abbie's to welcome his patrons.

"Pretty soon, people are going to start coming in just to see that picture," he said, adding three sugars to the coffee Abbie had passed around.

"That doesn't say much for your chef," Aretha said, obviously pleased at the compliment.

"You hear that, Louie? What have I been trying to tell you?"

"Let the man have his coffee in peace," Abbie said.

"I ain't bothering him. I'm just saying . . ." He sipped his coffee.

Abbie smiled at Louie. "You know, I'm glad Peachy didn't tell me he was bringing *the* Louie Baptiste to dinner or I might not have had the nerve to make such a complicated meal."

"Miss Abbie, you ain't got to apologize for nothin'," Louie said, adding a southern compliment to a great cook. "You put your foot in that paella."

"Thank you," Abbie said. "It was an honor to have you at my table."

"The pleasure was all mine," Louie said.

"Well, now that you two have formed a mutual admiration society, does that mean you'll consider my offer more seriously?" Peachy said.

During dinner, it had come out that Louie had been a much admired chef with his own small restaurant in New Orleans before Katrina. After the levees broke, he'd waited in water up to his chest for two days before the coast guard rescued him. He had escaped to Atlanta, assuming he'd go back and pick up the pieces when the water went down, but by the time he was allowed back to his Ninth Ward neighborhood, all that was left was the slab the restaurant building had been sitting on and a bunch of empty houses where his neighbors used to live. He stayed around for a couple of months, waiting for some signs of the recovery they kept promising and not seeing any.

Finally, when the smell of the bodies and the sewage and the broken promises got to be too much for him, he had come back to Atlanta with two friends of his, also chefs, and taken a job at a downtown hotel where, according to Louie, the man in charge couldn't have made a pot of decent gumbo if his life depended on it. One of his friends had moved in with a daughter, but he had lost his wife when the water swept through their house and he never got over it. His daughter, still grieving her mother, kept trying to get Louie's friend to talk about it, but he couldn't, or he wouldn't, and one day he left a note saying he was sorry, enclosed four thousand dollars in cash he had buried in his backyard and brought with him in a tin box, and just walked away.

Louie had tried to comfort the young woman by telling her that her father just needed some time, but they both knew he wasn't coming back. His other friend had tried and failed to find a job and finally went back to New Orleans because he couldn't think of anywhere else to go. Every now and then he and Louie would talk on the phone and his friend would say, *Don't come back here, man. Stay up there where you got it good. Ain't nothin' down here but broke niggas and stray dogs and neither one worth a damn.*

Louie knew his friend wouldn't lie, so he rented himself a small apartment just outside of West End and tried to cook the bland food that was required, but in his dreams, he still heard the sound of second-line bands and longed to add just a pinch of spice to the pot. When Peachy came to see him about the chef's spot at Sweet Abbie's, he had thought it was a dream come true until Peachy told him the place wasn't in Atlanta, but at the tip of a tiny little island where hurricanes were a fact of life.

He told Peachy he was sorry, but he couldn't do it. His desire to run his own kitchen was overwhelmed by his memories of all that water rising in the darkness. But he longed to be able to accept Peachy's offer, and Peachy knew it. That's why he had coaxed Louie into coming along this evening. By the time we all settled over coffee, no deals had been struck, but the fellowship and the good food and Abbie's easy hospitality had worked their magic. Louie agreed to consider the offer again.

It had worked on me, too. Our conversation early on before the others arrived had given me some hope for the house and Aretha had agreed to come with me in the next couple of days to take a look around so I'd know what I was up against when it came to repairs. Once I knew that, I'd be in a better position to evaluate Greer Woodruff's offer and decide whether I could afford to keep playing hard to get or whether I should jump on a plane back to Amsterdam and start begging François for that teaching job.

But none of that had to be decided tonight. It was late and Peachy was driving back to Tybee early in the morning. Aretha offered to give Louie a ride home but he said he'd rather walk. Me, too. I was looking forward to the short walk back to Zora's. She wasn't due back until tomorrow and the idea of a midnight swim had just presented itself to me as the perfect way to finish off a lovely evening. Maybe I could absorb the mermaid's serenity by osmosis and emerge filled with a newfound peace, an unshakeable clarity, and a plan for getting Zora back on track.

Abbie declined my offer to help clean up and walked me outside. Louie and Peachy were standing at the end of the walk. Peachy was still lobbying.

"Thank you," I said to Abbie, smiling at the soft scent of her everpresent patchouli. "I really needed this."

"Me, too," she said. "I'm so glad you had a chance to meet Peachy. Now we can talk."

"Talk about what?"

"About whether or not I should marry him," she said, laughing. "What else?"

Peachy came up on the porch, grinning at me as he put his arm around Abbie's waist. "I can vouch for that Negro's character if you accept his offer to walk you home."

Louie was standing on the sidewalk, holding his hat in his hand like an old-fashioned gentleman caller.

"You don't have to do that," I said.

"We go the same way," he said. "I'd be honored to have your company."

Peachy and Abbie had such signifyin' looks on their faces, I laughed out loud. "You two deserve each other!"

"You got that right!" Peachy laughed, too.

"Great to meet you," I said to Peachy, hugging Abbie goodbye.

"You, too," Peachy said, and kissed my hand just like Louie had done to Abbie a few hours ago and winked. "That Negro ain't the only one with the moves."

TWENTY-THREE

•

*L*ouie lived just outside of West End in a small apartment right on the MARTA line. He could catch the bus outside his front door and be at the downtown hotel kitchen where he worked in less than twenty minutes. His route home took him down our street and he matched his steps to mine easily, like a man who already knew what his feet would find. The night was cool and our nonstop, laughter-filled conversations at dinner had allowed us the luxury of enjoying each other's quiet company as we savored the walk home together.

There is no way to imagine the terror Louie must have felt watching the water rising with no possible escape. No way to understand the horror of the sounds and sights and smells that came after. The destruction not just of neighborhoods, but of a whole way of moving through the world. Some people could not survive it. Their hearts broke and rebroke too many times for mending, and so even if they lived through it, they were never the same. How could they be?

It was like that afternoon at the height of the plague years when Howard called in tears because he wanted to plan a brunch and realized all of his beautiful, fabulous friends were dead of AIDS, except me.

"What's the point?" he had sobbed, filled with the pain of loss and the guilt of the survivor. "What's the point?"

I never know how to answer that question. That one seems better put to a priest or a shaman than an actress who has never been very good at improvisation. Good food had been the point for Louis. He found his way by feeding people. I found mine by telling stories from the stage. But now things had changed and he found himself taking orders in someone else's kitchen and I found myself getting ready to fix up my wreck of a house and wondering how I would ever know the answer when I couldn't even seem to find the question.

That's when I saw the car parked out front. There it sat, a good foot and a half from the curb; the same dirty green Chevrolet that had taken Zora to the wedding had now delivered her safely home. Of course I was relieved, but the last person I wanted to see tonight was a fool who didn't even know that it's always bad manners to sit out front and blow your horn for a lady.

I stopped in front of the house and smiled at Louie. "This is me," I said. "Thanks for the walk."

"My pleasure," he said, touching the brim of his hat. "Good luck with your house."

"Thanks," I said. "Good luck with your kitchen."

"Good night, then."

"Good night."

He stood there while I strolled up the walk, climbed up the steps. I turned at the door to wave. He touched the corner of his hat and headed off down the street. Maybe Zora was winding up her weekend and her friend would be leaving now. Maybe we could still take that swim together.

No such luck. When I stepped inside, there she was, lying on the couch next to the fool I'd seen in the front seat of the car on Friday. He was shirtless and shoeless with one hand holding on to the nearly empty vodka bottle and the other hand holding on to Zora. There was an open pizza box on the coffee table, two roaches in the ashtray, and two big water tumblers that I assumed they had been using for their cocktails. They were both out cold.

The television was playing the late-night videos where the girls all look like strippers and the guys all look like gangsters and nobody seems to be having any fun, although they are all working really hard to make you think they are. For a minute, I just stood there looking at the two of them, wondering what the appropriate response might be. The way I figure, I had three options. One, I could wake her up and demand an explanation of such low-class behavior; two, I could wake him up and offer to kick his little ass if he ever showed up around here again; or three, I could go upstairs and close my door and deal with it tomorrow when she was sober and he was history.

To my credit, I took option three. It wasn't easy, but I turned off the TV, locked the front door, went upstairs, put on my pajamas, brushed my teeth, said my prayers (just in case), got in bed, and turned out the light. A lot of good it did me. Lying there in the dark, I was so aware of the two of them sprawled out downstairs that I couldn't relax. It was almost as if she wanted me to find them. She knew I'd be coming home late from Abbie's and there was no way not to see them on my way upstairs. What did she expect me to do? Ignore them? Be the outraged grandmother who would throw him out and force her to do the right thing? Pack my things and carry my meddling ass back to Amsterdam?

I had just about made up my mind that I was going to have to go back to option one and wake her up, when I heard a noise in the hallway. I sat up and listened. Someone was passing my door, headed toward Zora's room, but it only sounded like one set of footsteps. Had she left him downstairs to sleep it off alone? I slipped on my robe and stepped out into the hallway.

Zora's door was cracked and the light was on, but there was no sound. Something didn't feel right to me, and when I padded down to her room on my bare feet and peeked in, I could see why. Her friend, still sans shirt and shoes, was standing in front of her dresser examining a watch Howard had sent her from Paris. He picked it up, turned it over, and held it in his hand with a little smile like he had found something he liked.

"What do you think you're doing?" I said, too indignant to be afraid.

He turned around so fast he staggered a little bit, still too drunk to count on perfect balance. "Jesus! Who the hell are you?"

"I'm Zora's grandmother," I said.

His eyes flickered over my body in a way that made my skin crawl, then he smiled. "You don't look old enough to be nobody's grandmother."

"What are you doing up here?" I said, rephrasing the question he had yet to answer.

He looked around the room like he was almost as surprised to find himself there as I was and then decided his best course of action was to lie. The only problem was, he didn't have one.

"She . . . uh . . . wanted me to get . . . her watch for her. Yeah, she wanted her watch." He tried another grin on me.

"All right," I said. "This is what you're going to do. You're going to go back down those stairs, put your clothes on, and get out of here."

"You ain't gotta get all bent out of shape," he said. "Zora invited me."

"Well, I'm uninviting you," I said, wishing I was strong enough to pick him up and toss him bodily out into the night. "Get your things and get out now."

He frowned and it dawned on me that I didn't know a thing about this man, standing there in my pajamas, ordering him around like I was the assistant principal who had caught him between classes without a hall pass. "And what if I don't?"

Something in his half-drunk defiance made me mad. *Damn danger.* I just wanted him out. "Then the police will help you. I've already called 911."

That was a lie, of course. I hadn't called anybody, but he didn't know that and the idea of the police being on their way had the desired effect.

"Well, fuck it then," he said loudly, brushing past me and down the steps. "Fuck you and fuck your drunk-ass granddaughter."

The noise woke Zora who was struggling to arrange her rumpled clothing more appropriately as I followed him downstairs into the living room, watched him pull his shirt over his head, and stuff his feet into a pair of white tennis shoes.

"What's wrong?" she said. "What are you doing?"

"Ask your granny," he said. "She the one called the cops."

Zora seemed to see me standing there for the first time. "Mafeenie, what's going on?"

"I found your friend upstairs in your room going through your things."

"Going through my things?" She turned back to him, confused. "You were going through my things?"

"I was looking for the bathroom," he snarled. "When here she come talkin' about callin' 911."

"They're on their way," I said, pulling my robe tighter around me, pressing my advantage.

"You know where the bathroom is down here," Zora said. "I showed you where . . ."

"Okay, I was takin' a look around," he said, grabbing his 76ers Starter jacket off the floor. "Ain't no law against that, is there?"

"Taking a look around at what?" Zora said, still sounding confused.

"Nothing, okay? Nothing! I'm outta here."

I resisted the impulse to throw something as he headed for the door. Maybe I should have gone with my instincts, because he stopped as he stepped out onto the porch and looked back at us with a sneer.

"Both you bitches can kiss my black ass!"

And with that highly unoriginal exit line, he trotted down the walk, jumped in his car, and headed off down the street, squealing his tires as a final goodbye. I closed the door and looked at Zora.

"Did you really call the police?"

I shook my head and started collecting the detritus from the living room. "No."

She just stood there in her rumpled clothes and watched without offering any assistance. Fine with me. I was too mad to talk to her now anyway. I headed for the kitchen, clutching the pizza box and the two supersize cocktail glasses. Zora trailed behind me with the Stoli bottle. I stuffed the box in the trash and rinsed the glasses in the sink.

Zora sat down at the kitchen table. "I'm sorry if I offended you, Mafeenie, but this is my life."

"It doesn't have to be."

"Oh, yes it does," she said, her voice getting louder, slurring the words. "It does because it is. This sorry, sordid, scary mess is exactly the way I'm living. This is it, Mafeenie. Welcome to my world."

She was trying to be defiant, but she only looked sick and sad and unhappy, just like her father had at the end. Full of self-loathing and self-pity and straight vodka, and all of a sudden I got mad again. Really mad. This child seemed to think she was the only person in the world whose dreams hadn't come true in a timely fashion. The only one who felt lost and scared and alone. Looking at her sitting in this beautiful house, in a place where she was safe and warm and protected from everything except gossip, I couldn't help thinking about Louie waiting in that filthy water for two days, hoping somebody would find him before he suffocated or drowned or went crazy. I couldn't help thinking about all the time and energy and love she was wasting just because things turned out to be a little more complicated than she thought they would. She owed herself better and she owed me better.

"Let me tell you something," I said. "This is not your world. This is no world at all. I came here for two reasons, to see you and to take care of my business with that damn duplex. But before I will watch you do this, I will burn that piece of house to the ground, catch a plane back where I came from, and let you drink yourself to death alone because this . . . *this* . . . is just bullshit!"

And it was. All of it. Zora looked like I had slapped her across the mouth, and it made me feel so bad, I wanted to take her in my arms and apologize and tell her everything was going to be okay, the same way I had wanted to tell that kid on the elevator that the shot he was headed for wouldn't hurt on its way to healing. But that would have been a lie, so I left her sitting there, went back upstairs to my room, got into bed, pulled the covers up over my head, and wept.

It seemed the sanest possible response. I'd only been back a week and everything was shot to shit. If this was life in America, they could have it. I'd had enough.

TWENTY-FOUR

*A*t two thirty, I heard Zora come upstairs and take a long shower. I got up and went to sit in the chair by the window. I hadn't slept a wink. The yard was dark. There was no moon showing and very few stars. I closed my eyes and called on every spirit I could think of to help me help Zora. It was too easy to carry out my threat to leave her. All I had to do was hop on a plane and never look back. But what kind of granny did that make me? The one who could teach you how best to toss a drink in somebody's face but didn't have much practical information when the going got tough. The one who only knew how to love you when it was easy, but left you to figure it out for yourself if things got a little messy. That wasn't who I wanted to be, but I wasn't sure if I knew how to do better. So I expanded my prayer to include a promise that if Zora would let me get close to her, I'd never push her away again, even for a second.

At three fifteen, there was a soft knock.

"Come in," I said, and Zora pushed the door open enough to stick her head in.

"You awake?"

"Sure, come on in."

She had washed her hair and brushed it out into a soft cloud around her face. I recognized her blue silk pajamas as a pair we had bought two summers ago in Paris. She had grown a few inches since then and the pants were definitely high-water, but I knew she had chosen them to please me.

"What are you doing?"

"Nothing," I said. "I just couldn't sleep."

"Can I sit with you for a minute?"

"Of course."

She sat down on the floor right next to my feet and hugged her knees against her chest like she used to do when she was a kid.

"Are you cold?"

"No."

We sat in silence for a minute, earlier events hovering between us like a ghost. At least she didn't smell like vodka and cheap grass anymore. She smelled like talcum powder and toothpaste. I reached out and stroked her hair slowly, gently. We didn't have to talk at all. Her being here was enough. She leaned her head against my knee and sighed.

"You're not really going away, are you?"

"Not until you throw me out."

"Good."

I kept stroking her hair. Even bohemian grandmothers like me know the power of a laying-on of hands.

"I want to tell you what happened in Birmingham," she said.

"All right."

I kept stroking her hair. She sighed again and snuggled a little closer to my knee. She was silent such a long time I thought she had changed her mind. When she did start talking, her voice was so quiet, I held my breath so I wouldn't miss anything.

"The night before the wedding, we all got drunk," she whispered. "We were dancing and listening to music and acting crazy, you know."

I didn't know, but it was a rhetorical question so I didn't say anything.

"Then the bride threw up and passed out and then Jabari and I had a big argument and he passed out, too. That left me and his brother up all by ourselves. That's when he . . . he showed me his penis."

She was quiet again for a long time. I took a deep breath and tried not to say, *He did what?* Being the Las Vegas of grandmothers sometimes means you hear stuff you wish you hadn't, but that comes with the territory.

"He said he'd been clipping my pictures out of *Dig It!* for months and fantasizing about me while he had sex with his fiancée. He said if I didn't want to . . . touch it, I could just watch him and that would be almost as good. I told him to go to hell and he got mad and started threatening me, so I locked myself in the bathroom until Jabari woke up." She hugged her knees a little tighter. "I wanted to come home right then, but Jabari was the best man so he wouldn't leave and I didn't have any money, so I stayed, too."

In what parallel universe does he qualify to ever be called "the best man"?

"So we went to the wedding and then the reception and . . . I was drinking a lot to get through it and he was just drinking because that's what he does. But all the way home he kept apologizing and saying how sorry he was and when we got here, he asked if he could come in just for a minute so we could break bread, that's what he always says, 'break bread,' so I let him come in and then he had a couple of joints and I had the rest of that vodka, so we just started doing all of that . . . and I . . . I didn't even remember you were here."

That's when she started crying. Big, wracking sobs that shook her whole body against my leg.

"I'm sorry, Mafeenie. I'm so ashamed. I never meant for you to see me like that. I'm not like that!"

I reached down then and pulled her to her feet and then drew her down onto my lap like she was five years old and needed me to kiss a skinned knee.

"Shhhh! Hush now," I said. "Hush! It's over. It's all over, I promise."

She put her arms around me and buried her face in my neck. Her long legs were dangling to the floor and I'm sure we looked as awkward as we felt, but it didn't matter. I held her like a baby and just let her cry. After a while, she stopped sobbing but she didn't move, so I kept rocking her. Gradually, her breathing slowed down and she sniffed loudly and sat up.

"You okay?" I said.

She nodded and sniffed again.

"There's a box of Kleenex on the nightstand," I said, realizing she had put my left leg to sleep. I rubbed some feeling back into it while she blew her nose loudly and sat down on the bed. "That's too far away. Come closer."

She dragged the little desk chair over and sat facing me. We were sitting in front of the window, and in the darkness the glow of the pool seemed almost otherworldly. Our knees were touching lightly and I reached out for her hands.

"Listen, darlin'," I said. "The world is a very big place and maybe, maybe neither one of us is supposed to be calling this little pitiful corner of it home."

"What do you mean?" She sniffed again.

"I mean there's nothing to keep either one of us here if this isn't where we want to be. We can fix up the house, sell it to the highest bidder, pack our bags, and hit the road."

"Sell the house?"

"It's just a house," I said.

"Are you sure?"

"It's your inheritance," I said. "I'm sure if you are."

"Oh, Mafeenie," she whispered, "can we really go away?"

"We can do whatever we decide to do," I said, "but there's one thing we have to be clear about."

"What's that?"

"This is a choice we're making based on who we are and what we want. It's no good if we're just running away. If that's all it is, then they've won and we're just a pair of scared little rabbits looking for a place to hide. Do you understand?"

"I understand," she said softly.

"Good."

"How soon can we go?" Zora said, like she was ready to leave right then.

"As soon as we can get the house in shape so we put it on the market and Howard can get things back on track at the theater."

"When will that be?"

"Any day now," I said.

"You promise?"

"I promise."

"Can I sit on your lap again?"

"I can do better than that," I said. So she slept in my room that night like she used to in Amsterdam. I think we both needed that closeness. She went to sleep before I did and I watched her face in the darkness until I felt myself fading, too. I whispered my thanks to whatever gods were listening, and slept like a baby.

•

TWENTY-FIVE

When Aretha came by to pick me up in the morning, Zora had already headed off to work and I was preparing myself for a first look inside. The thing about the house is that it isn't just a piece of property to me. It represents my connection to a long line of women for whom home ownership was a requirement. My mother was a member of a large, messy, matriarchal clan whose family herstory begins with the story of an enslaved ancestor forced to bear the master's child. When the baby's facial features precluded the possibility of denial, the mistress of the plantation grew increasingly agitated at her presence until the master packed up our ancestor and her daughter and drove them to the outskirts of Montgomery, where he deeded them a small house and set them free.

That house represented the official end of their enslavement and was handed down from mother to daughter until the city of Montgomery grew up around it. Finally forced to sell to make way for progress, the great-granddaughter took the proceeds, immediately bought another house, and started the process all over again. When I was a little girl in Montgomery, all my aunts and female cousins owned their own houses. Men would come and go, but the houses and the freedom they represented remained constant.

When my mother divorced my father and moved us to Atlanta when I was twelve, she sold our house to her second cousin, once removed, and immediately bought the duplex. Her plan was for us to live on one side and rent the other to an older, single woman, preferably a schoolteacher or a retiree. She did this successfully for the whole time I lived in Atlanta, after I moved to New York, then Amsterdam, and up until the time she decided to go back to Montgomery and buy back her first house from the cousin who had decided she'd had enough of Alabama and moved to Florida.

She held on to the Atlanta house for my benefit, and when the rent money it continued to generate paid for Zora's education, I knew how pleased that would have made her. But Zora needed something else now. She needed a way to get far enough from the scene of the crime, and the coverage of it, to regain her perspective. There was no way she could learn any valuable lessons from a boarded-up house located smack-dab in the middle of—what had Greer Woodruff called it?—an undesirable neighborhood. If my mother's legacy was about continuing a long line of free women, this would be what she would expect me to do.

I hoped when Aretha and I got there, the indignant squatter wouldn't be around to greet us, but I had no way of knowing, and the prospect of being confronted by him again did not appeal to me. Aretha told me not to worry about it.

"You said he didn't seem dangerous, right?"

"More pissed off at me than anything."

We were riding down Martin Luther King in her beautiful red truck and, considering our mission, her expression was surprisingly serene.

"Maybe you woke him up," she said calmly. "He's probably not a morning person."

I looked over to see if she was kidding and she grinned to let me know she was.

"Don't worry. If he makes you nervous, we'll get one of Blue's guys to come back over with us."

Blue's guys, the army of well-dressed, soft-spoken, hat-tipping men whose presence made West End such a peaceful place. Too bad we couldn't clone them, I thought, as Aretha turned into the driveway and headed up to the house. As she parked the truck, she looked around, frowning.

"I can't believe they just let it go like this," she said. "This was a great house."

"The question is," I said, "can it be a great house again?"

"That's what we're here to find out, right?"

"Right."

"I'm just going to give a few blasts on the horn in case our squatter is sleeping in."

I nodded. "Good thinking."

She blew three long blasts and then three more. If anybody was in the house, they would know they had company. We waited a minute, but no one emerged. In spite of her confident demeanor, I think Aretha was as relieved as I was.

"You ready?"

"Absolutely," I said, opening the door and stepping down into the overgrown yard.

Aretha shook her head, her eyes surveying the bags of trash, piles of broken furniture, stained, rain-sodden mattresses, and other debris scattered all over the big front lawn and up to the front door. People had obviously been using the yard as an unofficial neighborhood dump site. I could smell the rank stench of garbage spilling out of a bag near the back fence. The idea of rats suddenly came crashing into my mind. One of my first official acts would have to be hiring a good exterminator.

Reaching into the truck for a black bag that she had stashed behind her seat, Aretha unzipped it and took out a small video camera.

"What's that for?" I said, immediately aware that I had applied no makeup and was wearing a pair of sweats I had borrowed from Zora. I never wore sweats, didn't even own any, but I realized the clothes I had with me were not really suitable for the task at hand. However, this borrowed finery was definitely not camera-ready.

"I thought it might be good to videotape what we find inside," she said. "I don't know what your legal options are, but it never hurts to have a visual record of the property's current condition."

That made sense, but I wanted to be clear. "So I won't be on camera?"

"Not unless you want to. We'll walk through and I'll make some comments about what we're looking at, sort of a running commentary, and you can add anything you want."

"On camera?"

She grinned again. "On or off. It doesn't matter, but for the record? You look great."

"Thanks," I said, knowing this was no time to explain to her that part of how I make my living is being able to make a dispassionate assessment of how I look at any given moment. Great was how I looked at the party after I opened the season with *A Raisin in the Sun* last year. I'd never played Lena, the matriarch, before, but I nailed it. When she picks up that pitiful little plant from the windowsill at the end and gets ready to go do battle with her new neighbors, there wasn't a dry eye in the house. But Lena is a poor woman eking out a living on Chicago's South Side doing day work. Her costumes, including an incredibly serious wig, are uniformly unattractive. For the party, I needed an outfit that would effectively banish Lena from the minds of all who saw me and reestablish me immediately as my real self.

Howard didn't let me down. I arrived in a bright red gown that clung where it was supposed to and gave me a break when it needed to, sky-high heels, ropes and ropes of pearls, and a faux-fur coat that looked so real I got an angry letter from the animal rights people which they later had to rescind. I was utterly fabulous, eliciting gasps whenever I floated by, pausing to offer a cheek or an air kiss somewhere in the vicinity of the recipient's ear. *That* was great. This is what it is.

"You ready?" I said.

The key I had gotten from Greer's office was completely unnecessary. When Aretha pushed the front door, it opened slowly like a bad moment in a horror movie. If it had actually creaked, I probably would have lost my nerve altogether. We stepped inside and just stood there for a minute while our eyes adjusted to the gloom. Inside was dim and dank, and I was glad Aretha had a big flashlight stuck in the back pocket of her overalls. There was lots of graffiti on the walls, some crudely pornographic, with various forms of fellatio being the cartoon subject of choice, and some scrawled signatures that seemed to be there strictly for identification purposes. Sir Smith and Kozmic Kat were two favorites.

There were mounds of trash everywhere, mostly fast-food wrappers and white Styrofoam food containers, but also some shoes, clothing, and lots of newspapers. Aretha handed me the flashlight and propped open the front door with a stick to give us the benefit of any available sunshine, but with most of the windows boarded up, we didn't get much help there. I flipped on the flashlight and swept it over the area we could see. Aretha turned on the camera and started walking around the house slowly, speaking clearly and calmly about what she saw.

"No locks on the front door. Trash uncollected. Walls defaced. Floors scarred." She turned on a switch but neither one of us expected light and we were right. Aretha kept walking and talking and I followed her, but I was in shock. It was so much worse than I had expected. They had bashed in the walls, ripped out the wiring, torn out the bathroom fixtures, and stripped the kitchen of both appliances and cabinets. Parts of the parquet floors were deeply scratched as if someone had deliberately gouged out the wood. The linoleum in the kitchen was just disgusting.

All the rooms were filled with more trash and whatever else the squatters left behind. There was no furniture to speak of outside of a few broken-down chairs and a couple of filthy mattresses that I wanted to douse with gasoline and burn right then and there. We had started on the rental side, but I was sure the family side would be no better. There was no sign here of recent occupancy so I assumed my squatter had been camped out next door.

Aretha finished the last bedroom: "Both windows gone, no overhead fixtures, walls defaced and damaged. Ceiling stained, but no sag." She turned off the camera and looked at me. I could see the concern in her eyes so I must have looked as stricken as I felt.

"You okay?"

"This is terrible," I said. "Just awful, awful."

"Calm down," she said. "Some of it is cosmetic and won't cost much to fix."

"What about the rest?"

She shrugged. "Let's look at the other side before I try to give you any estimates, okay?"

That didn't sound promising, but I agreed and followed her back through the wreck. The front door on the side we used to live on wasn't locked either. Aretha turned on the camera and I turned on the flashlight. My heart sank. This one was just as bad. The small dining room where my mother and I ate so many meals together. The living room where I'd entertained my first boyfriends to the sound of Motown music. The kitchen where I mastered a family recipe for macaroni and cheese. It was all trashed. Aretha was still describing what she saw, but she was also watching me out of the corner of her eye.

When we got to the two bedroom doors, both of them were closed. I opened the door to my mother's room and found nothing there that had belonged to her, just more mess and the strong smell of urine and mildew. I stepped out of Aretha's way and reached for the door to what had been my room. The room where I started my period. The room where I first had sex when my mom had to go to Montgomery one weekend and I stayed home alone to study. The room where I'd know it was Sunday by the sound of Ms. Simpson's voice singing, "And he walks with me/and he talks with me/and he tells me I am his own," on her side of the house. The memories were suddenly pouring out of that door before I even cracked it and I wasn't sure I could go in.

"Was this your room?" Aretha said.

I nodded as I stood there with my hand on the doorknob.

"Do you want me to do this one by myself?"

"No, I'm okay," I said. "It's just a little spooky. Makes me think about how long it's been since I lived here."

And how weird it feels to be back.

But then I opened the door. The room that had been my girlhood sanctuary was free of trash and as neatly organized as a prison cell. A narrow cot was covered with an old quilt, which was surprisingly clean, and a card table with one chair was in the corner. Sitting in the middle of the table, on top of a stack of what looked like old library books, was a saucer full of candle stubs, obviously the room's only light. There were books lined up around three of the four walls.

He also had a small red plastic cooler and a pair of black shoes with no shoelaces at the front of the cot. On the wall above the pillow, he had tacked up a small snapshot of a man and woman wearing their Sunday clothes, smiling into the camera. They looked happy and hopeful, the way people do on graduation days and election nights and honeymoons. There was also a calendar from the soul food restaurant around the corner with the days of the current month marked off in a series of neat red X's.

"I guess this is where your squatter has been hanging out," Aretha said, as surprised as I was by the sudden imposition of order in the midst of the chaos we'd been slogging through.

"Let's leave it," I said, pulling the door closed, suddenly feeling an entirely inappropriate rush of guilt for invading his privacy, even though he was squatting in my room.

Aretha wanted to get some footage of the yard and the exterior of the house. She didn't need me for lighting anymore, but I walked with her anyway, trying to sort things out.

"Did you used to play out here?" she said as she turned the camera toward a mountain of black trash bags down closer to the street. It looked like people had just walked up to the fence and tossed their junk right over into our yard.

"My mother had an amazing rose garden out here," I said, remembering. "Red, yellow, pink, white. She was always pruning them or feeding them or watering them. It would kill her to see it like this."

Aretha turned off the camera and looked at me. "Then I guess we'll have to do something about it."

·

TWENTY-SIX

*H*alf an hour later, we were back in West End, lingering over a cup of tea at the Soul Vegetarian Restaurant while Aretha tried to make the task I was facing seem routine and achievable. Neither one of us had ordered food, but all around us hungry diners were feasting on broccoli quiche, sweet potato soufflé, and lentil soup. I was too busy pouring over the figures Aretha had written on a yellow legal pad to think about food. She had listed all the repairs and estimated the cost, including labor and supplies, and at the bottom, the figure she'd written and underlined twice was eighteen thousand dollars.

"That's more than the whole place is worth," I said.

"Only according to Greer Woodruff," Aretha said. "But I think we can discount her opinion for two reasons. One, she let the place fall apart and didn't even call you, which is not only bad business but downright rude, and two, she's trying to buy up all the property around here fast for some reason that doesn't have anything to do with a desire to help rebuild anybody's nest egg."

"What is it?"

Aretha shrugged. "My guess is she's got somebody interested in that corner property and all the way down Wiley Street to the freeway. These hotshot developers are always trying to buy these problem properties cheap and then sell them to the highest commercial bidder. If there's some real interest and the owners are reluctant to sell, they've been known to use some pretty unsavory tactics to intimidate the holdouts."

"Like what?"

"Vandalizing vacant property. Encouraging squatters and break-ins. Most of the people on Wiley are old women by themselves. Their husbands are dead. Their kids are grown and gone one way or another.

Once they don't feel safe after a few of these incidents, they're much more willing to take what they're offered and make the best of it."

"How can they make the best of it on fifteen thousand dollars?"

"They can't. They've been trying to get preservation money, but there's nothing really historic about the neighborhood. It's just some little houses where people lived their lives and raised their kids and got old. It's sad, you know? Where are they supposed to go once Greer Woodruff buys them out? Fifteen thousand won't even be a down payment on anyplace they'd want to live."

"Do you think Greer Woodruff would do something like that? Just to make a profit?"

"Didn't you tell me your squatter was worried about predators?"

"Yes."

Aretha took a sip of her tea. "I think she's already doing it."

"Well, what if the people in the neighborhood refused to sell? What if we fix up these properties and make our own deal?"

"Well, you'll probably triple the value of your mother's investment, and your neighbors can stay put if they want to or take the best offer and move to Florida. Everybody wins."

"Except Greer Woodruff," I said.

"Exactly."

I wondered how this had suddenly morphed into one of those "reclaim the community" movies. I hate that pseudo-inspirational bullshit. In my experience, the target population usually remains intractable, no mater how many uplifting power ballads you pack onto the soundtrack. "So now I've got to redeem the whole neighborhood?"

"You don't have to redeem it," she said. "They want to stay. They just need . . ." Her voice trailed off and she frowned, searching for the right word. "*Inspiration*. They need some inspiration."

I rest my case. *Cue the ballad.*

"How much do you think the place is worth?"

"I'd say one hundred twenty-five thousand just for the land."

"One hundred twenty-five thousand dollars?"

"Two hundred thousand if you fix up the house and do a little landscaping."

"That's ten times what she offered me!"

"That's what I'm talking about. She figures you're not going to want to spend the time and money to fix it up or have the patience or contacts to find a buyer on your own."

"How much time are we talking about?"

Aretha shrugged and her eyes scanned the figures she had put on the legal pad. "Depends on how much work you want to do."

"All of it," I said. If I was going to sell the place and put my faith in hard cash instead of bricks and mortar, I needed to be sure I got a good return on my mother's investment. Otherwise, she'd never forgive me.

"Well," Aretha said. "I'd say two and a half, three months, to get it all done, once we get a crew."

"How big a crew?"

"The more, the merrier," she said. "Four is good. Five is better. Experience preferred but not required."

The only kind of crew I knew how to organize was the kind that puts a play on the stage, but that wasn't the same thing at all. "Where do I find a crew?"

"I'll pull one together if you want me to," she said. "I manage a lot of property for Blue so I always have some guys on standby. It'll take me two weeks to finish the door project, then I'm ready to come on full-time."

"The door project?"

She laughed. "That's a long story and I've got to pick up Joyce Ann."

"I'm sorry I kept you so long," I said. "You've given me a lot to think about."

"Well, don't just get stuck on the numbers, think about how great that house is going to be once we get it all fixed up. You won't recognize the place." She stopped and smiled across the table at me. "Or maybe you will."

TWENTY-SEVEN

•

*W*hat happened while I was gone? I don't mean just to my house. I mean to *us*. What happened to the idea we had about being a community of people on the move? Atlanta was a magnet once for every bright young black person with a willingness to work hard and a desire to share the vision of a city where we were the decision makers, the visionaries, the leaders, the ones who could already see that future where everybody got a slice of the seemingly inexhaustible pie. We walked proud and we felt free. We were free! Sure, there were some old folks on both sides of the great American racial divide who couldn't quite get it together about this new day, this new way of being and see-ing and doing what needed to be done, but their habitually negative energy was overwhelmed by the voices of men and women determined to change the face of business as usual *forever and ever, amen.*

But all that seemed like a cruel joke now. All those dreams have dovetailed into a community-wide nightmare where casual violence is the order of every day, vandalism is a spectator sport, and a strange sense of entitlement allows those unwilling to work at anything to still feel they have the right to kick in somebody's door to get the things they want. Young people are angry and confused. Old people are scared to leave their houses for fear of being mugged or worse. And in the middle, the rest of us look around and wonder how it all fell apart so fast.

Walking through my mother's house with Aretha was more than a revelation. It was a reinforcement of what I told Zora the other night. We don't have to stay here another second longer than we want to. There is no place for me in Atlanta anymore, if there ever was. This is no place to live free, laugh loud, and stay strong. It's too hard just to stay alive. I don't see myself in ten years, a little old lady, locked in her house, afraid to open the door for the mailman, or crack the window to let in the evening breeze.

No wonder Zora was floundering around, trying to hide from the scandal sheets, stop the war, and save the world, all at the same time. It was time for her to be in a place where every hand that reaches out is not trying to pull you down. All I had to do now was piece together enough money to do what needed to be done at the house, find a buyer who wouldn't insult me with such a low offer, and get me and Zora two one-way tickets back to where a woman can enjoy her freedom instead of just dreaming about it.

I pulled out Aretha's notes and got my own legal pad. My financial reserves, such as they were, had to support me while I waited for François's heart to grow fonder, keep up with my expenses in Amsterdam, and now, somehow, find a way to make major repairs on a house I didn't even want to live in. It was going to take some juggling, that was for sure. The sooner I got started, the sooner I hoped I could figure it out.

By the time I had covered three pages with "what-ifs," and was still no closer to really getting any balls in the air, Zora arrived with a pizza and a much needed infusion of positive energy.

"I gave them my notice," she said, putting the pizza on the kitchen table, where I was doing my calculations, and going over to the sink to wash her hands. "I told them I'd help interview a replacement, but after this week, I'm yours!"

"Were they surprised?" I was glad she had moved so quickly, but also a little nervous now that I had promised her I had the next move covered.

"I think they figured they were doing me a favor letting me work there at all, so I should be grateful no matter how they treated me," she said. "The thing is, I was grateful. But it doesn't feel like I'm helping anybody anymore. Like no matter what I do, people are still going to be fighting about nothing and coming home crazy, and nobody knows what to do about any of it."

"They're always fighting about something," I said.

She dried her hands and sat down across from me. "Okay, but what? What is it about?"

I smiled and opened the box, releasing the unmistakable aroma into the air. My stomach growled in response. "Who knows?" I said, taking a slice of pizza. "Maybe it's a man thing."

She laughed and reached for a slice, too, folding it expertly like Howard had shown her. "Then we'll never understand it."

"You got that right," I said. "But your timing couldn't be better. I'm looking for a crew and you'd be perfect."

"A film crew?" She sounded excited by the idea.

"Not exactly," I said quickly, reaching for the disk Aretha had given me with the video she took this morning. She assured me that Zora would know what to do with it. "Where's your laptop?"

"In my backpack," she said. "What's this?"

"A disaster movie," I said, while she withdrew the thin silver notebook and opened it for business.

She popped in the tiny disk and the video came up on the screen. You could hear Aretha's voice calmly ticking off the problems as we moved through the debris and darkness. "Walls defaced, floors scarred . . ."

Zora looked up at me. "This is terrible."

I nodded. "Yep."

"It's even worse than you thought."

I had told Zora we were gong to have to do some work at the place, but nothing prepared her for what she was seeing. We sat there, munching on our pizza and looking at our pitiful nest egg, rotting among the weeds. This was my first viewing of what Aretha had shot and it was pretty hard to take even though I'd been there. When we came back outside to get some footage of the yard, I heard her ask me a question and then my voice talking about my mother's roses. I was so saddened by what I was seeing that I didn't notice that she had turned the lens in my direction and suddenly, there I was, in all my borrowed sweats bunching around my ankles, no-makeup-wearing glory. To complete the picture, I was frowning.

Zora leaned closer when I came on the screen, listening intently. I was listening, too, but mostly I was looking. I assumed I'd hate myself on camera the way I looked this morning, but I didn't. I actually liked the way I looked and the way I sounded. Indignant. Incredulous. Outraged. Exactly the way I felt. And then it was over. The last freeze-frame was a long shot of that huge pile of trash bags, just sitting there, stinking in the sunshine.

Zora looked at me. "She put you in it."

"I told her I didn't want to be on camera."

"Why? That's what made it real. Listening to you talking about Great-gram's roses. I never saw them, but you made me care." Zora sounded like she was critiquing a performance. "That was the best part."

"The best part of a disaster movie," I said. "According to Aretha, the place is going to need almost twenty thousand dollars' worth of repairs."

Her eyes got big with surprise. "Do you have that much to put into it?"

"Do I have that much period." I pushed the legal pad across the table so she could see for herself.

"Does this estimate include the crew?" Zora said, her eyes scanning the figures.

"That includes everything."

"And if we do all this, do you think we'll be able to sell it?"

"We'll be able to put it on the market," I said, "but Aretha said we might still have a problem finding a buyer."

"Why?"

"Because people don't just buy a house. They buy a neighborhood."

"So we have to fix up the whole neighborhood?"

"No, but we have to be realistic. There's no guarantee that we'll find a buyer. We may end up right back at Greer Woodruff's office, hat in hand, asking if her offer's still good." Of course, that wasn't going to happen. Not the hat-in-hand part, anyway.

Zora thought about that for a minute, her eyes still studying my scribblings. Then she pushed the figures aside and looked at me. "I think we have to do it, Mafeenie. The bigger our nest egg, the freer we'll be. We have to consider this an investment."

Although I would usually argue that finances aren't the key to freedom, in this context, she had a point.

"I've got almost two thousand dollars in my savings account," she said. "We can use all of that."

My first reaction was to say: *Don't worry, honey. Hold on to your money. Mafeenie will take care of it,* but if we were going to be free women together, I had to stop thinking of her as a baby girl and realize she was a partner in all this. It was her future we were talking about, too. She should be allowed to invest in it. Besides, if things didn't work out, I could always replace her money later when I got back on my feet.

"I'll figure out how to piece together the rest," I said. "And we can save some more if we can both work crew. Aretha's going to help too as soon as she gets through with a project she's doing in West End."

"The door project?"

"That's the one. She said she accepted a lot of work based on having some help, but her assistant's reserve unit got called to Iraq."

"I know her. That's Alisa, the girl who was staying here before me."

"She's a painter?" The idea of a young artist fighting her way through the streets of Fallujah suddenly made me feel sad.

"She's a housepainter. Aretha's the artist, but the door project is different."

"She said we're on the list," I said. "What is it exactly?"

Zora smiled and closed up her laptop with a muffled click. "When Aretha first started working with Blue Hamilton, she painted a lot of the doors on his properties blue. It was a North African thing she had read about to ward off evil spirits, but people thought it meant they were down with Blue, so everybody wanted one."

I remembered seeing a lot of blue doors in the neighborhood. Turquoise, really, a nice splash of tropical color even on a cold gray day. "Did it keep away evil spirits?"

"It did a good enough job so that when the doors started fading, or got scuffed up, people wanted her to repaint them. The more she did, the more people wanted her to do. They even ran a picture of her in *Dig It!* painting the door of the twenty-four-hour salon up on Abernathy. The day after that, they got so many calls Aretha could have spent the next two years just doing doors. How many more does she have to do?"

"She said about another two weeks' work."

Zora reached for another slice of pizza and grinned at me. "Then I guess I didn't become unemployed a moment too soon."

"What are you talking about?"

"I'll be Aretha's crew so she can finish the doors and she'll be our crew to fix up the house."

I was a big fan of exactly that kind of bartering. Saved money and kept everybody connected.

"Fair enough," I said, pinching a mushroom off the pizza, but resisting another slice. "That way you'll get to our place much faster."

"You're not scared of the evil eye, are you, Mafeenie?"

"I'm not scared of anything," I said, "but why take a chance?"

TWENTY-EIGHT

·

*F*our hours later, we had figured out where the major pieces of our budget were coming from so we decided to save the rest for tomorrow and reward ourselves with a swim. It's funny how a new decision can give you the impetus you need to get moving. Once we decided we were going to sell, we had an organizing principle. We shared a goal that we had said out loud and we were in this together.

We slipped into our suits and padded out to the pool, slid into the water, and closed our eyes. We both sighed at the same time. That's the thing about being in warm water. It's hard to keep worrying. Which isn't to say my brain wasn't still sorting through strategies and solutions. I opened my eyes.

"Can we really list the house on the computer?" I said to Zora, who was doing a lazy breaststroke nearby.

She laughed. "I love the way you say it. 'On the computer,' like the Internet is this vast, mysterious thing that requires special attention and animal sacrifices in order to do your bidding."

"Don't make fun of me," I said, glad I was floating on my back so I could see the moon. "My whole generation is illiterate when it comes to computers. Even the ones with the BlackBerries. They're faking it."

"You all are just lazy," she said. "But the answer is yes, of course we can list it. All the real estate companies do it. That's the easy part. The hard part is there are thousands of houses listed. Probably millions. We need something to make ours stand out. Something to catch your eye that makes it special."

"Too bad we don't have a mermaid."

"That would definitely help."

"You never did tell me the story of how it got here," I said.

"You need to ask Amelia when she gets back," Zora said, kicking her feet gently so that we floated along side by side, talking easily. "All I know is that some of the rich guys who built these houses had a little competition going with giving extravagant gifts to their wives. The guy next door built a life-size playhouse. The one across the street put in a terraced garden with a waterfall. There's a house around the corner with beautiful stained-glass windows all around. But this guy drove them all crazy when he built this pool. It was one of the first ones in Atlanta and it got written up in the paper and everything."

"How come the beautiful mermaid is so brown?" I said, knowing there were no black folks living in West End way back then.

"The tiles were made at some special place in Morocco and they cost a fortune. The guy didn't specify color when he ordered it. He just said he wanted a mermaid, so when the tiles got here, he couldn't send them back."

"What did his wife say?"

"The story is that she refused to swim in it," Zora said.

"Just because the mermaid was brown?"

"I guess," Zora said, floating on ahead. "You should ask Amelia."

That must have been one angry white woman to give up the pleasures of swimming in her own private pool just because of a brown mermaid, or there was more to the story than met the eye.

"Do you think it was his mistress?" I called to Zora at the other end of the pool now.

"The mermaid?" She sounded shocked.

"Not a real mermaid," I said. "Whoever posed for the picture."

"I never thought about it," she said, laughing as she floated back alongside me. "You're always looking for a story."

"That's my job," I said. "You ready to get out?"

"Sure," she said.

We climbed out into the cool night air and wrapped ourselves in two big beach towels.

"That would kind of finish off the story right, wouldn't it?" I said. "The wife had looked the other way for years, and then, suddenly, in full view of her neighbors, she's confronted with the face of her rival, right in her own backyard."

"Right in her own backyard," Zora echoed, wrapping another towel around her head.

"Now that would be enough to make you concede use of this wonderful pool, but just a generic racial response? I don't think so."

"That's because you're not a racist," Zora said. "Remember they had to drain that whole pool in Las Vegas because Dorothy Dandridge put her toe in it."

"Dorothy Dandridge was a real live woman, not a bunch of Moroccan tiles and they didn't *have* to," I said, slipping on my flip-flops and leaning over to touch my toes just because I could. "They *chose* to. All those people who sat there and let that hotel manager act a fool are the ones who made it such an ugly story."

"What do you mean?"

"Think how differently that whole crowd could have gone down in history if they had all jumped in the pool when he insulted Dorothy to show their support for another human being. Then Dorothy would have jumped in, too, and they would have had the great pleasure of seeing one of the most beautiful women in the world laughing and playing in the water with all her new friends."

"I like your story better than the real one, Mafeenie," Zora said, slipping her arm through mine as we headed up the path to the house.

"Of course you do," I said. "Everybody likes a happy ending."

TWENTY-NINE

·

The next morning when Zora went to work, I called Greer
Woodruff's office. The pretty little receptionist told me nobody
was available so I left a message on the boss lady's voice mail.

"Ms. Woodruff? This is Josephine Evans. Thank you for your offer
to buy my mother's house, but it's not for sale at this time. I think she'd
want it that way."

•

$\mathcal{A}$ bbie was more confident of my decision than I was. She was making a pot of tea and telling me why.

"The first thing is, it's your mother's place, so you *know* you have to fix it up. Second, how can you pass it along to Miss Zora unless you do?"

She was pouring boiling water over the silver tea ball she had dropped into the round dark blue pot. "Plus, Dr. King deserves better."

She put the teakettle back on the stove and dropped a big dollop of Tupelo honey into the hot water.

"Dr. Martin Luther King?"

"That's the one," she said. "May he rest in peace."

"Rest in peace," I said, "but what does that have to do with this?"

"Only everything," Abbie said, taking down two round mugs in the same shape as the teapot. "Your house happens to be on his street."

That much was true, but so was Jake's Soul Food Shack and Miss Diana's Wig Parlor and Hakim's Bookstore and the building where the old Paschal's used to be down the street from the Busy Bee Café.

"The corner lot, too. It should be a showpiece."

"What are you talking about?" I said, following her down the hall to the living room where she had made what would probably be the last fire of the season. It was almost spring. Moving in a fragrant cloud of jasmine tea and patchouli, she put the tray down and we claimed opposite ends of the couch.

"I'm talking about showing some respect. I'm talking about how we've let a street that is supposed to honor a great American hero become a punch line for black comedians," she said, pouring two steaming cups of sweet tea and handing me one. "I just think he deserves better."

"Of course he does," I said, "but it's just one house."

"Peachy's friend Zeke always says all we can do is one house, one street at a time."

She looked so small and certain, sitting there cross-legged and serene. Abbie was always the idealist in the group, arguing for the goodness in people when the Marxists made her start feeling pessimistic. She was still trusting in the transformative powers of community.

"You haven't changed a bit."

"Neither have you," she said. "Riding in like the Amazon Queen to rescue everybody."

"Don't get carried away," I said. "I'm not rescuing anybody. I'm just cleaning up my yard like any good citizen would do."

I was teasing her about her recent breakthrough on the citizenship front, but she didn't take low.

"Then as one good citizen to another, I will volunteer my services for your crew."

"You don't have to do that," I said, immediately picturing those mounds of trash, those grossly graffitied walls. The smell in that place would render Abbie's patchouli null and void.

"Of course I do," she said calmly. "You said you needed five and with me, you, Aretha, and Zora, that's four. One more is easy. Besides, you don't think I'm going to let you have this adventure without me, do you?"

"Is that what this is?" I laughed. "An adventure?"

"Of course," she said. "What did you think it was?"

"Oh, I don't know. A wedding?"

She smiled and sipped her tea. "The jury is still out on that one."

"Well, until it comes in, will the gentleman in question let you stay away from Tybee Island long enough to get any work done?" I teased her.

"He'll survive," she said, and had the nerve to blush.

"You love him, don't you?"

"I do," she said. "I really do. It's crazy, but he makes me laugh, he's got a lot of sense, and the sex is amazing."

Five years of self-imposed celibacy had gotten me out of the habit of conversations where current sexual partners were routinely revealed and rated. I didn't know if I was more surprised that she spoke so frankly or that she was still having sex she described as amazing.

"Excuse me?"

"There is an art to making love to a postmenopausal woman, as I'm sure you know," she said. "And Peachy Nolan is an artist."

"You ought to quit," I said. "I'm talking about home repairs and you're talking about multiple orgasms. You're making me jealous."

"Yeah, right," she said. "How many sad-eyed leading men did you leave throwing roses on the tarmac as your plane lifted off?"

"Those were the days, but they are long gone."

"Nobody special?"

I shook my head. "Not for a while."

"No sex at all?"

"Not unless you count a little self-pleasuring now and then."

She laughed. "Why'd you stop?"

It was a question we could ask each other. Our long-ago lives had paved the way for an intimacy that came back immediately, like riding a bike. Or having sex.

"I don't know," I said. "It just got harder and harder to meet men I wanted to invest that kind of energy in. Then things started drooping down and drying up and I just got tired of all the prep work."

Abbie laughed, but not unsympathetically. She knew she was the exception, not the rule. The truth was, I missed having sex. It wasn't always great, but it was always something.

"You talk about it like major surgery!"

"Don't get me started," I said, rolling my eyes.

She laughed again, but I had a serious question. "Are you really going to marry him?"

"I think so. I just want to be sure. Half the reason I'm spending so much time off the island for a couple of months is to see how it feels to be away from him. We've been joined at the hip for the last year or so and I want to give myself a chance to look at what we are a little more objectively."

"Without all that great sex to cloud the issue?"

"Something like that. So you see, helping you with the house would be a perfect way to distract myself while I make up my mind."

"All right," I said. "You may consider yourself an official part of the crew."

"Thank you. I didn't know I was going to have to beg to help you take out the trash!"

"I'm glad for you," I said. "About Peachy."

"But a little surprised, huh?"

"A little. I can't imagine getting married at this age. I'm too set in my ways."

"Well, that's the trick, I think," she said, choosing her words carefully. "Love always removes an element of freedom. All the give and take, the compromises you make. That's just part of it."

"Which is probably why I'd be an awful wife. I'm not even a very good friend."

Abbie refilled our cups. "You're a great friend. I've been missing you for the last twenty years."

"I'm too selfish to be a good friend," I said.

"What are you talking about?"

"It's an occupational hazard. If you're going to be in theater, nothing can be more important than the show. Not friends. Not family. Not lovers. Nothing."

She was looking at me strangely. I knew it sounded harsh, but it was true.

"Well, I'll consider myself forewarned, but don't let the fact that I'm serving tea and cookies mislead you. I have my moments."

"You are the sweetest person I know!"

"That's because I usually get my way."

The way she said it made me laugh. "What happens when you don't?"

"Then I go someplace where I do!"

"Does Peachy know this side of you?"

"Of course," she said. "He's usually the place I go."

THIRTY-ONE

•

$\mathcal{E}$ver since Aretha and I had opened the door to his room a few days ago, I'd been thinking about the guy who was squatting at my house. There was something about the bleak orderliness of the room that moved me, but there was also something disturbing about it. What was the deal on all those books? Either this guy could be somebody whose life had taken a terribly wrong turn that he was trying to correct, or he could be another Unabomber. I dropped Zora at work so I could borrow her car to go pick up some cleaning supplies and drove straight to the duplex. Morning seemed a safer time to return to the scene of our earlier exchange, and somehow I knew it would go better if I came alone. When I turned up into the yard, he was sitting on the back steps smoking a cigarette. He looked in my direction, frowned, and stood up.

I turned off the ignition, hoping I wasn't crazy for coming up here all alone to talk to a homeless stranger. I stepped out of the car, but left the door open just in case.

"Good morning," I said, trying to sound like this was an ordinary exchange between new neighbors. "I'm Josephine Evans. I own this place."

"You think I forgot who you are that fast?" he said.

"I didn't remember if I said my name."

"Well, now you've said it."

I cleared my throat. "I don't think you said yours."

He looked annoyed. "Is this a social call or are you here to put me out?"

"Nobody's putting anybody out," I said quickly, ignoring the issue of whether this was a social call. "But I'm going to clean up the place so . . . so . . . I wanted to . . . let you know." Was I going to ask his permission?

He just looked at me for a minute. "Well, it's about time."

I took that to be an affirmation of my plans.

"And thank you for . . . keeping an eye on things."

"I didn't do it for you."

"But I can still thank you, can't I?"

He looked at me and pointed toward Wiley Street. "You see that little white house there, about midway down the block?"

From where we were standing on top of the hill, we could see most of Wiley Street below us."

"The one with the flowers out front?"

"I see it," I said.

The street had a few houses that were well kept and cheerful, but most of the yards were as overgrown as this one and the homes looked in need of some serious repairs and a new coat of paint.

"That's my mother's house," he said. "She's seventy-three years old and she lives alone. Last year, she got broken into twice. Both the guys who did it were living up here in your house. Just sitting up here watching her come and go. Deciding when to bust in."

He looked at me disapprovingly.

"Why didn't she call the police?"

"She did," he said. "They ran those two out, boarded the place up, and nothing happened for a couple of weeks. Then the police got busy someplace else, the robbers came back, broke in on Miss Mance across the street and Miss Thomas next door, and then back to my mother's house to get whatever the first two hadn't taken."

No wonder he was a little pissed off. What was a question of property to me was a question of his mother's safety to him. "I thought you said the police boarded up the place. How did they get in?"

He looked at me and shook his head slightly as if that was the dumbest question he'd heard all day. "It's not hard to get in when nobody's watching. That's why I started staying here. To make sure they didn't come back."

I didn't know whether he was telling the truth or just giving me a creative excuse for trespassing, but it sounded plausible, except for one small detail.

"Does your mother know you're staying up here?"

"No."

"Why not?"

"I've had some problems with drugs," he said. "She had to put me out."

He said it very matter-of-factly, but I knew it was never so simple for a mother to throw her child to the wolves, no matter what he had done. I remembered one disastrous visit when my son came to spend some time with me after Jasmine had left and told him she didn't want to see him again until he sobered up. He alternated between being maudlin and full of self-pity and being angry and full of accusations. My maternal guilt translated into a series of excuses for his bad behavior until the night he stumbled in late to a dinner party I had organized in his honor, drunk and disorderly to the point where Howard offered to throw his ass into the canal if I'd just give the word, but I couldn't. He was still my baby, and even when everybody else saw only a raging asshole, I saw the little boy who used to beg me to read him one more bedtime story or push him just a little higher on the swings in Central Park.

I hoped what I was getting ready to do was not just another attack of maternal guilt, but I'd come this far trusting my instincts. This was no time to start second-guessing.

"How are you doing now?"

"I'm clean."

"How long?"

"Four months." He hesitated. "And twelve days."

"Good," I said. "Then we can do business."

He raised his eyebrows. "What kind of business do you think I have with you?"

"You're living in my house. You want to keep living in my house, right?"

Even a righteously indignant squatter knows the question of sleeping indoors or outdoors is always serious business worthy of discussion.

"Yeah, so?"

"So this place is a mess," I said. "It's going to take a lot of work to fix it up right. I need a crew. You interested?"

"A cleaning crew?" He sounded like the idea was beneath him.

"An everything crew."

"Well, the place sure could use a coat of paint."

I wanted to say, *Why don't you tell me something I don't know?*

"Well, here's what I propose. You work on my crew and you can keep staying here until we finish the project."

"Then what?"

"After that, I'm going to put the place on the market, so you'll have to find some other place to stay."

"What are you paying?"

"I'm paying rent."

It hadn't occurred to me that he would turn me down. It seemed like the most humane way to deal with a bad situation. I didn't want to put him back out on the street, and the truth was, I did need a crew. "And fifty dollars a week."

He ran his hand over his beard and tugged it as if considering the question.

"How long?"

"Two months," I said. "Maybe three."

"Say three," he said. "That way I can make plans."

"It's a deal," I said. "But I need to ask you one more question."

He was instantly wary. "What's that?"

"What's your name?"

"Victor. Victor Causey."

"All right, Mr. Causey," I said. "Welcome to the team."

THIRTY-TWO

*P*ackages from Howard were always cause for celebration. I met the man from UPS pulling up in front of the house with one for me and one for Zora. I propped hers on the front table so it would be the first thing she saw when she got home and sat down in the front window with my own treasure. Inside was another box, tied with a silver ribbon, and an ivory-colored envelope sealed with a real red lipstick kiss. Howard was famous for sending all his most personal correspondence adorned with a smooch.

"*Ma chérie*," he had written in lovely violet ink just to make me smile, which it did. "I know the enclosed is extravagant, but what the hell? I saw it and couldn't resist. Wear it someplace they don't expect you to and cause a scene. Miss you more than words can say, as do your many fans. Hold yourself in readiness for a triumphant return. In the meantime, wear this one in good health. Yours in fabulousity, H."

I put the note aside and opened the box. There in a nest of tissue paper was a bright red kimono with long, richly embroidered sleeves. The silk was so light that it felt weightless when I slipped my arms in and went to take a look in the hall mirror. It fit perfectly, the ankle length not long enough to stumble over, but wide enough to swirl a little when you walked. The color was so rich and vibrant that it made you want to touch it to see if it generated warmth or just light. This truly was a robe fit for a queen, Amazon or otherwise, and I loved it just like Howard knew I would. Not that I had anyplace to wear it. I'd been spending my days at Home Depot, trying to get the best deals on the supplies we'd need next week when Zora was finally free and we could get started on the house. I smiled at my reflection, wondering what the folks in the paint department would say if I swept in tomorrow wearing this.

I was about to slip it off and put it back in the box when I saw Zora coming up the front walk, so I hurried over to beat her to the door, swung it open, and struck my best red-carpet pose for her. She laughed out loud and applauded as she took the stairs two at a time and hugged me gently, like she didn't want to damage my outfit.

"That's beautiful! You're beautiful! Where are you going?"

"I've been where I'm going," I said. "Howard sent it to me."

"I'm jealous," she said.

"Don't be. There's a package for you, too!"

"Hooray!"

She dashed inside, dropped her backpack, and opened the box with her name on it. Her letter was sealed with a kiss, too. She read it to me out loud. "Dear Lil' Bit, I think if Dorothy had had these, she would have simply kicked that witch's green ass and headed home a better woman for it. Enjoy! Love you madly, H."

Inside Zora's box was a pair of high-heeled, impossibly pointy-toed ankle boots in the softest red leather. She kicked off her Crocs and slipped them on immediately, smiling with pleasure at her suddenly stylish feet. "Only Howard would send me red shoes! I love them!"

"We look so fabulous, it's a shame we don't have anyplace to go," I said. "This neighborhood has got to develop some decent nightlife."

"Where would you go if you were back in Amsterdam?" she asked, leaning back on the couch, admiring her new red shoes and my flaming kimono.

"In this?" I said. "Actually, in this, I would probably have people in. I would make Howard fix something wonderful to eat and I'd put on music and tell people to come at midnight after their shows were over so they'd all be keyed up from performing and bring that energy with them. I'd invite the neighbors so they wouldn't be mad about the noise and encourage loud laughter, tall tales, and passionate kissing in the coatroom."

I twirled around for her amusement and my own. "I'd serve too much champagne and make everybody walk home or spend the night, and in the morning, we'd take our coffee out on the terrace and watch the canal boats go by, and everyone would say, 'My god, Josephine, where did you get that fabulous kimono?' And I'd say, 'Howard found

it' and he would say he knew it was extravagant, but he couldn't resist."
I plopped down next to her on the couch. "And there you have it. A day
in the life of Josephine Evans, superstar. Well, the former life, I guess."

"Your life is like the best telenovela in the world," she said, grinning
at my impromptu performance.

"A soap opera?" I rolled my eyes. "I was thinking more along the
lines of—"

Before I could finish that thought, Zora sat straight up. "Oh, my
God!" she said. "Oh, my God!"

"What? What's wrong?"

"Nothing's wrong! It's perfect! It's absolutely perfect!"

"What are you talking about?"

"It's you," she said. "Don't you see? It's you!"

"It's me what?"

"It's your story that makes our place special. The fact that it's you!"

"*Me?*"

"Don't say it like that, Mafeenie. You're a star."

"Not over here, I'm not. Over here I'm just another unemployed
actress."

She looked at me and frowned. "Well, all of that is about to change.
You're going to be the shero of your own story."

I groaned. "Shero? You're not going to start talking like a feminist,
are you?"

"I am a feminist, besides you're not unemployed. You're engaged in
an epic battle between good and evil on a conveniently human scale. A
struggle between the forces of light and the forces of darkness."

She was getting a little carried away. "All that because I want to
clean up one little house and sell it to the highest bidder?"

"No, Mafeenie, all that because you refuse to let your mother's
parting gift to you fall victim to the horrors of urban blight. Because
you left your glamorous life in Europe to reclaim your granddaughter's
inheritance and bring back beauty to this one small corner on a street
named for an American hero."

At first I thought she was just goofing around, but the longer she
talked, the more I began to see that this really was a terrific story.

"That sounds wonderful," I said, admiring her ability to find the coherent thread in the midst of the messiness. "Go on."

"We'll document the whole process on your YouTube site."

"What YouTube site?"

"The one I'm going to post for us," she said. "The one that is going to begin with you and Aretha walking around, talking about mildew and rodent droppings and all that other gross stuff."

"Great opening," I said.

"It ends with you talking about Gram's roses. About how she used to make you water them and how bad it would make her feel to see it today."

"That's where it ends?"

"Just that segment, Mafeenie. That's just the first one to show them what a big ugly job is confronting you."

"Then what?"

"Then we let them see you take it on, whittle it down to size, and emerge victorious."

"You're serious, aren't you?"

"Absolutely. It's perfect. All you have to do is be yourself. I'll take care of everything. I can see it now: *Actress Takes on Greatest Role, Comes Back to Rescue Childhood Home.*"

"That's true!"

"I know it is! You don't think I'd ask you to lie, do you?"

"You better not."

"I won't," she said, rushing ahead to her next idea. "How about that's what we'll call it. *Rescue on Martin Luther King: One Woman's Story.*"

I groaned again. "It sounds so melodramatic. Like a movie of the week."

"No, Mafeenie, like a reality show." She said that like it was a positive thing.

"I'm not sure this is such a good idea."

"It's a great idea," she said. "You said we needed a mermaid. Now we have one. *You!*"

"And what exactly do you want me to do?"

She leaned over and took my hand. "Tell me the story of this moment as we're walking through it. Talk about whatever's on your mind, just like you did about the roses. Just like you did about the party you'd throw for your friends."

I was sure my expression betrayed my doubts.

"Sometimes I'll ask you questions."

That was not particularly comforting. "Questions about what?"

She shrugged. "I don't know. The house. What you're thinking about. What it feels like to be back here after being gone for so long."

"And this is going to help us how?"

"Because we'll be building a story. We won't even talk about selling the house yet. We'll just talk about fixing it up because it's the right thing to do."

"That's true."

"It's all going to be true, Mafeenie. This is your real life."

She was right. The only thing that could make it a lie was me.

"By the time we finish, we'll have more buyers than we know what to do with."

"I'm not used to talking about myself," I said, almost convinced but not quite.

She grinned at me. "You're always talking about yourself."

I grinned back. "You know too much."

"No way," she said. "My grandma said that's not possible."

●

THIRTY-THREE

*T*he first phone call of the morning jolted me awake at 4 A.M.

"Hello?"

"Wake up, Miss Thing," Howard's voice crowed on the other end of the line. "I know it's early, but you have got to hear this."

I sat up and covered my other ear to shut out the birds noisily waking up outside my window. Sometimes it felt like morning in a Disney cartoon around here, where the big-eyed birds and adorable mice make friends with the princess in disguise by filling her garret with song.

"What are you talking about?" I said. "Hear what?"

"Listen! Stop saying *what* and just listen for a minute."

He held up his phone in the midst of what seemed to be a group of people shouting something. I pulled the covers over my head and strained to hear the words they were chanting more than shouting. It sounded like . . . like . . . *my name!*

"Howard!" I said. "Howard!"

"Did you hear it? They're chanting your name! It's crazy!"

"Where are you?"

"Outside the board meeting. There are five hundred people here trying to get in. They had to move it to the theater because so many people were crammed into the conference room and they refused to leave! They just stood there chanting, '*Josephine! Josephine!*' It was fabulous. Absolutely fucking fabulous!"

"They're demonstrating about me?"

"When I got here at seven there were already people standing around out front. You're a cause célèbre, missy. What do you think about that?"

"I think it's great," I said, loving the sound of chanting demonstrators receding in the background, still filled with artistic indignation. *Josephine! Josephine!*

"The idea that you would be held accountable for George Bush's sins is just not fair and everybody knows it. When the board tried to talk about security concerns, people shouted them down, grabbed the mikes and recited your many artistic triumphs, endless good works, and selfless devotion to this theater ad nauseum."

"All that stuff is true!"

"Of course it is. Who do you think provided them with the necessary information in the first place?"

Howard had done exactly what he promised to do.

"I owe you."

"You owe me big-time, so what else is new? The point is that they had to adjourn the meeting in order to review your case."

"I'm a case now?"

"A case, a cause, let's call the whole thing off," Howard sang. "They're meeting again in a month. Can you hold out that long?"

"What makes them think I'll still want to come back there in a month?"

"Because they know I can't live without you," he said. "I gotta go! People are amassing outside. Got any messages you want me to deliver to your fans?"

"Tell them I said . . ."

"Hang on, sweetie. You're breaking up. What?"

"Tell them I said . . ."

"I'm losing you, sweetie! Love you!"

Before I could say "love you back," the line went dead. *Damn!* This was my big moment, a chance to actually rally the troops in the field. I had a great line, too. I was going to say, *This is the price we pay for life in wartime.* I scribbled it down on my dream catcher pad beside the bed and hoped he'd call again before I went back to sleep, but he didn't.

The second call of the morning was from Greer Woodruff and came in at a much more civilized hour. When the phone rang, I was sitting on the back porch swing trying to figure out exactly what I had agreed to do last night. *Just be yourself,* Zora had said, as if that is the simplest thing in the world, which it ain't. For me, the beauty of acting is all that time I get to spend being somebody else. Being on camera as myself was going to require a strong story to carry me through. Otherwise, there's too much *me, me, me,* even for me!

"Hello?" I said. "Temporary Evans residence."

"I'm trying to reach Josephine Evans," Greer Woodruff's voice said.

"This is Josephine Evans."

"Ms. Evans? Greer Woodruff. I was hoping I could catch you."

"Well, you did."

A long time ago, I learned that the best way to get more information than you give is to agree as much as possible and keep conversation to a minimum. The silence blossomed.

"Ms. Evans," Greer said finally. "I don't think it's exaggerating to say that we got off on the wrong foot last week."

"Yes," I said. "I think we did."

She waited for me to say more. When I didn't, she cleared her throat delicately. "So I was wondering if we might have lunch and see if we can't come to some better understanding of each other. Say Friday at noon?"

"Fine," I said.

"I'm a member of the Commerce Club," she said. "They have a lovely lunch buffet."

No way was I going to meet her on her turf. "Paschal's is more convenient for me."

"I'll look forward to seeing you at Paschal's then," she said smoothly. "Until Friday."

"I'll be there."

I wondered what had made her decide to call me. Maybe she wanted to make me a better offer. Maybe she wanted to clarify the old one. Or maybe she'd heard people were chanting my name on the streets of Amsterdam and she just wanted an autograph.

THIRTY-FOUR

•

I think I let Zora talk me into doing a reality show," I said to Abbie as we headed over to the West End News for some cappuccino.

"I don't think I can respect you if you eat bugs for money," she said.

"Ain't that much money in the world," I said, and laughed. "Zora wants to document the process of fixing up the house."

"On television?"

"The Internet."

"Ahhhh. . . ," said Abbie in the same awed tone that Zora finds so funny in me. "The Internet."

We were both usually fast walkers, but today we were strolling through the neighborhood, trying to wrap our imaginations around the Internet.

"She wants to call it 'Rescue on Martin Luther King: One Woman's Story.' "

"Are you the woman?"

"Yes."

We passed a high-school-aged girl holding a child by the hand with a faraway look in her eye and then a kid on a bike who waved at Abbie as he rode by. She waved back.

"I like it. Did you tell her we'd been talking about Dr. King?"

I shook my head. "Nope."

"That makes me like it even more. I love it when things kind of come in clusters. She was thinking about Dr. King, too. We all are."

"We all who?" I said. Abbie tended to think and talk in big, inclusive circles. My tendency is to try and keep it specific.

"We who believe in freedom," she said.

We shared a love for a song whose lyrics quote the indefatigable civil rights worker Ella Baker: "We who believe in freedom cannot rest until it comes."

"You're quoting Sweet Honey in the Rock before nine o'clock in the morning?"

"I couldn't resist. I love the way they sing that song, but it's true in a way, don't you think?"

Talking to Abbie was always a process of surrendering to her unique conversational rhythms. She takes the long way home, but she always gets there.

I picked up my cue. "Don't I think what?"

"That it's significant for me to be thinking about Dr. King and for Zora to be thinking about Dr. King and now your project is named after him."

"Yes," I said. "I'm sure it's significant."

We turned onto Abernathy and became part of the morning energy of people on their way to work or school, still energetic and hopeful just like we were.

"I've been thinking about my work with your crew," Abbie said.

"You're not backing out, are you?"

"Of course not. I decided I'd like to work on the outside rather than the inside, if that's okay with you."

"Fine with me, but the yard is a total wreck. It's going to be a big job."

She smiled. "I want to restore your mother's roses."

Just the idea made me feel sentimental, but it wasn't practical. "That's a lovely idea, but right now, we've really got to stick to the basics."

"I think a garden is basic," she said calmly. Abbie was never argumentative. Just certain.

"Not on our budget," I said as we stepped inside the West End News and headed for a corner table. Henry waved good morning from behind the counter where he was busy with people in need of early-morning caffeine. "We just don't have the money for a garden."

"Think of it as an investment," she said. "Just like the paint you're going to buy."

"That's the point," I said. "I have to paint. I don't have to plant roses and feed them and water them and prune them." All the tending of my mother's beauties came back to me in a rush.

Abbie grinned at me. "Your mother worked your last nerve with tending those roses, didn't she?"

"Yeah, I guess she did," I said.

Henry came over with a cappuccino and an espresso and the news that Mr. Charles and Mr. Eddie had taken a gambling excursion to New Orleans with the blessings of Miss Iona, Mr. Charles's wife, who declined to accompany them because of what she calls angry spirits roaming the city. I thought about Louie's ordeal and wondered if post-Katrina tourists ever felt like they were dancing on bones.

"So roses are out," Abbie said, stirring her cappuccino slowly.

I nodded, glad she wasn't going to press the point. "Yes. Roses are definitely out."

"Well, then, how about we grow sunflowers?" she said cheerfully. "They're big and bright and wild and you don't have to do much to keep them happy."

I put down my cup and looked at her across the small table. "Why are you so determined to have a garden? You've seen my place. There is already plenty of stuff to do."

Abbie nodded sympathetically. "I know. It's a huge job, but the garden is a big part of it, don't you see?"

At the counter, Henry was wiping down the gleaming cappuccino machine and whistling "Lift Every Voice and Sing."

"Convince me," I said.

"All right, I will." She shrugged off her coat and leaned forward in the chair. "Last year, while I was living in D.C., some kids broke into my house while I was home. They didn't rape me, but one of them peed on me and the other one . . ." She took a deep breath. "The other one masturbated on me."

I reached across the table and took her hand and she let me.

"Then they took what they could carry, which wasn't much, and left me tied up naked for one of my students to find in the morning."

"I'm so sorry," I whispered. "Oh, Abbie, I'm so sorry."

"Yes, me, too, but here's the thing. That part was awful, but the worst part was afterward. I couldn't stop thinking about their eyes.

They had no feeling in their eyes at all. None. They didn't think about me as another human being with thoughts and feelings and family. They didn't think about me as a woman old enough to be their grandmother. They were just out, taking stuff they hadn't earned, terrorizing people they didn't know, and waiting for something to excite them or surprise them or satisfy them, but nothing can, Jo, nothing can." She stopped and took another breath. "That's what I saw in their eyes. That's what we have created in our own children and it terrifies us to the point where we can't tell the truth about it, even to each other. Even to ourselves. Because we're afraid it's gone too far and there's nothing we can do about it. Not a damn thing."

We sat for a minute, her words hanging there between us.

"Then what's the point of gardens?" I said softly, bringing us back to the problem at hand.

"Defiance!" she said with such sudden vehemence that Henry's eyes flickered in our direction reflexively, then away without ever interrupting his soft whistle, which had now segued into "My Girl." "Absolute defiance. In the face of all the madness, and the meanness, and the dead-eyed boys, and the desperate girls, and the endless, insane wars, I still think life is a gift and struggling for freedom is the obligation of any thinking human being and . . . and . . ."

She was picking up speed, but there was no way I was going to try to slow her down.

". . . and that ultimately most people are good and all that Anne Frank, sixties bullshit *that I still believe.*"

Abbie stopped. I could tell she was trying to collect her thoughts, but I knew where she was going, and now I was right there with her. I got it. Her response to the evil she had seen in her fellow human beings had been to put her hands in the dirt and help something grow. Of course, we needed a garden.

"So," I said, "you think we'd do okay with sunflowers?"

She looked at me and her smile was definitely worth a few budget adjustments. "Sunflowers would be perfect," she said. "And think how great they'll show up on camera."

I laughed. "You and Zora ought to go into business together."

She laughed, too. "I think we just did!"

·

THIRTY-FIVE

Zora wanted me to talk about the house without actually being there. She needed the footage and she hoped it would be easier for me to think about the place in a positive way if I couldn't see it. That made sense. Looking at it made me mad and sad and semi-hysterical. Not exactly the preferred states for conjuring up childhood memories that could make this wreck of a house seem like a home. It was my idea to wear the kimono Howard sent, even though Zora thought it was a little too theatrical.

"I am a little too theatrical," I said. "I don't want them to think I've spent my life scrubbing out the bathroom sink."

She conceded the point. "You're right. There's plenty of time for that later. Okay. Where do you want to sit?"

We agreed that outside by the pool would make people want this house, not our place, and the kitchen was a little too informal for my outfit. We finally settled on a cozy corner of the living room. There was a big brown chair with an arm I could perch on without feeling or looking uncomfortable and a nice little Tiffany lamp giving off what would probably be my last good lighting until this project was over.

"Ready?" said Zora, after checking to be sure her technology was doing as she intended.

"Should I introduce myself?"

"Yes."

"And then just start talking?"

"That's all there is to it."

"Okay. I'm ready. Roll 'em!"

She laughed. "Nobody really says 'roll 'em.' "

"They used to," I said. "What do they say now?"

"*Hit it!*" she said, so I did.

"Hello," I said, looking where she had told me to look. "My name is Josephine Evans. I'm an actress and I grew up in that house you just saw. It didn't look like that then, of course. It was a lovely house. Nice neighborhood, too."

What the hell was I talking about? I took a deep breath and smiled at the little red light on the tiny little camera.

"So when I first came back, I had been away a long time . . ." How much detail did I need? Did I need to say where I had been? "I had been away working, but this house was special to me in a lot of ways, so when I saw it, I was shocked. I couldn't believe it."

This was harder than I thought it would be. I stopped again. Then Zora came to my rescue.

"Tell me one special thing about this house," she said.

"Special to whom?" I always sound snotty when I'm nervous.

"I'm asking you, Mafeenie," Zora said gently. "Special to you."

That was as good a place to start as any. I tried to put myself back in the mind of that twelve-year-old girl arriving from Montgomery with my mother, already missing my family and friends. What had appealed to me about this house back then?

"Well, at first I hated that it was a duplex," I said. "Even though there were two separate entrances, and no shared living space, I could never get over the fact that somebody who was not related to me was sleeping on the other side of my bedroom wall."

Zora nodded encouragingly like this was the kind of stuff she wanted. I relaxed a little.

"The tenants were always quiet and well behaved," I said. "Mostly they kept to themselves. I don't remember ever hearing them talking on the phone or laughing out loud, although one of them used to sing hymns once a week while she got ready for church. That was Miss Simpson."

As soon as I said her name out loud, I could see her face in my mind. A sweet face with a sad smile.

"She was about forty years old and she worked as a secretary at Spelman College, but that was all I knew about her. She never went out except to go to work or to church and, as a child, I found myself wondering about the story of her life. I would sit on the side of my bed on

Sunday morning, listening to her singing, and make up little stories about who she might be and write them down in a little notebook. My mother found one of the notebooks once and said I shouldn't make up things about people because it might hurt their feelings. I didn't stop doing it, but after that, I made sure I hid the notebooks."

Zora was still smiling and nodding and I felt like I was telling her something she really wanted to know.

"I didn't know it at the time," I said, "but what I was doing would stand me in good stead once I became an actress because the key to acting is the ability to fully imagine another human life, and that's what I learned how to do in this house. That's what I learned, all those nights lying in bed, wondering about Miss Simpson's childhood and trying to figure out why she was crying in the backyard that day I came outside and saw her standing in the middle of my mother's yellow roses, clutching a letter and sobbing loud enough for me to hear her, see her standing there, and run back to my room to write it all down."

When I heard myself say that, I realized I had walked up on the answer to Zora's question.

"That was the gift this house gave me," I said. "An understanding and appreciation of the mysterious, private, unknowable lives of other human beings, and that is a very special thing. And that is why I'm not going to let it go. Not now, not ever."

I looked at Zora, who waited a couple of seconds to see if I was through, and then said, "Cut."

"Was that enough?"

"Yes, Mafeenie," she said. "That was perfect."

·

THIRTY-SIX

*E*ven though I had picked the place, Greer Woodruff had claimed it as her own by the time I got there a few minutes after noon. The lunchtime crowd was already gathering around the hostess stand, listening to their stomachs growling in anticipation and wondering why there was only one woman at that big old table in the back where the hostess could have seated that group of five and moved things along a little more quickly. I didn't have to wonder. I realized this was Greer Woodruff's turf, too.

She stood up to greet me and I shook her hand and slid into the booth across from her. She smiled at me and raised her hand for the waiter. It was MacArthur. When he realized I was the guest for whom Greer had been waiting, his stricken face confirmed Zora's suspicions. I smiled as if seeing him was the pleasure of my day. That's the thing about Atlanta. You are always going to see the person you are trying the hardest to avoid.

"Hello, MacArthur," I said, enjoying his discomfort. "Got your camera with you today?"

"Good afternoon," he croaked. "Welcome to Paschal's. Can I bring you something from the bar?"

I decided against a drink and asked for iced tea instead. Greer had a cup of black coffee. I wondered if our picture would make the magazine. *Atlanta businesswoman meets with expatriate actress at historic Paschal's restaurant.* It didn't sound very sexy. And unless I miss my guess, we're too old to make the tabloids. MacArthur brought my tea immediately without making eye contact.

"Thank you for agreeing to see me," Greer said. "I was sorry to get your message and I wanted to let you know that I'm still very interested in that property. I think in my haste to acquire it, I may have been insensitive to the fact that the parcel . . . *the house* has an emotional component as far as you are concerned that I didn't factor in before we spoke."

"That's one way to put it," I said.

"I meant no disrespect to your mother," she said. "Or to your memories of the house itself. Please accept my apologies."

"Certainly," I said, wondering if her apology included making me a better offer. "And I apologize for my abrupt departure from your office. You see, my mother gave me that house when she died so that I could always finance my own freedom. When I heard your offer, I was a little concerned. Fifteen thousand dollars doesn't buy as much freedom as it used to."

She nodded, looking so sympathetic I almost believed she was. Except for the eyes. They were too busy watching me to feel anything.

"May I be candid with you?" she said as MacArthur headed our way with a vegetable plate for me and a chicken salad for her.

"Please."

She waited while he presented our food efficiently and glided back out of sight. We both ignored the plates he had put before us.

"I've been a power player in this town for longer than I care to remember," she said, leaning forward as if she was going to share a secret with me. "And because I am a woman, a black woman, I've had to fight for everything every step of the way."

She was trying to see if we could bond on the basis of our mythical sisterhood. Not a chance. I wasn't mad at her for doing business. I was mad at the way she was doing it. If she wanted my house, all she had to do was make me a decent offer for it, not run it into the ground so I wouldn't have any other options.

"The reason I am so interested in the land around your house is because, Ms. Evans, a very large conglomerate wants to put a major piece of commercial development right there on Martin Luther King Drive." She paused dramatically and pushed her untouched chicken salad in the little tomato half with the scalloped edges to the side. "If they can get a parcel of land at a price that makes sense. The piece you're sitting on is key."

"Sounds like you may have undervalued it just a little," I said.

"Exactly." She smiled as if she had found the opening she needed. "Is it time to talk about money, Ms. Evans?"

"I'm not sure," I said. "I thought we already did that."

She pursed her lips as if she was disappointed in me for bringing up our off-on-the-wrong-foot meeting.

"Name a price you think is fair, Ms. Evans. You'll find I'm a reasonable woman."

"Well, sometimes I'm not," I said. "Which is why my house is not on the market."

"Everything has a price."

"Everything or everybody?" I said.

"Ms. Evans," she said firmly, sounding like she was speaking to a stubborn child. "This is a very good deal and there is a very finite window during which you can take advantage of it. These people aren't going to give me much longer to put this package together, and frankly I can't in good conscience recommend it."

"Well, I wouldn't want you to go against your conscience," I said.

"Taking care of your property was not my responsibility. It was yours," she said. "Blaming me for your own neglect isn't going to help either one of us."

"I'm not asking you for your help," I said, realizing I should never have come here. Zora and I had made another plan, a better plan, and Greer Woodruff wasn't part of it. Besides, there was something about her attitude that brought out the worst in me, and even though I didn't know exactly what it was, at this point, I didn't really care. It was time for me to go.

"Well, maybe you should be."

That was enough. Who did she think she was talking to? I stood up, wishing I had ordered that drink so I could toss it.

"I'm sorry I wasted your time," I said. "But I don't think we have anything to talk about."

She stood up, too. "I'm sorry you feel that way, but before you go,

I think it's only fair to tell you that there are people interested in that land who won't be as open to discussion as I've been."

"I'll keep it in mind," I said, "but just between us, what are they going to do? Wreck the place?"

It wasn't as good as a well-thrown drink, but as exit lines go, it wasn't half bad.

•

 walked back to West End from Paschal's trying to decide whether
Greer Woodruff was going to be a problem or just a minor irrita-
tion. She was clearly a woman who was used to getting her own way,
but so was I. It was too early to tell what cards she was prepared to play,
but so far I felt like I was holding my own. All I needed now was some
work clothes that didn't make me look like Granny Gump. If Zora was
going to be around playing *Candid Camera,* I needed something practical, but with what Howard called "the possibility of panache."

My route took me right by the West End Mall. Zora had warned
me that my choices would probably be limited to generic sweats or
low-slung jeans that showed more meat than I was prepared to share
with strangers, but there was no harm in just passing through to see
what I could find. I had to find something to wear while I was hauling
all that trash around.

As I passed by the grocery store, headed for the mall, I heard somebody call my name.

"Miss Evans!"

I turned to find Louie emerging from the store wearing his lovely
gray suit and a big grin on his face. I smiled and waited for him to
catch up.

"Good afternoon," he said. "I didn't mean to startle you. It just
shocked me to see you walking right by."

I laughed. "I live here, remember? How are you?"

"Fine, fine," he said. "I'm cooking a special meal and I needed to
put in an order for some mussels. This place has the freshest seafood in
town."

Why didn't that surprise me?

"Did your chef finally realize who he's got in the kitchen?"

Louie shook his head. "Not yet, but he has finally agreed to let me cook a meal for him. I told him I'd pay for everything if he would just eat my food one time and then consider adding some of my signature dishes to his menu."

"That sounds great," I said. "Good luck."

"Thanks," he said. "I'm going to need it. This boy thinks he can really burn and he don't know a roux from a ratatouille. My problem is going to be trying to educate his taste buds while I leave them wanting more."

"From what I hear, that's your specialty."

He smiled. "I'll have to cook for you one day so you can decide for yourself."

Was he flirting with me? Maybe I had spoken too soon about the men not looking anymore. I think Louie had seen me just fine.

"I'll look forward to it," I said. "Which way are you walking?"

"To the bus stop," he said, looking embarrassed. "I lost both my cars in the flood. Haven't been able to afford another one."

I wondered how long it took to get over it when you lose everything. I wondered if you ever do.

"You started work on that house?" he said.

"We start on Monday morning," I said. "I'm on my way to the mall now to find some work clothes."

He grinned at me, strolling beside him in a long, black trench coat, black pants, black sweater, and my signature silver jewelry.

"I thought those were your work clothes."

He was definitely flirting. I just smiled. The bus stop was right outside the mall entrance and unless I was going to wait with him until the bus came, it was time to be about my business.

"It was good to see you," I said. "The guy's taste buds won't know what hit them."

"Thanks," he said. "Good to see you, too."

We both saw the bus turn the corner a few blocks away.

"You could really do me a big favor."

I looked at him, but his easy smile told me nothing except he had a very pleasant face and very sad eyes.

"You should get Miss Abbie and Miss Aretha and your granddaughter and come for dinner on Monday night after your first day at work."

"Oh, you don't have to do that," I said.

"I'm the one asking for the favor," he said. "I don't know how to put on a pot for less than ten people, so whatever happens, I'm going to have a lot of really high-class leftovers."

That made me laugh. "How can I turn down an invitation like that?" I said. "I'm sure my crew will be delighted. What time?"

"Eight o'clock."

"We'll be there."

The bus rocked to a stop in front of us and people hoisted themselves and their packages slowly aboard.

"Good," he said. "Knowing you ladies will be the ultimate recipients of this food will make me able to add the most important ingredient in any real New Orleans cuisine."

"What's that?"

"Love," he said, touching his hand to his hat lightly. "What else?"

THIRTY-EIGHT

·

*A*fter I looked at the video of myself talking about the house, I didn't know whether to laugh or cry.

"What is it?" I said, turning to Zora for some explanation that would make me feel better about my ramblings.

"It's you, Mafeenie. In all your beautiful, unedited glory."

"That's just what I mean. What the hell am I talking about?"

"You're talking about yourself. You're letting us get to know you since we're going to be spending the next couple of months with you. Once I put it together with the other footage, it will draw people right in."

"Right into what?"

The whole reality idea was starting to spook me. I couldn't just talk off the cuff and be expected to make any sense at all. That's what writers were for!

Zora realized I was getting agitated. "Calm down, Mafeenie. This is the way it is now. Listen, there's this old guy from England, he's about eighty or something, and he made this little video about himself. Who he is. What he likes. His grandkids. He's just standing there talking, needs a shave sometimes, but it's so real, you can't take your eyes off it. He gets hundreds of thousands of hits every day."

She sounded excited, like an ingénue on the first day of rehearsal.

"There's a way to do it live, too, and that's even better because it's really taking place right then, while you're watching it. Anything can happen."

That seemed to be the main draw of these excursions into reality entertainment.

"So what happened to the old guy?"

"Nothing happened to him. He's still doing it. He's a star!"

"What's his name?"

Zora grinned at me. "That's last century thinking. We don't have to know his name. We know him."

My head was spinning. There was a whole new way for people to communicate with each other and I was clueless. Zora looked sympathetic.

"Think about it this way, Mafeenie. How many performances of *Medea* have you done?"

"All together?"

She nodded. I started trying to add them up in my head. Let's say thirty productions over the years. Thirty performances for each production. That would be about nine hundred performances? Could that be right? Almost a thousand nights saying the same words over and over? Doing the same blocking? Killing those two innocent little actors again and again, who I'm sure had to pay for years of therapy after the show closed.

Zora was still waiting for her answer.

"Close to a thousand."

"Let's estimate a sold-out house of five hundred a night."

That was fair. All my *Medea*s were sellouts. "Okay. That's about four hundred thousand people?"

"If you did it on YouTube, you could hit twice that many people in one day."

"You can't put *Medea* on YouTube."

"Of course you can't," Zora said, looking disappointed in my inability to grasp what she was saying. "You have to put *you*."

That was what happened to us technophobic old farts. Whenever we actually glimpsed the power of this new stuff, we freaked out and started telling you what it *couldn't* do. Zora was patient, but firm.

"Mafeenie, things are different now. It's not better or worse, it just is. You're an artist. You have to be open to new ideas."

It's worse, my old-fart brain said, but I held my tongue. She was trying to tell me something important if I could just listen to her.

"Go on."

"What hasn't changed is that people are still looking for stories, like you always told me they would. They're just finding a lot of differ-

ent ways to tell them, like you did when you were riding around Paris
on that horse talking about the Amazon Queen. That was new and it
worked great!"

"There was a war on," I said. "I had to do something to get people's
attention."

"There's still a war on."

I couldn't argue that, but I also didn't see what that had to do with
me talking about Miss Simpson and my childhood notebooks.

"Have you talked to Miss Abbie about what she wants to call the
gardens?"

"Where did you see Abbie?" I said, glad for a change of subject.

"Coming home this afternoon. She said you okayed doing a garden and we were going to call it the Martin Luther King Peace Garden
Number One, but she couldn't remember if she'd told you that yet."

I laughed. "She's already named it and hasn't planted the seed first."

"It's a peace garden, Mafeenie, and she gave it a number. That
means she expects there to be others."

"Other gardens?"

"Of course. That's the kind of stuff the Internet can do best. Give a
bunch of people something to do that some other people are already
doing. It makes them feel connected. Part of something. Abbie calling
this garden 'number one' connects her to number two, which inspires
number three, and on and on. Soon you got people all over the world
planting gardens for peace because they saw you on our video planting
sunflowers where Great-gram had her roses."

"She told you I vetoed the roses?"

"Sunflowers will be fine," Zora said.

I looked at her. "You're good at this."

She grinned at me. "Good enough for you to trust me?"

"I do trust you, it's just that this is a lot to ask of one little video of
one little woman on one little corner."

She came over and plopped down on the couch and put her feet in
my lap. "Listen, Mafeenie, you remember that Woodstock DVD we
used to watch all the time?"

Zora and I watched all the sixties classic concert films during one
memorable summer when Howard threatened to abandon us if we

didn't stop playing the Jimi Hendrix version of "The Star Spangled Banner" every morning as loud as we could crank it up.

"Of course," I said, giving her a little foot massage.

"You remember that guy who was singing the antiwar song where everybody was supposed to join in?"

"Country Joe and the Fish," I said, kneading the ball of her foot gently.

"Yeah, and when people wouldn't do it, he got mad and said, 'Listen, you fuckers, you gotta sing better than that if you want to stop a war.' "

"One of my favorite moments of the whole concert," I said.

"Well, this is sort of like that. People just aren't singing loud enough and anything we can do to make them sing louder is a good thing."

"How long did you talk to Abbie?" I said, hearing the voice of the visionary coming through strong in the middle of a project that was supposed to be about getting a better price for a piece of real estate and now seemed to be about putting an end to war around the world.

"Long enough for her to tell me she wanted to make a short statement on the video about the gardens before we start on Monday."

"What did you tell her?"

Zora stretched her toes. "I told her absolutely."

"So I guess this means you're the director?"

"Yep," she said, grinning. "Which means you have to do everything I say."

I grinned back. "You're new at this, huh?"

•

THIRTY-NINE

*A*retha brought T-shirts. We didn't think she was coming since she had a few more doors to do, but when Zora and I pulled up bright and early Monday morning, she was standing in the yard talking to Victor, who was wearing a pair of jeans and a white T-shirt that said RESCUE ON MLK in big red letters on the front. Aretha was wearing one, too.

"I love it," Zora said, pulling in behind Aretha's truck and grabbing her little black bag of technology. She had tried to explain it to me a couple of times, but I was hopeless, so she gave me permission not to understand *how* she did it as long as I approved of *what* she was doing. I got out of the car and waved at my assembling crew members. The only person not here yet was Abbie and she had called to say she was on her way.

"Good morning," Aretha said, giving Zora a hug and handing each of us a T-shirt. Victor stepped back a little and looked at Zora since they hadn't been properly introduced yet. "I think a crew works better when it looks like a crew."

"Me too," I said, plucking a T-shirt from the pile she was offering. "These are great! I'm a sucker for a good costume."

Zora pulled hers over the T-shirt she was already wearing and walked over to Victor. "I'm Zora Evans, Josephine's granddaughter. Are you Victor?"

"Yeah. Victor Causey."

She stuck out her hand and he looked over at me before he reached out to shake it. I realized that he had found a way to shave and removed the scraggly beard he had been sporting the other day. I smiled my approval.

"Thanks for working with us on this," Zora said. "This house means a lot to me."

"Not enough to live in it," he said, still a little surly, even in his crew T-shirt.

"Not yet," Zora said.

Before I could tell her she didn't have to take any guff from Victor, Abbie pulled up in her little Volvo and tooted the horn like we might miss her. Victor sighed and sat down on the back porch steps. His quiet sanctuary had suddenly become a veritable beehive of noisy new arrivals, high expectations, and brand-new T-shirts. Zora sat down beside him and unzipped her bag.

"Am I late?" Abbie had on bright yellow sweats and a pair of red rubber boots.

"Of course not," I said, glad for her familiar smell as she reached out to hug me.

"Who did the T-shirts?"

"I did," Aretha said, handing her one, which she immediately pulled on just like Zora and I had done. We had all just added the T-shirts on top of whatever layers we were already wearing, so now we looked a little lumpy, but it didn't matter. Aretha was right. We were now officially a crew. It was time to get started.

FORTY

·

The five of us gathered on the lawn, surrounded by the job that lay ahead of us. This was our crew: me, Zora, Aretha, Abbie, and Victor. The first thing I did was say a brief welcome and thank them for agreeing to help. Victor was getting paid, but I thanked him anyway. Zora had already gotten everybody's permission to videotape any- and everything. Everybody except Victor, who objected vehemently until I suddenly had a flash of inspiration and offered him another twenty-five dollars a week. Zora promised to keep him off camera as much as possible. He still grumbled, but he agreed. I had made peace with the whole reality idea by informing Zora that I didn't care how much footage she shot of me, I didn't want to see any more pictures of myself doing whatever this was we were doing. All it did was make me feel self-conscious. She kept telling me how great I looked and sounded, but I was adamant, so she finally agreed.

"It's important that we tell the story not just of this house," I said. "But of this moment."

They all nodded, except Victor, who rolled his eyes.

I looked over at Abbie. "Did you want to say something about the garden?"

"Yes," she said.

Zora, who had been standing next to her, checked the technology and nodded.

"Okay," Abbie said, smiling at all of us, but talking to that unseen audience Zora had assured us would be watching too. "I'm not going to make a speech or anything. I just want to say that a lot of you may not think of yourselves as gardeners, but your country is at war. You have to do some things you might not do otherwise, just because it is your country, too. The first thing is, you have to love it, the essence of it, the goodness of it, not the people we have allowed to call themselves our leaders, but the country itself. We have to help each other the way good people always help each other. The same way good people always know when something is wrong because you can always tell if you're really looking." She stopped and looked at Zora and frowned slightly. "What was I talking about?"

The mysterious, private unknowable nature of human beings, I thought. Of course Abbie and I were still friends. We were still doing the same work.

"Loving your country," Zora said softly.

"Yes!" Abbie said, pleased to be reminded. "Of course. We have to find a way to do whatever it takes to reclaim our country. And it doesn't have to be something big. It can be something that seems small. Something that helps you remember the good things. Focus on your neighbors. Focus on the mountains behind your house. Focus on any grandbaby you can find. Focus on music you sing with other people. Focus on growing something. That's why we're making a garden here and that's why we're going to call it the Martin Luther King Peace Garden Number One. Because if we can grow sunflowers on Martin Luther King Drive, maybe we can grow sunflowers in Baghdad, too."

"And Fallujah," Aretha said.

"And Kabul," Zora said, behind the camera.

"And New Orleans," I said, for Louie.

Victor didn't say anything, but he didn't roll his eyes either.

"Anything else?" Zora said.

Abbie shook her head and smiled. "No. I think that's it for now."

"Okay," I said. "Then let's get to work."

FORTY-ONE

By the end of the day, we were almost too tired to take Louie up on his offer to feed us. *Almost*. Aretha had plans with her daughter and Victor brushed off our invitation before I could fully extend it, but Zora and I went home to shower and change before Abbie picked us up at just before eight. It had been a long day's work, but we had already made a visible dent and that was enough to satisfy me.

It was going to be a big job, even with all of our hands working, but we had a plan to keep us on track. Aretha had worked out a schedule of what needed to be done in what order so we wouldn't be doing drywall before the electrician finished. But all of that came later. Today, all we had done was bag and re-bag trash, inside and out, load up Aretha's truck and let her haul it to the dump. Abbie and I worked outside and Victor and Zora worked inside.

By six o'clock, we were all exhausted. The water wasn't on yet and I worried about where Victor would go to clean up, but I knew better than to ask him. I got the feeling his pride was all he had to call his own and anything that threatened it touched off some serious alarms. He and Zora seemed to get along fine. They tossed enough trash out of that house to fill two loads on Aretha's truck all by themselves.

Louie lived on the second floor of a well-kept four-unit building on Ashby Street, and we pulled into the driveway as we had been instructed to do. As soon as we stepped out of the car, we could hear zydeco music coming from an upstairs window, along with the aroma of something that made me know how hungry I was. Zora found Louie's name on the mailbox, and we rang the bell. He buzzed us in without requiring any verbal ID and stood smiling at the top of the steps, holding a wooden spoon and wearing a big white apron. The sounds of zydeco king Clifton Chenier were pouring out of the door behind him.

"Ladies," he said, "welcome, welcome, welcome!"

We followed him into his apartment, which was so small, the four of us seemed to fill up the place like a party when everybody arrives at the same moment. Or maybe it was just the music. Or the smells wafting in from the kitchen. Louie's place was offering the two things New Orleans is known for—good music and good food.

I introduced Zora and thanked him for having us.

"Thanks for doing me this favor," he said to me when Abbie had stepped into the small bedroom to return a call from Peachy. Louie had just spoken to him and conveyed Peachy's apologies that he couldn't get away from the restaurant to join us. Zora was in the living room, dancing by herself, and Louie was moving around in the cramped kitchen with a grace that was almost as sensual as the smell of food. It was like watching a really good dancer. I sipped the champagne he had offered and enjoyed the show. He was dishing out steaming bowls of gumbo and cutting huge hunks of steaming corn bread that had been cooked in the skillet the old-fashioned way. There was also a big pot full of steamed shrimp and crayfish, a pan of blackened catfish, another of jambalaya, and one more pot of red beans which I was sure would provide the perfect topping for the fluffy white rice he had just removed from the heat.

I surveyed the feast and my stomach growled again. No way Louie's chef could resist this offering. If he liked good food, this probably made him weep.

"So how many of these fabulous dishes will we now be seeing on the menu at that hotshot hotel you work for?"

Louie carried two bowls of gumbo over to the tiny kitchen table. "None of these made the cut, Miss Josephine."

"None of them?" *Impossible.*

"Not a single one." He set the other two bowls down and put the plate of corn bread in the center of the table. "That's why this is really kind of a celebration."

"I'm all for that," I said. "What are we celebrating?"

He looked at me and untied his apron. "I quit."

"You quit your job?" I was surprised. He had told me at Abbie's that Atlanta had a surfeit of good chefs and that he was lucky to have found a position, even if it was less than perfect.

"The thing is, cooking's not just a job to me," he said. "It means something. How it looks, how it smells, how it tastes. How people feel when they eat it. All that matters to me."

"I can see that," I said, smiling at the beautiful table he had laid out for us.

He smiled back. "I've given up just about everything else I can think of already. This is the one thing I figure I gotta keep doing the way it's supposed to be done or I'm not what I say I am."

Zora's dance must have come to an end at the same time Peachy and Abbie said their goodbyes because before I could say another word, both my crew members suddenly poked their heads around the door, their noses quivering like rabbits'.

"Anything we can do to help?" Zora said. Abbie was grinning at me over Zora's shoulder.

"You can sit down and eat this food," Louie said, pulling out a chair for her with one hand and one for Abbie with the other.

"Peachy's sorry he can't be here," Abbie said. "He said to tell you, and I quote, 'If you have enough time to cook for us, you could be down there cooking for him.' "

Louie laughed, pulled out another chair for me, and sat down, too. "Duly noted," he said, reaching for my hand and Zora's on his other side. We lowered our heads.

"Bless this food," Louie said, "and these friends who come to share it. Amen."

"Amen," we all said, glad Louie hadn't felt the need for a longer communication with the Almighty. The food he had put before us was a beautiful, aromatic distraction and we were only human. We helped ourselves to the corn bread and picked up our oversize gumbo spoons. After that, there wasn't much conversation for a while. Not that we didn't have anything to say. Just that it's rude to talk with your mouth full.

•

FORTY-TWO

I like him," Zora said, after Abbie dropped us off and we had taken our showers and climbed into bed together in my room for what had become our nightly ritual.

"Me too," I said. "He's been through a lot."

"Abbie told me," she said, snuggling down a little deeper into the pillows. "He didn't seem to be too upset about quitting his job."

"They don't deserve him."

"Maybe he'll come and work with us."

The idea hadn't occurred to me. "As a chef?"

Zora giggled. "We can't afford a chef yet, Mafeenie."

I loved that "yet." Showed confidence, always a big part of projects like this. Faith was a big help, too.

"Well, what did you have in mind?"

"I don't know. Maybe he can be a part of our crew," she said. "Abbie said he told her he used to have a big garden behind his restaurant. He grew everything on the menu."

"Did he ever grow any sunflowers?"

"I think they grow wild in New Orleans," she said, yawning.

"Everything grows wild in New Orleans," I said, pulling the spread up around her.

"Even Louie?"

"I'm sure he had his moments," I said. "Are you sleeping in here tonight?"

"Can I?" She was half asleep already.

"Of course." I leaned down to kiss her goodnight.

She was asleep before I had a chance to turn out the light, but I just lay there for a minute trying to imagine what Louie being wild might look like. By the time I dozed off, I wasn't any closer, but the next morning, I remembered the sound of zydeco in my dreams. Old habits are hard to break.

FORTY-THREE

.

On Wednesday, our crew expanded by one. Aretha and Zora were trying to finish up the last of the blue front doors, so another pair of hands was right on time. Abbie and Victor and I were raking up the endless detritus that still cluttered the front yard when I glanced up and saw Louie getting off the bus at the bottom of the hill. He was wearing jeans, an army jacket, work boots, and a cap. He was carrying a bigger version of the red cooler in Victor's room, which he had reached back into the bus to retrieve.

"Is that Louie?" Abbie said.

"Sure is," I said. "Did you know he was coming?"

She shook her head. "Nope. Did you?"

"Nope."

Her signifyin' look returned. "Maybe he wanted to surprise you."

"The more, the merrier," Victor grumbled, watching Louie starting up the driveway.

Victor worked hard, but he complained hard, too. And continuously. I hoped his disposition would improve as we all got to know each other, but so far, he seemed to move between sullen and surly with equal regularity.

I waved at Louie and so did Abbie, but his hands were full with the cooler so all he could do was nod and smile.

"What's all that he's carrying. Lunch?"

"Cross your fingers," I said, mentally crossing mine. "This brother can burn."

We headed up the lawn to the house as Louie gently deposited the cooler on the back steps.

"Welcome to my wreck," I said.

"It's a work in progress," Abbie said. "I'm so glad you came."

He smiled. "Since my services are no longer required downtown, I thought maybe you might be able to put me to work."

Victor was looking at the cooler, and suddenly I wondered if he was hungry. Was seventy-five dollars a week enough for him to feed himself? Maybe I should make it a hundred.

"I think we've got a rake with your name on it," I said.

"I'm your man," Louie said. "I'm a rakin' somethin' when I put my mind to it."

We were taking entirely too much time with chitchat to suit Victor. We had already agreed that noon would be our regular break, and it was eleven forty-five. Louie turned to Victor and held out his hand.

"I'm Louie Baptiste."

"Victor Causey." They shook hands. "What's in the cooler?"

"A little of this and that," Louie said, popping off the top to reveal a veritable feast. He had thick sandwiches in plastic bags, deviled eggs, potato salad and cole slaw in Tupperware, and a jar of huge red dill pickles. Everything was neatly packed on a bed of ice. We had been raking and hauling since early this morning and I was suddenly so hungry, I almost swooned. "Anybody want lunch?"

"Now you're talking," Victor said, with his first smile of the day.

"You look like a roast beef man," Louie said, handing Victor a hearty sandwich that could have fed a small family.

Abbie had a blanket in the trunk of her car and she spread it on the ground like we were guests at a Sunday school picnic. Abbie and I both had turkey and we split the biggest pickle between us. Louie said people in Louisiana and Mississippi soak the pickles in red Kool-Aid and then eat them. It started off with kids and now everybody was eating them. He couldn't resist trying it. This was his first batch, and while it sounded awful, the taste wasn't bad at all.

The weather was cooperating with enough sunshine to warm up the afternoon like it was already spring and we ate like we never would again. I suddenly missed Howard. He would have laughed to see me sitting on an old green blanket, in front of a broke-up house, eating red dill pickles, and loving every minute of it.

"What are you planting?" Louie said, looking down the lawn at the plot we were clearing.

"Sunflowers," Abbie said. "Maybe some roses since that's what used to grow here."

He looked surprised. "Nothing to eat?"

I shook my head. "Not this time."

"Not even some herbs?"

He sounded like the idea of having a garden that didn't feed you even a little bit was inconceivable.

Abbie looked at me. "We hadn't really thought about herbs."

Of course the idea appealed to her. I had to nip this in the bud. If I let Abbie start adding things, my whole budget would be spent at the nursery buying tiny little tomato plants and a few sprigs of basil.

"I don't think so," I said. "We've already got our hands full, don't you think?"

"They grow real easy," Louie said. "Some basil, a little sage, maybe some rosemary."

It sounded like that Simon and Garfunkel song.

"That would be lovely," Abbie said. "Especially since it's a peace garden."

"What do herbs have to do with peace?" I said. "I thought the flowers were symbolic."

Abbie smiled and turned to Louie. "Do you think herbs have a place in a peace garden?"

Louie smiled back. "Well, I never saw anybody fighting when they're eating good."

"Amen, brother," Victor said, and looked at me. "You weren't kidding when you said he could burn."

Louie glanced over at me, and suddenly I felt embarrassed that I had paid him a compliment.

"So how much is it going to cost me to grow these exotic spices?" I said.

Abbie laughed. "Don't worry. I'm sure Louie and I can work something out."

Knowing them, they already had.

•

FORTY-FOUR

*F*riday morning when we got to the house, a city inspector had already come by to drop off a stop-work order. Zora scanned it quickly while I read over her shoulder.

"It says we aren't displaying the necessary permits for the work we're doing."

"You gotta have a permit to clear out the trash?" Victor said.

"You have to say where you're going to dump it and tell them what's in the bags."

I looked at the big green Dumpster half-full of bags already. Some we had filled with trash from inside the house, but the ones other people had just left here, we were tossing in with no intention of exploring the contents. This was a classic case of letting sleeping dogs lie.

"That's crazy," I said. "I'm not opening the bags."

"It says we have to prove that there's no lead or asbestos involved before we can dump it anywhere," Zora said.

It was amazing to me that there were rules that could keep us from cleaning up the place, but none that had seemed particularly effective in keeping it from becoming the dangerous eyesore that it was.

Abbie was reading over Zora's shoulder, too. "It says we can come down and file the necessary papers and if it all goes through, we can start up again on Monday."

This was ridiculous. The last thing I wanted to do was twiddle my thumbs all weekend. "So what are we supposed to do until then?"

"It says stop work on the house and unauthorized removal of trash," Abbie said, looking at me without the slightest sign of stress or agitation.

"So?"

"It didn't say we couldn't work in the garden."

FORTY-FIVE

·

$\mathcal{J}$ knew that kimono was perfect for you," Howard said, waking me up on my first day off in the last five. We had been working like dogs, but we could finally see a tiny little dent in all we had to do. I gave everybody a day off to rest. "You looked fabulous!"

"You saw me?"

"Not all of us are living in the Stone Age, missy! Of course I saw you. You're all over the Internet."

"I am?" I sat up and tried to focus on what he was saying. Had Zora put us out there already? Was I floating around somewhere in cyber-space in my beautiful kimono talking about Miss Simpson and promising to save my house from urban blight or else?

"You are, in the finery I sent, thank you very much, as well as work-ing away in those ridiculous T-shirts that I assume are required for rea-sons which remain mysterious to me, but it all works, sweetie. Stroke of genius. People are already addicted to it."

Addicted to us on our knees ripping up old carpet and scrubbing out the bathrooms?

"We're pretty much working all the time," I said, "so I haven't had much time to really look at it."

It hadn't occurred to me that people in Amsterdam would see it. Was this what they meant by a global community? It was a little too early for me to comprehend it all.

"Are you kidding?" Howard said. "People here are loving it. They're quoting what you said about the mysterious, private unknowable na-ture of human beings in acting classes all over town."

"Maybe I can be a good teacher after all."

"Don't bother," he said. "Those who can *do,* and you will be able to do pretty much whatever you want after the board meeting next month. That demonstration shook them up bad, and this rescue mission is only adding fuel to the fire. It's such a noble mission, sweetie. Very Princess Diana. Nothing about it smacks of ugly American. Miss Zora is a genius. Nobody here can understand why all the streets named after Martin Luther King aren't national shrines or something."

"That's what Abbie keeps saying."

"I know. It's all on there. She looks great, by the way. I could practically smell the patchouli."

That made me laugh through a great big yawn. "I'll tell her."

"Here's my news and then I gotta go. I've fallen in love."

"Howard!" Howard's last great love had broken his heart in about ten different places and taken off for parts unknown. Nursing him back to some semblance of sanity had taken the better part of a year.

"I know, I know. I swore I would never do it again, but he's not an actor. That should count for something."

"Is he a designer?"

"Don't laugh."

"I'll do my best."

"He's an acrobat."

"An acrobat?" Even for Howard, this was something new.

"A Chinese acrobat, thank you very much. He's in one of those acts where there are like a thousand of them on one bike."

As a kid, I remember wanting to do that for about ten seconds. The amount of trust, athleticism, and smiling required struck me as daunting. "Is this the part where I'm not supposed to laugh?"

"I know, I know, but who would have thought you'd be planting sunflowers on the lawn of the ruins of your family home?"

He made it sound like I was Scarlett O'Hara coming home to rebuild Tara after the Yankees had marched through with Sherman on their way to the sea.

"Point well taken. Is he nice or just beautiful?"

"I didn't say he was beautiful."

"He's a Chinese acrobat. They're all beautiful."

Howard laughed. "He's a god. And really funny, and he thinks I'm as fabulous as you and I know me to be. What's not to love?"

"What indeed," I said. Howard may as well have been calling from another planet. The presence of Chinese acrobats was not unexpected in my other life. In this one, it would have been like saying, *Look at the T. rex coming up Cascade Road.*

"Well, that's all the news from here. Keep doing what you're doing. It adds to your overall fabulousness and makes my job as easy as falling off a log."

"Or a bicycle."

"Go to hell. Love you!"

"Love you more!"

For at least thirty seconds, I was tempted to turn on the computer downstairs and look at what we were posting. The feeling was strong, but then it passed. We still had a lot of work to do, and watching myself do it didn't make it any easier to scrub down those walls and cart those bags of trash to the Dumpster. But this was my day off. I turned over and went back to sleep. When I dreamed of Howard on a bicycle, holding tight to the back of his new lover, the only little chocolate face in the midst of all those smiling Chinese acrobats, I wasn't even surprised.

•

FORTY-SIX

Z ora and I used our first day off to compare notes on our
progress. The cleanup was going great, and when I told her
about Howard calling to say we were a hit in Amsterdam, she just
grinned an I-told-you-so grin at me.

"Abbie's already gotten more than a hundred requests for information about the garden," she said. "How cool is that?"

Abbie and Victor had almost cleared the garden space of trash
bags, but they were still a week away from putting anything in the
ground.

"What kind of information?" I said as we walked down to the pool.

"What to plant based on where they are. How to know if you've got
enough sunlight. Basic stuff. We've got a link to the West End Growers
Association so everybody gets a response in twenty-four hours."

"I am almost ready to admit that the future might not be so bad,"
I said.

"You know what else they want to know?" She slipped out of her
robe and eased into the water. The smiling mermaid's flowing locks
seemed to ripple as the water lapped around the edges of the pool.

"What?"

I followed her with a sigh. A week of scrubbing walls and tossing
trash bags had left me aching and exhausted. The warm water felt wonderful.

She grinned at me again. "Where have *you* been all their lives?"

"I told you I was an unknown quantity over here," I said, lying out
on my back and kicking lazily down the pool toward the deeper end.

"Used to be, not anymore. You're becoming a cult figure, Mafeenie.
Abbie, too, but with her, they want to know about soil samples. With
you, they want to know about *you*!"

"So me and the old guy are taking the Internet by storm," I said. "What do you tell them?"

She turned over in the water and started her easy breaststroke. "I tell them you're a star."

I held that thought as I did one lap to Zora's four, and by the time we climbed out and toweled the water off, I felt like a star. Rested, refreshed, and almost fabulous. I took the chair beside Zora, closed my eyes, and sighed deeply. She did, too.

"Mafeenie?"

"Yes, darlin'?"

"Can I ask you something?"

"As long as it doesn't have anything to do with dumping permits and the rising cost of cleaning supplies."

"Nothing like that."

"Good, then fire away."

"Have you ever had a female lover?"

The question didn't surprise me. We had been talking about sex since Zora started her period in the middle of her visit with me the summer she turned thirteen. In response to her questions, we had talked about her body, her soul, caring for her clitoris, the challenge of the vaginal orgasm, and AIDS. She wasn't sexually active yet, but she was curious and I was prepared to answer any question she wanted to ask. Knowing that discussions about sex are almost always about a lot of other things, too, I always kept my ears open.

"Yes," I said, without opening my eyes. "I've had lots of lovers. Men, women, never children, and I was never into groups. Too hard to focus."

"So how was it?"

I opened my eyes and looked at her. "Are you interested in a specific woman or are you just thinking of expanding your horizons?"

She laughed. "I should be taping this."

"This is our day off," I said. "What's going on?"

"I don't know. This guy from Morehouse called me up. I had some classes with him and he seems nice, but men are just so hard to deal with. There's always so much drama. I thought maybe women would be easier just because there wouldn't be all that man stuff."

Like the woman stuff is any less complicated. "So you're thinking about women as a kind of fallback position?"

"I don't mean it like that," she said. "Or maybe I do. What do you think?"

"Well, the truth is, the only time I had sex with a woman was when we were both going out with the same man and she hit on me. I knew it would really piss him off when she told him."

"Why'd you think she would tell him?"

"Because that's why she did it in the first place," I said, remembering how awkward the experience had been for both of us. We would have done better to just have lunch and tell everybody we had sex. "My best sex has always been with men, but my best relationships have always been women. Look at me and Abbie. We haven't seen each other for a hundred years and our friendship picked up right where it left off. That never happens to me with men."

"Why do you think that is?"

"Because I could never get used to telling a man the truth."

"Never?"

"Not if I could help it."

"What about Howard?"

"Gay men are exempt," I said, "because you're probably not going to be having sex with them."

"So are you saying you never tell straight men the truth?"

I shrugged, amused at her surprise. "Well, it's different now, but in my prime, it just wasn't done. My generation was trained to lie. Telling a man the truth is a very recent phenomenon. Like the Internet."

Zora's cellphone rang on the table beside her and she reached for it. I resisted an impulse to grab it and toss it in the pool. The mermaid would probably have jumped right out.

"I thought this was our day off."

She looked at the caller ID and frowned. "It's Victor. I gave him this number for emergencies."

I sat up.

"Victor? This is Zora. Everything okay?"

The frown deepened, which was not a good sign.

"Did you see who did it?"

"Did what?" I said.

She held up her hand, listening. "Okay. Don't touch anything. We'll be right there."

So much for an off day.

•

FORTY-SEVEN

*W*e could see it from the street. A smelly mountain of trash where we had worked so hard all week to clear a space. Victor was standing near the house next to a neatly dressed woman who turned in our direction when we pulled up in the yard, but Victor said something to her and she stayed where she was as he hurried over to meet us.

"What happened?" I said.

Zora was already turning her technology toward the pile, but she was standing close enough to pick up Victor's response, too.

"Somebody dumped a truck of trash on us," he said.

I looked at him, annoyed at the obviousness of his answer. "I can see that," I said, sounding as pissed off as I felt. "But who? When did this happen? Did you see anybody?"

Victor shook his head. "It was here when I got back. I went to church with my mother," he looked embarrassed to say it. "And then . . . I wanted to show her what we were doing, cleaning up and everything, but when we got here"—he gestured helplessly at the mound— "there it was. They must have known I wasn't here."

The woman was still looking in our direction, clutching her purse to her stomach like it might fly away or get snatched if she didn't hang on tight. She was a small woman, but she had a big presence, and the intensity of her dark eyes made it seem even bigger. Her dark blue coat, small, flowered hat, and sensible, low-heeled pumps completed a picture of churchgoing-black-womanhood that was as familiar to me as my own face in the mirror.

It dawned on me that this was Victor's mother. The woman who had put him out when the crack made him unrecognizable, even to her. The woman who had climbed up this long driveway to let her son show her that he had permission to be here now. That he was working.

That he had turned a corner. That he was doing this as much for her as for me. If I felt bad, he probably felt ten times worse. And my mother wasn't standing right there looking at me, either.

"I should have been here," he said.

Victor's mother came toward us slowly, picking her way across the uneven yard.

"They probably would have dumped it anyway," I said, turning toward her as she approached. "People have been throwing stuff over that fence so long they probably think that's what it's for."

Victor's mother cleared her throat. "That's just what I told him."

He looked at her and ducked his head the way he probably did when he was about ten years old and she caught him at some mischief.

"There's no law against going to church on Sunday," she said.

"None I feel bound to obey," I said, smiling and extending my hand. "I'm Josephine Evans. This is my house."

"I'm Betty Causey," she said, shaking my hand with a grip that was surprisingly firm for such a small woman. "That's my house down there on Wiley. The one with the flower boxes."

"You ever have any problems with people dumping trash in your yard?"

She looked at Victor. "You didn't tell her?"

"I told her," he said, heading down by the fence to take a closer look at what we'd be up against first thing tomorrow morning. Zora was already there with her camera.

"I've had problems with people doing everything," she said, watching her son poking at the bags gently with a stick. "Trash in my yard. They stole my car. Broke my front window. Kicked in my side door. Tore up my garden."

My heart sank. Was this just the beginning? "Is it kids?"

She shrugged, still looking at Victor, who was talking to Zora as they walked around the mound. "No kids can drop that much trash in one day."

"Then who do you think it was?"

She turned to me with an exasperated expression that made her look exactly the way her son did when he was pissed off. "I think it's Woodruff."

"Greer Woodruff?" I had an immediate mental picture of the boss lady at the wheel of an overflowing dump truck. "Why?"

"She made you an offer for your place, right?"

"Yes."

"Why didn't you take it?"

"The offer was ridiculous. I told her my place wasn't for sale."

"*Bingo!*"

"Bingo?"

"She wants these last four houses, yours and the three of us down on Wiley. She wants them *bad*. Her business is tied up with a lot of shady people. Now it's time to pay the piper and she needs our houses to do it."

"What kind of shady people?"

Victor, now close enough to hear his mother, grimaced slightly. "You don't have any proof that it's her."

"Stop talking like a lawyer," Betty snapped. "I'm just saying—"

"It's getting late," Victor interrupted her before she could say more. "We should start back."

Betty Causey pursed her lips and rolled her eyes, which seemed to be a family expression of disgust.

"Would you like a ride?" Zora said.

"No, thanks. I need the walk," Betty said, accepting the arm Victor offered. He managed to look courtly even in his worn jacket and frayed white shirt. I wondered what the minister thought when he showed up at church this morning. Knowing Betty, she had had the whole congregation praying for her prodigal son. They probably welcomed him back with high hopes and prayers of thanksgiving.

"This is my granddaughter, Zora," I said as they moved slowly toward the sloping driveway.

Betty smiled and nodded her head. "I could have guessed it. She's the spitting image of your mom."

"Did you know my mother?" The idea had never occurred to me.

"Everybody knew your mother," Betty said, stopping to look at me like I was forever missing the obvious. "She was always talking about how important it was for a woman to own the place she laid down in every night. Even if you were married, she was always telling us to be sure our name was on the deed right alongside our husband's." Betty smiled to herself. "They didn't appreciate it either, but we made them add us anyway just so we wouldn't have to keep hearing her fussing about it. And she loved her roses. She's the one that made us all start gardening, too."

Those were my mother's two major passions, all right. Roses and real estate.

"Why did people stop doing their gardens?"

She shook her head sadly. "Too dangerous. We can't be outside like that. Not anymore."

"I'm sorry," I said, wondering if Greer Woodruff was responsible for that, too.

Betty Causey held a little tighter to Victor's arm as they started down the driveway, but then she turned back to me.

"I remember you, too," she said. "Always writing stuff in your little notebooks. Do you still do it?"

"No," I said. "I'm an actress."

She raised her eyebrows. "An actress?"

I nodded, loving her surprise.

"Well, Miss Actress," she said, putting one foot down carefully in front of the other. "Welcome home."

FORTY-EIGHT

•

$\mathcal{I}$t took most of the next day to even make a dent in the new trash pile. We would fill up Aretha's truck and she'd haul it away and then we'd fill it up again. What Betty had said kept popping into my head as we worked. *No kids can drop that much trash in one day.* Abbie and Zora were downtown filing a complaint report with the city, and at noon one of Aretha's friends arrived with another truck. By five o'clock, he and Victor were loading up the last of the mountain before heading for the dump. Aretha and I were sitting on the front steps, trying to decide what to tackle next, when a navy blue Cadillac pulled up in the yard and slowed to a stop. The vanity tag said SERVANT. I looked at Aretha, who just shrugged, as the door opened and a tall, thin man wearing a brown silk suit stepped out and smiled in our direction.

"Councilman Rogers," Aretha said, as he reached back inside for his hat and what looked like two yard signs. I wondered if he was here to do a little campaigning.

"He's Greer Woodruff's boy," she whispered to me as we stood up to greet him.

"Ladies, ladies, don't get up!" he said, coming across the yard like he owned it, his voice a booming baritone that enjoyed the sound of itself a few decibels louder than could be called conversational. I knew a lot of actors like that. They throw their voices at you, convinced you will be powerless before its sheer ability to fill up a space.

"I'm Josephine Evans," I said, raising my own voice just a little to be heard over the truck which was idling nearby. "The property owner."

The councilman extended his hand. "I'm Councilman Julius Rogers, serving the people of this district for the past twenty-two years. May I first apologize for the less civilized among my constituents who have been using your place for dumping. There is no excuse for it and I will work with you to make sure it doesn't happen again."

"Thank you," I said.

"Glad to do it," he said. "In the meantime, you should post these signs in a prominent position to let people know that there's a new sheriff in town."

He chuckled at his own joke and handed Aretha two official-looking No Dumping signs as if that settled that.

"Thank you," she said, heading for the toolbox in her truck. "I'll post them right away."

"Glad to do it," he said again, then turned back to me. "Ms. Evans, I wondered if I might have a word with you privately, as the property owner."

"Certainly," I said.

Victor and Aretha's friend were backing the truck into position for departure and Aretha was loudly pounding the first sign into the ground near the fence.

"Come inside."

He smiled and followed me into the house. I took him into the dining room where we had established a kind of crew room with a table and four mismatched chairs. We had scrubbed down everything inside, but the real work was still to be done. As a stopgap measure, Aretha and Zora had put a cheap coat of white paint over everything, but the outlines of some of the more garish bits of graffiti were still vaguely visible in the afternoon sunlight as ghostly images of too many bad drawings of too many oversize penises. Councilman Rogers's eyes flickered over the walls and then back to me. I turned on the hurricane lamp we were using until electricity was restored, and the images faded in the light. He smiled in a way that made me want to slap him now and get it over with.

"Squatters did a job on these walls," I said calmly. "We'll need a few more coats of paint to cover their artwork completely."

"I see," he said, pulling up a chair like a man who was used to focusing on the matter at hand, regardless of surroundings. "Well, I may be able to save you a whole lot of paint and a whole lot of trouble."

"What kind of trouble?"

"Why don't you sit down, Ms. Evans? It makes me feel like I'm being rude to sit, but my dogs are barking today. It feels good to take a load off."

I took the chair across from him. "What kind of trouble?"

"Just what you had the other day. Trash in your yard. Vandalism. Robbery. Home invasion. All the things for which my constituents are deservedly famous."

I wondered what he wanted. "You mean you don't think the signs you gave us will turn the tide?"

"I think they will be helpful, but let's lay our cards on the table, shall we?"

Aretha stuck her head in before he could answer. "Excuse me, Jo, if you don't need me in here, I'm going to go on and get started on the front door."

She held up a gallon of paint that I knew was the same turquoise she had used to adorn all those front doors in West End.

"I'm fine," I said. "Go ahead."

Councilman Rogers waited until we heard her close the front door behind her and cleared his throat. "Greer Woodruff is an associate of mine. We have done business over the years, always for the betterment of this community and rarely for her own financial gain."

"She's doing all right for herself," I said. "Lovely offices."

"Yes, well, she is on the verge of doing a very important development deal here that I believe she outlined for you."

"Yes, she did."

"Then you understand how important such development can be to a depressed area like this one."

He was waiting for me to argue, but I just looked at him. I was waiting to see those cards on the table. "Yes, I do."

"Ms. Woodruff would like you to revisit your decision in regard to the sale of your property."

"Or what? She'll arrange to have some more trash dumped in my yard?"

"That's hardly the way Ms. Woodruff does business," he said. "I just thought when I heard about your misfortune that . . ."

"I think it's exactly how she does business," I said, talking over him, "and I'll tell you just like I told her. My house is not for sale."

He took off his hat and laid it on the table between us. "How long have you been away from Atlanta, Ms. Evans?"

"What does that have to do with anything?"

"Twenty years? Thirty?" He touched the edge of his hat lightly. "Thirty-five? That's a long time to be gone. A lot of things have changed. This town doesn't run on high ideals and big dreams anymore. It runs on big money, the quicker the better."

Outside I could hear Abbie and Zora pulling up. The delighted squeal that accompanied their arrival meant they had picked up Aretha's Joyce Ann, who always greeted her mom with a whoop of the purest delight. Just the sound of it made me feel good. Councilman Rogers made me feel tired.

"This particular deal has ramifications far beyond what you may be able to see right away," he said. "All of us can benefit if we can move with dispatch."

There were the cards I'd been waiting to see. Whatever deal Greer was in the midst of trying to make, part of the proceeds were clearly going into Councilman Rogers's silk pockets. I stood up.

"I do appreciate your concern," I said, "but I'm not interested in making any deals."

He stood up, too, although you could tell that wasn't the response he was looking for from me. "Greer Woodruff has some powerful friends in this town."

"I'll keep it in mind," I said, leading him out the back door so we wouldn't disturb any painting going on out front.

Joyce Ann was squealing again. She had dipped her hands in the paint with her mother's blessing and was now making handprints all over the front door. Abbie was applauding their efforts, and Zora was capturing it all on video.

When we got to his car, Councilman Rogers tossed his hat in and gave me one last chance. "You know, Ms. Evans, I understand you have quite a reputation as an actress."

"I have my moments," I said.

"I'm sure you do," he said, "but the thing is, this is real life."

"It's all real life," I said. "Thanks for stopping by."

As he headed back down the driveway, I wondered how long it would take him to report back to Greer Woodruff.

"It's good luck," Abbie said as I joined them at the front door.

I had met Joyce Ann only once before, but she gave me a big smile and held up her turquoise hands.

"I'm good luck!"

"Yes, you are," I said, laughing.

They had pinned one of our big T-shirts around her like a chef's apron.

"Blue never let me do the handprints in West End," Aretha said. "He never really got it, but Zora said you didn't mind."

"I love it," I said. "Do the handprints make it stronger medicine against the evil eye?"

"Absolutely," Aretha said.

"Good," I said. "Something tells me we're going to need all the help we can get."

"You've already got it," she said, watching her daughter carefully putting more prints on the door with Abbie's encouragement.

"Show us your hands, Joyce Ann!" Abbie said as Zora moved in closer. "Show us your good-luck hands!"

FORTY-NINE

·

The next day Aretha came by to tell me that a friend of hers called to say she had heard a rumor about what Greer Woodruff's people wanted to put over here. A prison. That meant we'd have the cemetery on one side of the street and the living dead on the other. Martin must be spinning in his grave.

FIFTY

·

I couldn't wait to tell Abbie what Aretha's friend had said about the plans to put a prison right there on our corner.

"That's a rumor," she said calmly. "You can't put a prison right in the middle of a neighborhood like that."

We were sitting in the kitchen looking through seed catalogues. The garden had gone from strictly sunflowers to a more eclectic mix of sunflowers, collard greens, herbs, and tomatoes. Abbie liked the idea of growing things that were beautiful to look at right beside things that were good to eat, and the idea of Louie cooking a meal with our very own produce made all of our mouths water. I had no idea there were so many different kinds of tomatoes to choose from, but Abbie was considering them all.

"Councilman Rogers didn't even mention it," I said. "He was too busy telling me how much respect he had for Ms. Woodruff."

Abbie looked at me. "You know what we need? A dedication ceremony."

She wasn't fully engaging in my rant against the powers that be. I had a lot more to say about the nerve of them, the bad intentions of them, the stupidity of them, but Abbie was smiling happily and looking at a paperback copy of *The Farmers' Almanac.*

"A what?"

"A dedication ceremony. For the garden. I'll get Aretha to make us a sign. We can unveil it or something, you know. Just to make it a little more dramatic."

"The garden isn't even up yet. The house still needs lots of work, inside and out, and the way things are going with the Woodruff crowd, we might be hit with a plague of frogs at any moment."

"Exactly when you need a dedication. Some kind of sacrament to pull everything together."

I groaned. "You and Zora are always trying to institute mystic rites of the sea."

She laughed. "Last time I checked, that corner was landlocked, but I am looking for the next full moon, if that's what you mean. If I was at the beach, I'd already know when it was due, but up here, I lose track. Too much artificial light."

"How is a dedication ceremony going to help stop a prison?" I said, feeling peevish and ignored.

She looked surprised. "Is that what we're doing?"

That had all the earmarks of a trick question, so I hedged a little. "Aren't we?"

"You said we were fixing up the house so you could sell it and get back to Amsterdam in time to open your season."

I hate it when people quote my inconsistencies back to me so accurately.

"Oh! And Zora was going with you."

"That's still the plan."

"Then why are you worrying about whether or not somebody wants to build a prison?"

She had me there. "I don't know," I said. "It just seems a shame to do all this work and then let them use it that way, but you're right. It's not my job to worry about it."

"But you are."

I wanted to deny it, but I couldn't. Working at the house every day, I had begun to think of it as my place again. I had begun to remember all the good times I'd had there and how much it meant to my mother.

Abbie turned a page and then looked at me. "You don't have to be ashamed of starting to care about this place, Jo. Everybody's rooted somewhere."

The idea of being rooted on a little corner of Atlanta, Georgia, had never been my intention. I was a citizen of the world, just passing through on my way back to the life I'd created for myself in a place where nobody ever dumped trash on my lawn and people celebrated my presence with complimentary bottles of expensive champagne. What was it about this house that was starting to pull at my heart-strings in a way I had never intended and didn't really understand?

"Are you?"

"Of course," she said, tapping her heart as if it was a place you could go to like Detroit or Chicago. "I'm rooted here."

FIFTY-ONE

•

When Victor told me his mother wanted to see me, I was happy to hear it. We hadn't had enough time to talk the other day, and I knew she had a lot more to tell me. I told him to tell her I'd look forward to it. On the appointed day, he offered to walk me over, but I asked him to stay at the house instead since we were the only two there and somebody was coming over from Georgia Power Company. Betty had sent the message through Victor, but he was not invited and I thought it would be less awkward if he didn't show up at all, hoping to be invited in.

When I walked up on the porch and rang the bell, I could hear her unlocking several dead bolts and at least one chain. It reminded me of living in New York before I went to Amsterdam. It took people twenty minutes to unlock their apartment doors. Those moments always made me nervous. If the building was so bad you needed that many locks, how safe did I feel cooling my heels in the hallway with both eyes peeled for predators?

Betty's front windows, including the large picture window, were covered with elaborate white burglar bars that looked more like New Orleans's famous wrought-iron balconies but not quite so welcoming.

"Come in, come in," she said when she finally opened the front door, and the burglar door, and stepped aside to let me in. The house was neat as a pin and smelled vaguely of pine-scented cleaner. She ushered me into the living room where a small television in a big cabinet occupied one corner and a matching couch, chair, and love seat were carefully angled for the best view of the screen. A low, glass-topped coffee table had several issues of *Ebony* and *O, The Oprah Magazine* carefully fanned out in the manner of doctor's waiting rooms. On top of the TV, there was a black-and-white photograph of a much younger Betty and a man in an army uniform standing arm in arm and smiling into the camera with the full confidence bestowed upon them by their youth and beauty. Beside it was a color photograph of a much younger Victor, graduating from college, or maybe high school, and looking appropriately serious.

The sound was turned down on the television, but I saw the Fox News commentator giving the latest grisly details of some poor woman whose only claim to fame was as the victim of a man she thought could love her. Betty took a seat on the couch. She had already laid out a tray with a pot of coffee, two cups, and half a pound cake. I turned my back on the mug shot of the accused ex and smiled at Betty.

"Thank you for inviting me to stop by," I said. "It was good to meet you the other day, even if it wasn't such a good time to talk."

"It was all right," she said. "Sonny was just talking like a lawyer."

Sonny.

"Would you like some coffee?"

"Thank you," I said. "I'd love some."

She poured two cups and handed me one.

"He's been a big help as part of our crew," I said.

"Well, that's good to hear," she said, pouring a little splash of cream in her coffee from a small silver pitcher. "He's a good boy, but it's time for him to be a good man. You've heard of tough love?"

I nodded.

"Well, that's what I'm giving him," she said. "It'll make him stronger or it'll kill him. Either way, we'll know what we're dealing with."

There was no denying that, so I just smiled and sipped my coffee.

"I saw you the first day you came over here," she said.

"You did?" I wondered if she had binoculars. Maybe while Victor was keeping an eye on her, she was keeping an eye on him, too.

"Of course," she said. "You were driving down the street so slow, looking at everything so hard, I wanted to make sure you weren't planning something. It used to just be the boys, but now it's the girls, too, and you can't be too careful."

The idea that anybody would mistake me for a dangerous juvenile would have been funny to me, except that she was serious. It struck me as a terrible way to have to live, hiding in your own house, peering out between the bars to see who might be casing the joint. It sounded like being in jail.

"I was just trying to get a feel for the neighborhood," I said. "It didn't look like this last time I lived here."

She put her cup down and looked at me. "How long do you think it takes? People's kids grow up, they move away, sometimes they die. Things change a little at a time, then one day you wake up and you're living in a different place. You're living someplace where people will steal everything that isn't nailed down, and sometimes that doesn't help either. A place where you can't even go out and work in your garden for worrying about these knuckleheads bopping you in the head for the money you got in your pocket."

"That's terrible," I said. "What about the police?"

She snorted a little. "They ain't no better. You didn't hear how they shot a woman ninety years old because they said she was dealing crack out of her house?"

"The police shot her?"

Betty nodded. "When it started getting real bad around here, I went over to West End and met with Bea Grimes at the Growers Association to see if we could become members so maybe their group could address some of our security problems, but Bea said they don't do anything outside of West End." Betty frowned and pursed her lips at the absurdity of the answer. "I said I understand Blue Hamilton can't be everywhere, but we still have a right to live, don't we? We still have a right to grow some collard greens."

That sounded like the chorus of a postmillennium urban American freedom song: *Ain't we got a right to grow some greens?* So far, she was describing the perils of living in almost any inner-city community, but what did this have to do with Greer Woodruff?

"Who do you think is responsible for the things that have been happening?" I said, hoping she would identify the enemy.

"I don't *think*. I *know* it's that Woodruff woman."

"How do you know?" I thought so, too, but I needed more than a feeling.

"Because once she got involved in it, things changed. We always had the break-ins and the robberies, but nobody was messing with your house. Nobody was dumping garbage on the grass or spraying nasty pictures on your front walk or sending the fire inspector out to tell you how dangerous your place is if you don't spend all the money you've got to redo everything."

The association between Greer and Councilman Rogers was becoming clearer by the minute. Betty was getting more agitated the longer she thought about it. She put her cup down.

"Crackheads crawling in the window are one thing. That's when you get burglar bars. But this stuff, this city stuff, all that is because we won't give her our houses so she can tear them down and sell this land to whoever wants it, just like we never lived here and raised our families and did the best we could with the blessings we were given."

She was leaning forward now, trying to share her feelings and keep control of them at the same time.

"She can't make you sell your houses if you don't want to," I said. "What she's offering isn't even close to what they're worth."

"They aren't worth anything now," Betty said. "Not with things around here like they are. People are scared if we don't take what she's offering, we won't be able to get anything better."

I put my cup down, too. "I think we can do a lot better."

She looked at me with a ghost of a smile. "So do I."

"Then let's work together," I said. "How many neighbors do you have who want to stay?"

"Three are strong," she said. "Daisy's a little shaky since she got broken into a couple of weeks ago, but I think if she sees we got something going, she'll come around."

"So that's four houses down here and mine makes five," I said. "If we all agree we're not selling, Greer Woodruff will get tired of trying to intimidate people and go find some land to steal that nobody's living on."

"That's what I keep telling everybody, but they act like I'm just talking crazy."

"Crazy or not," I said, "I just think if you let them run you out of one place, they'll run you out of another."

"Exactly," she said, refilling our cups. "And in spite of everything? I still like it here. This is home."

"Me too," I said, surprised by how much I really meant it. "Me too."

•

FIFTY-TWO

Zora had a date with her friend from Morehouse. Victor was having dinner with Betty for the second time this week, and Abbie had gone to Tybee for a weekend visit with Peachy, who had stepped up his lobbying efforts with Louie. For his part, Louie had agreed to finally come down and see the place after three days of watching the Weather Channel to be sure there was no sign of a tropical storm. With everybody so scattered, Aretha and I decided to use the time to do some detail work on the inside of the house. We were painting the trim in the dining room a delicate shade of ivory. The pornographic graffiti was a distant bad memory, and the new windows we opened wide allowed light and fresh air in abundance.

I was sitting cross-legged on a cushion, painting an old-fashioned floorboard, and Aretha was perched halfway up an aluminum stepladder touching up the ceiling trim. I liked working with Aretha. We talked about everything and nothing with an ease that surprised me, given the thirty-year difference in our ages. Sometimes we didn't talk about anything at all, like today, but the company still made the job go faster. We'd been working in silence for a couple of hours when Aretha suddenly asked a question as if we'd spent the afternoon in conversation.

"Your son was Zora's father, right?"

"Yes," I said. "His name was Ira. He was an actor, too."

"Can I ask you something?"

"Sure."

"Did you find it hard to balance being an artist with being a mother?"

I laughed. "Impossible."

She laughed, too. "Thanks a lot!"

"I was lucky. Ira's father was able to take on the primary responsibility for raising him and did a much better job than I ever would have done." *Although he blamed himself for Ira's drinking until the day he died.*

"Joyce Ann's father is really hands-on, too. "

"Well, then she's a lucky little girl."

"Did you ever regret it?"

No point in lying to the girl. She already knew the answer to that question. "Constantly, but I never thought I could be a great mother. I *knew* I could be a great artist."

And that was the unvarnished truth, in all its selfish glory. "And I was."

"And you are. " She smiled.

I smiled, too. "Do you miss spending more time on your work?"

"I do," she said, "but I had a lot going on in my life and I needed to take some time and sort things out."

I remembered the pictures of her and her husband in *Dig It!* It couldn't have been easy to come back from that with sanity and optimism intact, but she had done it. I wondered how.

"Abbie helped me realize that it takes time to figure it all out and that the most important thing for me to do was to be patient with myself and take the time I needed to heal."

"Easier said than done."

Aretha grinned and turned back to her painting. "Not once you start doing it."

FIFTY-THREE

•

We spent the day refinishing floors inside the house. Buffing off all the gunk was hard work, but at the end of it, we could finally see the beauty of the wood again. I congratulated Victor on a job well done and he actually smiled at me. He was spending more time with his mother, and although he hadn't said it, I think they were both circling around the idea of him moving back in with her again.

Zora was babysitting for Aretha so I had the house to myself for a few hours. My plan was to take a nice hot shower and then fix myself some dinner, but first I decided to retrieve two messages that had come in to the cellphone I never carry with me.

Howard's was the first one. "Oh, my darling, I can't believe you're not picking up! What is the point of a cellphone if you never take it out of the house with you?"

He sounded stressed and annoyed.

"Well, they have lost their minds over here. Everything is up in the air. I'm on my way to Paris for the weekend, but I think that weasel critic from the paper has your number and will probably call you. Somebody at the theater gave it to him. Three guesses who, but do not talk to him! No matter what he says, do nothing until you hear from me!"

I wondered what the hell was going on.

"You're a star," Howard said, his voice trembling with indignation. "They don't deserve you!"

That didn't sound so good. I couldn't even imagine what he was talking about. I saved the message and went on to the next one.

"Hello, Miss Josephine," said a voice I recognized as belonging to the snide little drama critic who was François's girlfriend's biggest booster. I realized that it had been days since I'd ever thought about the theater wars and wondered what kind of progress Howard was making. "Are you there? Well, call me back as fast as you can. I'll pay, but I can't go to press without a quote from you since The Human Theatre Company has just announced that they'll be closing their season with a brand-new mounting of *Medea*."

I sat down. *Do nothing until you hear from me.*

"François will direct, of course."

Of course.

"Consuelo Rivera will be starring, which is the big news!"

The really big news.

"So call me, please. I need a reaction and I'm on deadline. Oh, and congratulations on that reality thing you're doing. Everybody's talking about it. *Ciao!*"

The house was quiet and empty. Zora wasn't around and obviously neither was my good sense. Here I was, scraping years of crap off a bunch of filthy floors, and my artistic life was being snatched right out from under me. It was time to fight back. I picked up the phone and punched in the number. He answered on the second ring.

"It's Josephine Evans," I said. "I didn't miss your deadline, did I?"

•

FIFTY-FOUR

I think I just burned a very big bridge," I told Abbie the next day as we strolled along the aisles of the nursery Abbie had dragged me to at the crack of dawn. She justified the insane hour by telling me that all the best plants would be gone by nine o'clock since the West End Growers Association gardeners all knew about this place, too.

"And you know how they are," she had said and rolled her eyes. I had no idea how they were, but that didn't save me from having to accompany Abbie on her early-morning mission.

Of course, I grumbled, but only because I didn't want her to make a habit of these outings. I'd been getting up earlier since I was usually too worn out to stay up very late, but I still considered myself to be a night person. Repairing old houses was a temporary blip on my screen. I didn't want to undo a lifetime of getting acclimated to theater hours by turning everything around. The truth was, I enjoyed these early-morning excursions. The smell of the wet dirt, the racks and racks of seeds, and the tiny seedlings that always looked too fragile to safely leave the greenhouse were all exotic to me. The only thing that was familiar was the absolute nature of the whole process.

Theater is like that, too. There is room in some performances for a little improvising, but that is a tightwire act best left to geniuses. For those of us who are merely mortal, the theater is a place of absolutes. You either know the line or you don't. You either understand the character or you don't. You can hit your mark, pick up your cue, and arrive for rehearsal on time, or you can't. Ultimately, whether you do or don't, at eight o'clock on any given evening the house lights will go down, the spot will find its mark, and the audience's collective wish that you will indeed make magic hangs in the air like the smell of hashish in an Amsterdam coffee house. Abbie had explained to me that gardening is like that, too. If you don't get the plants in by Good Friday, no amount of good intentions will produce tomatoes by the Fourth of July.

"Sometimes you have to burn a few bridges to keep from crossing the same river twice," Abbie said. "What'd you do?"

"I told the biggest drama critic in Amsterdam that François had completely lost his mind and his vision, that his board was clueless, and that his girlfriend couldn't act her way out of a paper bag."

Abbie looked surprised only by the last point. "I thought you said she was talented."

"She wants to close the season with *Medea.*"

"François would never do that."

"He's directing."

Abbie stopped in her tracks. "You're kidding, right?"

"I wish I was."

"Well, that's just tacky. What are you going to do?"

"I don't know," I said, watching two women who were easily eighty-plus pushing along a cart filled with potted calla lilies. Despite their age, their gait was more stride than stumble. They nodded as they passed us and we nodded back. "I guess I'll have to wait and see what Howard says. He's kind of my general on the ground."

"What do you want to do?"

Once again, Abbie hit the damn nail on the head. She knew it, too. I could tell from the grin that was slowly spreading across her face. *What do I want to do?* Be invited back to do one more *Medea* in a long line of *Medeas?* Work with François on something we had already explored fully, and then some? Throw cold water on his girlfriend and hope she'd melt like the witch in *The Wizard of Oz?*

"I have no idea what I want," I answered her honestly, surprised at how comfortable I was with such real uncertainty.

Abbie nodded. "Well, you'll figure it out."

"I better figure it out," I said. "I'm out of work, in debt, and in doubt."

"You left out the most important thing," Abbie said, picking up a calla lily to put in our cart.

"And what is that?"

"Free," she said happily. "You're absolutely free."

·

FIFTY-FIVE

*Z*ora and I left work on the house to Victor for the day and went over to the antiwar demonstration in West End. It was an over-cast morning and both of us were quiet on our way to the park. I don't know what I expected, but the crowd was pitiful. A few old radicals, some students, a few curious bystanders, and a homeless man whose rest we were disturbing. We were gathering in the community park on Abernathy, but nobody seemed to be in charge. There was a small stage set up with a podium and a microphone, but no one had approached it, even to play roadie and say "test, test," to see if it was working. Every-body was kind of standing around waiting for some more people to show up and feeling a little foolish for being there.

I felt a little silly myself. Where were all the throngs of angry, politi-cized people, come to do battle with their government and emerge righteously victorious? These folks looked frail and tentative. There was none of the energy of the antiwar demonstrations in Paris and Amsterdam. There was none of the feeling here that our presence as citizens could really affect anything our government did one way or another.

"They should have tried to flash it," Zora said, breaking into my woolgathering.

"What?"

"Where you put it on the Net that we're all going to gather at a cer-tain time and place and do a certain thing and then go home."

"You call that flashing?" I said. My use of the word ran more to-ward seedy men in trench coats, opening them to treat innocent passersby to a glimpse of the family jewels.

"Not flashing," she said, smiling as she always did at my continuing ignorance when it came to all things Internet. "Flash mobs. It's just something people were doing for a while. They would all show up at a store or something and just do something together."

"Something like what?" I said, watching the homeless man gathering up his things, muttering darkly about us all being a bunch of communists.

"I don't know. Clap their hands, sing something. They went to a toy store in New York and everybody gathered in front of this big elephant they had and bowed down to it."

"That's crazy."

Zora shrugged. "It wouldn't have to be for something silly. People could come together for something like this. Something good."

I nodded. "Well, then I'm sorry they didn't do it, too."

When Abbie and Aretha pulled up together in the truck, they saw us immediately in the small group and waved. Zora and I waved back as they got out and started in our direction. Aretha had on her overalls and work boots. Abbie was wearing an orange jacket and purple pants. She had on turquoise Chinese shoes with pink roses embroidered on the toes. In the middle of more conservatively dressed people, she looked like a tropical bird that had just flown in to jazz up the proceedings.

"Who's in charge?" she said, after we all hugged our greetings and she had a chance to look around. Four or five more women arrived, two carrying signs that said WAR IS NOT THE ANSWER.

"You are," I said, only half kidding. "We've been waiting for you."

"No problem," she said, without a moment's hesitation and headed for the stage, which was really just a slightly elevated platform.

Zora reached into her bag for her technology and started taping.

Abbie walked up to the mike and smiled at the valiant few. "Good morning," she said. "I'm Abbie Allen Browning. I am an American citizen and I am against all the wars that are currently being waged in my name around the world."

There was scattered applause. Aretha and I clapped loudly and Aretha even whistled like people do at baseball games. I smiled to myself. Abbie was working her citizenship show again.

"I am a peace activist," Abbie said. "That means I am always active for peace. As a citizen of a country at war, I am determined to show by my words and my actions that I do not support violence as a solution to human problems."

More scattered applause. Still sparse, but people were moving forward a little at a time. Abbie smiled encouragingly.

"So does anybody else want to say anything about why you're here?"

Everybody looked around like kids do when the teacher asks a question about an assignment nobody's read. I looked around, too, but Aretha was already moving to the microphone. Abbie smiled at her and stepped aside. Aretha smiled back and faced her fellow citizens.

"I'm Aretha Hargrove and I'm here because my daughter Joyce Ann is only four and I want to make a better world for her to grow up in."

Aretha moved over next to Abbie and they both looked at me. I headed for the mike.

"I'm Josephine Evans and I'm here because people in other countries need to know that not all Americans support the war."

I stood there for a minute, wondering if there was something else I should say, but another woman was already heading for the mike, so I stepped aside.

"My name is Margaret Hudson," she said. "I'm here because my daughter is stationed in Iraq and nobody can explain to me what she's doing there other than getting shot at by a whole bunch of people she doesn't even know."

People were starting to line up at the foot of the stage. The impromptu testimonials were starting to draw a modest crowd. I looked at Abbie and she grinned at me.

"Be careful what you ask for," she whispered.

"My name is Harold Hoskins," said a man with dreadlocks and an old green army jacket. "I'm here because I was in Nam and this is the same damn thing all over again, 'scuse my French, ladies."

"Tell the truth, brother!" a man said from the front of the platform. "Tell the truth!"

As each person said why they were there, they joined the group of us standing with Abbie, nodding at each other like you do at Sunday-morning church services.

SEEN IT ALL AND DONE THE REST · 239

"My name is Tamara Williams and I'm here because my brother is in Afghanistan."

"My name is Edward Dennis and I'm here because we got no business over there in the first place."

"Excuse me," the woman behind me whispered as we applauded Mr. Dennis. "Don't you have a messed-up house on Martin Luther King?"

I turned to look into her face. "Yes," I said, wondering how she knew me.

"Well, I think it's great what you're doing," she said. "It's about time somebody took a stand. We watch you all the time."

"You do?"

She nodded. "Keep up the good work."

"Thanks," I said. "We will."

By the time we got to the end of the line of people who wanted to testify, there were almost fifty people on the stage and everybody was grinning like we had just marched over to the Pentagon and shaken our finger in some general's shocked face. I guess we hadn't done much if you measure the morning objectively. Gathered up a few people for an antiwar demonstration in a neighborhood where almost nobody seemed to notice. Nobody except those of us who showed up like the good citizens Abbie keeps telling us we have to be and spoke up for peace. In public. In the company of our neighbors. One by one until we all stood together. Stronger, even if just for that moment. A little stronger.

Zora was the last one in line, her technology still in hand. She swept it over the group and then stepped up to the mike.

"I'm Zora Evans," she said. "And I'm here because there's no place else I'd rather be."

FIFTY-SIX

•

"Miss Thing, the town is on fire!" Howard said. "I thought I said do nothing until you hear from me and now I get back from Paris to find all hell has broken loose."

"Good," I said. "They deserve it. Welcome back."

"Welcome back? Do you know what this means?"

"It means I told the truth and let the devil take hindmost."

"A charming saying from the old country," Howard said, "but hardly relevant. The board is furious about the story that fool wrote after he interviewed you."

"They're furious? I'm the one who should be furious. *Medea*, Howard? They're going to let her close with *Medea*?"

"Of course they're wrong, and trust me, there was no way it would have happened, before this! Now it will be a miracle if they don't set your things out on the street!"

"You're exaggerating."

"They are demanding an apology, Miss Thing. And right away!"

"An apology? For what?"

"Oh, maybe for calling them all a bunch of idiots who wouldn't know good theater if it bit them on the ass!"

"That's not what I said!"

"Then what did you say, sweetie? And make it good. I've got to do some serious damage control if we're going to pull this thing out. First thing you have to say is you're sorry!"

The idea was inconceivable. "I can't apologize, Howard. Everything I said was true."

He didn't say anything for a minute, and then he sighed. "I know that, and you know that, but truth ain't all there is to it, sweetie.

They're positioning you as the aging American diva who doesn't want to pass the baton to the new generation."

I winced. "An aging American diva?"

"I'm sorry, sweetie. It's a mean old world, but if you want this gig to support you, *and me*, in our old age, you gotta bend a little."

I didn't say anything.

"Are you sulking?"

"She told the man I had been too old for *Medea* for more than a decade," I said. "Don't I get to respond?"

"She would have told the man you had two heads if she thought it would get her a lead," Howard said. "And of course you get to respond, sweetie pie, every time you set foot on that stage and not a moment before."

"I just don't understand why she had to say all that. She made me sound like a washed-up hag."

"She made herself sound like an ungrateful wretch," he said. "But that's just the way of it. Remember us when we were thirty?"

"We were dedicated idealists," I said. "We wanted a theater that would change people's lives so they would change the world!"

"We were ruthless little fiends," Howard said, "who wanted nothing more than a chance to holler our unappreciated genius at the moon."

He was right, of course, but I wasn't that way anymore. *I didn't deserve this.*

"I miss you so much," I said. "Am I ever going to get to come home?"

"I miss you, too. Don't worry. I'll figure out something. Just don't do any more interviews, okay?"

"I still want that, you know?"

"Want what, sweetie?"

"That howling at the moon thing."

"And you shall have it," he said soothingly. "I promise."

"I believe you," I said, because he expected me to, but the truth was, I was beginning to have my doubts.

"Except for one thing."

"What's that?" I said.

"Your genius will never be unappreciated. You are still, and always will be, a star."

•

FIFTY-SEVEN

*B*etty Causey called to tell me that Daisy Turner, one of her neigh-bors, got robbed last night. They cut her alarm and came through an unlocked back window. They didn't have to break anything to get in, so the woman slept through the whole thing. She didn't even know she'd been robbed until she got up this morning and realized her television set was gone. The one in her bedroom. The thought that somebody had been in her room scared Daisy so badly she fainted and hit her head on her dresser. Now she was staying at Betty's, scared to go home, vowing to take whatever she could get for what she was now calling "that little broke-up piece of house" and go move in with her daughter.

Although Betty said that wasn't likely since they had never gotten along very well, and probably weren't going to start now, the point was everybody was scared, and Betty thought I ought to know. I thanked her and she told me there was one more thing she wanted to tell me. Greer Woodruff had called Daisy yesterday to repeat her offer to buy the house. Daisy had refused and gone to bed early, but Betty didn't think it was a coincidence that the break-in had happened later the same night, and what did I think? I told Betty I didn't believe in coin-cidence. She said she didn't either.

This was not working out like it was supposed to at all. I only came here to check on Zora and wait out the storm back home. After that, my round-trip ticket was supposed to take me back to my real life. The one I made up from scratch and nurtured and shaped and poked and polished until it looked just like me. And now, here I was, working like a young slave, paying a homeless guy to live at my house so he could earn his way back into his mama's heart, and trying to help save a neighborhood that couldn't be saved.

The real problem was none of this stuff was going to help us attract any buyers. People weren't watching us on the Internet because they wanted to live here. They were watching us because they were glad they didn't.

•

FIFTY-EIGHT

*Z*ora tried to talk me out of it, but I knew Greer Woodruff was the kind of woman who probably liked to get an early start, so I drove over to her office at seven thirty. I pulled into the almost empty parking lot and went upstairs. The glass door was still locked, so I pounded on it as hard as I could without breaking it, to let her know she had company.

Greer Woodruff emerged from her inner sanctum with a small frown to let whoever was knocking at her door with such determination know that she did not appreciate being disturbed. When she saw me, the frown got bigger.

"Ms. Evans," she said, opening the door a little, but not inviting me inside. "You're out early."

"They know it's you," I said.

"I'm sure I don't know what you're talking about."

"I'm sure you do." I stepped into the office even though she didn't want to step aside to let me pass, content to let me stand in the hallway and plead my case. "And this is where it's going to stop."

"Do you want to tell me what you are raving about?"

"I'm not raving," I said. "I'm talking about terrorizing old women in their beds."

"As you recall, I told you there were other people interested in those properties. Perhaps you ought to take your complaint up with them."

"I'd be glad to," I said. "Who are we talking about?"

She narrowed her eyes slightly and I could see her debating how she wanted to play this. "You know I had pretty much convinced everybody to sell before you got here, and now, all of a sudden, people are canceling contracts and having second thoughts."

"Second thoughts? None of these women wanted to sell their houses any more than I did."

"That's their choice," she said.

"Then why don't you let them make it? There must be other properties your client could buy. This city is full of vacant houses."

She smiled her non-smile. "But that would be a different deal that would in no way benefit me or my company."

There was not a shred of compassion in her voice. "Is that all that matters to you?"

Her face was hard and her tone was cold. "The thing about you is that you're used to lots of options. Lots of offers to do what you want to do. That's not my experience. I've had to make my own luck. Opportunities like this don't come along often at our age."

If she thought we could bond on the basis of our proximity to the golden years, she was as wrong as she could be.

"This is the deal that will secure my future and the future of my company. The one that makes up for all those years when the boys wouldn't let me pull up a chair at the table. When they made their deals on the golf course and expected me to be a minor partner whenever they decided to throw me a crumb."

This was a woman with a lot of axes to grind. It was clear that our little houses were having to bear the weight of a lot of other stuff that didn't have anything to do with us or our properties.

"This is the deal that will guarantee that I'm not one of those broke old ladies who lived longer than they were supposed to and don't have anyplace to go to come in out of the rain," she said. "It can do the same thing for you."

"I'm not broke and I'm not old," I said.

She smiled as if to say *not yet.* "At this point, I am prepared to offer you considerably more than our initial discussions might have indicated."

Her partners must really be leaning on her. "How much more?"

"Fifty thousand dollars."

The irony of it was that if she had made the same offer the first time I came into her office, I would have taken it, grabbed Zora, and headed back to Amsterdam in style. But there was no way to take it now, even if she had offered a hundred thousand. She had made herself the villain of this story we were telling. My character was the *shero*. That meant I could never, ever make a deal with the devil. Even a bad script would never make a mistake like that.

"I don't care how much you offer me," I said. "Nobody is going to run me off."

Jesus! I sounded like a Hollywood western, but it felt good. It felt real good to say it that way.

"If I want to sell it, I will. If I want to live on it, I will. If I want to roam the world just because I can, I will, but as long as my name is on the deed, that house and that garden belong to me and nobody is going to run me off," I said, heading back out into the hallway and punching the button for the elevator. "Not even you."

She just watched me through the glass as the doors hissed closed behind me. Walking out to the parking lot, I was exhilarated. I had practically told her to get off my land by sundown. I was just sorry Zora wasn't here to get it on video. John Wayne would have been so proud.

FIFTY-NINE

·

*L*ate that night, after our swim when we were sitting beside the pool, wrapped up in our robes, reviewing the day, Zora made a great suggestion.

"You know it's fine to go shake your fist in Greer Woodruff's face . . ."

"I didn't shake anything in her face."

Zora looked at me. "Okay. It's fine to *verbally* shake your fist in her face, but that's not going to do much for those old women."

"Daisy filed a police report."

"I know," Zora said, "but I think they need to be a bigger part of the story."

"*Our* story?"

"It's their story, too," Zora said, turning on her side to face me. "Aren't you the one who said people don't just buy a house, they buy a neighborhood?"

Zora was getting as good as Abbie at casually tossing my own words back in my face. I always made sense when they quoted me, which was part of the frustration. How can you argue your own good sense just because you're moving through a moment of weakness when it's hard to keep an eye on the big picture?

"Aren't you the one who cringed at the idea of trying to save the whole neighborhood instead of just our little piece of it?"

Zora sat up and hugged her knees, gazing into the pool where the mermaid, as always, maintained her mysteriously aloof watch over the proceedings.

"That was before all this stuff started happening," she said slowly. "I don't think they can hold out if we don't help them."

"I'm not sure they can hold out even if we do," I said. "But what did you have in mind?"

"Well, we're still telling the same story, right? The good guys rescuing this corner from the bad guys? Like the westerns?"

"In a nutshell," I said.

"And isn't part of that story the townspeople rising up and deciding to fight back, even when the bad guys are scary?"

She had that right. There's no payoff in a story where the hero stands up and nobody stands up with him. Or in this case, with *her*.

"Go on."

"I think we should invite them to join us. I'll get some video of them describing what they've been through, telling us about their personal journeys from wherever they came from, to this very moment when everything they have is being threatened."

There was no denying that their story would add some depth and texture to our own. Betty was a great character, and nobody could hear Daisy talking about the break-in and not feel angry and protective, two emotions guaranteed to pull you into the story and refuse to let you go.

"What makes you think they'll let you tape them?"

She turned to me and smiled. "Don't worry, Mafeenie. I'll make them an offer they can't refuse."

SIXTY

•

*W*hat she offered them was a great meal in a beautiful setting and a free set of custom-made, sky-blue burglar bars for anybody who needed them, underwritten by Peachy, who told Abbie it was a damn shame that old black women had to barricade themselves in their houses to feel safe. Abbie, never a fan of burglar bars, had made peace with them at her D.C. house after the break-in, but she could only bear it if they were painted blue and installed with a prayer and the hope that they would keep in love as much as they kept out harm. When she told Peachy about the break-in at Daisy Turner's house and all the things Betty had been through, Peachy immediately told her to order the bars and have the company send him the bill. Abbie said she had never loved him more.

Having the women come to Louis and Amelia's house was another stroke of genius from Zora. Abbie and Aretha went to pick everybody up. When they walked in, Louie was in the kitchen making magic, Al Green was on the CD player, and there was a sign-up sheet so they could schedule their appointments to be measured for their baby-blue burglar bars. They accepted the wine I offered them and tried to get Louie to tell them what smelled so good. He politely but firmly shooed them out of the kitchen and told me he needed another twenty minutes to get everything on the table.

According to our plan, Zora suggested that we go down by the pool so she could show them the mermaid. A few minutes later, they had accepted her invitation to put their feet in it and sighed with pleasure and surprise at how warm it was. They sat on the blue tiled bench that allowed them to dangle their toes in the water without dampening their dresses, sipped their wine, and relaxed into a moment clearly constructed for their comfort.

"Must be nice," Thelma said.

"I'm going to miss it when the owner gets back," Zora said, making it clear that we were all visitors in this particular peaceful garden.

"So tell me some more about this story idea, Miss Zora," Betty said. "You gonna make us all movie stars?"

Zora smiled. "Something like that. Are you ready for it?"

"Not without some Botox," Thelma said. "I could use a little help in the close-ups."

"It's not that kind of movie," I said.

"What is it, then? A horror movie?" Daisy said, and they all laughed.

"No, it's nothing like that," Zora said. "Let me ask you something."

"As long as I can keep my feet in the water, you can ask me anything you want."

"How many of you own your houses?"

"We all do," Thelma said. "But they ain't worth the price to put 'em up for sale."

"But what if they were?" I said.

"What do you mean?" Daisy kicked her feet lightly back and forth in the blue water. The ripples made the mermaid's curls flutter delicately.

"I mean," I said slowly so they'd have time to wrap their minds around the idea I was putting forward, "I mean, if we fix up these houses, I believe we can get no less than one hundred thousand for each of them."

There was a collective gasp of disbelief.

"Maybe more," I said calmly.

"From who?" Thelma's voice was dripping doubt.

"From the people who are tired of being stuck in Atlanta traffic every day. The people who want to move back into town to raise their families."

"Those people never come down here looking for houses," Betty said. "Besides, I want to keep my house, not sell it."

"Yeah," Juanita said. "What's the point of all those fancy burglar bars if we're not going to hang around for a while?"

"Listen, ladies," I said, "I'm not going to kid you. I'm fixing my house up for sale and I want to sell it fast for the most money I can get.

The best way to do that is to make fixing it up part of a bigger adventure. Make the whole process a story that potential buyers can follow, then when I get ready to sell, they won't just be buying a house. They'll be buying a story. The same will be true when you get ready to sell yours, or even if you don't sell, the light we shine on this neighborhood will make it impossible for Greer to keep doing the things she's been doing."

They liked the sound of that, but they were still not sure what we were talking about. "So how you gonna get 'em down here to see the place?"

"We don't have to get them down here," Zora said. "We'll go where they already are."

"Where's that?" Daisy said.

"On the computer," Zora said, smiling.

Juanita snorted. "I don't even own a computer. None of us do, so how's that gonna help us?"

"You don't have to own a computer," Zora said. "I'll put everything we need on my computer and we'll send it out as part of the same story."

They thought about that for a minute, then Betty spoke for the group. "So what exactly are you asking us to do?"

"Nothing," Zora said quickly. "Just be a part of the story you're already moving through every day. Let me put you on video so people can see you, listen to you, get to know you, the same way people watch their other stories on TV."

"We ain't no actors," Juanita said, but she didn't sound nearly as skeptical.

"You don't have to act," Zora said calmly, just like she had when she talked me into this. "Say whatever you think and show me whatever you want me to see."

They looked at each other. "So it's sort of like a reality show?"

"Exactly," Zora said. "I'll be taping all the time and I'll use the best of what we get and erase the rest."

"You gonna let us see it first?" Betty said.

"Anytime you want," Zora said. "Don't worry. I'll make you look good."

They all smiled at that and swung their feet in the warm water.

"So what's the name of this story?" Thelma said.

"It was *Rescue on MLK*," I said. "*One Woman's Story*. But now it's all of us, so I think we can change it if you want."

"Change it to what?"

"Whatever you want," I said. "It can either be *Neighborhood Residents Join Beautification Efforts* or, *Neighborhood Residents Wish Meddling Actor Would Carry Her Ass Back to Amsterdam and Leave Them in Peace*."

They all laughed at that, including Abbie and Zora.

"How about let's try the first one," Betty said, looking around at the others to be sure she spoke for the group. "If it works out, maybe you can stay around for a while."

"If what Baptiste is cooking tastes as good as it smells, you can stay around as long as you want to," Thelma said.

"It tastes even better," I said.

"Well, don't make me take your word for it," Daisy said, standing up carefully and shaking the water off her bare feet gently. "Let's see what Louie is putting down."

So that was what we did.

SIXTY-ONE

•

$\mathcal{A}$t the end of the evening, after Louie had carefully divided and wrapped the leftovers, everybody piled in with Abbie or Aretha for the ride home. Victor took Betty's arm on the steps and she smiled gratefully and patted his hand. Zora went to review the video she'd just shot while we were eating, and Louie and I made short work of the cleanup. He wiped the pots down carefully and put each one in its place.

"This is a good kitchen," he said, nodding approvingly.

"Thank you for doing this," I said, untying the big apron I'd wrapped around me while I worked. "Everything went so well, for a minute there I thought you might have put something in their food."

"Neighbors are supposed to eat together," he said, smiling slowly. "Back home, we ate together every Friday. My mama would boil some shrimp and my aunt Lynette would bring the gumbo. There must have been a dozen cousins running around. Uncles, aunts, friends, there were so many of us. People who weren't even related would think it was a party and stop off, too."

When Louie talked about New Orleans it was always with a mixture of pleasure and pain. All of his memories had an artificial endpoint, stopped by a wall of water rolling toward his front porch in the dark. Even when he started a story that began in the sweetness of love and family and food, it would end in destruction and abandonment and madness and death.

"You really miss it, don't you?" I said, not because I didn't know the answer, but just to let him know he still had the floor if there was more to say.

"You remember my friend who told me not to come back to New Orleans?"

I nodded. That was the buddy who said the city had nothing to offer any more "broke niggas and stray dogs." Louie's attempts to get him to move to Atlanta had been unsuccessful. For him, there was no other city.

"He killed himself."

"Oh, Louie," I said, "I'm so sorry."

"He couldn't make peace with it," Louie said softly. "It was like every day when he got up, he still couldn't believe it. He kept figuring, he'd wake up one day and we'd be right there on that corner again, laughing and talking and drinking a beer."

"I'm so sorry," I said again, feeling helpless to comfort him, wishing Abbie were here to say something that would help him make sense of it. I wondered if I should call her.

"Are you okay?" I said.

He nodded. "His nephew called me last night. I'm going to rent a car and drive down tomorrow."

It dawned on me that he had gone through with all the cooking and presentation and fellowship that helped make the meal we'd just shared such a perfect moment for all of us without saying a word about his loss.

"You should have told me," I said, feeling guilty, like I should have known. "You didn't have to do all this today."

He looked at me a long time and I looked right back. The death of a friend is a profound moment of loss and vulnerability, but also of reaffirmation, celebration, and tenderness. I saw all that in Louie's sad eyes.

"Yes, I did," he said, "because that's the way we do it in New Orleans. We bury the dead, but we always feed the living."

SIXTY-TWO

*T*he letter came from François by FedEx:

> Dear Ms. Evans,
>
> Due to what the board perceives to be the aggressive and adversarial posture you have adopted toward The Human Theatre, both artists and administrative staff, and your unwillingness to answer questions from this body concerning your unwarranted actions and whereabouts, we can no longer extend to you the level of support you have enjoyed for many years as an important member of this company. We are therefore terminating your artistic residency stipend with the enclosed check and requesting that you instruct Howard Denmond to turn over all keys and information pertaining to the apartment you currently occupy by the end of the month. The delivery of the keys and your cashing of the enclosed check will constitute the formal end of the relationship between you and this theater company.

At the bottom of the page, François had scrawled: *Josephine, it didn't have to be this way.* He had enclosed a check for five hundred dollars.

SIXTY-THREE

·

$\mathcal{W}$e had Abbie's blessing of what I kept calling "the leaves and shoots" on the day of the full moon, just as she wanted, but we did it in the morning, so we couldn't actually see the moon. Our usual crew was going to be in attendance, and Peachy had driven up from Tybee especially for the occasion. Louie was in New Orleans, but I also invited Betty Causey and her neighbors, who had become part of our extended family. In addition to what we were doing at my place, we were also doing a little fixing up at theirs, and they were very grateful. Just knowing we were keeping a more conscious eye on them made them feel a little safer. Thelma had come over a couple of times to talk to Abbie about her garden, and Juanita was toying with the idea of planting some tomatoes in her own yard. Daisy was still staying at Betty's, but she was almost ready to go back home.

A half an hour before we were due to begin, they all walked over together, wearing their church dresses and Sunday shoes, since Zora had told them we were shooting video and everybody wanted to look their best. They settled into the chairs Victor and Peachy had dragged outside for them and sipped on lemonade that Zora brought from the soul food restaurant.

Abbie had on a purple tunic, a pair of bright green pants, and her trademark Chinese shoes. Aretha brought Joyce Ann who, as always, first made a beeline to the front door to check on her handprints. Zora, wearing a simple white dress and her hair pulled off her face with one of Aretha's red ribbons, was shooting everything. Victor, who was standing on the porch when we got there, giving everything the once-over, was, to my amazement, wearing a dark blue suit.

"Good morning," he said, looking a little embarrassed when I walked over to say hello. Under the suit he was wearing one of our crew T-shirts.

"Nice suit," I said. "You look great."

The pleasure on his face made me glad I hadn't teased him. I was wearing a pink dress I had borrowed from Abbie. It was too hot for turtlenecks and I was getting tired of all that black anyway. She also loaned me a beautiful pale gray shawl with mile-long fringe. I loved it.

"You look okay, too," which from Victor was high praise.

"Abbie said she was going to have something green showing by the end of the month," I said. "Looks like she knew what she was talking about."

"Miss Abbie has a green thumb and then some," he said.

Working with Abbie seemed to agree with him. No longer the angry squatter who had first confronted me about being an absentee landlord, Victor had become an integral part of our crew. After a month of seeing him almost every day, I still didn't know much about him, but I was beginning to consider him a friend.

"Can I ask you something?" he said.

"Sure," I said, wondering if anybody ever said no to that question, which would, of course, be an answer itself.

"Do you ever miss what you do in real life?"

I smiled at him. "Isn't this real life?"

"You know what I mean," he said. "The other part of it."

I thought about it, as much to give myself an honest answer as to give him one. "Sometimes," I said. "Not as much lately. I've been having too much fun playing in the dirt."

He nodded, smiling. "Yeah, me too."

"Can I ask you something?"

He hesitated long enough for me to want to take back the question, but I didn't.

"Go ahead." He said it almost like a challenge.

"What do you do in real life?" I said.

He ran his hands over his face, brushed a piece of imaginary lint off his blue lapel, and looked back at me. "In real life, I used to be a lawyer. I had a wife and a daughter and a house and an SUV. Then I started smoking crack and in two years, I smoked it all away. Every bit of it."

Abbie was walking Joyce Ann through the garden, pointing out the slim green shoots that were going to grow up to be seven-foot-tall sunflowers.

"My wife left me and took my daughter and when my mother put me out, I started staying up here with the other crackheads. I knew they were breaking into people's houses because they always had stuff to sell, but I wasn't doing that yet. I was doing day labor work, hanging with the Mexicans because I could speak a little Spanish, but then, one night, I heard them talking about how they were going to rob this old lady's house on Sunday while she was at church, and I realized they were talking about my mother. That's when I knew I had gone down as far as I needed to go."

Betty and her friends were talking to Zora and laughing into her camera like they weren't even aware of it. Victor looked over at them and then back to me.

"So I told them if anything happened to my mother's house I would slit their throats." He took a deep breath as if waiting for my permission to continue.

"Go on."

"They must have believed me because they stopped coming up here and everybody else did, too. I stayed around here to make sure and I got myself off that shit one day at a time. I would cross off every day that passed and then the next one and the next one. After a while, I didn't want it anymore, but my old life was gone and I knew it wasn't coming back, even if I wanted it to. So I just kept working with the Mexicans and waited to see what would happen next. That's when you got here."

He smiled at me then and I smiled back. That story is the reason terms like "the homeless" don't mean anything. All the stuff that ends up with somebody on the street happens one person at a time.

"You weren't much of a welcoming committee."

"At first I thought you weren't serious," he said. "I thought it was probably just a bunch of bullshit."

Zora's almost-a-beau had just arrived, also dressed in white and carrying a single yellow rose. She smiled and turned the camera in his direction. He waved and the old ladies rolled their eyes at Zora and nodded their approval.

"What do you think now?"

He looked at me and grinned. "Well, working with you got my mom to give me one of my old suits back, so I'd say, so far, so good."

"Good enough," I said, laughing and turning to ask Abbie when we were going to get this show on the road. Victor's story made me want to hug him, but I knew better. We weren't quite there yet, but so far, so good.

•

SIXTY-FOUR

The ceremony was nothing like I had been afraid it would be. It was more like what Abbie did at the peace demonstration. She gave a little informative statement and then she invited everybody to do the same. It was just our usual crew, plus Betty and company and Peachy, who wasn't going to miss it even if he did have to close the restaurant for two days, and Zora's friend, who seemed like a genuinely nice guy.

Abbie didn't need a mike in such a small space so we all sort of gathered around the edges of the garden and grinned at one another, suddenly shy in the face of our accomplishments and our hopes.

"Good morning," Abbie said, and we all answered her like good little children.

"Good morning."

"*Great* morning," said Peachy, grinning at Abbie.

"Yes," Abbie said. "It is a *great* morning because we are here to dedicate a garden for peace, right here on the corner of Martin Luther King Drive and Wiley Street."

"Amen," said Betty Causey, and her friends nodded their heads. "Amen."

"We also dedicate this first effort to the mother of Josephine Evans, Doris Evans, who first looked at this yard, imagined a garden, and then made one."

"Amen," said Peachy, with a wink and a nod in my direction.

"Amen," said Victor, obviously feeling ministerial in his blue suit.

"Now I'm not here to make a speech," Abbie said, like she had at the park. "I just want to thank Josephine for what she's doing on this corner."

"What we're doing," I said.

Abbie smiled. "That's right. Because this isn't just a little piece of garden, or a little patch of dirt that doesn't mean anything to anybody. This garden is part of a street and this street is part of a community where Miss Betty can take an evening stroll with Victor and Miss Thelma can braid her grandbaby's hair on the front porch and me and Peachy can sit on Jo's back steps and eat some watermelon he brought from the island while Zora tells us what the rest of the century's going to look like and Joyce Ann puts her handprint on every door she can find."

Hearing her name, Joyce Ann grinned at Abbie. "For good luck," she whispered loudly in case Abbie had forgotten.

"Yes, baby, for good luck and good friends and the blessings of home," Abbie said. "Because this garden is only the first one. There should be gardens like this on every street and boulevard and byway in this country that carries the name of Martin Luther King, Jr., because we owe him that much."

She stopped and looked at all of us. I could see that she was getting a little emotional.

"Take your time, baby," Peachy said. "Tell the truth to the people."

Abbie took a deep breath. "Every time somebody puts in a garden, it casts a vote for peace. It reaffirms a faith in a future where things can grow and bloom and remind us of who we really are and who we can be." She paused again and then grinned at Zora's camera. "Okay. That's enough talking. This is garden number one. *Where is number two?*"

SIXTY-FIVE

*D*riving home later, Zora seemed a little distracted.

"I thought that went well," I said. "Didn't you?"

"I thought it went great. I just hope whoever buys this place knows how to take care of a garden."

"Me too."

"Maybe they'll hire Victor to do it."

"Maybe."

She turned off MLK onto Ashby Street and headed toward West End. There was a narrow, trash-strewn vacant lot across from the Mc-Donald's Express. I wondered how long it would take Abbie to start making inquiries about its ownership. She was the one who had told me Blue Hamilton wasn't interested in expanding his operation, but if he wasn't careful, by the time he got back from Trinidad, Abbie would have strung together an archipelago of new gardens, connecting West End to the newly forming Martin Luther King Jr. Peace Garden District.

"Couldn't we put that in the contract?" Zora said. "That they have to keep him on as the gardener?"

"I don't think you can require that kind of stuff unless you're selling one of those English country manors where the whole staff of loyal servants comes with it."

Victor wasn't exactly like those everything-by-the-book butlers that Anthony Hopkins can play better than any actor alive, but I knew what she was getting at. I think that was the first time we realized we were going to miss this place once we cashed in and headed back out into the world. Neither one of us said it out loud, but we both knew it. We just didn't know what to do about it. Not yet, anyway.

"I guess you're right," she said. "It's just pretty amazing to watch it grow, isn't it?"

"Yes, it is."

"People love the scenes where you and Abbie are in the garden with Louie talking about the herbs."

That startled me. I didn't remember Zora videotaping any of that extended conversation about whether we should grow basil and sage or add some rosemary and maybe a half a row of hot peppers. Mostly they talked and I listened and wandered up and down the rows where Victor and Abbie had already planted the sunflowers and the roses and a variety of tomatoes whose names sometimes sounded a little like porn star monikers to me: Juicy Jumbos, Sweet Reds, Big Beefy.

Of course, I didn't say that to Abbie in front of Louie. If you're not looking for any sexual involvement, it's usually better not to introduce the topic of pornography into the proceedings. Good thing I didn't. Zora, and her stealth camera would have captured it for all the world to see and while my Amsterdam audience is pretty much unshockable, I didn't want to offend any potential peace gardeners.

"Louie said as soon as there's enough of anything to cook it or add it to something, he will make a big pot of something to celebrate," she said.

I laughed. "Those plants aren't hardly out of the ground yet. It's going to be a while."

"Worth the wait," she said, turning onto our quiet street.

The thing was we both knew there was no chance we were leaving until those sunflowers came up. We needed what the Juicy Jumbo crowd calls "the money shot." The one that makes your investment of time and feeling worth the wait. Once the flowers were in bloom, our tomatoes were big enough to eat, and Louie's herbs and peppers were ready to grace his gumbo, then we'd get the footage we needed to generate the sale we were looking for. Until then, Victor wasn't going anywhere, and neither were we.

·

SIXTY-SIX

The next day at the grocery store, a woman looked up from the seafood counter and asked me if I didn't have a house on Martin Luther King. When I said I did, she hugged me like we were long-lost pals.

"Oh, my God," she said. "I watch your videos all the time." As if to prove it, she stepped back and adopted a more serious tone. "*Rescue on MLK: One Woman's Story.* That's it, right?"

"That's it," I said. "I'm glad you like it."

"Like it? We love it! We look at it every day before we do a lick of work. My boss tried to get mad, now we got her watching it, too."

I laughed with her. Zora kept trying to tell me how popular the story was with people, and I was beginning to think she was right. I gave the woman four autographs: one for her, one for each of her friends, and one for the boss.

"This should get me a raise," she said, posing beside me for a shot on her cellphone before she hugged me again and moved off down the produce aisle.

The other people in the store were giving me sidelong glances, trying to figure out who I was that I had provoked such a reaction. I smiled at them, but offered no explanation. Now this was more like it. This was what I was used to. Recognition and approval. I could learn to live with this. The funny thing was, even though I was still counting on Howard to pave the way back to Amsterdam, it was becoming less and less urgent that things work out there. I was feeling more at home here every day. Maybe Abbie was right about everybody being rooted somewhere.

When I got home and told Zora what had happened, she grinned at me. "I told you, didn't I? You're a star, Mafeenie. I wish you'd let me show you the footage."

"Wait until we're done," I said. "Once we've sold the house and signed off the airwaves, you can show me everything."

"You promise?"

"I promise."

"Mafeenie?"

"Yes?"

"Don't say 'airwaves.'"

SIXTY-SEVEN

•

*L*ouie had been gone almost a week and a part of my brain was spending lots of time trying to imagine where he was and what he was doing. Abbie said Peachy hadn't heard from him either, but she wasn't worried.

"I think he went to say his goodbyes," she said when I asked her why. "That always takes more time than you think it will."

Peachy was here for the weekend and Abbie was coming by to pick me up for dinner at a new place they wanted to try. I had just zipped up my dress and chosen a pair of turquoise earrings a poet friend of mine made for me as part of his second career as a jewelry designer when the doorbell rang. I glanced at the clock and smiled to myself. Twenty minutes early. They must be starved. I grabbed my blue shawl and headed downstairs. Black was still my mainstay, but hanging around Abbie sometimes made black seem so unnecessary.

When I opened the door, I was ready to start signifying about island Negroes who can't tell time without a tide clock, but it was Louie. He had on a white shirt, as always, but no tie, brown pants, and a sport coat. He was carrying a small plastic leftover container and looking apologetic.

"I'm sorry," he said. "This is kind of spur of the moment, I guess. I should have called you, but I don't have the number with me and I haven't called it enough to remember it, so . . . here I am."

"Welcome back," I said, relieved that he didn't look any the worse for wear. His eyes didn't look as sad as I remembered, or was that wishful thinking?

"Come in, come in," I said. "When did you get back?"

"Just this minute," he said. "I was on my way back to my place, but I wanted to thank you."

"Thank me for what?" I said, surprised.

"For helping me say goodbye."

He didn't know he was quoting Abbie exactly, but I did. I sat down on the couch. He took a chair and gently put the plastic container down on the coffee table. I didn't ask him what it was. When the story required it, he would tell me.

"You're welcome," I said. "Is that what you were doing?"

He nodded. "Not just to Catfish, he was ready to go, but to all the stuff I had down there that made it home. To all the stuff I kept thinking in the back of my mind that I didn't have to let go because it was all coming back, sooner or later, just like it was before." His hands gently squared up the container like it hadn't been placed perfectly before him the first time. "My whole family living on the same street or just around the corner from each other. Living upstairs from my place and watching people start lining up every night before we even open because they know whatever I'm cooking is the best they ever had. Mardi Gras . . ."

He looked at me and sort of shook his head and smiled a little. "We had some good times, me and Catfish and Eddie and Arno. Now all of them are gone but me, and I don't care what anybody says, they'd be alive today if everything had stayed the way it was before the water wiped it all away one time for good."

He shrugged and sat back. "But it didn't stay that way. All that stuff that used to mean home to me isn't even there anymore. I went over to where my house used to be, my restaurant, my neighbors, the house I was born in, and I got out of that rented Chevrolet, and I stood there trying to see it like it used to be, but I couldn't. It was what it was, and it is what it is, and that's when I started thinking about your place."

That wasn't what I was expecting. He picked up the plastic container again and balanced it on his knee. "The duplex?"

He nodded. "I started thinking about the garden we're putting in over there and about how nice it's going to be once you get it all fixed up the way you want it. About how much I'm looking forward to picking those herbs and making us all a pot of something we can eat together."

For Louie, all the significant passages are marked by the cooking and eating of favorite dishes in the company of people you love. "We're already looking forward to it," I said.

"Me too," he said. "That's how I realized I wasn't thinking about what *was* anymore. I was thinking about what was *next*. I was looking at my past, but I was thinking about my future."

He stopped and looked down, a little embarrassed at having his feelings so close to the surface where I might be able to see them. "I'm not saying it right."

"You're saying it just fine."

He looked up to see if I meant it. Of course I did.

"What I mean is, I'm never gonna let New Orleans go, it's in me. In *here*." He tapped his heart like Abbie had done to show me where she lived. "But I can't keep one foot there and one foot wherever I happen to be standing."

What he was saying made perfect sense to me. I'd been straddling my old life and this new one ever since I got here.

"No," I said, "you can't. That never works."

"You got that right," he said. "So now I need to ask you a favor."

"Of course."

That's when he popped the top on the plastic container and extended it lovingly like a forkful of key lime pie to share with a dining partner who ordered the flan.

"Dirt?" I said, not so much disappointed as intrigued.

He nodded. "I took it up from where my garden used to be." He reached in and sifted a handful like cornmeal before you put the eggs and the buttermilk in and stir gently. "It was a good-size plot, too, but I don't see myself growing there again anytime soon, so . . ."

He picked up another handful of dirt and let it fall through his fingers. I was surprised at how black and rich it looked. He didn't have to say any more. I knew exactly what he wanted. I was big on rituals and this was a perfect opportunity for one.

"Do you want me to scatter the dirt in our new garden?"

When he looked up at me, his eyes were still sad, but they were peaceful. "If it's okay with you, and with Abbie, I surely would."

"Then that's what we'll do."

"And you don't have to worry," he said quickly. "I had it tested, you know, because of all the bad water standing around, but it's clean. They even irradiated it just to be sure."

"I think that would be wonderful," I said. "It sort of ties everything together."

"Good," he said, popping the cover back into place and sliding the New Orleans dirt over to me. "That's real good. Will you hold on to this until I have a chance to talk to Abbie about it?"

As soon as he said her name, the bell rang and I could hear laughter on the porch.

"Here's your chance," I said. "That's her and Peachy right now."

"Perfect," Louie said, smiling. "I need to talk to him, too."

That could mean only one thing. I stopped on my way to the door. "Are you considering his offer seriously this time?"

"I've been considering it," he said. "Sometimes it just takes a minute to see when something good is staring you in the face and nothin' but fear is keepin' you from it."

We looked at each other for a minute and I had the unmistakable impression that Louie was talking about more than a move to Tybee Island.

The bell rang again and Louie grinned at me. "That Negro has no sense of timing whatsoever."

I laughed and opened the door. My friends were laughing, too. Abbie shaking her head and blushing like a bride.

"You ought to quit," she was saying.

"No chance of that, Sweet Thing," he said. "I am in it to win it!"

"Well, your luck is holding," I said, stepping aside so they could see Louie standing behind me. "Look who's back."

"Louie!" Abbie said, leaving Peachy's side to give Louie a welcome-home embrace and a smile of real pleasure at his return.

Peachy and Louie made no move toward each other, but both were obviously pleased to be unexpectedly in each other's company.

"I thought you had put us down, brother," Peachy said, feigning surprise.

"You know I had to come back."

"Why is that?"

"Because," Louie said, "I hear you got a little old piece of restaurant that needs a chef."

Peachy's eyes lit up as a grin spread slowly across his face with the realization that he was finally going to get what he wanted, but he shook his head.

"You're late, man. I just hired a stubborn old fool who thinks he's the only person who knows what to put in a gumbo pot."

Louie looked at Peachy and then he grinned back all the way up to and including his big brown eyes. "If his name ain't Louie Baptiste, he's a damn lie!"

They both laughed and Peachy reached out and grabbed Louie in one of those big backslapping hugs that men do because they have a hard time just hugging and holding on. Abbie and I, who had no such problem, hugged and held on tight, feeling the round softness of each other and loving the sweetness of these men we were just beginning to know.

SIXTY-EIGHT

•

*P*eachy had to go back to Tybee early in the morning, and Louie was going with him. Abbie said we'd wait until he came back to add the dirt he'd brought from New Orleans to the peace garden. That made sense to me. He'd probably want to say something. Or *cook* something.

Later that day, Abbie transferred the dirt from the container to a lovely ceramic bowl that she set on the mantelpiece in the dining room, which had become the house's common space. She lit a few candles and even laid a yellow silk flower nearby like an offering. I had been working outside and when I came in, I smelled the candles first. *Patchouli.*

Abbie was an inveterate altar maker. Any available space would, if left unattended, begin to sprout candles, incense, seashells, small photographs, and silk flowers. She was a firm believer in the power of positive spirits to guard the perimeters and after a while, I got used to it. Between the altars and the good-luck handprints on the front door, I told Abbie we were probably as protected as we could be, considering.

"Considering what?" Abbie said, coming up to stand beside me as I contemplated her latest handiwork.

"Considering the random nature of bad luck and the presence of true evil in the universe."

She looked at me. "I withdraw the question."

I laughed. "I'm sorry. I didn't mean to sound so gloomy. All I really meant was I'm glad Louie's back."

She nodded. "Much better. See how easy that was?"

"Easy as pie." And it was.

Two days later, the duplex burned to the ground.

SIXTY-NINE

•

I had already cried at the heap of rubble where all our hard work had been, comforted Victor who had been visiting his mother when he saw the flames and burned his arms badly trying to put them out himself, apologized to my mother's spirit for whatever I had done to bring this on, and worried myself into a forty-eight-hour headache from hell when the fire investigator showed up. In real life, the people who come to call when something really awful happens to your property are as matter-of-fact as the doctors who bring you the bad news about your body. They don't weep for your misfortunes. They list your options and dismiss your theories, not necessarily in that order. The weary-looking man from the fire department came by to tell me that their initial investigation pointed toward faulty wiring and looked surprised to hear me say that I thought Greer Woodruff might be involved.

"Ms. Evans," he said, "I understand your frustration, but you have no proof of arson, much less anything that points to Ms. Woodruff."

"She has been pressuring people around here to sell their houses."

"She's in the real estate business."

"When they won't sell, there are burglaries or trash dumping or vandalism. This is not the first fire, either. There have been others."

He flipped through his folder, reviewing the facts. "As I understand it, those fires were set by squatters on the property. Reports were always filed while you were away." He looked up. "You were absent from this property for quite a while, is that correct?"

He said it like I had left a puppy in the middle of the road. "It was a rental property. Ms. Woodruff's company was responsible for the management."

"I see," he said.

"The point is," I said, "I would like to accuse Greer Woodruff of arson."

It sounded like a reasonable request, but he stood up and handed me my copy of his report.

"Ms. Evans, this is America. It's not illegal to do business. This form will clear you for any insurance claim. If you want to accuse people of crimes, call the police department, but everything I found points to faulty wiring."

There was nothing else to say, so Zora walked him to the door and came back.

"So," she said, sitting down across the kitchen table from me, sipping her cold coffee. "What do you want to do?"

I looked at her and there was no option but the plain, unvarnished truth. "I think, Munchkin, that it might be time to throw in the towel and let these people have their corner," I said. "The insurance and whatever Greer's still offering for the land will pay for your school or take you to Europe if that's what you want."

"What are you going to do?"

"I don't know," I said. "I got run out of Amsterdam for being an American at war and now I'm being run off this corner for being an American at peace."

"It's still a war," she said.

That statement was no comfort to a woman whose only tangible asset had just burned to the ground.

"You're right," I said. "So what is the free woman's role in wartime?"

"Well, what if something happened so we didn't have to sell the house at all?"

"There is no house, remember?"

"I remember, but couldn't we build another one?"

She wasn't making any sense. "Listen, darlin', this whole thing was about *selling* a house, not building one. This story is over. We're going somewhere we can be the women we were born to be."

"Where's that, Mafeenie?" Her voice was very quiet.

I looked at her, unsure of what she was trying to say. "What's wrong, darlin'? What's the matter?"

She stood up and walked over to the window. "When we first started working on the house, I couldn't wait to get everything done so we could sell it and get on up out of here. I hated Atlanta, hated that so many people knew me, or thought they did. Every time I went out, I was worried somebody was going to take my picture and sell it to *Dig It!* or put it on YouTube. My life felt like one big pile of shit and I didn't have a clue what to do about it."

Watching her talking about those days, I realized how far she'd come in just a couple of months. Her face had filled out with the weight she'd gained back, her skin was glowing, and her eyes had their old sparkle again. She turned back to me.

"But I don't really think that much about leaving anymore. It all feels different. Like maybe there's a bigger reason why we're doing this." She stopped trying to find the right words.

"I'm listening," I said. "Go on."

She smiled and took my hand, holding it lightly. "It's just that, when people see me now, they don't care about all that stuff that happened last year. They want to ask me about the house, or if they can start a garden at their church, or do we need somebody to help with the painting, and I want them to help. I want them to feel like if we can do it, they can do it, too. It's not even about selling it to the highest bidder anymore. It's more about all of us working together, about seeing the house go from what it was, to what it could be, to see those sunflowers Abbie planted coming up in Great-gram's garden."

She squeezed my hand a little tighter. "I guess what I'm trying to say is, I don't even care if we go to Amsterdam anymore. Just doing what we did, refusing to leave just because somebody told us to . . . we're already free." She grinned at me and I grinned back. "Isn't that really what you came all this way to tell me? That I'm already free?"

"Yes," I said, claiming the advice as my own immediately. "Exactly."

When I hugged her, it felt so good, we just stood there for a minute, holding on to each other for dear life.

"And I think Miss Abbie's right about the gardens, too," Zora said when I finally released her. "Every time somebody plants one, they'll feel more peaceful just for doing it, and if we have enough of them, it will change people's lives and that can change the energy on the planet, and . . ." She stopped, suddenly hearing her mother's voice in her mouth as clearly as I did.

"Attack of the sixties," she said, laughing. "So sue me. You and Mom are to blame for this insane optimism."

"It looks good on you," I said, remembering how sad and strange she'd been when I first got here, loving how strong and happy she was now.

"It looks good on you, too."

"So, it's your inheritance," I said. "What do you want to do?"

"You said it doesn't count as free if you let them run you off."

"That's right."

She grinned at me again. "Then let's build a house."

SEVENTY

·

*T*here wasn't much we could do on the site until we finished the basic demolition of the burned house. Our crew of amateurs couldn't handle that, so Aretha got some guys from West End to tackle it. It would take about a week. In the meantime, Zora had been responding to all the attention we'd been getting, and Abbie had been trying to talk me into a tour. The day she first suggested it, I thought I had been invited over for tea and sympathy.

"I'm sorry about the garden," I said, wandering around her kitchen while she adjusted the flame under the kettle. Whoever had burned the place had taken a few minutes to run through the garden and kick up all the things that were growing.

She shrugged and turned on the flame under that bright blue kettle. "It'll grow back. That's why gardens make such wonderful symbols. They have all the great lessons present in every cycle. If they grow up beautiful, bug free, and bountiful, you can tell folks that nature is a generous host and to count their blessings. If there's drought or blight, you can tell them the universe is a cruel and arbitrary place and they better get right with God."

Abbie was very pragmatic for a visionary.

"What will you tell them this time?"

She handed me the honey. "That when we replant, we'll probably put some Roma tomatoes in there with the Sweet One Hundreds. That some of the sunflowers survived and they'll be back in no time. Louie's putting in some herbs this afternoon."

Her calm willingness to get on with it was typical of her. She often said there were only two questions worth considering: what is and what is next. I smiled as she got out our cups. "You don't have to be so wise all the time."

"Yes, I do. That's my job, remember? It's the trade-off for not being twenty-five anymore."

"Do you remember twenty-five?" I said. "It seems like another lifetime."

"It was," she said, dropping a mint tea bag in each of our cups.

"You got that right," I said. "It's the life we used to have before we realized that in every setting, we're the oldest women in the room."

She nodded. "The problem is, people have really weird ideas about that old woman. About what she needs and thinks and feels, but the truth is, they don't know any more about any of it than we do, because it's all new again, just like when our breasts came out and our periods started."

"Seems like we got here faster than I thought we would."

"And not a moment too soon," she said, laughing in a way that made her look about fourteen years old. "This is when it really starts to get interesting."

Abbie had one of those faces that has spent a lot of time laughing, even if sometimes it was just to keep from crying.

"I'm glad you and Zora decided to hold on to the house," she said, pouring the hot water into our cups and replacing the kettle on the stove. There's something about the whole ritual of making tea, even just cups of tea, that is soothing. Abbie had it down, and I felt myself relax into the warmth of her kitchen and her spirit.

"Me, too, although I have no idea where we're going to get the money to rebuild anything."

Abbie sat down across from me. Behind her head the big map of the United States on the wall was a fitting backdrop for what was coming next, even though I didn't know it yet.

"When you first came back," she said, "I knew we had some work to do together. The house and the garden were just the way to get it started."

"What kind of work are you talking about?"

She grinned at me. "The same kind we've been doing for forty years. Trying to survive our own adventures so we can talk about them later."

"Nice work if you can get it," I said, laughing at her description of our lives. "We've seen it all and done the rest."

She laughed, too. "That's where you're wrong."

"And why is that, my visionary friend?" I said, sipping my tea.

"Because you've never been to Amarillo."

"Amarillo, Texas?"

"Don't say it like that," she said. "It's not the end of the world. See?" She turned to the map behind her, pointed to a spot in the middle of the Texas panhandle, and smiled affectionately like you might if you were talking about your hometown. But Abbie is from D.C., which is a long way, in every way, from the Lone Star State.

"It's close enough," I said.

"You can say what you want," she said. "But it's the place where I finally got it."

"Got what?"

"The secret of life."

Even from Abbie, this was a lot to swallow. "In Amarillo?"

She laughed again. "Deep in the heart of Texas."

"I'm sorry," I said. "I just thought people usually had spiritual awakenings in places with names like Kathmandu and Machu Picchu."

"There is no specific place, Jo. That's part of the mystery of it. You just have to keep moving around until you feel it."

We were deep in the Abbie zone now, but I was determined to figure out what the hell she was talking about.

"Until I feel what?"

"Connected."

The idea of my patchouli-smelling friend finding a cosmic connection in the middle of cowboy country was so far-fetched I thought she might be kidding, but she was dead serious sitting there, smiling serenely with Amarillo hovering behind her head like a sign.

"Listen, Jo, I know it sounds crazy, but I think you need to do a tour. You wanted to see America. Well, now it wants to see you, too."

This was getting weirder and weirder, even for Abbie. A tour? I leaned back in my chair and took another sip of my tea. "Okay, but only if you and Zora will go along as backup dancers."

"Very funny," she said, "but I'm asking you to tell the story, not sing it."

"What story would that be? The story of the house that burned down before we could even get it fixed up pretty? Not very inspirational."

"You're looking at it all wrong," she said, sounding more urgent than annoyed. "The story is about the fact that you and Zora didn't give up. You're going to rebuild. You didn't let the bad guys win."

Why was it that most discussions of honor and courage ended up sounding like the plots of Hollywood westerns? Maybe we should have bracelets made that said: *What would John Wayne do?*

"They've been watching you live it on all their little computers, in all their little individual rooms, now they want to come together to hear you tell it. They want to be part of the story, not just observers," Abbie said. "Zora said we've got invitations for you to come and speak from all over the place. She put some pictures up two days ago, right after the fire, and people want to help you rebuild. They want to give you money for supplies. They want to send me clippings for the garden. They want to buy T-shirts!"

"T-shirts?"

"Zora said people have been trying to buy them for months. It's a classic story. People love it!"

"So what does this have to do with a tour?" I said, speaking hypothetically. "A tour means New York, Chicago, San Francisco, L.A., Atlanta."

Abbie blew on her tea and set the cup down. "Do you know why Peachy and I really took that trip in the first place?"

"I thought you set off in search of America."

"That's part of it," she said. "But not everything. When we first started, I was feeling so sad, I could hardly get up in the morning."

"Sad about what happened in D.C.?"

"About that and about what was happening to people in New Orleans. About the war. About kids like the ones who broke in on me. Everything seemed to be falling apart at the same time and everything I thought I could do about it seemed too little, too late. Once I went to

Tybee, I got so I didn't want to leave the island at all. I was too afraid of what I'd find out there, roaming around waiting for me. I told Peachy I was afraid I'd lost something important and he said maybe we ought to take a trip and see if we could find it."

Of course she wanted to marry him.

"So we just hit the road, like I told you. No destination. No agenda. No timetables. We were just riding through America. One night, it was about seven o'clock and we'd been traveling all day. I was tired so Peachy pulled off at this tiny motel right outside of Amarillo. We took our suitcases in and found a little Mexican restaurant a block away full of big families and first dates and friendly waiters who spoke English to us and Spanish to each other. We ordered two margaritas and laughed and talked our way through some of the best fajitas I ever had in my life. Nobody was arguing or fussing about politics or minding anybody else's business. It was just people, out in the middle of Texas, being people. *Together*.

"It was sunset when we left the place, and as we walked back to the motel, the sky was turning the most amazing shade of purple. I still had the sound of those happy people in my head, so I took Peachy's hand and we just stood there at the edge of the parking lot and watched the sun go down. That's when I felt the connection. Not just to Peachy, but to something bigger than just him and me. Something about the idea of what a country like this could be if people could figure out a way to just be people."

She took a deep breath.

"Go on," I said, wondering if that was what it felt like to be a real American. "I'm with you."

"I think that connection was what I was looking for," she said. "And the weird thing is, that great big feeling brought me back to something much, much smaller. It brought me to Tybee and West End and now to your garden because I realized that you can only be a good citizen one step at a time. That's all I have to do. Tending my little corner of America is all there is to it. If I want to stop the war, the first thing I have to do is make sure nobody's fighting at my house. And you have to make sure nobody's fighting at your house and on and on and on . . ."

She sounded like Zora, optimistic and determined. A hard combination to beat, even if you want to, which I didn't. I couldn't argue with the idea of cleaning up your own backyard, but there was one problem. In the movies, once the idealist states his case, John Wayne rides in with a great big gun to make it stick. Could it work without that?

"The other thing about the bad guys," Abbie said, "is that they're always outnumbered by the good guys. No western worth its salt omits the scene where the people, energized by the one who stepped forward to protect them in the first place, rise up and stand together to save their town."

"You think that's going to happen this time?"

"It happens every time," she said.

"Well, what am I supposed to do until they get themselves together?"

"Oh, I don't know," she said, grinning at me across the table. "Put on a strapless dress. Sing something."

∙

SEVENTY-ONE

When we told Zora about the tour, she was beside herself.

"That's a great idea," she said. "We've gotten so many hits since the fire. I've just been showing the burned-out shell, no statement from you or anything, and people are going crazy. They want to do something!"

Abbie just smiled.

"Then I guess we ought to let them," I said, surrendering.

"It's time for you to make a statement."

"A statement about what?"

"About what happened," Zora said, glancing at her watch. "Let's do it now. I can get it on tonight at our regular time."

"Regular time for what?"

"Live?" Abbie said.

Zora nodded. "If we hurry. Come on, Mafeenie. I'll explain on the way."

"Do I need to change?" I was wearing jeans and a T-shirt, our crew uniform that had become my new outfit of choice.

"It's perfect," Abbie said.

The three of us drove over together. I was thinking about what I wanted to say and how I wanted to say it. Talking to Zora about freedom and talking to Abbie about connections made me feel good. It didn't make me stop worrying about our finances or feeling bad about the loss of the house, but it made the struggle we were in a bigger one. Even if Greer Woodruff never had to answer for her role in any of it, even if we couldn't prove it, our continued presence there would thwart her plans without a need to call her name. And for all those people who seemed to be watching, it would give them a visual image of our little group doing what free people always have to do if they're going to stay free: fight for it.

Zora had been posting live feeds twice a week, sometimes new video, sometimes just her assessment of what was going on. Because of my self-imposed prohibition on looking at what she was doing, I had never seen it and was only vaguely aware that it had taken on a life of its own. Abbie said people all over town made it a point to be there for the live feeds to see what she had to say.

When we got to the property, I jumped out and went to stand in front of where my house used to be. Zora turned her little camera in my direction, and I tried to imagine how many people could see me standing there with just a click. I looked out into their collective eyes.

"We had a fire here last week," I said. "I think somebody set it. Somebody who decided this house didn't need to be here. That whatever this house represented doesn't need to be represented here. Whatever this garden represented doesn't need to be represented here. That this neighborhood doesn't need to even be here. Well, they're wrong. We live right here because we want to, and we won't be run off. We're going to put another house here, and another garden, and every time they burn it down, we're going to put it right back."

Okay. I needed to wrap it up. I took a deep breath. "We all know there are people who don't want us to reclaim this community," I said. "People who have made deals that they think are more important than our lives. People who think a neighborhood can be bought and sold to the highest bidder. People who think money can buy everything, and when it can't, the strong one gets to take it anyway because nobody can tell her no."

I said *her* just so Greer Woodruff would know I was talking about her.

"But it doesn't have to be that way. Not if enough people who know what's wrong will stand up whenever they see it and say *no*, as loud as they can every chance they get."

I was channeling Tom Joad's speech at the end of *The Grapes of Wrath.* I wondered if anybody watching me had read it or seen the movie. Probably not. I was as close as they were going to get to that kind of determined idealism.

"Because America isn't some big, weird, abstract thing. It's just us. And we love this house, and this garden, and we're going to find a way to live on it in peace because . . . that's what citizens do."

I said that for Abbie because I knew she would appreciate it and because I finally understood what she meant.

"The rebuilding," I said, "starts now."

Zora was nodding and smiling, and I didn't have on a strapless dress, but it was definitely time to sing something. I had just the song. Everybody knows it and everybody feels better when they sing it.

"This little light of mine," I sang. "I'm gonna let it shine." My voice sounded stronger than I thought it would, so I sang a little louder. "This little light of mine, I'm gonna let it shine."

From where she was standing next to Zora, Abbie joined in, too.

"This little light of mine, I'm gonna let it shine. Let it shine, let it shine, let it shine."

We sang the whole song twice and then Zora turned off the camera and we sang it again just for the three of us. It's that kind of song.

SEVENTY-TWO

·

$\mathcal{I}$ made the cover of *Dig It!* The story was entitled "Burned Out Actress Vows to Rebuild." The headline wasn't clear about whether the burned-out part referred to me or the house, but the story was breathlessly supportive in its coverage, so I couldn't complain. Abbie and Zora were busy putting together an itinerary for what they were now calling The Sea to Shining Sea MLK Rescue Tour, which would start in Tybee and end in San Francisco. Aretha had managed to talk the T-shirt company into donating a bunch of shirts, and I realized I was becoming a community spokeswoman by default.

I studied the cover of *Dig It!* for a long time. There I was in a still they had taken from Zora's video at the house the other night, looking serious as hell. I had my eyes closed and my head thrown back, singing "This Little Light of Mine" for all I was worth. It was very sixties, warm and fuzzy, but I knew anybody who was serious enough to burn down a building to get what they wanted wasn't going to be put off by a few freedom songs. We hadn't heard anything from Greer Woodruff since the fire. I was waiting for that other shoe to fall.

I wasn't the only one waiting. Greer's associate Duncan Matthews was waiting, too, and he was afraid to wait any longer. He wouldn't have presumed to call, he said, after I assured him I remembered our first meeting during one of my early visits to Woodruff and Associates, unless he had some information he thought I needed right away. When I told him to meet me at four and he said the sooner, the better, I knew he wasn't kidding.

SEVENTY-THREE

·

We met at Soul Vegetarian. Once we sat down and ordered iced tea, Duncan Matthews said he didn't know where to begin.

"Start anywhere," I said. "I'll keep up."

"It's not her fault," he said.

"Sure it is."

He was miserable. During all those performances he had seen of *Medea,* he never for an instant thought he'd be sitting across the table from me like this, but here we sat at Soul Veg, a tiny restaurant for vegans and those who love them. No chance either one of us was going to run into anybody we knew in here. We took a table near the back, surrounded by the smell of grilled tofu and broccoli quiche.

"May I speak frankly?"

"Please."

He sighed like he was already exhausted by the effort to get through these next few minutes, reached into his pocket, and pulled out a small silver disk. I recognized one of the tools of Zora's technology. Duncan was holding it gingerly between two fingers.

"You know how easy it was for you to get those pictures of your house out on the Web?"

"My granddaughter does all of that," I said. "I never even look at the footage."

"Well, you'll want to take a look at this," he said, and handed me the disk.

I turned it over and saw that the word *Birmingham* was printed on the front side.

"It can go out just as easy."

"What is it?"

He fiddled with his water glass. His herb iced tea was untouched. "Did your granddaughter go to Birmingham with a couple of guys a month or so ago?"

The way he said it sounded nasty. *A couple of guys.*

"She went to a wedding."

"They had a party," he said. "From the looks of it, things got pretty wild. Out of control, maybe?"

Zora's whispered confession came creeping back into my head: *I want to tell you what happened in Birmingham.*

"What's that got to do with you?"

"The thing is, it has to do with you," he said. "Somebody at that party shot some video. Of your granddaughter."

My heart felt like it was going to explode in my chest. I closed my hand around the disk as if I could obliterate it if I just squeezed hard enough. I looked at Duncan. "Is that what's on this thing?"

"It's a copy," he said. "She has the original."

There was no reason to be more specific. We both knew who he was talking about.

"And what does she intend to do with it?"

"Your granddaughter's pretty well known because of the project you've been doing. All the coverage she's gotten. And then all that other stuff that happened last year, you know."

"I know."

"Well, that video in your hand will fly around the Web. If it got out."

My first reaction was to see if my drink-in-the-face throwing skills had eroded due to lack of recent practice, but I knew this was no time for theatrical gestures. This was Zora's worst nightmare. An insane moment that you somehow manage to stumble out of and survive, suddenly blasted around the world for all to see, judge, discuss, dissect, and commit to memory. If Zora had been freaked out by all the coverage she got in *Dig It!*, this would be more than she could take. *And for what?*

"My granddaughter doesn't have anything to do with this."

"I know, I know . . . ," he said, his voice trailing off. He sighed again. "Look, Ms. Evans, I hate being the one she asked to do this, but

288 · PEARL CLEAGE
288 · PEARL CLEAGE

in a way I'm glad because I admire you so much as an artist and as a person."

I cut him off. "Then why are you involved in this?"

"Because it's not just her. We all need to do this deal."

"What does that mean?"

He looked around furtively. There were only a few other people in the place, absorbed in their conversations and their dinners. Satisfied that we were not being eavesdropped upon, he still leaned closer. I did, too.

"Last year, when that police scandal exposed a lot of the cocaine connections in this town, everybody went underground. All of the ways they'd been laundering their money dried up or were under such close scrutiny that nobody could do any real business."

He said it like he was talking about General Motors and Chrysler.

"Some of us were having problems at that time due to fluctuations in the real estate market, some bad investments, things that didn't work out the way we hoped they would." He gave what I guess he thought was an ingratiating smile. "Atlanta is a very volatile market, I don't know if you know that."

I just looked at him. I was not interested in a seminar on the buying and selling of property in this city. I was interested in why any of this was happening.

"So Greer had the idea of approaching some of these guys . . ."

"The cocaine dealers?"

"Yes, well, not the street guys. The other ones. The ones who handle the real business of it."

I remembered the men I'd seen with Duncan in Greer's office that first day. Were those the guys who had burned my house?

"I don't know how she even knew who these guys were, but she made them a proposition where we could wash a lot of cash for them if they would let us use their money while we were holding it to clear up some of our own problems. They said they didn't care what we did with it as long as we had it ready when they needed it back. Greer told them that wasn't a problem because she had some deals working that would take care of everything in plenty of time."

He took a swallow of his water and ran his hand over his hair nervously. "So she asked some of us to come in with her and it sounded like a good solution all the way around—and it could have been. But we thought it was going to be a three- or four-year thing, you know nothing happens fast in this business, but they got their network back together faster than that, and now they want their money."

If Greer Woodruff didn't have any better sense than to go into business with cocaine dealers, the men weren't keeping her out because she was a woman. They were keeping her out because she didn't have good sense.

"How much money does she owe?"

"Well, it's really all of us together, but the deal for this corner would be enough to put everything right. She figured you'd be willing to sell cheap when your place stopped generating any income, and the others weren't going to be able to hold out much longer. But when you came back and then you wouldn't sell, that presented a real problem, you see, because we don't have anything else in the works. This is pretty much it if we're going to fit within their time frame."

"Why don't you just pay the dope dealers the money she keeps offering us?"

He squirmed uncomfortably when I said "dope dealers." "The debt is a little more than that."

How big a fool was she? "How much more?"

He looked around again. "Three million," he whispered.

"Three million dollars?" Who borrowed three million dollars from gangsters and hoped for the best? Didn't these people ever go to the movies?

"I know it sounds like a lot, but this one deal that you, Ms. Evans, have been holding up will clear everything. Our share is five million. That takes care of our partners and puts all of us back in the black."

He looked at me and had the nerve to smile like I would share his relief that there was a plan on the table by which his company could be saved at the expense of my granddaughter's reputation and her inheritance.

"You should be ashamed of yourself," I said, knowing a deal like this required shamelessness as one of its key components.

"I am," he said, wiping the smile off his face. "I am deeply, deeply ashamed, but these guys are losing patience with us and we need to close this deal right away. We're out of time. You have to name a price."

"And if I don't?"

He clasped and unclasped his hands nervously. "Ms. Evans, your granddaughter is a very beautiful young woman. She's at the beginning of her life, probably has a bright future, but if this video hits the Web, that will be the defining moment of her life. It will be like Paris Hilton's sex video or Monica Lewinsky's dress. No one will ever meet her without remembering it. They'll remember how shocked they were." He looked at me. "Or how turned on."

I stood up and he did, too. "I'm sorry, I shouldn't have said that. I apologize."

Several of the other patrons in the restaurant glanced our way.

"All I'm saying is"—he lowered his voice—"these guys don't care where they get their money or how. If we don't pay, there's no telling . . . I'm sorry, Ms. Evans, I truly am, but I have a family."

The irony of defending his family by threatening mine was lost on him. "So do I."

"We have to make this deal, Ms. Evans. We're out of options." His voice was almost a whisper. "And once you and your granddaughter see this tape, I think you'll see that you are, too."

That noise I heard was the sound of the other shoe dropping.

·

SEVENTY-FOUR

Zora was at home, working on her computer, when I got there. She took one look at my face and knew something was up.

"What's wrong, Mafeenie?"

There was no way to tell it but to tell it. "I just met with one of Greer's partners. They've got a video of you. In Birmingham." I took it out of my jacket pocket and handed it to her the same way Duncan had handed it to me, gingerly.

She turned it over in her palm while I told her what he had said. When I finished, she looked at me, but I couldn't read her face.

"Do you think she'd really do it?"

"Yes," I said.

She was turning the disk over in her hand slowly. "Did you see it?"

"No, darlin'," I said. "I didn't see it."

"Well, you know what?" Her voice was soft but not shaky. "I'm not going to see it either." She sounded strong. Determined.

"Are you sure?" I hoped she was. Once you start running scared, it's hard to slow down.

She laid the disk down on the desk like it was too hot for her to hold anymore. "You know, a couple of months ago, I would have said take the money. Tell them we'll give *them* money, anything they want, just don't . . . *don't ever* put this out there where people can see me on the absolute worst night of my life. Don't let people see me drunk and crazy and nasty and stupid and sad. Don't let strangers make judgments about who I am because of who I was."

"What would you say now?"

She looked at me and I was amazed to see that she was smiling. "Well, my grandmother taught me that if you let them run you off, you're just a scared rabbit looking for another place to hide."

"Your grandmother is a wise woman." Zora didn't want to agree to this blackmail any more than I did. I'd never been prouder of her. "So what do you say?"

"I say fuck them!"

"Are you absolutely sure?" I said, wondering suddenly if maybe we should look at it before she made a final decision. "It might be . . ."

Zora held up her hand. "I know exactly what it is. I was there, remember?"

I nodded.

"I'm sure," she said.

I hugged her. "Then I say fuck them, too!"

She laughed and hugged me back. "Nice language from a grandmother!"

"Okay," I said. "But if we're going to do this, I think we should call your mother so she'll know what's coming."

"No way," Zora said.

I was surprised. Jasmine is not a technophobe like me. She might actually see the footage somewhere and that would be awful.

"Don't you think you should warn her?"

"Remember what I told you about flash mobs?"

"I think so."

"You will. Call Greer. Tell her you'll come by tonight around seven to make the deal."

"What are you going to do?"

"Don't worry. They're the ones out of options. Not us."

"But we can't really prove anything," I said.

"We don't have to prove anything. All we have to do is shine the light."

SEVENTY-FIVE

•

W hen I got to Greer's office, everyone had been sent home as I requested. I told her I didn't want anybody to see us together. I had built up a certain image, I said. It wouldn't help it to see me selling out. Since that image is all I've got left, I thought the least she could do was allow me to be discreet. She agreed, sounding smug that she had finally brought me around to her way of thinking. It was almost seven. She met me at the door without a smile and got right down to business.

"Let's go in the conference room, I've got the papers all laid out."

I followed her down the short hallway and she closed the door behind us. The large window looked out over the parking lot, but Greer walked over and closed the blinds. That was fine with me. I was the one who had said this kind of deal was one that was better done in darkness. Besides, if Zora was right, she'd be opening them again soon enough.

"Have a seat," Greer said, and sat down herself, opening a folder full of papers.

I took a chair across from her and put my purse on the table exactly as Zora had told me to do. I hoped my brilliant granddaughter knew what she was doing, but if she didn't there was nothing I could do about it now. My job was to stall Greer Woodruff as long as I could until our troops arrived. I wasn't sure yet how I was going to do that, but I was sure something would come to me.

"I am so pleased that we've been able to come to terms," Greer said, when she seemed satisfied that she had the necessary papers in front of her.

"I wouldn't call this coming to terms," I said. "You're a blackmailer doing business with drug dealers."

"I'm a black woman doing business in America," she said.

"What does that have to do with it?"

Her non-smile was closer to a sneer. "That's a funny question coming from a woman who had to leave the country to find work."

"So if I had stayed, I'd have the right to be a blackmailer, too?"

"No, you'd have the right to be self-righteous. But you didn't, so you don't." She pushed the papers across the table along with a fat black fountain pen.

"Do you have the disk?" I said.

"Of course. I have it right here."

It looked just like the one Duncan Matthews had. I took it and dropped it in my purse.

"You should be glad you took the deal," she said. "Some of my partners had a real interest in this disk. Your granddaughter is a beautiful girl. Even when she's drunk."

I swallowed hard. Only a few more minutes to go.

"This is the end of this neighborhood," I said. "Don't you even care?"

"This isn't the end of this neighborhood," she said. "You missed that by a couple of years. You were just too far away to notice. And whether I care or not is beside the point. If I don't do it, somebody else will."

"What happens to Betty Causey?"

"She'll get twenty thousand for that little beat-up house she's got." Greer leaned back in her chair. Now that she had me in her office, she wanted to toy with me for a while like a cat before it eats that mouse. "See, I do have a heart, Ms. Evans. I added five thousand dollars for her pain and suffering. She can go find some relatives in the country who will be glad to take her and her crackhead son in for that kind of money."

"He's not a crackhead." I couldn't let that go unchallenged. "What about the others?"

"They'll get fifteen apiece. All in all," she said, "it's not a bad deal. They were going to have to go sooner or later."

"Because the cocaine dealers need the money you borrowed?"

"I didn't borrow it. I agreed to perform a service vital to anybody who does the bulk of their business in cash." She twisted her mouth into a smile. "Besides, it's not my fault they lived longer than they were supposed to."

That's when we heard the first horn. It was one long blast and then two short ones. It sounded like a signal and it was. Greer frowned slightly. There was a moment of silence and then, out of nowhere, an explosion of horns, a cacophony of horns. I stood up. Greer took three short steps over to the window and raised the blinds with one angry motion.

The parking lot was full of cars. They were all blowing their horns and flashing their lights and the noise was deafening. I could see Betty and Daisy standing beside Abbie, who was leaning in her own car window, blowing the horn for all she was worth. Thelma and Juanita were standing with Victor, who was leaning on Aretha's truck while she laid on the horn like a champ. Zora was standing in the back of the truck with her camera pointed toward the window where we were standing.

Greer turned to me. "What the hell is going on?"

"We're just doing business," I said, reaching into my purse and pulling out Zora's other little camera. I set it down on the table, out of her reach, able to get a shot that included us both. "Twenty-first-century business. It's called the Internet."

She stepped away from the camera like it was about to explode. She was as clueless about this stuff as I was, but she knew this was bad. Very bad. "You sent this out live?"

"Live and in living color, but don't worry. You didn't say anything incriminating. You were just being yourself."

"You can't prove a thing! Not a thing!"

"I don't have to prove anything," I said, pointing to the parking lot. "As far as they're concerned, you're guilty as sin."

I picked up the unsigned contracts and tore them in half. I knew it was corny, but I was on a roll. Zora had sent the feed out live and asked people to come and bear witness and blow their horns at her signal. And they did it! They actually did it! At the very least, Greer Woodruff was going to have some explaining to do.

"Guilty of what?" She snarled, too mad to realize this was still going out live. "Trying to buy up some houses from a bunch of scared old women? Trying to hang on to a business I built from the ground up?" She raised her voice to be heard above all those horns blaring outside her window. "For doing what the white boys do every day of their lives and nobody says a thing about it?"

"There aren't any white boys here," I said. "Just two black women doing business in America. And for the record? *Ain't nobody scared around here but you!*"

SEVENTY-SIX

•

T he next day, we made the cover of *Dig It!* again, and we led the six
o'clock news on all three local stations. Zora and I held hands on
the couch as the anchorwoman smiled her best you-won't-believe-this
smile.

"Good evening. Our top story is one for the books," she said. "Or
maybe for the movies. A prominent local businesswoman is being accused of money laundering and an array of related charges stemming
from a local reality show exposé that has become a cult favorite on the
Web."

We grinned at each other and I squeezed her hand. Zora had just
thrown a big old bucket of water on the witch. We could practically
hear her melting.

"Called *Rescue on MLK,* and featuring the reclamation of a corner
lot on the historic thoroughfare, the show's regular live video feed featured a meeting last night between Greer Woodruff, owner of
Woodruff and Associates, and the show's star, Atlanta actress Josephine
Evans. Let's take a look."

"They're going to show it, Mafeenie!" Zora said. "Now you'll get to
see the woman the world has been looking at all these weeks."

It was finally time for me to look, so I did, and there she was, Citizen Evans, reporting for duty. A wild woman with wild eyes, a wild
face, a wild gypsy heart that had finally found a home where she least
expected it. *Is that what I look like now? Full of righteous indignation
and courage and joy?* I leaned closer and what I saw was an absolutely
free woman looking back at me. And I loved her. I loved her fiercely.

SEVENTY-SEVEN

•

*Y*ou are fabulous!" Howard's voice on the other end of the line was falling all over itself with delight. "Beyond fabulous! Everybody saw you in that scene with that awful woman last night. The way you tore up those contracts! All those horns blowing. My God, people were calling me all night. They can't get enough!"

"That was no scene," I said, laughing at his excitement. "That was my life."

"*Was* your life is right," he crowed. "It's time to come home in triumph!"

"What are you talking about?"

"I talked to François a few minutes ago. All is forgiven! The theater is prepared to pay you whatever you want for as long as you want. Come home!"

Home.

"Why the sudden change of heart?"

"Because you are the toast of the town, honey! The absolute, hot buttered toast! Anything you put your name on is a guaranteed hit! Open the season, close the season, pick a new season. You're free to do whatever you want."

And suddenly, there it was. The moment when what you want is the only real question, and you absolutely must know the only real answer because you are the only one who can, and, of course, you do.

"I'm not coming back, Howard," I said.

"What do you mean 'not coming back'?"

"I'm going on tour."

"On tour?" His voice was incredulous. "On tour where?"

I hoped he was sitting down. "Would you believe Amarillo, Texas?"

ACKNOWLEDGMENTS

Most special thanks to my husband, Zaron W. Burnett, Jr., for his amazing generosity as a constant collaborator and his ability to make every road trip a life-changing adventure; to my grandchildren, Michael and Chloe, for always being as happy to see me as I am to see them; to my sister, Kristin Williams; her husband, Jim; and their children and grandchildren; and to my friends Lynette Lapeyrolerie, Walt and Lynn Huntley, Cecelia Corbin Hunter, Ingrid Saunders Jones, Jimmie Lee Tarver, A. B. and Karen Spellman, Shirley C. Franklin, Ray and Marilyn Cox, Gary and Helen Richter, Ayshia Jeffries, Marc and Elaine Lawson, Kay Hagan, Donald P. Stone, and Maria Broom; and the West Coast branch of my extended family, Zaron W. Burnett III, Meaghan V. Underwood, Skylar and Griffin Underwood; Ron Gwiazda for taking care of business; Howard Rosenstone; and Bill Bagwell, just because.

SEEN IT ALL
and
DONE THE REST

Pearl Cleage

A READER'S GUIDE

A CONVERSATION WITH PEARL CLEAGE

Pearl Cleage sat down to talk with Carleen Brice, author of the novel, *Orange Mint and Honey,* about the art of writing, the business of publishing, and the inspirations found in the world between.

Carleen Brice: You started out writing plays, correct? What led you to the theater?

Pearl Cleage: I have always loved the theater. My mother and my father used to take us when I was growing up in Detroit. We saw everything from Ossie Davis and Ruby Dee in *Purlie Victorious* to Dame Judith Anderson in *Agamemnon* to Rudolf Nureyev with the Royal Ballet to José Greco and his passionate flamenco dancers to an updated version of Shakespeare's *The Taming of the Shrew*—where they drove real motorcycles on the stage—to Alvin Ailey's *Revelations.* I loved it all! I loved the movies, too, but the immediacy of live theater was always so exciting. Anything could happen! So I started writing short plays when I was really little.

I was one of those kids who always put together a Christmas play or a Thanksgiving play that everybody had to watch after they'd eaten that huge holiday meal and they were powerless to move. I'd recruit my cousins and my big sister, and we'd do the Christmas story or the Pilgrims' landing at Plymouth Rock. I doubt that we were very good, but we always got an enthusiastic response from our captive audience, and I was hooked! I acted and wrote plays all through school, but when I got to college, I stopped acting and concentrated on writing. I have written thirteen plays, and I'm really happy to say they have all been professionally produced.

CB: How is writing a novel different than writing a play? Do you have a different process?

PC: I never intended to write novels! I had been happily writing my plays, and then I had an idea for a story that would not fit on the stage. It was too long, there were too many characters, too many settings, too much internal dialogue. So after weeks of trying to change it enough to make it fit the stage, I gave up and decided I'd try to write it as a novel instead. Since I had never written a novel, I was intimidated by the form. I didn't know where to start, how to proceed, how to wrap things up. As a playwright, I had been working to develop my craft for years. Now here I was, facing something totally new. I took a deep breath, and calling on the spirits of Alice Walker and Toni Morrison to help me, I plunged in.

This, of course, was a mistake. Anytime you try to conjure up great writers to work on your book with you, there is bound to be some confusion. For me, it was trying to write third person like they do. I was used to writing dialogue, not description. When you write a play, you say: "It is a Sunday afternoon on the sidewalk outside of a Harlem brownstone. The year is 1930." Then the set designer does the research and creates a set that looks like that Harlem sidewalk. The costume designer creates authentic period costumes, the lighting designer makes it look like a sunny city afternoon, and the actors bring their charisma and skill to making the characters come alive. Now, as a novelist, I had to do all that myself, in addition to creating characters and making them walk, talk, and move through their story.

I was overwhelmed and, after a few months, I was floundering around with two hundred pages that I hated. I was trying so hard to be a serious novelist that I wasn't having any fun, and reading my pages, I knew the reader wouldn't have any fun either. So I took a bold step. I said a mental apology to Alice and Toni, threw away all those pages, and started again, but this time I was writing first person. It worked like a charm. As a playwright, I'm used to letting the characters speak. Once I started writing in the main character's voice, the book came alive. Ava Johnson had a story to tell, and all I had to do was get out of the way and let her tell it. I had a ball. The book turned out to be *What Looks Like Crazy on an Ordinary Day,* and I've been writing novels ever since.

CB: Are you still writing plays? What about screenplays for any of your books?

PC: I still write plays. I just wrote one last year called *A Song for Coretta*. It takes place in Atlanta as five women wait in line to go and pay their respects to Mrs. Coretta King, who lay in state at Ebenezer Baptist Church. When I saw the television coverage, I was very moved by the picture of all those folks, standing in the rain at midnight, waiting to say goodbye to someone they admired and respected so much. The play was done at Spelman College, where I was teaching at the time, and then at 7 Stages Theatre. We had a great cast and a wonderful director in Crystal Dickinson. We sold out every show! The play is currently going into production in several other cities. *A Song for Coretta* was the first play I had written in ten years, and it felt good to be working in theater again. I am thinking about another play already!

As far as screenplays are concerned, my husband, Zaron Burnett, who is also a writer, is working with me on screenplays for several of my books. I am curious to see how they will translate. People are always casting the movies for me, especially for Blue Hamilton! Of course, Denzel Washington in blue contacts is always the first one they mention!

CB: Your books always include messages about social justice and just being good to one another. Is that a conscious plan on your part when you start writing?

PC: I am a true child of the sixties so I'm always trying to make the world a better place! I am convinced that if every person would just do their part, we could solve any problems we have, worldwide! I grew up in a very politically conscious and politically active family, and I'm sure that's part of why the people in my books are always so deeply rooted in their community. The southwest Atlanta neighborhood I'm writing about has been my home for thirty years so I am acutely aware of our problems, but I am also aware of what a vibrant place it is. I hope the books encourage people to look around at their own communities and get involved in something to make it better. The women in my books work with young people, support refugees, help new mothers, employ the homeless, grow peace gardens, and participate in anti-war demonstrations. They also find time to fall in love, have babies, raise families, go to the beach, fly kites, and laugh with their friends. I never thought you had to give up romance to be a revolutionary!

CB: It's been awhile since I've been to Atlanta. Is the West End you describe in your latest books really the way you describe it: well kept with all-night businesses and men who tip their hats to ladies and women who feel safe walking at night? Or is this an urban African American neighborhood as you'd like to see it?

PC: I wish I could say that West End is exactly as I describe it, but we're not there yet. One of the things I'm always trying to do in my books is to create the kind of neighborhood I want to live in. I want to be able to walk at midnight fearlessly. I want to be able to sit on my front porch and not hear gunfire, and I sure want to have some men around who tip their hats and know how to say "Good morning!" I want to eat fresh vegetables from the bounty of community gardens. So I try to paint those pictures. I try to make readers remember how it feels to be safe and happy and loved and free. If we can see it, we can be it! (I told you I was a sixties child!)

CB: A lot of writers (published and not-yet-published) read [my] blog. What's the best advice anyone ever gave you about writing?

PC: My father gave me some wonderful advice when I was working full time and raising my daughter and keeping up an active social life. I was spending my time doing everything but writing and, of course, I was whining about it. My father listened to me for about fifteen minutes and then he said, "Nobody's going to give you permission to write. They're always going to have other things for you to do. If you want to write, you better start writing." My feelings were hurt because I was looking for some sympathy, but he was right. Nobody is going to give anybody permission to write. If you want to do it, it is up to you to make a way to do it. The best book about the writing process that I've come across is Anne Lamott's *Bird by Bird*. It's widely available in paperback, and it's got lots of good advice and laugh-out-loud stories about the craziness that all writers think is theirs alone, but which is really just part of the process.

CB: What changes have you noticed in publishing since your first novel, *What Looks Like Crazy on an Ordinary Day*, which was an Oprah's Book Club pick?

PC: I think the biggest difference I've noticed in publishing is that there is a lot more emphasis on business and a lot less emphasis on the artistic development of the authors. Publishers are struggling to find a way to make books commercially viable in an age when people are getting so much of their information from electronic sources. I think writers feel this pressure, too, and sometimes it gets in the way. The craft of writing doesn't have anything to do with the business of best-sellers. When the two get confused, nothing good can come of it.

CB: Those of us who are black female writers sometimes feel especially discouraged about the current book scene. Any words of encouragement?

PC: There exists a vibrant community of black women writers. Some of these writers are commercially successful and some are less well-known, but many of them are working at the top of their game. They are writing wonderfully, and their work deserves to be widely read, reviewed, discussed, and enjoyed. The problem is that we don't have viable publishing houses with viable distribution systems that are dedicated to publishing black women authors and aggressively marketing their work. What we need are some businesswomen who can see that publishing can be both culturally significant and commercially robust. There are so many avenues for marketing the work of black female authors that have not been fully explored, including book clubs, churches, sororities, and professional organizations. To my sister-writers who are feeling downhearted about the current book scene: I suggest that maybe we should start trying to find some bright young women with business degrees and see if we can make them see the possibilities for a future in publishing. In the meantime, our job is to keep telling our stories. If not us, who? If not now, when?

CB: Thanks, Pearl, for your time!

QUESTIONS AND TOPICS FOR DISCUSSION

1. Why does Josephine decide not to stay and fight the theater and the backlash that she is receiving because she is an American? How does she just walk away from it all? How do you think the rest of the world views Americans since the Iraq War began? How do you think Americans view themselves?

2. How is the issue of responsibility, both public and private, central to the book? How do the characters carry out their responsibilities to each other—Josephine to Zora, Zora to Josephine, Howard to Josephine? How do the characters carry out their larger responsibilities to society? To Atlanta? To the United States?

3. The relationship between Josephine and Zora is complex. Many of the same personality traits can be seen in both granddaughter and grandmother. How do you think this both helps and hinders their relationship? Both wanted to run away from their lives at the beginning of the story; how did they change their ways of thinking by the end?

4. Why does Josephine decide to call the reporter back even after Howard warns her not to? How is Howard an enabler for Josephine?

5. There are many symbols in the book that seem to tie together the major themes of the story. What does the mermaid in the pool represent? Josephine's abandoned house? The garden?

6. What is Victor's role in the story? How does his story mirror those of others in the book?

7. Abbie found the "secret of life" in Amarillo, Texas. How do you think she helped Josephine find the secret of life? Do you believe that people find their bliss in a certain place on a map?

8. Why does Josephine stand up to Greer Woodruff, when she ran from her problems in Amsterdam? What keeps her in Atlanta besides Zora?

9. Some people have been inspired by this novel and have planted peace gardens. What does a peace garden mean to you and what would you plant in yours?

10. Family plays an important part in this book. What are the various types of families portrayed? How do neighborhoods create family?

PHOTO: © ALBERT TROTMAN

PEARL CLEAGE is the author of *Baby Brother's Blues*, *Babylon Sisters*, *What Looks Like Crazy on an Ordinary Day . . .*, which was an Oprah's Book Club selection, *Some Things I Never Thought I'd Do*, and *I Wish I Had a Red Dress*, as well as three works of nonfiction: *Mad at Miles: A Black Woman's Guide to Truth*, *Deals with the Devil and Other Reasons to Riot*, and *We Speak Your Names: A Celebration*, in collaboration with Zaron W. Burnett, Jr. She is also an accomplished dramatist. Her plays include *Flyin' West* and *Blues for an Alabama Sky*. Cleage lives in Atlanta with her husband, writer Zaron W. Burnett, Jr.